PRAISE FOR THE NOVELS
OF ANYA BAST

CRUEL ENCHANTMENT

"An enchanting, magical entry in a superior series."
— *Genre Go Round Reviews*

WICKED ENCHANTMENT

"[The] Dark Magick series is intriguing, intense, and powerful, a unique mixture of today's world with fantasy. A great read!"   — *Fresh Fiction*

"If you like dark faery tales filled with intrigue, politics, backstabbing, lying, and outright betrayals, you will like *Wicked Enchantment*. I loved it and I can't wait for the next book!"   — *Manic Readers*

"A superb romantic fantasy . . . Wickedly enchanting."
— *The Best Reviews*

"*Wicked Enchantment* will draw the reader in from the very start and I absolutely can't wait to read the next installment in this great new series."   — *The Book Lush*

"I love Anya Bast's books. Her imagination is incredible and her ability to share the worlds she develops is out of this world . . . This book was excellent."
— *Night Owl Romance Reviews*

WITCH FURY

"Full of action, excitement, and sexy fun . . . Another delectable tale that will keep your eyes glued to every word."
—*Bitten by Books*

"Hot romance, interesting characters, intriguing demons, and powerful emotions. I didn't want to put it down and now that I've finished this book, I'm ready for the next!"
—*Night Owl Romance Reviews*

WITCH HEART

"[A] fabulous tale . . . The story line is fast-paced from the onset . . . Fans will enjoy the third bewitching blast."
—*Genre Go Round Reviews*

"Smart, dangerous, and sexy as hell, the witches are more than a match for the warlocks and demons who'd like nothing more than to bring hell to earth and enslave mankind. Always an exhilarating read."   —*Fresh Fiction*

"*Witch Heart* is a story that will captivate its readers. It will hook you from the first few pages and then take you on a wild ride. It is a fast-paced story but it is also a story that will make you feel emotion. Anya Bast uses words like Monet used paint. It's vibrant. It's alive. Readers will be able to see the story come to life as it just leaps out of the pages."   —*Bitten by Books*

WITCH BLOOD

"Any paranormal fan will be guaranteed a Top Pick read. Anya has provided it all in this hot new paranormal series. You get great suspense, vivid characters, and a world that just pops off the pages . . . Not to be missed."

—*Night Owl Romance Reviews*

"Gritty danger and red-hot sensuality make this book and series smoking!"
—*Romantic Times*

WITCH FIRE

"Deliciously sexy and intriguingly original."
—Angela Knight, *USA Today* bestselling author

"Sizzling suspense and sexy magic are sure to propel this hot new series onto the charts. Bast is a talent to watch, and her magical world is one to revisit." —*Romantic Times*

"A sensual feast sure to sate even the most finicky of palates. Richly drawn, dynamic characters dictate the direction of this fascinating story. You can't miss with Anya."
—*A Romance Review*

"Fast-paced, edgy suspense . . . The paranormal elements are fresh and original. This reader was immediately drawn into the story from the opening abduction, and obsessively read straight through to the dramatic final altercation. Bravo, Ms. Bast; *Witch Fire* is sure to be a fan favorite."
—*Paranormal Romance Reviews*

DARK
ENCHANTMENT

ANYA BAST

BERKLEY SENSATION, NEW YORK

THE BERKLEY PUBLISHING GROUP
Published by the Penguin Group
Penguin Group (USA) Inc.
375 Hudson Street, New York, New York 10014, USA
Penguin Group (Canada), 90 Eglinton Avenue East, Suite 700, Toronto, Ontario M4P 2Y3, Canada
(a division of Pearson Penguin Canada Inc.)
Penguin Books Ltd., 80 Strand, London WC2R 0RL, England
Penguin Group Ireland, 25 St. Stephen's Green, Dublin 2, Ireland (a division of Penguin Books Ltd.)
Penguin Group (Australia), 250 Camberwell Road, Camberwell, Victoria 3124, Australia
(a division of Pearson Australia Group Pty. Ltd.)
Penguin Books India Pvt. Ltd., 11 Community Centre, Panchsheel Park, New Delhi—110 017, India
Penguin Group (NZ), 67 Apollo Drive, Rosedale, North Shore 0632, New Zealand
(a division of Pearson New Zealand Ltd.)
Penguin Books (South Africa) (Pty.) Ltd., 24 Sturdee Avenue, Rosebank, Johannesburg 2196,
South Africa

Penguin Books Ltd., Registered Offices: 80 Strand, London WC2R 0RL, England

This is a work of fiction. Names, characters, places, and incidents either are the product of the author's imagination or are used fictitiously, and any resemblance to actual persons, living or dead, business establishments, events, or locales is entirely coincidental. The publisher does not have any control over and does not assume any responsibility for author or third-party websites or their content.

DARK ENCHANTMENT

A Berkley Sensation Book / published by arrangement with the author

PRINTING HISTORY
Berkley Sensation mass-market paperback edition / April 2011

Copyright © 2011 by Anya Bast.
Excerpt from *Midnight Enchantment* copyright © 2011 by Anya Bast.
Excerpt from *Dragon Bound* copyright © 2011 by Teddy Harrison.
Cover design by Rita Frangie.
Cover art by Tony Mauro.
Interior text design by Kristin del Rosario.

ISBN: 978-0-425-24053-3

BERKLEY® SENSATION
Berkley Sensation Books are published by The Berkley Publishing Group,
a division of Penguin Group (USA) Inc.,
375 Hudson Street, New York, New York 10014.
BERKLEY® SENSATION and the "B" design are trademarks of Penguin Group (USA) Inc.

PRINTED IN THE UNITED STATES OF AMERICA

10 9 8 7 6 5 4 3 2 1

This book is dedicated to my readers.
Without your devotion, all the stories and characters
that crowd my imagination would be forever trapped inside,
making me crazy. Thank you for all your emails,
for buying my books, for chatting with me on Facebook
and Twitter, and for showing up at my book signings
with your lovely, smiling faces. I appreciate each
and every one of you more than I can express.

ACKNOWLEDGMENTS

Thank you to Brenda Maxfield and Reece Notley for being there to do read-throughs and offer opinions and suggestions. I value your input highly.

Thank you to Axel de Roy for creating the incredible map of Piefferburg that appears on my website, www.anyabast.com.

Lastly, as always, thank you to my beloved husband and daughter who forgive the hours I spend at my laptop and the detached way I walk around the house sometimes, lost in another world. I love you both more than anything.

ONE

HE made her want to be bad, and Charlotte Bennett was never bad.

She lay on her side in bed, eyes slowly coming open, the remnants of an amazing nocturnal adventure still clinging to her mind. In adulthood her dreams had a tendency toward monotone colors and were about as interesting as the act of folding towels. This dream had been real enough to make up for a lifetime of black-and-white snorefests.

She rolled onto her back, stared at the ceiling fan over her bed, and groaned. Apparently her body was trying to tell her something. She was still tingling in places that hadn't tingled in a very long time. Considering she hadn't had sex in nine months, the reason for the dream probably wasn't all that surprising.

That man! She'd never met anyone like him in real life. That was because men like the one in her dream didn't exist. Her subconscious had probably fashioned him from bits and pieces of the heroes she'd read about in romance novels, or characters she'd seen in movies. Longish dark hair, muscular build, strong jaw, deep brown eyes, hands that—

The phone rang.

She closed her eyes for a moment, cursing it inwardly. Just a few more minutes cuddled under the covers, immersed in her dream would have been nice. Reality was about to steal away the clinging vestiges of the luscious, sensual experience—and the delicious man who'd given it to her. Ah, well. It couldn't be helped.

She rolled over, grabbed the phone, and gave a sleep-husky "Hello." At the same time, she groped for her glasses and shoved them on.

Pause.

Charlotte sat up a little. "Hello?"

"Charlotte? Is that you?"

"Harvey?" She sat all the way up, clingy dreamy deliciousness now completely eradicated. Panicked by the only reason her boss would be calling on a Monday morning, she glanced out the window—daylight-bright, she now noticed—and then at the clock. Shock rippled through her.

"Are you all right? It's—"

She smacked her forehead with her open palm. "It's ten AM, I'm not there, and I haven't called."

"Ah . . . yes."

She threw the blankets back and bolted from the bed, her bare feet going cold on the hardwood floor. "I don't know happened. I'm so sorry! I guess my alarm never went off. You must think I'm a total incompetent." She stared accusingly at her alarm clock, which was set to play Tchaikovsky's "1812 Overture" every morning.

"That's okay, Charlotte. This isn't like you at all. You've never even been late, not once since you started working for us. Remarkable, really." Harvey chuckled. "So we knew you hadn't suddenly gone crazy and were sleeping off a bender or anything." Chuckle. "Or that you'd had a hot date and were—"

Charlotte gave a forced laugh and tried not to grind her teeth. "Right, yes, of course. That would be crazy."

"Of course it would. No, we just wanted to make sure you were all right. So, you're coming in?"

"Absolutely." She'd missed only two days of work in the last five years. Flu. Hand washing was so important. "I'll be there within the hour."

"Great, Charlotte. You know we're lost without you."

She smiled, warmth from the compliment suffusing her.

It didn't take her long to get dressed, throw her hair up into a clip, and dash on a minimum of makeup. She grabbed her purse and headed out the door. It was now almost ten thirty. Her in-box would be growing more unmanageable by the moment.

Charlotte.

She stopped with her hand on the doorknob, the low, shivery voice blowing through her like a breeze. That had been the voice of her dream man and it had been coming from . . . *inside her house.*

Blinking rapidly, as she did when she was nervous, she scanned the kitchen to her left and the formal living room to her right. Then she peered up the stairs to the second floor. All was calm, silent. The house was empty.

She gave her head a shake. "Crazy," she muttered and headed out the door.

JUST as she'd presumed, the papers on her desk had multiplied like rabbits. The problem with being a capable employee was that your boss had lots of confidence in you, and that was a double-edged sword.

She paused in the entrance of her cubicle and stared at the pile of work for a moment, sighing. Then she firmly reminded herself that this was why she'd obtained her MPA from the University of Illinois, cheating herself out of a personal life while she'd done it. It was true that her position here at Yancy and Tate wasn't her ultimate dream, but it was a stepping-stone to the career she really wanted. Everyone had to pay their dues, and she was no exception.

"Charlotte?"

She jerked a little, startled, and turned to see Harvey behind her.

"Sorry." He grinned, transforming his plain face into something close to handsome. He studied her for a moment. "You're wearing glasses."

Glancing at him, she touched the frame, readjusting it on the bridge of her nose. "I didn't want to waste time with my contacts today."

"Ah, well, glad to see you made it in."

She walked into her cubicle, setting her purse onto the one free space on her desk, and sank into her chair. "Glad to be here."

"Just stopped by to remind you that we have a client meeting at one thirty."

Panic shot through her veins as she remembered. "Tricities, Inc.?"

He nodded meaningfully.

She stopped herself from lunging at her desk. She'd totally forgotten and she had so much to do! "I'll be ready, Harvey."

He smiled at her. "I know you will. I have complete confidence in you."

She spent what was left of her morning cutting through the pile of work on her desk and then, instead of taking a lunch, prepared for the meeting with Tricities.

By the time early afternoon rolled around, she felt caught up and prepared to consult with their client. Knowing she must also *look* prepared, she headed into the bathroom with her makeup bag and examined her face in the mirror.

"Ugh." The sound echoed into the empty room.

With hardly any makeup, her face looked white and gaunt. She hadn't had much time to fuss with her hair that morning and was decidedly "pillow-styled." She undid the clip, extracted her brush, and went to work. There wasn't much she could do with the thick mass other than straighten it up and put the clip back in. That accomplished, she set her glasses aside and worked on her makeup.

Then she stood back and took a critical appraisal of her clothing. She'd thrown on a white button-down shirt, a plaid cardigan and a pair of black pants. Frowning, she saw the top two buttons of her shirt were undone. She corrected it, put her glasses back on, and gave herself a critical head-to-toe sweep. *Marginally better.* She gave her shirt one last downward tug to settle it more smoothly in place and smiled at herself in the mirror to practice for the meeting.

Grabbing her makeup bag from the counter, she walked to the bathroom door.

Charlotte.

She stopped short, her entire body going cold. The voice of her dream man again. At work. In the bathroom. Oh, God, was she going insane?

Charlotte, come to me.

Images flashed through her mind. An airplane ticket, destination Protection City, Carolina. A flash of heavy, tall gates— the gates of Piefferburg, if she wasn't mistaken. She'd only ever caught glimpses on the TV program *Faemous*, but she thought she recognized them. Piefferburg was the huge warded detainment area where the fae were kept imprisoned by the Phaendir.

With the flashing images came a nearly irresistible compulsion to leave work *right now*. Drive to the airport *right now*. Buy a ticket to Protection City *right now*. All of a sudden she *had* to get to Piefferburg, no matter what.

Dropping her makeup bag onto the floor since it no longer mattered—nothing except getting to Piefferburg mattered— she went for the bathroom door. If she hurried, she could make it to Protection City by evening.

"Wait a minute!" She stopped cold with her fingers wrapped around the door handle, and then yanked her hand away, scrubbing it on her pants as though she could wipe the germs off.

What was she doing? She couldn't leave; she had a financial consultation to give. Anyway, she had no reason to drop everything and fly to Protection City, Carolina. Even less reason to go to Piefferburg.

The fae? *No way.*

She shuddered, remembering the nightmares she'd had of them as a child. When she'd been six she'd woken night after night screaming, soaked in cold sweat. Her father had been there to reassure her that no goblins lurked under the bed, no joint-eaters peered at her from the cracked open closet door, but it had been close to her mother's death and she'd cried for her.

Night after night she'd screamed and thrashed in her father's arms realizing anew that her mother wasn't there to hold her . . . and never would be again. The grief of that still lay heavy in her chest and the nightmares had forever linked the fae with it.

No, she wanted no part of the fae. They were right where they belonged and she had no wish to consort with them. She was quite happy to live all the way across the country from that place and nothing was going to force her there.

Still, the compulsion lingered. She gritted her teeth and furrowed her brow, fighting it. It eased a little, and she sagged against the door. What was wrong with her? It had to be the dream she'd had. It must've jarred something loose in her subconscious that she hadn't known she needed to deal with. Find the root of the problem, address it, and she'd be able to continue with her job. She just needed a little time to sit down and think, analyze the situation. Unfortunately she wasn't going to get that, not right now.

Feeling suddenly sick, she backed away from the door and leaned down to pick up her makeup bag. Just then Erica, one of her colleagues, came into the bathroom.

"Oh, my gosh, Charlotte, are you all right?" Erica breathed, her blue eyes wide. "You look like you're about to vomit."

She glanced into the mirror. Her pale face had taken on a distinctly greenish hue and she was covered in a light coating of sweat. Lovely. She blinked rapidly, searching for a response.

Charlotte, you cannot ignore me. Come to me now.

Compulsion filled her once again. The only thing that kept her from bolting for the door was her willpower. She bowed her head, closed her eyes, and grabbed the edge of the bathroom counter to stop herself from complying with the mystery man's wishes.

"Charlotte? Should I call someone? Are you all right?"

Come now.

Charlotte forced her eyes open and returned Erica's panicked stare. "Did you hear that?"

"Hear what?" Erica's frown deepened and she shook her head. "You really don't look good. You should go home, Charlotte." She entered one of the stalls.

Go home? In the middle of the day? She'd never done that in her entire life. She touched her forehead and found it warm and feverish.

Charlotte.

Letting go of the counter and not bothering with her makeup bag, she lunged for the door and raced all the way back to her cubicle. Her watch showed it was exactly one twenty. Past time to get to the conference room. Scooping her papers into her arms, she raced across the office toward her destination.

CHARLOTTE LILLIAN BENNETT, COME TO ME.

Strong compulsion filled her. She fought it, but this time nothing stemmed the tide of *must*. Ten times stronger than what she'd felt in the bathroom, there was no denying this. Right outside the double doors of the conference room, she dropped all her files.

Leave. Yes, that's exactly what she should do. Harvey could meet with the clients solo. He had all their financials and could consult with them just fine on his own. She needed to get to Piefferburg right now.

The heavy wooden doors of the conference room opened

and Harvey stuck his head out, surveying the mess of paper on the floor and then looking up at her. "Charlotte?"

Alien persuasion crashed through her. *Tell him you've received an urgent call from the Piefferburg Business Council and you must leave right away.*

She bent down and gathered the files into her arms. "I just got a . . . a call. I need to leave. I'm so sorry, Harvey." She stood and fled.

Stopping only long enough to drop the files at her desk and grab her purse, she went to her car and drove immediately to the airport. In her head shouted the refrain, *What am I doing?* Yet she was completely unable to stop herself from handing over her credit card to the clerk at the Transnational Airlines service desk for a seat on the next flight to Protection City.

The lady behind the counter looked up at her with a bland smile on her face. "Do you have any luggage to check?"

She glanced down at her side as if a suitcase had magically appeared there. "No." She had nothing with her. No extra clothing, no toiletries. She'd even left her vitamins behind, drat it all. This was obviously fae magick of some kind. The prospect terrified her almost as much as it angered her. What if she'd had a critical prescription she'd needed to take? What if she'd had a pet at home? Or kids!

Fae magick. Fear made a cold sweat break out on her forehead.

The lady gave her the boarding pass and soon she'd passed through security and reached her gate. She collapsed into a chair and stared at the waiting plane, every fiber of her being straining to get on it *now* so she could get to Piefferburg *now*.

Her father would kill her if he knew what she was doing. Whether or not she was under some magickal fae mind-control, her father would skin her alive. Her family had a dark and sordid history with the fae and she'd been fed stories about their treachery since she'd been a child. Never consort with the fae, her father had warned her. Stay away from Piefferburg at all costs, he'd said. Don't be seduced by the glittering images that *Faemous* feeds the public. The fae are bad. Evil.

"The only good fae is a dead fae," had been a familiar utterance in her home.

Her opinion was far more varied than her father's. In her mind it wasn't so black and white as all that. The HFF, Humans for the Freedom of the Fae, had some very valid points, in her opinion, though that was an opinion she would never share with her father. Especially since her father was the head of the HCIF, Humans for the *Continued Incarceration* of the Fae, the HFF's flip side. The HCIF gave scads of money to the Phaendir and helped them lobby Congress for legislation that would keep the fae right where they were.

She glowered at the airplane. She had no idea what was going on here, but once she found out, there was going to be hell to pay. Of course, mostly that was the fear talking. She knew she lacked the ability to bring hell to a fae. The weakest one was twenty times more powerful than she was.

And this man was powerful, indeed.

Her mind strayed to the dream. At the time she'd thought it had just been a vivid dream, harmless. She'd played out all her fantasies with that luscious man. Now it turned out . . .

Oh, hell. The realization slammed into her.

That had never been an innocent dream and the man she'd committed all those erotic acts with was probably real. He had to be the one holding her leash at the moment, the one who was yanking it so forcefully.

Her hand strayed to the collar of her shirt. The things she'd done in that dream . . .

A man swathed in the traditional attire of the Phaendir sat down across from her. Many of the magickal sect of druids wore ordinary clothing, dark suits, dress pants, and polo shirts. Usually you couldn't tell a Phaendir from an ordinary man, but this one wore the heavy brown robes of a monk.

Still holding the collar of her shirt, she gave him a tentative smile, which he returned with a stern look. Almost as if to say he knew what she'd done last night.

She slid down into her chair and looked away from him.

The Phaendir were always male and mostly all big and imposing. And one could never forget the powerful magick. Magick enough to keep all the fae of the world imprisoned. They deserved everyone's utmost respect and were not to be trifled with.

Except she was about to both disrespect and trifle with them.

How was she supposed to get permission to be admitted into Piefferburg? It used to be that any human could enter at their own risk, but now that Gideon Amberdoyal had become archdirector, every human needed to be personally approved by him, their backgrounds thoroughly checked.

Lie.

She blinked several times. "Excuse me?"

The Phaendir looked at her sharply, his eyes narrowing. The action reminded her of a hawk that had just caught sight of a juicy mouse.

Don't say anything out loud. Speak to me in your head.

Her mind whirled for a moment. She chewed her lip. Finally, she tried it. *You're real?*

As real as you are.

Oh, God. *You're fae?*

Pause. *Do you know any human capable of long-range telepathy and dream invasion?*

She went silent for a minute, processing everything and trying very hard not to freak out in front of the brother.

When you arrive in Protection City it will be very late. Stop at a store and buy a suitcase, clothes, and toiletries. Find a hotel and stay there for the night. In the morning, go to Phaendir Headquarters and ask for entry into Piefferburg.

What will I tell them?

Tell them your company is doing some work for the Piefferburg Business Council and you're coming in at their request. They need help with their accounting system and a few other issues. Tell them you'll be there for an extended period of time, two weeks at a minimum to complete the project.

She forced herself not to react physically to his words. *Two weeks? I can't be gone from my job for two weeks. Anyway, the Phaendir will check my story and discover I'm lying.*

We've got you covered.

What was that supposed to mean? *What's going on? Pause. Are you going to hurt me?*

There was no reply for several moments. *We have no plans to harm you.*

That was not exactly a comforting answer.

I hate you with all that I am. Even in her mind, her voice shook with emotion.

Silence.

TWO

BROTHER Gideon P. Amberdoyal stared across his desk at Charlotte with his watery brown eyes. Slight of build and average in height, Mr. Amberdoyal was hardly the imposing figure his position might lead someone to believe him to be. In fact, he was far slighter in physical stature than the majority of his Phaendir brethren. With his thinning hair and cheap gray suit, he reminded Charlotte more of a used car salesman than the leader of the Phaendir, one of the most powerful group of individuals in the world.

She'd met his predecessor, Brother Maddoc, at a fundraiser the HCIF had held for the Phaendir a couple of years ago. She hadn't wanted to attend, but her father had guilted her into it. The former archdirector had been far more physically impressive and much more charming.

She smiled politely. "It's an honor to meet you, Mr. Amberdoyal."

He gave her a cold smile, his flat brown eyes flashing dangerously for a moment. Her smile faded. Ah, so there was strength behind the unassuming visage. "Your father is the illustrious Jacob Arthur Bennett, head of the HCIF. I think it's an honor to meet *you*, Miss Bennett. It's always nice to encounter humans who care so much about our cause."

"I do care." *Just not as much as my father.* "My whole family is very grateful to the Phaendir. I'm not sure my father's genetic line would have survived if the Phaendir hadn't stepped in during the fifteen hundreds and created Piefferburg. In fact, I might not even be sitting here if you hadn't imprisoned the fae."

"Yes." He templed his fingers on the top of his desk. "Your father told me the story."

She shuddered and looked down into her lap. "Believe me when I say I'm not looking forward to spending time among them." She hadn't lied yet, but it was coming. The magickal persuasion lay heavily on her will as it had since yesterday.

Brother Gideon smiled his hard, dangerous little smile again and leaned toward her from behind his desk. "That's why I find your request so odd. Why would someone with a history like yours take an assignment that put her in Piefferburg City for two whole weeks? Why didn't you request that Yancy and Tate send someone else in your place?"

The wave of compulsion was so strong that when she opened her mouth to tell Gideon the absolute truth, no words came out, only little puffs of air.

Brother Gideon's eyes narrowed.

"Sorry, I'm a little overwhelmed." She blinked a few times and smiled. "I don't like it, but it's my job and I'm looking to be promoted. I couldn't turn this assignment down, not at this point in my career. You can call my boss if you're suspicious of my intentions." She opened her purse, extracted one of her business cards, and handed it to him over the desk.

She hoped he called. Her boss would tell him the truth—he had never assigned her any such special project—and she could get out of this mess somehow. Even if it meant she went to jail or the loony bin, anything was better than Piefferburg.

He took the card, stared at it for a moment, and then set

it aside. As he moved, she noticed the thick, white mottled skin peeking from his shirtsleeve cuffs. Scar tissue, it looked like. Charlotte knew that the most pious of the Phaendir self-flagellated. Apparently this man was really into it.

Licking his thin lips, he steepled his fingers on his desk and raised his gaze to hers. "I can see no possible ulterior motive for your entrance into Piefferburg, Miss Bennett. I'm satisfied after performing a very thorough background check that you have no sympathies with the HFF, especially since you're the daughter of Jacob Bennett."

She shook her head. "No, I don't."

He smiled. "Still, you must understand we need to be very careful these days. My predecessor, Brother Maddoc, allowed the fae to recover several magickal artifacts, ones that might be of use to them. It's why we checked your luggage and purse when you arrived this morning."

"Yes, I know. I read all about it in the paper. There's a possibility the fae could break your warding and run loose." A shiver went up her spine at the thought.

She wasn't alone in her fear. After the news had broken there had been a run on survival supplies and weapons that could be used against the fae. Things like goblin repellant, red cap deterrent, and big guns that stopped just about anything with a pulse. Her father even kept a charmed iron sword in his library for such an event, a weapon that had cost him over fifty thousand dollars. The media had, of course, shamelessly hyped the hysteria.

Brother Gideon's face went hard. "No, Miss Bennett, there's no possibility that such a thing might occur. Not on my watch."

She nodded. "I believe you."

"But in order to keep it from happening, we need to analyze every entrant into Piefferburg. My predecessor's methods were too lax and people got in who shouldn't have. Our processes are not meant to offend."

"I'm not at all offended." Part of one of her nightmares flashed into her head—the bloody open mouth of a red cap. "I'm happy to see such strong controls in place."

He smiled at her and picked up the business card. "I'm glad you understand." Then he reached for the phone.

Oh, thank God. He was going to call.

Say this, "As Labrai wills, so shall it be."

Charlotte jerked at the abrupt intrusion of her puppet master's creepy psychic link. His words were accompanied by coercion so strong that the phrase tumbled from her lips before she could even think about uttering it. Smiling serenely, she said, "As Labrai wills, so shall it be."

Brother Gideon paused with the phone halfway to his ear. She could hear it ringing on the other end. Her office was in Oregon, three hours behind Protection City, and had just opened. Brother Gideon almost set the receiver back into the cradle. Instead, he lifted it all the way to his ear.

Ha! Take that, puppet master. She received no reply. The magick man was probably shaking in his boots right now.

She smiled smugly as Brother Gideon connected with one of her superiors and attempted to verify her story. Any moment now and the jig would be up. Brother Gideon would—

He hung up the phone and gave her a wide smile. "Everything checks out. I hope your project in Piefferburg City is successful, Miss Bennett."

Her smile faltered.

Still under the magickal mojo, she stood smoothly and offered her hand across the desk. "Thank you very much, Mr. Amberdoyal. It truly was a pleasure to meet you."

He stood and shook her hand. "I'll walk you to the gates. Shall I order a car to meet you once you're inside? You're not dressed for a hike through the Boundary Lands and I don't advise it. It's very dangerous."

"Yes, a car to Piefferburg Square would be lovely."

They made their way out of the office, headed toward the exit. Her hands were shaking as she picked up her suitcase, packed with clothes and other items she'd bought as soon as she'd reached Protection City, and followed him. In a mere matter of minutes she would be in the one place on earth she'd never wanted to go.

"I understand you're going to the Piefferburg Mercantile Exchange, among other locales," Brother Gideon said mildly as he led her to the gates.

"Yes. They're having trouble with their accounting system and need me to consult."

"Yours is not the first human company to be doing business in Piefferburg City, of course. Piefferburg has done well in creating an economy." Brother Gideon's teeth barely kept from gnashing. "And the government allows them to do it. They've even gone so far as to allow the Piefferburg Business Council to make phone calls into the human world to arrange for people such as yourself to enter. Of course we closely monitor their communication."

"Of course. Business is business, I guess."

"Indeed."

Gravel crunched under her shoes and the wheels of her suitcase as they walked in silence for a moment. Outwardly she appeared calm. Inwardly, she seethed. As soon as she met this man pulling her strings like she was some marionette, she was going to let him have it. Now she understood that expression about blood boiling with rage.

When they reached the huge gates, they were already opening. The hinges made a low moaning sound, a little like what she imagined the gates of hell might sound like. Her stomach churned.

Her eyes skirted the tall stone wall that ran around Piefferburg, but her human gaze couldn't see the magickal warding that imprisoned the fae. An almost organic thing, the warding existed in a subconscious, hive portion of the Phaendir's collective mind—fueled by their breath, thoughts, magick, and, most of all, by their very strong belief system. It wasn't that wall or those gates that kept the fae separate from the world— it was the druids.

Brother Gideon bowed. "Safe travels. May Labrai always be at your side."

She bowed in response, a little stiffly. "And also at yours."

"Call the front gates when you're ready to leave. Your

name will be on the list of approved exiters. They'll send a car for you if you ask them."

"Thank you." She stood staring at him for a long moment. Stalling. The compulsion was pushing her toward the gates and she was resisting, but her ability to do so flagged more with every second.

Brother Gideon fidgeted, motioning at the entrance. "You're free to enter now."

She closed her eyes briefly. "So I am." The magickal pressure forced her to turn and walk through the partially opened gates, leaving her world behind. The gates closed with a metallic clang that made her jerk.

The other side of the gates looked much the same, though the trees and foliage around her seemed to have extra color—like she'd stepped into a painting in which the artist had used slightly unreal hues. She stood on a paved area with a dark brown gravel road that led off into what appeared to be an enchanted forest beginning not far away.

All she could see past the paved area, other than the road stretching away to what had to be Piefferburg City, were trees. Huge, towering, ancient trees. She'd never seen the California redwoods, but this is what she imagined they must look like. She felt dwarfed by them, and they seemed almost sentient. As though they were watching her, judging her, and found her . . . inferior.

"Miss Bennett?"

She turned to meet her first fae and froze, staring. Terror raced through her veins, made her eyes open wide in panic, yet her feet were rooted in place. It was a red cap, of all things. One of the creatures from her nightmares. The images that had haunted her nights as a child flooded in a rush to her mind's eye. Jaws snapping. Snarling. Blood dripping from sharpened teeth.

She drew a deep, shaking breath to get hold of herself. The nightmares had never been real. It had only been the imaginings of a small child's mind drawn from her father's horrid warning-filled stories about the fae.

Just a nightmare. Not real . . .

She drew a second breath, closed her eyes, and collected herself. She felt light-headed.

"Miss Bennett?" the red cap asked again.

Never real. She opened her eyes and her heart skipped a beat.

He was a hulking monster of a humanoid fae with a dark red "cap" of skin on his otherwise bald head. A swirl of black tattoos marked his massive face, swarming down one side of his neck. If she could see inside his mouth, she would find viciously pointed teeth—all the better to tear the flesh from the bones of his enemies.

Red caps needed to kill periodically to survive—luckily *periodically* was every few hundred years. It was also lucky that they kept their restorative murdering to their own kind in elaborate gladiator-like tournaments that all the fae turned out to see. *Faemous* was always trying to get permission from the FCC to air the tournaments and, luckiest of all, the FCC always denied them.

But they didn't just attack indiscriminately, she reminded herself. They weren't vicious, murdering creatures. They had rules, a system in place to fulfill their needs.

Of course, she could argue logically with herself all day . . . there was still a red cap standing in front of her.

"Please don't eat me," she whispered and then snapped her mouth shut. Her fear had just pushed the words she'd been thinking right out there.

The red cap guard leered at her and smiled. Oh, yes, there were the teeth. Wooziness and nausea made her take a step backward. "You're not to my taste," he growled.

Another guard motioned with an excessively long arm toward a classy black sedan waiting at the curb. "Your car."

"Th-thank you." Honestly, she couldn't wait to be out of their presence. She walked quickly to the vehicle and opened the back door. Peering within, she hoped for something that wouldn't make her want to pee her pants.

A man with artfully tousled, thick dark hair and a face fit

for a men's magazine cover grinned charmingly at her from the behind the wheel. He had dimples, a trait that gave him an innocent air that was immediately offset by the mischievous— maybe even dangerous—glint in his eyes. He was devastatingly handsome. He was not, however, the man from her dream.

"I'm Niall Daegan Riordan Quinn. Get in and I'll take you where you need to be." His voice reminded her of warm honey.

She paused, leaning into the car with one hand on the handle of her suitcase and the other on the door. "I'm nowhere close to where I need to be." Her voice shook with badly controlled rage. "Tell your friend to let me go back to my life."

His eyebrows rose. "You have more guts than your looks imply."

"Gee, thanks for the compliment."

He grinned again. This time it was far more irritating than charming. "Get in already, would you? You've got no choice but to go to Kieran, and you know it."

Kieran? "Is that his name?"

"Get in and I'll tell you more."

She hesitated a moment longer, then pushed her suitcase onto the backseat and climbed in after it. No way was she sitting in front with this guy.

Once she'd closed the door, he pulled away from the curb. "Normally the goblins drive the cars to and from the gates, but we figured getting into a vehicle with one of them behind the wheel might be a little too much for you."

She shifted impatiently. "So Kieran is the"—she struggled to find the right word. She never swore, but the urge to do so now was nearly overwhelming—"jerk who did this to me?"

"Whoa, Nelly. That's some strong language there, girly." Sarcasm dripped from every syllable. He chuckled . . . irritatingly. She was really starting to hate this fae.

"*Fine.* Bastard! Asshole! Dick!" she yelled at him. Her cheeks heated.

"Ah. Now that's more like what I'd expect from a woman who's had all her free will taken away." He gave a genuine laugh this time. "Still, take a tip from me. I wouldn't be calling Kieran Aindréas Cairbre Aimhrea an asshole or a dick to his face. He's got somewhat of a bad temper. Calling him a bastard is okay since he is one in the literal sense of the word." He paused as if thinking. "In the figurative sense, too."

"Will he hurt me?"

"Kieran's got a bad temper, but I've never known him to harm a woman. Still, he's holding your leash, so to speak, so it's probably wiser to keep him happy."

"What does he want from me?"

"All will be revealed once we reach the Unseelie Court."

Her spine snapped to attention and she gripped the seat in front of her, leaning toward Niall. "The *Unseelie* Court?"

He cast a look of disbelief over his shoulder. "Did you think we were going to the Rose, the tower of sunshine, lollipops, and unicorns that poop rainbows? No fae with juice dark enough to bind and compel a human all the way across the country is going to be Seelie, woman."

THREE

AND, of course, if she'd thought about it, she would have realized that.

She sat back in the seat with a thump. This was getting worse by the second.

Niall glanced at her in the rearview mirror. "It's not that bad. The Unseelie aren't all the boogeymen the media has made us out to be."

She blinked. "An entire *Faemous* crew was once *eaten* in the Black Tower."

"Oh, yeah, that." Niall shrugged one impressively broad shoulder. "It was the goblins. What are you going to do?"

She sat for one shocked moment, then attempted to sputter out a response.

He met her eyes in the mirror. "Humans enter Piefferburg at their own risk. That *Faemous* crew knew goblins work in the Black Tower. They should have been aware of and respected goblin culture. They knew the dangers, but their stupidity and greed made them take chances." He shrugged again. "And they paid the price. C'est la vie."

"You're okay with people just . . . getting eaten?"

"No, I'm not okay with it. It was a damn crying shame." He distinctly did not sound like it was a damn crying shame at all. "But that's the nature of goblins. Piss them off and you might get eaten. They stuck their video cameras into goblin faces over and over, even when they were told not to do it. They filmed goblin women and children when they were warned to never, *ever* do that." He shrugged again. "Male goblins are very protective of their females and offspring, offspring especially. Threaten their young and you become a meal. As far as I'm concerned, that *Faemous* crew pretty much invited themselves to be dinner." He peered at her in the mirror. "Cultural sensitivity, you know? Now why don't you look outside for a while and enjoy the view. We'll be in the *ceantar láir* soon, then the city and there's not much green there."

Grinding her teeth, she glanced out the window and did a double take. The Boundary Lands had an ethereal glow caused by tiny sparkling lights in the treetops and the foliage, lighting the forest so she could see the huge tree trunks that seemed to go on forever. They shadowed a carpet of lush green grass that was scattered here and there with clumps of bright flowers or the occasional moss-covered log or gigantic stone. Flowers should not have been growing on the forest floor. Normally there wasn't enough sunlight there for them. It had be some sort of magick that kept them—

"The birch ladies."

Apparently she'd been talking out loud. Fabulous. "The birch ladies are responsible for the flowers and grass that shouldn't be there?"

"Yes. They're the caretakers of the forest. Their job is also to take care of anyone who loses their way, especially women."

"What are all those twinkling lights?" She paused, trying to make sense of them. "Are they—"

"Please don't say Tinkerbell."

She snapped her mouth shut because that's exactly what

she'd been about to ask. If they were very small faeries like Tinkerbell.

"The lights are sentient and they're fae, but they're more like what you might think of as plankton. You can't really interact with them. They're called sprae and they provide magickal energy to the living things in the forest."

"That's incredible," she breathed, staring out the window. For a moment, she almost forgot about her plight.

"You're in Piefferburg. Everything is incredible here."

The word *Piefferburg* brought her back to reality. She closed her mouth and sank into the seat, facing forward. After a moment, she asked, "Why didn't Mr. Aimhrea come to pick me up himself? It seems like the least he could have done."

Niall raised his eyebrows suggestively in the mirror. "I think after the dream you shared with him you can call him Kieran."

Her cheeks heated and she looked out the window.

"He didn't come because the bond he forged with you is weaker according to proximity. The closer you get, the more he loses his hold on your free will. Once you two meet face-to-face it will pretty much disappear."

Finally, some good news.

"We couldn't have you kicking a fuss at the gates. We needed to get you to the Black Tower so we could make sure you're secure when the compulsion part of the bond breaks."

Or maybe not.

Her breath came fast and shallow. She closed her eyes, fighting to gain control of an impending panic attack. "You intend to keep me prisoner?"

"It's unfortunate and we're sorry we need to do it." His eyes met hers in the mirror. "But it's the only way."

"Oh, God."

"We're not going to hurt you." His voice was softer, filled with something that sounded like genuine empathy. "Really, we're not. Stop worrying about that."

She panted a few times, got herself under control, and glanced out the window. They were entering what had to be the outskirts of Piefferburg City. Was this fae suburbia? What had Niall called it . . . *ceantar láir*?

Like human suburbs, the lawns were all carefully manicured with neat little fences and a car in every driveway. However, instead of every house being more or less the same, each one was drastically different. A very small house might sit next to an enormous one, for example. And all of them were just odd. Some looked like the houses she'd always known, but others were underground or were shaped like a deranged octopus or completely made of glass or had no windows at all.

She guessed it must be because all the races of the trooping fae lived side by side here. Each type of fae had different living requirements.

It wasn't long before the suburbs began to give way to more commercial areas. Soon it became clear they were in the city, though it had far more the feel of a European city than an American one. She'd been to Brussels before and that's what it reminded of her of—narrow back streets and old, uneven cobblestone that made the car shake when you drove over it.

Here most of the houses were tall and slim, clearly ancient and probably had winding, twisting staircases within. The city had retained its sixteenth-century roots, though a more modern city had been built around and on top of it. It created a mix of old and new that gave the city a unique feel—as unique as its inhabitants.

Niall guided the car through a series of narrow, curving roads, deeper and deeper into the heart of the city. With interest, she examined the fae they passed on the streets. To think they had once lived in secret alongside humans. Some of them were hideous; how had they managed to remain incognito? Of course, by the fifteen hundreds, they hadn't been. That's when they'd been outed as a result of their internal strife and Watt Syndrome. Then, when the fae had been at their weakest, the humans and Phaendir had allied to capture and imprison them.

The neighborhood seemed to take an upscale turn and she assumed they must be near the Black Tower. The driver pulled up in front of a tall, multiturreted shiny black quartz building and her question was answered.

"I don't want to get out." She imagined her back was glued to the seat.

"Ah, well, you know he'll make you."

"I hate him."

"To know Kieran is to hate him. He's not exactly all sunshine and puppies." He opened his door, got out, and threw his keys to a tall, spindly gray thing . . . that had to be a goblin. Her heart rate sped. All she needed to see today was a joint-eater and she'd hit her nightmare trifecta.

Niall opened her door and leaned in. "Come on, princess."

"I'm not getting out while he's there." She stared at the goblin.

"He's not going to hurt you. He just wants to take your bag." He sighed and rolled his eyes when she didn't move. "I won't let anyone eat you, I promise." He waved the goblin away.

Still, she couldn't make herself move. Fear had driven an icy spike down her spine.

Kieran cut into her mind. *The goblin means you no harm and neither do we. Come to me, Charlotte.* This time, along with the magickal persuasion that coaxed her to leave the car came a wave of calmness.

She closed her eyes for a moment, absorbing every ounce of that manufactured calm, took a deep breath, and climbed out of the vehicle. She eyed the retreating goblin so hard she almost tripped on the curb. "I'll take my own bag."

"*I'll* take your bag." Niall grinned his annoyingly charming grin at her, took her suitcase, and walked through the wide black quartz double doors of the tower. "Follow me."

Holding her arms over her chest, she followed Niall through a large foyer that seemed oddly empty of people . . . beings, as the case may be, and then took an elevator up several floors. It let out into a corridor with—surprise— black quartz walls and a black marble floor shot through with veins of silver. Accent tables set with pretty vases of flowers decorated the wide hallway, along with artwork and recessed lighting. Evil posh.

They stopped outside a heavy wooden door that was carved with symbols she didn't recognize. Whatever they were, they made her skin want to run away without her.

Niall slanted a grin at her. "Ready to meet your master?"

She snarled inarticulately at him.

Niall ignored her and opened the door.

The most gorgeous man she'd ever seen in her life rose from a black leather couch and walked toward her. His thick, longish tousled dark hair shadowed moody dark eyes. His face was handsome, but not in a *GQ* kind of way. His features were a little rougher, a little less refined. He looked like he hadn't had much sleep in the last twenty-four hours or so, and a brutal, wild light lit his eyes. That light warned her to be careful of him. His chest was well defined under a navy blue sweater, the hint of the black tribal tattoo that covered his side and snaked up one muscular upper arm and broad shoulder peeking at the collar. His narrow hips were snuggled into a pair of well-worn jeans.

She knew that well-defined chest, that tattoo, those narrow hips, intimately. This was the man from her dream.

Face grim, he came to stand in front of her. "I'm Kieran Aindréas Cairbre Aimhrea."

At first look, the compulsion that had held her prisoner eased to the point of almost nonexistence.

Charlotte drew her fist back and let fly, popping him right in the mouth.

FOUR

PAIN exploded in Kieran's jaw and mouth. His head whipped to the side. He put a hand to his lip and drew it back to see blood on his fingertips. Immediately the coppery, salty flavor of it hit his tongue. She'd split his lip. He looked at her through the fall of hair across his forehead. He guessed he must've looked pissed, since she took a step backward while holding her hand like it hurt.

The merry sound of Niall's laughter filled the air.

With a sharp shake of his head, he flipped his hair back and tried to get the animosity out of his eyes. It was hard, considering who her father was. She'd been raised to hate the fae, to want to keep them imprisoned. It was difficult not to feel anger toward her, even though he'd essentially enslaved her.

Guilt flickered.

After all, he'd pulled her from her life, dragged her all the way across the country, and eradicated most of her free will.

His tongue snaked out to taste blood on his lip. "I guess I deserved that."

She raised her chin, though fear lit her eyes. Some people cowered when they were terrified, other people punched. He was pleased to find that Charlotte was a puncher. She would need strength for what was to come. She cradled her fist in her opposite hand. "You sure did. A whole lot more, too." She dropped her hand to her side and adopted a challenging body posture, looking ready to leap at him and tear him limb from limb.

He grinned, and it cost him. Pain shot through his mouth and he winced. He took her in from head to toe. Black hair, small, curvy. Glasses on the bridge of her narrow nose and black slashes of eyebrows above them. Freckles across her cheeks. She wore little makeup, but she had beautiful skin and didn't need it. Pretty hazel eyes. Nice mouth. A seriously dowdy dresser—as though afraid someone might notice her, or, heaven forbid, find her attractive. From the way she dressed he guessed that humans must completely underestimate her, but there was steel in her. Not many in this world dared to hit him.

Of course, that just proved she didn't know him very well.

She hadn't looked like an undersexed multiple cat owner in their shared dream. That was typical, of course. Humans in dreams tended to appear as they saw themselves in their heads, or as they wished they were, or sometimes as a representation of their innermost selves. In her case, he presumed her dream self was the latter, considering the hellcat way she was acting right now. Maybe extreme anger and fear had brought it out of her. This behavior was incongruous with her appearance and everything he knew about her.

Interesting.

In the binding dream he'd initiated with her, her hair had been loose and a little longer. She hadn't worn her glasses and her eyes had been a beautiful hazel that had alternately looked green or brown, flecked with amber. She'd worn light makeup that had made the most of her lovely skin and full lips. The clothes she'd worn—for the short amount of time she'd been wearing them—had been far less drab than the ones she had on now. His mouth went dry at the memory.

He wiped away the last bit of blood. "Nice to meet you, Charlie."

She frowned at him. "Who said you could call me Charlie?"

"You did. In the dream." He paused, blinked slowly, and smiled. "Remember?"

She turned an interesting shade of red.

"We got close enough for nicknames." His grin widened. It hurt, but it was worth it. "If you recall."

"You bastard. You . . . you seduced me and then hijacked my will." She stalked toward him. "You used my body and then bound me by some *magick*"—she said *magick* like someone might say *vomit*—"that may have cost me my career." She poked her finger into his chest. "Not to mention you made me lie to the Phaendir and enter the one place in the world I never wanted to go."

"Yeah, that about sums it up." He grabbed her finger and used it to push away from her. "Except I never used your body. I've never even touched your body until now. All that was only in your head. It wasn't real."

"Semantics."

"By the way, you were pretty willing to be seduced."

She opened her mouth, but no sound came out. "It was only a dream!"

He stared at her for a pregnant moment, then winked and walked away. "Exactly."

"The magick that binds me seems pretty real."

He turned toward her and pointed. "That's real as death and you can't break it."

Her jaw worked and her eyes snapped. "Why are you doing this to me?"

Opening his arms, he gave her a mocking half bow. "It's my magick. I'm a dream wraith, among other things. I can enter people's dreams, influence them, make the pretty into a nightmare or nightmares into the pretty." He grinned. "But where's the fun in that? I can even steal dreams if I choose."

She paled. Her voice shook. "You know that's not what I meant."

"Oh, I'm sorry. What did you mean, love?"

She stared at him, looking as though on the verge of tears. Even though he knew how much she hated him and his kind, he felt like an asshole for taunting her. What he'd done to her hadn't been right.

But it had been the only option.

He hadn't wanted to do it. He'd had magick enough to bind one person to him through a dream, only one. He'd been saving that magick for centuries, hoping to never have to use it. He had a right to feel grouchy, too.

Just then Niall cleared his throat. Kieran had forgotten he was even there. He set her suitcase down in the foyer. "The queen is going to want to see her."

Kieran met Charlotte's eyes with a small amount of satisfaction. No sense in cutting short the agony. She could wait a little longer to discover her purpose in being here. "All right. Let's head up there."

Charlotte's eyes bulged and he could hear her breath catch from way across the room. "I haven't slept in close to twenty-four hours. I need to rest, maybe take a shower—"

"Worried about your appearance before our queen?" Kieran lifted a brow. "I thought you hated the fae. Why would you feel the need to show respect to our monarch?"

Her hands twisted in front of her. "I don't . . . *hate* the fae."

"Really?" That was from Niall. "Could've fooled me."

"We know about your father, Charlotte." Kieran gave a slow blink of satisfaction. "We know you were raised with certain prejudices. Come on, admit it, you're a bigot."

"That's such an ugly word."

"An ugly word for an ugly thing, yes."

"You're not being fair. You don't even know me." She rolled her eyes. "I'm not a bigot. Just because my father is head of the HCIF doesn't mean I hate the fae. I have a mind of my own."

It was true that she was not active in the HCIF, but, by all accounts, she never seemed to turn down a fund-raiser when her father asked her to attend. "You don't love them either."

She gestured in frustration. "Well . . . should I? Look at the situation I'm in!"

Niall broke in. "I saw the way you froze when you were confronted with the red cap at the gate and the goblin at the Black Tower. We scare the snot out of you."

She put her hand on her hip and glared at Niall. "Is there any particular reason you shouldn't?"

Kieran shifted, growing impatient. "Don't worry; we're not going to feed you to Queen Aislinn." He winked at her. "She's a vegetarian."

"That's so comforting."

He pushed past her and walked out into the corridor after Niall. "Stop acting like a two-year-old and follow me. Maybe Queen Aislinn will tell you why you're here."

She hesitated a moment, then, leaving her suitcase in the foyer of his apartment, followed them.

CHARLOTTE told herself not to be intimidated by these fae or their pretend queen, but it was much harder than she'd anticipated. Especially when she entered the royal receiving room and met Queen Aislinn.

It wasn't that the queen was imposing. In fact, aside from her formal attire, she seemed very accessible, with a pretty face and warm smile. She sat in a well-to-do rose and white living room with a cozy fire burning in an enormous creek stone fireplace that stretched all the way into the vaulted ceiling of the room.

The queen sat in a comfortable-looking white chair, her husband, Gabriel Mac Braire, sitting next to her in a similar one. She smiled warmly as Charlotte, Niall, and Kieran entered the room, though her handsome husband's face remained stony.

Charlotte prided herself on not watching *Faemous* or being privy to much of the fanatical information about the fae royalty. However, it was impossible not to know a little of it. It filtered through human culture and was imbibed almost through osmosis. So she knew the queen's story and it was, admittedly, a compelling one. Queen Aislinn had spent her life in the Seelie Court, keeping the fact she was Unseelie a secret in order to spare her mother embarrassment. Her biological father had been the Shadow King himself.

When the Shadow King had discovered Aislinn was his daughter, he'd feared her, knowing she was the rightful heir to his throne. So he'd had an incubus—the man who was now her husband—seduce her to the dark side. The Shadow King had intended to kill her, in fact had planned to eradicate her very soul, but his plan had backfired when the incubus had fallen in love with her. Together they'd defeated the Shadow King and Aislinn had taken the Unseelie Throne. Something, of course, she'd had no intention of ever doing.

In the end, the Shadow King had brought upon himself the very thing he'd meant to avoid. The story was almost poetic.

"Come in." Queen Aislinn motioned to her. "You don't need to be afraid of us."

Yeah, right. Charlotte lingered in the small foyer for a little longer, then stepped into the room and took a seat—the chair farthest from Kieran. She did not bow to Aislinn. After all, she wasn't her queen.

Charlotte's gaze rested on the tattoo of the Shadow Amulet around Aislinn's throat. She knew that the amulet was an actual physical object, becoming solid at the wearer's death. When passed to the new recipient, it sank into the body, leaving the tattoo behind. It imbued the wearer with powerful magicks, making the royal the strongest fae in the court.

The queen looked pointedly at Kieran's split lip. "What happened?"

Kieran's jaw locked and his gaze flicked to Charlotte.

The queen's silver blond brows rose. "Ah."

Charlotte folded her hands in her lap and shot a poisonous look at Kieran. "I would appreciate it if *someone* would tell me why I'm in this godforsaken place with you people."

The entire room went silent and an icy sensation stole over her. For a moment she imagined the windows had actually rimed with frost. She glanced at the queen, who wore a frigid little smile.

Magick? She shuddered.

She knew that the Summer Queen, ruler of the Seelie Tuatha Dé Danann, possessed magick that sometimes spilled through her emotions. Perhaps that was the way it worked with the Shadow Queen, too.

The queen drew a slow breath, as though trying to gather her patience. "You know what the *bosca fadbh* is, I presume?"

"A puzzle box consisting of three pieces. Once joined, it acts as a key to open the back of the Book of Bindings and gives the fae access to magick that could possibly break the warding around Piefferburg and set you all free. You'd have to live in a cave not to know what it is."

She nodded. "Your family has quite the history with the fae, Miss Bennett. A history with the *bosca fadbh* as well." She paused. "Did you know that?"

Charlotte frowned. She was aware of her family's twisted past with the fae. It was a source of great shame for them. "The *bosca fadbh?* No."

"You haven't heard any family stories? Something passed down from generation to generation? It would have been on your mother's side."

"My *mother's* side?" Way to hit a sore spot with her. She shifted impatiently. "There are plenty of family stories, but nothing about the *bosca fadbh*. I've been told the fae systematically targeted my father's genetic line almost to extinction before Piefferburg was created. Please, can someone tell me what I have to do with any of this? I'm an accounting executive from Portland, Oregon. I'm not fae-struck. Hell, I never even watch *Faemous*. I never asked for any of this, never wanted it. My life should have nothing to do with yours. Just let me go."

The queen smiled sadly. "I'm sorry, but that's not going to happen."

Icy fingers of dread clenched around her spine. For a moment her anger faded to despair and she let her gaze drop into her lap.

"You're our only hope, Charlotte Lillian Bennett," she continued. "You're going to have to stay here with us until we can figure out a way to unlock the memories of your ancestors."

"Memories of my ancestors?" Her head jerked up. "What do you mean?"

The queen pursed her lips, her brow knitting. "I mean that you carry memories in your bloodline, in your maternal memory. Somewhere in the depths of your genetic material is the key, possibly, to the location of the third and final piece of the *bosca fadbh*."

"That's impossible," she breathed, her hands curling around the armrests of the chair.

The king's sensual lips curled in a mirthless smile. "You're in Piefferburg now. Under the faery mound. In the hollow hills." His smile widened. "Anything is possible."

"How long is this expected to take?" She crossed her arms over her chest, tapped her foot, and tried desperately not to ask *will it hurt and will I survive it?* She was not going to roll over and show these people her tender parts.

"We don't know." The queen smiled gently. "Perhaps you can take this opportunity to open your eyes to us. Maybe you'll see we're not that bad."

She snorted. Not that it was funny—none of this was even remotely funny. Still, it was either laugh or dart across the room and attempt regicide or queenicide or whatever the term was for killing a queen. She gave Aislinn a withering look. "Please. How can you even say that after what you've done to me?"

"We are truly sorry it has to be this way and will find a way to compensate you for it."

"You can never make this up to me."

"We've already helped arrange things with your employer. The Piefferburg Business Council is aware of what we've done and has called your boss, telling him they've summoned you. In fact, it should be great for your career, since the business council is making it very clear that no one but *you* will do for the job." The queen nodded her head at Charlotte's enemy. "You'll be staying with Kieran until we can get the details figured out."

She sucked in a breath and bolted to her feet. "No. No way." She pointed at Kieran. "There's no way on this planet that I'm staying anywhere near that man, let alone in the same apartment. You can pull me out of my life, force me to come here, endanger my career, but you're not making me spend any more time with him."

The room erupted into verbal chaos, but she wasn't listening to any of them. She worked her jaw, feeling for the tight tether she'd had around her mind for the last twenty-four hours. What was it that Niall had said? Once she came face-to-face with Kieran the compulsion part of the bond would go poof? Seems it had, since she'd been able to punch him.

"In fact," she announced. "I'm not staying here another minute. I'm out of here and you"—she glared at Kieran— "can't stop me." She whirled and went for the door.

Niall immediately shot up from his place and tried to block her way, but she pushed past him.

"Let her go," she heard Kieran say lazily. "She won't get far."

FIVE

HER steps were light, almost euphoric, on the slick, polished marble floors of the Black Tower. Remembering where Kieran's apartment was because of those creepy markings on the door, she ducked in and retrieved her suitcase. Apparently no one bothered to lock their homes here. She didn't want to leave anything of herself behind—not even quickly purchased clothing and toiletries from Walmart.

She saw no one as she sped along the corridor toward a door at the end, hopefully one that would lead her out of this madhouse. If she could find her way back to the gates, she could make it to the Phaendir and be saved.

The door opened into what appeared to be a tall, spiraling staircase. Statues of men, women, and . . . well, creatures stood in dimly lit alcoves. In fact, the whole staircase was dark. Her foot hesitated on the first step, but she couldn't retreat now. Kieran's words rang in her head, *She won't get far.*

Oh, yeah? Watch this. She started down the stairs, suitcase in hand. Her footsteps echoed as she pounded her way into the semidarkness. The suitcase got heavier with every step, but her resolve remained strong.

It was an educated guess that she would find a way out of the Black Tower when she reached the bottom, since she'd seen the four corner towers when she'd pulled up to the massive building. Indeed, judging by the view from a small window near a heavy wooden door many flights down, she'd guessed right. An exit. *Thank God.*

Pausing with her fingers wrapped around the cool metal of the handle, she peered up the staircase, brow crinkling. Why hadn't they come after her? Apparently she was pretty important to their plans, so it seemed unlikely they'd just let her walk away. Yet, here she was, walking away.

With a shrug, she opened the door.

"Oh, good, a dark alley," she muttered. It was still afternoon, but, as she peered up into the sky, she saw that the storm that had been threatening all morning was just starting to get revved up. "And rain. Fabulous."

Well, in for a penny, in for a pound. She was going to make Kieran eat his words. She stepped into the alley, letting the door close behind her. She stood for a moment in the cloud-shaded murk. The alley nestled at the foot of the Black Tower. The tower's heavy, smooth quartz walls rose on her right and a brick wall rose on the left, Dumpsters, doors, and barred windows scattered the stretch to the street.

Something made a low scratching sound and she froze. A thin cry went up from somewhere close and she whirled, her hands finding and yanking down on the door handle to go back into the tower. *Locked.*

She closed her eyes for a moment, taking a deep breath. "I'm fine," she whispered. "Just fine. Nothing to be afraid of." Then she headed down the alley. Fast. There was only one direction to go, the alley dead-ending at the foot of the Black Tower. The wheels of her suitcase made a comfortingly mundane sound on the pavement. A sound like they would make anywhere—Portland, Chicago, New York . . . Piefferburg City.

Rain started. First just a light *pitter-pat*, then getting harder. She quickened her pace.

Brighter light glimmered from what had to be the mouth of the alley and she double-timed it there, practically running. Another light emerged from an open door ahead of her on the left. A dark shape quickly blocked it.

Her steps faltered as she approached. An old, gnarled woman stood on the crumbling stoop. A cackle like a pile of broken rocks issued from her ancient throat. Charlotte shivered as she hurried past. Glancing over as she walked, she swore the old crone changed into a beautiful young woman, a slightly older pregnant lady, and then back again to the elder, cackling all the while.

God, this place was creepy.

But the scary old lady wasn't half as bad as what she found when she hit the mouth of the alley.

Charlotte came to a skidding stop. If her heart palpitated any more she was going to have a heart attack. Stark, raving terror cemented her in her shoes.

Tall, spindly gray beings regarded her with large alien eyes from their late afternoon bustle down the sidewalks of what had to be Goblin Town. She knew these creatures were mostly nocturnal, but regardless of the daylight, all the shops were open and the streets were packed with flesh-eating monsters.

And here she was right in the middle of them. Smack-dab in the center of a waking nightmare.

This had to be what Kieran had been talking about when he'd said she wasn't going to get very far. He couldn't know about her bad dreams as a child, but most humans had been fed on boogeyman tales about these things from the cradle.

Her immediate impulse was to turn and run, but the alley only led back to the Black Tower and defeat. Her pride wouldn't allow it.

She closed her eyes for a moment and concentrated on getting her breathing and heart rate under control. She would not let this visceral reaction from her childhood rule her. She had hard facts about the goblins at her disposal. Niall, as much as she hated to admit it, was right about respecting their culture. Respect their culture and they would leave her alone.

It was beginning to rain pretty hard now. Charlotte's hair and clothes were fast growing soaked. The goblins seemed not to mind; they strolled the streets as though bright sunshine shone down on them. A goblin female with heavy breasts and a small goblin baby strapped to her midsection by a large swathe of multicolored fabric stopped and looked at her. "Can I help you?"

Charlotte tried to answer and failed. She'd known many of the goblins spoke English . . . she just hadn't been expecting to converse with any.

"You look lost." The goblin shifted the weight of her sleeping child a little and pointed down the street. "If you're trying to go somewhere, there's a line of cabs down there in front of the Royal Amber Hotel." She nodded and smiled. "We don't get many humans here." Then she continued on her way.

The word *cab* made it through Charlotte's shock. A cab. Perfect. That was exactly what she needed. She eyed the distance between herself and the tall white building down the block that the goblin had pointed at. All she had to do was walk down a street filled with things from her nightmares that might decide to eat her. The alternative was Kieran Aindréas Cairbre Aimhrea.

She'd take the monsters.

"WHAT were you saying about how she wouldn't get very far?"

Kieran tried not to snarl at Niall and failed. He was weakened by fighting the human woman's formidable will and her proximity had sapped the strength of his ability to compel her. Indeed, Charlotte had fled much farther into the *ceantar dubh* than he'd expected.

"*Goibhniu*, looks like she's gotten herself a cab," said

Aeric O'Malley, coming up on his right side with his wife, Emmaline, beside him. The rain was starting to come down really hard now, plastering their clothing to their bodies. Somewhere in the distance, thunder boomed.

"I can see that far perfectly fine on my own," Kieran growled.

"Is that her?" asked Emmaline, shouting over the pounding of the rain. "The woman in that really ugly sweater?"

"What gave her away?" he drawled. "The fact she's the only human around?"

Emmaline shot him an annoyed sidelong look. "Touchy, touchy."

Once upon a time, he and Emmaline Siobhan Keara Gallagher had not gotten along. In fact, he'd tried his best to kill her once. Back in the day, before Piefferburg and during the fae wars, Emmaline had been an assassin for the Summer Queen and she'd killed his twin brother. Of course, his twin brother had really needed killing, brutal and sadistic fuck that he'd been. Still, when he'd found out she'd been in the Black Tower, he'd gone a little ape-shit and tried to strangle her.

But then Emmaline had risked her life for the second piece of the *bosca fadbh* and he'd forgiven her. These days they were even friends.

They watched while the cab with the human in question drove away. He never would have believed Charlotte would have balls enough to get all the way to the Royal Amber Hotel, not to mention get into a cab driven by a goblin. Apparently the threat of his presence had been enough to force her to it. He supposed he should be proud.

Niall cleared his throat. "Kieran, I hate to point out the obvious, but she's getting away."

"I'm aware." Kieran stepped onto the street and made his way toward the hotel. Getting a cab to follow her was faster than going all the way back to the Black Tower to collect his motorcycle. "Don't worry, I still have a little compulsion left in this bond. Anyway, we all know where she's headed, right?"

THE cab was driven by a goblin.

It had almost been the last straw. The only thing that had kept her from running away as soon as she'd opened the back door of the vehicle and been confronted by the driver's goblin face was the fact she'd have to run the monster gauntlet again to make it back to the Black Tower. So, figuring she'd made this far, she'd sucked it up and got inside.

"The front gates, please." Her voice was shaking. Brilliant.

He looked back at her for a long moment, his alien eyelids blinking slowly. The windshield wipers *thwick thwacked* against the rain.

She ground her teeth together, fear rising like bile to the back of her throat. Did he not speak English, perhaps? She didn't know any of their language. Whatever was going on, she just hoped his plans didn't include her liver and a nice Chianti.

He looked at her a moment longer and then faced the front and began to drive. She sank down against the seat with a slow breath of relief, closing her eyes for a moment. If she could just get to the gates, she'd be okay.

Turn around.

Her whole body stiffened.

"You get the hell out of my head!" she yelled.

The goblin regarded her silently in the rearview mirror.

"Sorry. I wasn't talking to you."

Turn around, Charlotte, or it's going to get ugly. The burst of compulsion that accompanied that sentence nearly made her spine bow with the effort not to command the driver to return to the hotel.

She screwed her eyes shut and took a few measured breaths, using every ounce of her willpower not to succumb to him.

Her mental reply sounded furious in her own head. *I thought you couldn't compel me anymore.*

No one ever said that. It begins to wear off once we come face-to-face, but it's not completely gone yet. You probably should have waited a little while before you made a break for it. I'm not done ordering you around.

The magickal persuasion did feel less intense than before she'd met him in person, and now it was much less evenly applied. But it was still strong.

"Oh, God!" she cringed and put a hand to her head as another wave hit. It seemed to be getting more powerful the farther she got away from him.

More deep breathing. More control. She could do this.

She glanced out the window. They'd left the city and were traveling through the Boundary Lands. Trees whipped past her window. The rain had stopped. Thank heaven for little miracles. It wouldn't be long before they'd be where she wanted to go. Kieran couldn't stop her now. She was strong enough to get away from him.

Seems like I can resist you, Kieran, she finally replied. *I'm still headed to the gates.*

You won't make it.

"Ma'am," said the driver. "We're being followed by another cab and they appear to want us to pull over."

She blinked, momentarily stunned by the goblin's very educated-sounding voice. Not to mention the politeness. Then she twisted to look at the headlights blinking madly behind them. She should have known Kieran wouldn't just let her go.

"Don't pull over," she ordered the goblin.

Pull over now. The sudden, strong burst of compulsion made her cry out.

"Pull over!" she yelled, putting a hand to her temple.

The goblin's gray, wrinkled face managed to look confused. "Which is it, ma'am?"

"Pull over," she wheezed, buckling over onto the seat. She knew that to comply was the only way to make it stop.

The cab pulled over to the side of the road, and the coercion eased. She dropped limply the rest of the way to the seat, rested her cheek against the cool plastic, and breathed heavily. She heard the sound of a vehicle pulling up behind them and doors slamming. The goblin cab driver got out of the car and spoke in a strange language, all clipped vowels and guttural words, with a man whose voice she didn't recognize. What was the name of the goblin language? She searched her memory. *Alahambri*. That was it.

Then Kieran's voice filtered to her ears. He sounded exhausted.

She pushed herself up and looked out the window at the group outside the car. Kieran looked even more fatigued than he had before, sagging against the back of the car and with dark circles marking the skin under his eyes. Compelling her must take its toll. Physically, Kieran didn't look a day over thirty-five, though she knew he was hundreds of years old. Right now he looked like a haggard thirty-five. She couldn't help the petty satisfaction she felt.

Kieran's tired eyes found hers through the window and her satisfaction left her in a rush. This man terrified her. More than the goblins. More than anything. She did not want to be tied to him in any way.

Yet running was futile right now, at least until this stupid bond thing ran its course. The most rational thing for her to do, even though she hated it, was to go back with Kieran and bide her time. Surely sooner or later she would have another opportunity to escape.

She opened her door and stepped out on the tree side of the car, as far from Kieran as she could get, pulling her suitcase behind her. An embankment cut sharply down the side of the road, ending in a rainwater-filled ravine. Her hair and clothes were plastered to her and she was freezing. Her foot squished deeply into mud. *Oh great.* Her suitcase was stuck in the cab, too. Curling her lip and shivering, one foot sunk into the mud, she gave her suitcase a vicious tug.

And tumbled backward.

She yelped, her arms windmilling and her suitcase *thunk-*

ing down beside her and rolling down the incline. It took her a nanosecond to follow it, sliding down the small hill at the side of the road. Icy water closed around her head and body as she fell into the ravine.

Sputtering, swearing, and splashing, she found her footing and pushed to her feet. She stood there dripping while her pursuers watched from the edge of the road. Niall wore a little smile she would have loved to knock off his mouth.

Kieran leaned against the back of the car as though he could barely stand, but was trying to hide it. He shook his head. "See what running gets you?"

She ground her teeth, dripping and shivering. Pushing her hair out of her eyes, she realized her vision was fuzzy. "I lost my glasses!" She searched in the murky water, but they were nowhere to be found.

The dark-haired woman with them carefully made her way down the embankment and held out her hand. She wore a bemused, yet sympathetic look on her pretty face. "Hi. I'm Emmaline. Come with me and we'll get you cleaned up and settled in. We're not as bad as you think, promise." She paused and grinned. "Well, maybe Kieran is."

Charlotte shook her head, taking a step backward. Her suitcase and her glasses were submerged somewhere in the muck and she wasn't up for fishing around for them. She wasn't up for sticking around with these people, either, enchanted forest at her back or not. She took another step away from Emmaline.

"Charlotte." Kieran's voice came out low and dangerous. A warning. Yet the compulsion had eased. His grip on her had to be slipping. She bet if she kept running, kept pushing against it, it would snap.

She scrambled up the other side of the embankment. Not far away lay a pile of jagged stones and she used a couple of the larger ones to pull herself up onto the other side of the ravine.

"Sorry, guys," she said, turning and giving them a mock sympathetic shrug and smile. "It's time for me to go."

She took a step backward, intending to fade into the forest behind her. Let Kieran try and catch her now. The road led straight to the gates and she knew she wasn't far away. All she had to do was hide until they left and then follow it.

Emmaline reached out a hand toward her. "Charlotte, look out for that—"

The ugliest being Charlotte had ever seen jumped from the pile of rocks and bared razor-sharp bloodred teeth. Swiping at her with a green gray gnarled hand and baring claws sharper than a cat's, he gazed up at her from about the height of her knee with a wrinkled face and bulging red eyes. "You'll not be getting my treasure, missy!"

Charlotte screamed and stepped backward, slipped in the mud, and tumbled—for the second time—down the slope and back into the filthy cold water of the ravine. She came up sputtering and terrified. Her gaze searched the pile of rocks but the creature was gone. "What in bloody *hell* was that?"

"Spriggan." Emmaline held out her hand again. "These woods won't treat you well, Charlotte. I suggest you come with us."

Charlotte wiped a hand over her face and gazed up at Kieran, who stood looking down at her like some dark god who controlled her fate.

Because, apparently, he did.

SIX

CHARLOTTE sat on his couch with Emmaline nearby. Kieran studied her. She looked different with her hair down and loose, glasses gone, and those awful clothes off her. She wore Emmaline's slightly too large clothes, a dark green sweater that set off her eyes and a pair of jeans. Charlotte's hair was still damp from her shower, her fair skin scrubbed free of makeup. She'd crossed her arms over her chest in a protective fashion, her legs crossed as well. One bare foot bobbed in anger.

His jaw still ached from her punch.

He had to admit, part of him admired her. Passive she was not. The woman had a spine of iron and she wasn't afraid to get in his face and defy him. He'd anticipated that she'd be sniveling and crying by now, but there hadn't been a teardrop in sight yet.

She was pretty, too, once you got the bad clothes off her and her hair down. She no longer looked like she wanted to blend into the wall behind her. Her expression was still hostile, however. He suspected that would be the case whenever he was near her.

He did tend to have that effect on women, in general, not just with this one. That was fine by him. For the most part, unless they were in his bed for the night, he didn't want much to do with them anyway.

"You look terrible." She gave him a head-to-toe perusal and then looked away, her nose up.

He felt terrible, too. He'd never used his magick to forge a bond with anyone before and the compulsion part of it was exhausting to maintain. She'd fought him so hard. He hadn't expected that, not from a human. And, of course, a dream wraith's bond magick wasn't really meant to be used on a woman who'd be so damned difficult.

"I think you gave Kieran a rough time today, Charlotte." A small smile played around Emmaline's mouth. Apparently she found this amusing. That rankled him. Still, he was grateful that Emmaline had stepped in and taken the human in hand.

"Yeah, well, I'm tired." He glanced toward his bedroom door. He was normally a nocturnal being, but the magick he'd been forced to expend had laid him low. It was only early evening and he was ready to snore. "I need sleep and I'm sure you do, too."

Charlotte made a frustrated sound. "I need sleep, but I doubt I'll be able to get any."

"You'd be surprised how your body takes over when you need to rest." Emmaline stood. "I'll go then. If it's all right with you, Kieran, I'll be back in the morning to see how Charlotte is doing."

"You're leaving?" asked both Kieran and Charlotte in unison.

The fact they'd said the same thing in the same moment made Charlotte flounce back in aggravation on the couch and recross her arms over her chest.

"Do you have to go?" Charlotte looked up at Emmaline hopefully. "I'd rather not be alone with . . . *him*. Or maybe I could come be your prisoner instead? Somewhere there's no men at all?"

"Sorry, Charlotte, but where I live there's definitely a man in residence. Remember the big blond guy from the Boundary Lands? That's Aeric O'Malley and he's my husband. As for you staying with anyone other than Kieran, I'm afraid the bond he's forged with you makes that impossible. At least for now. You're stuck with him for a while."

Charlotte looked devastated.

"That means I'm stuck with you, too." His voice came out a low growl.

Charlotte shot him a dirty look. "Yeah, but this was *your* choice, buddy. Not mine. I'm the one who gets to play the wounded party in all this. Not you."

"Look, *princess*, you have no idea what I've sacrificed—"

"Kieran," snapped Emmaline, "shut up."

He pushed a hand through his hair and grunted. She was right. He needed to shut his trap.

At least there was one good thing about all this—no way was he going to fall in love with Charlotte and activate the curse hanging over his head. That's what the bond magick was truly meant for, of course, to draw a mate. That was why he'd never used it before. He was the last man on earth who should attract love. Luckily he'd bonded this bitter, angry woman. There was a greater chance he'd fall in love with Abastor, the head horse of the Wild Hunt.

Emmaline held out a hand as if to stay their bickering. "I'm going now . . . okay?"

"Yeah, okay, Emmaline." Kieran pushed tiredly up to his feet and saw her out the door.

Once it was closed, he leaned against it and spoke without looking back at Charlotte. "We're on the top floor of the Black Tower. All windows lead to bloody tragedy on the cobblestone of Piefferburg Square and this is the only door." He shot the dead bolt, turned, and dropped the key down his pants. "Come get the key if you want it bad enough." He grinned and winked at her. "Maybe you do."

"You're a bastard."

"So they tell me. Try to escape and you'll find yourself thrown into Aeric O'Malley's forge down in the depths of this tower. Ask Emmaline how pleasant it is to stay there, she's spent many nights."

"I thought she was married to him."

"She is. They weren't always married, though. Once they were mortal enemies. Kind of like you and me."

"Yeah, but I guarantee we'll *stay* enemies."

He bared his teeth at her. "That's for certain, princess."

She only shook her head and sank back against the cushions.

"If you're hungry, there's the kitchen." He jerked his thumb to the left. "Don't expect me to cook tonight. Oh, and I don't think you're the type, but don't get any bright ideas about slitting my throat while I'm sleeping. The bond will kill you if you do."

"What?" She sat bolt upright. "What are you talking about?"

"The bond." He pushed a hand through his hair. He didn't want to get into this now. "It's a sort of mating thing. Man and woman, bound by magick, drawn together in the hope caring will blossom."

"Mating . . . bond? Caring?" She swallowed hard.

He grinned at her. "Yeah. You remember the mating part, right?"

She blushed, but it was clearly from rage, not maidenly apprehension. "Is it like a love spell or something?"

"Have you fallen in love with me already?" Normally love was meant to evolve from the bond—organically, not through magick—but not in this case. Love was something he wanted no part of—*could not have* any part of.

She narrowed her eyes at him and spat out, "Hardly. In fact, my emotions for you are decidedly on the opposite end of the spectrum."

"Yeah, same here, princess. Don't sweat it, okay?" He walked toward his bedroom. "Guest bedroom's over there. Sleep well."

"Hey!"

He stopped.

"You still haven't explained the bond thing to me."

"I'll tell you more in the morning. I need to sleep now. Like I said, just don't kill me. To kill me is to kill yourself." He gave her fake bright smile. "Night!"

CHARLOTTE stretched and yawned, sunlight streaming in through the huge windows of Kieran's living room. Once Kieran had retired for the night, she'd face-planted on the couch before she could assuage the hunger in her belly or make it to the guest bedroom. The stress of her situation had been no match for going so long without sleep and her body had just shut down.

Now her body was demanding food. Her stomach rumbled. She couldn't remember the last time she'd been this ravenous.

She sat up, working the kinks out of her shoulders and eyeing the throw pillow she'd crashed on for any drool spots. She felt dirty—again—because she'd slept in her borrowed clothes. Before heading to the kitchen, she went to the window. The sun was high in the sky, so it had to be around noon. A wave of guilt hit her for sleeping in so late. What would her father think?

Suppressing a laugh at how absurd a reaction that was under the circumstances, she gazed around the apartment. She could definitely tell Kieran was a bachelor. The place was clean and comfortable, but somewhat spartan and definitely lacking a woman's touch.

She thought of her own house. How she loved that place. It was her own space, away from her job and the demands of her family. She'd enjoyed decorating it just so, selecting everything to please only herself. It was her haven and she wished like crazy she was in it right now.

She looked out over Piefferburg Square below her. It bustled with activity. Kieran's apartment was very high, but she could still make out the mélange of various fae creatures that hurried like ants below her to work, school, lunch, or wherever. Not that much different than a square filled with human beings.

Directly across from the Black Tower sat the Rose Tower. Her breath caught looking at it. Rose quartz and crystal glimmered and blinked in the bright rays of the sun. Over there were the more benign kind of fae. All humanoid, it was said. Purebred Tuatha Dé Danann, the gentle sidhe race from which it was said all fae sprang. They were white magick practitioners. Their magick didn't maim or draw blood, not like the Unseelie.

The Unseelie took all fae, no matter their lineage or fae breed. As long as their magick could harm in some way, could injure or kill, they were in. Kieran Aindréas Cairbre Aimhrea was most assuredly of the dark magick variety, considering what he'd done to her. She wondered what the full extents of his powers were.

She wondered about this damned bond he'd drawn her into.

Where was he, anyway? Still sleeping? She entered his bedroom, making as much noise as she could to wake him. It was past time he gave her some answers. She slammed the door open. He didn't stir.

He lay sprawled lengthwise across the mattress as though he moved a lot while he dreamed—or invaded other people's dreams. An empty vase stood on the night table near his bed. She picked it up and dropped it on the hardwood floor. It didn't break, but it made a nice *thunk*. He still didn't wake up.

Doing something like deliberately dropping a vase was not normally in her character. Normally she was far meeker. She'd never *punched* anyone in her life. This situation was bringing out the worst in her. Or maybe it was just Kieran.

She stepped closer to the bed, examining her enemy while he was in such a vulnerable state. He was definitely good-looking. He was what her friend Marcie would have called *beefcake*. He wore a pair of dark blue sweatpants. She could just see them under the sheet twisted around his waist. His upper torso was bare, revealing a powerful chest and muscular arms. His longish dark hair lay tousled around a face that was compelling in its masculinity. He was not what she would call handsome, but the brutal lines of his face were intriguing, appealing . . . attractive, if she didn't know any better. And she knew better.

Oh, yes, he was quite pretty . . . until he opened his mouth.

She leaned over the bed near his head, her gaze tracing the strong line of his jaw with its slight cleft and his full lips that seemed not to fit with the rest of him. The lips were expressive, emotional. They were like a puzzle piece that didn't groove with the others. Especially not his eyes when they were open. His were the first pair of brown eyes that she'd ever known to look hard and cold. Normally eyes like that always appeared warm. Clearly life had not always been kind to him.

What had happened in this man's life that would cause pain to be so apparent?

Of course, her first mistake was thinking he was a man. He wasn't a man. He wasn't even human; he was fae.

Just then Kieran opened his eyes and looked straight into her face.

She opened her mouth to demand he tell her more about this bond, but she found herself flying through the air instead. Giving a surprised scream, she landed flat on her back on the bed beneath him, his big body pinning hers. The position brought back a flood of memories from the dream.

Smooth muscled chest sliding against her bare breasts, the heat of his breath on her throat. Teeth nipping at her skin and making her shiver with pleasure. His knee sliding between her thighs, parting them . . .

Except this was no dream. This was real. His real body on her real body.

SEVEN

AFTER a heartbeat of complete and utter shock, she screamed and flailed, raining hits and kicks against him.

His grip found her upper arms and tightened. He straddled her waist and bore down on her until she couldn't move. "Stop it," he commanded. "Be quiet. I'm not going to hurt you."

She took a deep, measured breath. "Then *get off* me." Her voice came out a low, spitting mad growl.

He rolled off her and swung around to sit on the edge of his bed. "If you don't want me to grab you and throw you down on the bed, don't hover over me while I'm sleeping." He ground the heel of his hand into his eye.

She sat up and pushed her hair out of her face. "Are you saying I surprised you?"

He looked at her and rolled his eyes. "Of course you did."

She made a scoffing sound. "I made so much noise walking in here, the idea I surprised you by merely leaning over you is ridiculous."

He gave her a suspicious look. "Why were you leaning over me, anyway? Couldn't get enough of me from the dream?"

Giving him a glare, she pushed off the other side of bed. Sitting on the edge, she muttered, "You wish."

His gaze swept her appreciatively, his pupils growing dark. "Maybe I do."

Heat rushed through her body at the look in his eyes. Her face flushed with anger at the answering little thrum of desire that pulsed through her. *No, Charlotte. No.*

His head dropped and he pushed his hand through his hair. "Why *did* you wake me up, anyway?"

She stood, ready to launch into her demands, but instead immediately became light-headed, and staggered back. She sank down on the bed before she fell. "Whoa."

"Did you eat anything last night?"

"No. I crashed before I could get to the kitchen."

"You need to eat."

"I need answers more than food." Her jaw worked. "My primary concern right now, among so many, is the blasted bond thing you tricked me into."

He studied her for a long moment. "Come on. I owe you answers. You'll get them over breakfast." He got up, and without another glance in her direction, walked out of the room.

Fine. If she had to break bread with him to get an explanation, she would. Anyway, she really needed coffee.

She followed him into the kitchen where he was busy pulling things out of the refrigerator and cupboards. She walked to the kitchen window, pulled her hands up into the sleeves of her sweater, and hugged herself. Every room of his apartment seemed to offer a good view of the square. While he cooked, she gazed outside. Below her, the area was much less packed. The lunch crowd must have gone back to work.

The kitchen was lovely, white cabinets, stainless steel appliances, center island, wine rack. This was the not the sparse kitchen of a bachelor; it was the kitchen of a cook. That had to be an accident. She couldn't imagine Kieran being particularly domestic.

Soon the wonderful smell of crackling ham on the stove reached her nose. Her stomach growled and her mouth watered simultaneously.

"I hope you like ham and oatmeal."

She turned. "I would eat a boiled tire right now, but, yes, I do like ham and oatmeal."

He motioned to a place set at the table for her. A bowl of thick, creamy oatmeal sat on a placemat with a heavy dollop of honey in the middle. To the side rested a small bowl of raisins. She tried not to dash across the small distance and bolt the whole meal.

She sat and raised a spoonful of the oatmeal to her lips. Closing her eyes, she stifled a moan. The oatmeal she'd eaten in the past had been bland, but this was full of flavor and texture. Better than cake. Or maybe she was just hungry.

She looked over at him. He stood at the stove tending the ham. Barefoot and bare-chested, his hair a tangle, he made a nice picture—if she chose to see him that way. Which she didn't.

"Is it good?"

"It's delicious. The best oatmeal I've ever had." She dug in with gusto.

"Coffee?"

She nearly swooned. "Please. Black."

He put a cup down near her, along with a plate of thick, cooked ham. After fixing himself a cup of coffee, he sank down across from her.

She looked up from her oatmeal. "Aren't you going to eat?"

"Later." He cleared his throat and leaned forward a little. "About the bond."

She set her spoon down and sipped her coffee, waiting expectantly to know her fate. The food that had tasted so good a few moments before turned to rock in her belly.

"I told you it was a mating bond, but that does not make it a love bond."

She leaned back in her seat. "What does that mean? Whenever you want to get laid, you use this bond thing?"

He gave a humorless chuckle. "I don't need a bond *thing* to get laid, Charlotte. I can do that just fine on my own. This is something different. It's a magickal perk of being a dream wraith. It's meant to draw a woman into a romantic relationship. Love *is* normally its primary objective." A cold smile crossed his mouth. "Not in this case."

No kidding. "So, do you do this often? Use this bond on humans to force them into Piefferburg?"

"The bond magick can only be used once. You're the first, will be the last, and, believe me, I did it under duress."

"Sex with me was really that bad, huh?"

His dark brown eyes went immediately molten gold. His gaze lingered on her, filling with erotic promise. She shifted in her chair and cleared her throat, suddenly feeling warm. "Actually, that was the best part of this deal. You were surprisingly . . . energetic that night."

She went crimson. Then she picked up her fork and waggled it at him. "Except it wasn't real sex, remember? It was a just a mind f . . ."

"Fuck. Go ahead, you can say it."

She ducked her head and dug into the ham.

"I have had the ability to forge this kind of a bond all my life. It's part of my magick. I am the only Unseelie alive who is able to do it, but I never intended to use this gift. However, when it became clear that the only way to lure the human woman we needed—*you*—was to use the bond, I did it. It is a risk for me. Not a large risk, but a risk."

"Risk?" She frowned at him. "Does that mean it's a risk for me, too?"

He leaned back in his chair. "Only if we—you and I—fall in love."

"Oh." She leaned back in her chair with a relieved *thump.* "Well, no risk then. You're not exactly my type."

"Nor are you mine."

She studied him. "What would happen if we did ever . . . fall in love?"

"You and I would both die a slow and horrible death and be claimed by the slaugh." He smiled. "I'm cursed, you see."

"*Oh.*"

"Oh."

She made a face. The slaugh was an army of unforgiven dead, the worst of the fae sentenced to live out eternity as enslaved warriors as punishment for their misdeeds. "That would suck."

"Yeah." He shrugged and took a sip of coffee as if they were discussing a bad weather forecast and not eternal damnation.

"Of course you're under a curse." She shrugged. "Why wouldn't you be?"

"Was that sarcasm?"

"Maybe a little. I'm not really sure how to respond to all this. So, how does one become cursed, anyway?"

"You become cursed by a witch or a fae with the ability. In my case, it was a witch hundreds of years ago. Cursed to never be able to know love."

She studied him for a long moment. He said it like it didn't matter, or maybe he'd just had a long time to get used to it. "God, I really am in faery now, aren't I?"

"Deep in the heart."

She chewed her lip. "Wait a minute. Hypothetically speaking, since neither of us have any interest in the other—"

"Except for sexually."

She almost swallowed her tongue. He was interested in her sexually? "Uh. Okay, anyway, since we're not falling in love anytime soon, but even if we did . . . fall in love, I'm human. How could I be claimed by the slaugh after my death? The slaugh is only for the fae."

His lips twisted and he raised his gaze to hold hers. "If a human falls in love with a fae, the deep way it would take for this curse to take hold, you'd be considered fae enough for the slaugh. It's happened before. I am not the first man to suffer a curse like this one."

Her jaw locked. "I want the hell out of this place."

"I want you to get the hell out, too, but not yet." He stood and started clearing the dishes away. "The upside is that the compulsion part of the magick is now dissolved. The downside is the bond magick will force us to stay together for the next few days. I don't like it either."

"Your mother never sent you to charm school, did she?"

"My mother died while birthing my twin. She never sent me anywhere except out into the world as an orphan." The slightest note of bitterness tinged his words.

"I'm sorry." She looked down into her lap. Having lost her mother at six, she could relate to that. It forged an unwelcome connection with him.

"It was a long time ago." He put the dishes in the sink and began to rinse them.

She frowned. "I thought fae fertility rates were so low. You and your brother, having been twins, must have been very rare."

"Fae fertility is in the hands of the goddess Danu. Nothing sways her will. Birth control doesn't work, nothing we can do influences whether or not a fae woman will conceive. Danu alone decides. Siblings are very rare. There are Ronan and Niall Quinn, me and my twin brother, and the Three Sisters."

"The Three Sisters?"

"No one knows what happened to them for sure. We think two of them escaped the Great Sweep. No one knows what happened to the third. They're the only set of three biological sisters known to the fae. All three of them are highly magicked. The middle sister possesses all the magickal traits of her older and younger siblings. They're also the only known set of siblings to share a psychic connection, the way my brother and I did."

"Ronan and Niall don't have anything like that?"

He shook his head. "Lucky them."

"Speaking of psychic phenomenon." She pulled her sleeves over her hands and looked into her lap. "How do you intend to access these supposed memories I have? It's not like I have a direct line into the heads of my ancestors. They're long dead, after all, and it's not like I ever met them."

"Ah, but you share their DNA. You have a latent psychic connection that threads from you, to your mother, to your grandmother, to your great-grandmother, and so on down the line."

"Through the maternal line?" She didn't feel any sort of connection to her maternal line, psychic or otherwise. Grief twisted in her stomach, making her go cold.

"Of course. Humans don't believe such things are possible." He snorted. "Humans would like everything magickal to disappear from this earth, leaving everything black-and-white and totally simple. But nothing is simple. The memories we need are there in your mind. We just have to find a way to get you to access them. The problem is you lack faith."

"Excuse me? You don't even know me."

"I know enough to see you're going to fight it because you don't believe it. You don't believe in magick and that's an extra block we'll have to plow through."

"Magick, in case you've forgotten, is what bound me to you and brought me here. I kind of have to believe in it, right? I'd be crazy if I didn't."

"That's not what I mean."

She rolled her eyes.

"The very fact I need to explain what I mean makes my point for me."

She made a cutting motion with her hand. "Fine, Mr. Vague, forget it. You're right. Stop now because you're giving me a headache."

He only smiled at her. That knowing smirk made her want to storm out of the room. God, she couldn't remember the last time anyone had riled her up as much as this man. She drew a careful breath and let it out. She had a feeling she'd be doing a lot of deep breathing and counting to ten while this guy was around. "Why did the witch curse you?"

His annoying smile faded and a muscle in his jaw twitched. He walked out of the kitchen. "We have work to do."

Hmmm.

After a moment, she got up and followed him. "What kind of work?"

"The kind where you change your clothes and hit the road with me. Today is the day we attempt to get you past your bigotry."

"I really wish people would stop calling me a bigot." She crossed her arms over her chest. "I'm a tolerant and open-minded person. My father would kill me if he knew I listened to the HFF's rhetoric and actually agreed with it sometimes." She shifted. "It's just I've had these . . ." she trailed off, pressing her lips together, not willing to share her nightmares with him.

"Had what?"

She bit her lower lip and shook her head. "Never mind, just please stop calling me a bigot. I don't think all fae are bad."

"Just some of us."

She shot him a look to kill. "You have to admit some of you are dangerous."

"So are some humans."

"Point taken, yet most humans who are dangerous don't have teeth sharper than knives."

"No. They have actual knives, or guns, or legislation that imprisons entire races of innocent people."

"Look, Kieran—"

"Go get ready. Take a shower, change your clothes, brush your teeth. Do whatever it is you do to get ready for the day." He half turned toward her, his dark hair falling across his forehead.

God, why did he have to be so pretty? She even thought he was good-looking when he was saying ugly things about her. This was so not fair.

"And then?"

"I'm going to give you a tour of Piefferburg." He smirked. "All the parts you didn't see yesterday, anyway."

Yes, she remembered the ravine quite well. And the stupid sprigat or whatever it was. She put a hand on her hip. "And my job? I'm supposed to be there right now, you know."

"Yancy and Tate can spare you for a little while. This is more important."

She sputtered for a moment, but he didn't stick around to hear her response. He closed his bedroom door.

"What's important to you is not necessarily what's important to me!" she yelled at the closed door and then stomped into the room where she should have slept the night before.

EIGHT

AFTER she'd taken care of her morning toilette, she decided what she'd wear. Emmaline, who was very nice for a fae, had lent her a wide selection of clothing since they were about the same size. All of it was pretty, but none of it was Charlotte's style. Bright colors and flattering, body-hugging cuts were not the kind of clothes she felt comfortable in. Her father had always encouraged conservative clothing and dark colors when she'd been growing up, and it was a habit she'd taken to.

She fingered a light green spring dress that had a small sweater to match, and then let it fall to the bed. Instead she chose the most comfortable outfit she could piece together from the offerings, a pair of faded jeans and a lightweight black v-neck top—the only dark clothing option she had. Emmaline had provided her still-in-the-package panties, socks, and a bra, and had also left her with a few pairs of shoes that almost fit her. She chose a pair of black ankle-length boots.

She wondered if that spinnett or spriglet, or whatever that

being had been, now counted her soaked suitcase and glasses among his "treasures." Good thing her eyesight wasn't so bad she needed her glasses to function.

If she was going to be a prisoner here for a while, she supposed she needed to buy new things. The thought of going bra and panty shopping with Kieran didn't make her feel warm and fuzzy, however. Maybe she could get Emmaline to take her. Kieran could pay for it; it was the least he could do.

When she went back into the living room, Kieran was lounging on the couch with his head back and eyes closed. He wore a tight dark blue jersey shirt and a pair of jeans . . . that he made look really good. She allowed herself to drink in the picture during the few moments it took for him to realize she was there and open his eyes. A girl could admire, couldn't she? She was human, after all. Even if the man she was admiring wasn't.

She twisted her hair up on top of her head and began to knot it there, wishing she hadn't lost her hair clip in the muck the night before.

"Leave it down."

She stopped midmotion and stared at him. "Why?" She always put it up because she couldn't stand the long tendrils brushing against her cheeks when it was down. She'd cut it short, but her mother had loved her long hair and had spent hours fussing with it when she'd been a child. It was one of the few good memories she had of her mom.

"You have beautiful hair. Don't hide it."

She blinked. "I do?"

"You do."

She twisted it up anyway. "I just want it to stay out of my face."

He shrugged and stood. "Ready?"

She scowled. "No."

"Great. Let's go."

"Listen—"

But he was already walking out the front door.

She followed him out of the Black Tower and fell into

step beside him on the street outside. It was a nice day in mid-spring and the streets of this section of town were packed with people.

All kinds of "people."

Kieran nodded as they passed a very tall, thin woman with green-tinted skin . . . who had gills. "A bean-fionn. They don't leave the Narrows much."

She tried not to stare as the woman continued on down the street. "We're not going back to Goblin Town, are we?"

"The apprehension in your voice makes me think we should, but, no, Goblin Town was not in my plans for the day." He paused. "It must be so boring living in a place where everyone appears humanoid."

She frowned. "I never really thought about it before. Anyway, you should remember what it's like. You did it once upon a time, didn't you? When the fae were all incognito and underground? How old are you anyway?"

"I'm five hundred and three."

She almost missed a step.

He stopped beside a big silver and black motorcycle in a small parking lot near the base of the tower. Unstrapping a helmet from the back, he tossed it to her. "Better put that on." Then he swung his leg over the bike and sat down, looking at her expectantly.

"We're riding *that*?"

He nodded. "I'm a very good driver, don't worry."

A little thrill of anticipation went through her. She'd never ridden on a motorcycle before. God, her father would have a heart attack if he knew she was even thinking about it. She dropped the helmet to her side. "I can't ride on that."

"Sure you can."

"No, I can't."

"Does everything have to be a big battle with you?"

"Apparently. Look, those things aren't safe."

His eyes went dark. "*Life* is not safe. Put the helmet on."

His tone seemed to allow no further disagreement, nor did the look on his face. Fine, she'd protested and been vetoed.

She had been kidnapped, after all. Her father couldn't blame her for being coerced by her abductor. She hesitated a moment longer, then gave in.

Once her helmet was secure, she threw her leg over and sat down behind him on the now gently purring machine. Her chest and stomach made immediate contact with his very warm, very muscular, very nice back. The same back she remembered exploring with her hands during the dream while he'd been over her . . . inside her. His hot mouth sealed to hers. . . . She drew a deep breath and looked for somewhere to hang on that didn't involve touching him any further.

Oh, this was so not a good idea.

He gunned the engine and took off from the parking space. She yelped and grabbed on to him, her hands finding each other around the tree trunk of his chest. So much for not touching him; she was plastered to him now.

He rode down the streets around the Black Tower, which seemed high-end in an Unseelie kind of way. Expensive-looking stores and automobiles. Nicely dressed fae, though most of them were nightmarish.

Then he rode down the street to the opposite end of Piefferburg Square, where the gleaming rose quartz tower of the Seelie Court ascended into the heavens. This was a high-end part of town, too, but there were far fewer of the scary-looking fae here. Most of the people walking the streets in this area were humanoid—Seelie Tuatha Dé, she guessed. The nonhumanoid seemed to be of the small, adorable, and nonthreatening variety. They had to be what were called trooping fae, all the fae who didn't fit into either court. These troop, as they were called, must be the kind that gravitated toward white magick.

She instantly decided she liked the Rose Tower better.

They passed through the area around the Rose Tower and into a poorer part of town. Eventually they hit the part of Piefferburg that she recognized as the burbs. He guided the cycle into what must have passed for a fae subdivision and traveled down a series of streets. All the lawns had tall hedges, shielding them from view of their close neighbors. Like the suburbs she'd seen yesterday, the houses were not uniform, instead all different shapes and sizes with various levels and number of windows. He pulled the cycle up outside a small rounded brown home with a grass-covered roof.

"We're visiting smurfs?" she asked after he cut the engine.

He cast a dark look at her over his shoulder. "We're visiting friends of mine, friends from way back."

Way back for Kieran probably meant centuries.

She got off the cycle a little regretfully and took off the helmet. She'd really enjoyed the freedom of the bike, even though her hair was mussed. Casting a look back at the cycle, she followed him up a small stone pathway lined with vibrant violet flowers that she didn't know the name of. They passed through the yard gate that was buttressed with more of the tall, thick privacy hedge that the suburban fae seemed to favor.

A small, short, brown-skinned man met them at the door. His wizened face was deeply wrinkled. He wore a pair of dark green trousers with suspenders over a plaid shirt. Charlotte couldn't tell how old he was since the ages of the fae could be deceptive. He gave her an easy, welcoming smile, even though she was a stranger. "Did you finally convince a woman not to run away from you, Kieran?"

Kieran glanced at her. "She's trying to run away, Eian, I just won't let her."

Eian laughed, obviously not aware of the truth of the statement.

"Eian, please meet Charlotte. Charlotte, Eian. Charlotte is human."

Eian grinned. "I'd gathered. She looks a little pale. Am I the first brownie you've ever met, dear?"

"Yes," she managed to answer. Never in her life had she thought she'd ever meet a real, live brownie. Even though she'd known they really existed, they'd seemed like the stuff of faery tales. Which, of course, they were.

"Well, come on in." Eian motioned them into the house. "I just brewed some good brown beer. Lillian is not having a very good day, but I think visitors might just make her feel better." Eian winked at her. "Especially a human, of all things. It's been a long time since we've seen one of those in the flesh."

While Eian bustled off into the kitchen, she tried not to gawp at the brownie's home. It was a snug place filled with blooming flowers and plants. The house was circular and the kitchen and living room were open, separated by a mahogany dining bar. Windows were abundant, showing off a neatly manicured yard that burst with green growing things. Everything was brownie-sized—the chairs and tables were small, the kitchen counters low—and comfortable looking. Human children–sized.

Eian returned with two big mugs of beer.

She accepted hers with hesitation. She never drank alcohol. Never.

"Oh! I have a cheese that would go wonderfully with that!" Eian hurried back into the kitchen.

Charlotte stared at the beer mug in her hand. "Um."

Kieran elbowed her and whispered. "Don't ever refuse the hospitality of a brownie, it's an unforgivable insult."

Darn it. There wasn't anything not to adore about the little brownie and she had no wish to offend him. And the mug was not brownie-sized, unfortunately. It was very much human-sized—large human-sized. Motorcycle riding and beer all in one day. What would her father say?

Eian returned with a plate of cubed cheese and a huge smile on his face. "Lillian is still sleeping, but I'm sure she'll wake up soon. Why don't we sit a little while in the living room?"

She looked doubtfully at the small chairs, sure she'd break one if she tried to sit. Following Kieran's example, she sat on the floor around the coffee table. She admired the piece of mahogany furniture, running her finger along the carved edge.

"I made the table myself." Eian set the delicious-looking cheese near them and sank into a chair with a sigh, his own brownie-sized mug in hand. "My family have been furniture makers for eons."

"It's absolutely gorgeous."

"Thank you. Don't do it now, though, I'm too old. And my children . . ." He trailed off. "Well, it looks like the tradition will die with me."

"That's too bad."

Eian smacked his lips together and nodded. "It is what it is."

A silence fell over the room. It was like a living thing, the weight of the unsaid. She looked between Kieran and Eian, not sure what had just happened.

Then Kieran raised his mug. "To Lillian."

A soft expression overcame the brownie's face and he raised his mug. "To my dear Lillian."

Okay, when in Rome. Not knowing who Lillian was or why they were toasting her, she nodded solemnly and lifted her mug. "Lillian."

The men took a deep drink. She looked down at the dark liquid, and when she couldn't stall any longer, raised the mug to her lips. The cool beer filled her mouth and slipped down her throat. It was like nothing she'd ever tasted before. Full, flavorful, nutty, just the slightest bit bitter.

She loved it.

Before she drained the mug down to its dregs, she forced herself to stop and set it back on the table. Kieran was watching her with a bemused expression on his face. Gee, she was glad she could provide entertainment. Giving him a cool look, she focused her attention on Eian. "Your beer is delicious."

"I'm so glad you're enjoying it. Watch out, though, it packs a bigger wallop than human beer."

She could already tell. A curious, yet very nice warmth had begun to spread through her body.

He pointed at the plate in front of her. "Have some cheese."

She plucked a cube of cheese and popped it into her mouth. Creamy and wonderful, it seemed to have three times the flavor of any cheese she'd ever eaten. "Oh, that's good. Why is it that everything here seems to taste better than it does out there?"

Kieran took a piece of cheese. "Because you're essentially in faerie, Charlotte. All food in here tastes like ambrosia to a human tongue." He popped the cube into his mouth. As he chewed, he waggled his brows at her. "Other things seem more pleasurable, too."

She gave him a slow blink and a cold look.

Eian laughed. "Don't mind Kieran, dear. He's always been wicked. Since this is your first time to Piefferburg, do you have any questions you'd like to ask?"

"Thank you." She pointedly turned her attention to Eian. "What I don't understand is how all the fae stayed hidden from humans for so long. I understand that you used glamour, but it's still hard to believe."

"Actually," said Kieran. "That's an old wives' tale. Glamour is a skill only some of the fae possess. The fae that looked nonhumanoid were forced to hide from humans, usually deep in the woods in small communities or literally underground. Back then it was easier. Even if the Fae Wars, Watt Syndrome, and the attack of the Phaendir had never occurred, the fae would have eventually been outed to the human world because of the advances in technology and the decline of the wild places. Essentially, the fae's habitat would have been destroyed, they would have been forced to move toward the city, and they would have been caught on video."

"What made the fae think they had to hide from us?"

Kieran's lips quirked. "Because the fae were so few in number and the humans so many. We knew that if they feared us we were doomed. Even with our skills in magick."

She looked down in the last little bit of her beer. "And we feared you."

"And we were doomed."

"Some of us still fear you."

Kieran grunted. "They're going to have to get over it. We're tired of being doomed."

The room fell silent for a little while. Finally Eian cleared his throat. "So what brings you into the hollow hills, my dear?" Eian took another sip of his beer. She noticed now that he had a slight trace of a Scottish accent.

She jerked her thumb at Kieran. "Him. Against my will." She took another drink of her beer.

"Against your will? What's this story about, Kieran?"

Kieran shifted on the floor. "One of her maternal names is MacBrehon."

The entire room plunged into icy silence.

Eian's gaze fell on her. "Oh."

Charlotte choked on her beer. Kieran pounded her on her back. "What don't I know?" she finally was able to ask, pushing the beer mug far from her.

Eian gave her a kind smile. "It's nothing, dear. I just haven't heard that name in a long, long time."

"What does the name mean to you?" she pressed.

Eian held Kieran's gaze for a pregnant moment and they communicated without words. She knew what they were saying—don't tell the human anything.

"You'll find all that out later." Kieran's voice held a note of finality.

She raised her eyebrows and popped a cube of cheese into her mouth. If Kieran thought she was done pushing for information on this subject, he was mistaken. *MacBrehon.* She'd had her genealogy done, but she didn't remember that name. It was true, though, that genealogy tended to trace the paternal line rather than the maternal.

Gosh, despite being stonewalled, she was feeling warm and tingly and just plain nice. She glanced at the almost empty beer mug.

The brownie stood. "I hear that Lillian has awoken. Would you like to meet my wife, Charlotte?"

She glanced at Kieran, having the feeling that Lillian was the reason they'd come. "I'd love to meet her."

They walked through a tiny doorway that she and Kieran had to stoop to get through and entered a bedroom that had an enormous window on the far wall, giving a stellar view of the well taken care of backyard. Lillian was short and slender, her skin reminding Charlotte of wood bark—brown, and textured with age. Her hair lay like a downy white cloud against the pillow and she wore a pair of fragile gold glasses on the bridge of her nose. She reminded Charlotte of the stereotypical grandmother, something she had never known, and she immediately warmed to her.

Lillian's eyes opened behind her wire-rimmed spectacles and widened when she caught sight of them entering the room. "Kieran, you've brought me a guest. Oh, a human." She reached out tiny hands. "It's been so long."

It felt completely natural for Charlotte to go to Lillian and take her hands. She smiled down into the older brownie's face as Kieran found a human adult–sized chair and slid it beneath her so she could sit at Lillian's bedside. She wasn't sure why she found these brownies so enchanting. Perhaps because, unlike so many of the other types of fae she'd seen so far, they were so nonthreatening.

"Lillian, please meet my friend, Charlotte." Kieran pulled up another larger sized chair beside her.

She shot him a look. *Friend?* That was going a little too far. Charlotte turned her attention back to the brownie. "It's a pleasure to meet you. My middle name is Lillian, in fact."

"How lovely!" Lillian squeezed her hand, but it was weak. "The pleasure is mine. I used to take care of the nicest human family's gardens back in the old days. I would allow their youngest daughter to catch glimpses of me in the hedgerow from time to time." Lillian giggled. "She was a sweet little thing, believed in faeries, thanks to me."

Charlotte studied the older woman for a moment before replying, her brow knitted. She knew she might not like the answer to the question she was about to ask, but the beer was sitting so pleasant and warm inside her, and she was feeling so light and free. "How can you still have such positive feelings for humans, Lillian, when we've done so many bad things to you?"

Kieran's gaze sharpened on her. Charlotte glanced at him, frowned, and gave her attention to Lillian once again.

"Oh, my dear, all the races do horrible things to each other. It's part of growing up." Lillian patted her hand. "One day, many eons from now, perhaps all of us will grow up enough to realize attacking each other is truly attacking ourselves."

Charlotte smiled into the woman's face. "I hope so."

Lillian looked at Kieran. "What a lovely woman you've brought to us. Is she HFF?"

Kieran coughed, maybe trying to stifle a laugh. "No, Lillian, she's not affiliated with them. I just thought she might provide you with a little distraction. How have you been feeling?"

"Old." A smile broke Lillian's face. "But that's what happens to all of us, right?" She patted Charlotte's hand again. "And it comes even sooner for others of us, doesn't it, Charlotte? My old is your ancient."

Charlotte smiled back at her. "Yet you're still beautiful."

"Oh, thank you, child, but you're ten times more beautiful than I ever was, even when I was in the blush of my youth."

She leaned forward a little, shaking her head. Physical beauty hadn't been what she'd been talking about. "No, I mean you are *so* beautiful." She frowned. Had she said beautiful or boofootal?

"Uh." Kieran eyed her and, scowling, she eyed him right back. "I think we should get going."

"Gave the human your beer, didn't you, Eian!" Lillian yelled. She muttered for a moment in Old Maejian. "Man loves to sow chaos."

"Come on, Charlotte," Kieran said, rising. "We better get you out of here."

She swatted his hands away when he tried to help her stand. "Leave me be."

"Oh, dear." Lillian pressed a hand to her mouth. "Will she be all right?"

Kieran put a hand on her hip to steady her and she moved to the side, knocking his hand away. "She'll be fine, Lillian."

"Lovely girl, Kieran." She winked at him. Then her face fell as though she realized she'd said the wrong thing. "Oh, I'm sorry. My mouth ran away with me."

"It's okay."

The brownie reached out and touched his hand. "You don't deserve the curse, you know. We all think that."

We all? Charlotte frowned, trying to figure out who *we all* could be.

"I do deserve it. I could've stopped him."

"No." She shook her head. "You couldn't have."

Now Charlotte was more confused than ever. She shifted to the side and nearly fell over. Kieran grabbed her before she collapsed.

"We better go. Good-bye, Lillian." Kieran guided her out of the room.

NINE

ONCE outside, he pushed her toward the bike and threw her the helmet. "Are you sure you can hold on well enough to ride this thing?"

She slid the helmet onto her head. "What do you mean? I feel great."

"Yes, I'm sure you do."

She grinned. "Beer is delicious."

He rolled his eyes. "We have one more stop today." He threw his leg over the bike. "Get on, drunkard."

"I'm not drunk." She got on behind him and molded herself to his body with a sigh. His body was so warm and had that soft hardness of a man in great physical shape.

He stiffened against her. "Honey, you're toasted. You're a lightweight, too. You only had one beer, even if was fae-brewed."

"Hey! You are raining all over my first beer parade. Stop it!"

"First beer?" He glanced over his shoulder at her. "That was your first beer? As in, before today you've never drank any? I thought most humans went to college."

"I went to college; I just never drank there. That was indeed my first beer." She stabbed her finger in the air. "Not only that, it was my first alcoholic drink ever."

"Good Danu, woman. Next you're going to tell me you're a virgin."

"I—"

"No. Don't. I don't want to know." The bike revved to life and he guided it away from the curb, making her yelp and cling to him again.

They traveled through the suburbs and back into the Boundary Lands. Navigating small gravel roads slowly and carefully, he led her through the forests and down an even narrower path that must have been meant only for walking. The trees finally opened up and revealed a gorgeous forest glen with a canopy of majestic oaks. The colors seemed extra vibrant here, like every leaf and flower had been hand-painted in a totally pure color. A tranquil forest lake backdropped by a cliff and fed by a waterfall sat in the middle of it all.

Kieran cut the engine and she clambered off the bike, pulling the helmet from her head and letting it drop to the soft earth as she stumbled toward the lake. "It's beautiful, like something out of a dream." She tripped and went down onto her knees. The ground seemed to sparkle and shine with tiny blue and green dots. "What is that?"

"Fae." Kieran came to stand behind her.

Suddenly she realized that he meant the little dots were living creatures . . . the sprat? . . . and she was kneeling on them. She bolted to her feet and tripped backward, gasping. Then realizing the dots were everywhere, she yelped and picked up her booted feet. There was nowhere safe to stand or walk.

Kieran laughed. "Don't worry about it. They're more like molecules than mammals."

"Niall explained them to me on the way to the Black Tower. They're not aware?"

"They probably have some type of awareness. When the Phaendir imprisoned the fae in Piefferburg, they followed us from all over the world. They alone can pass through the warding the Phaendir have erected, but they never leave. They seemed to be drawn to us. They're the lifeblood of the Boundary Lands, the magick in these trees and plants."

"I saw them on my drive into the city, but why are there so many concentrated right here?"

"No one knows." He rotated in a slow circle, admiring the tiny fae floating through the air. The edge of the tattoo peeking at his collar seemed especially dark against his skin. "We just enjoy it."

She held out her hand to a clump of them. "Pretty, pretty sprat."

"*Sprae.*" He held out his hand and thousands of the little beings seemed to adhere to it. "We call them sprae."

"Huh." She waved her hand and the sprae came to her, too, covering her fingers and palms. She couldn't even feel them on her skin. "Why do they do that?"

He moved his hand this way and that, admiring the tiny beings. "They're attracted to fae blood."

"But I'm not fae."

He was already walking away, his head up as he took in the environment and a faraway look on his face. He hadn't even heard her.

Frowning, she moved her hand and the sprae shot away. She walked to the edge of the pool and sat down on a rock. Small orange, green, and blue fish darted through the crystal clear water. Just sitting here, hearing the waterfall not far away, feeling the tranquility of this place—it made everything okay, even the bad stuff. Just for this one moment. "This place is magical." Then she blushed, realizing what she'd said.

"Yes, it is." Kieran sat down on the rock next to her.

"I mean, of course it's magical," she muttered.

"This place is more so than the rest of Piefferburg. I brought you here so you could see its beauty."

"And why did you take me to Eian and Lillian's?"

He gazed up at the sparkling fae orbs above him. "So you could meet a nonthreatening fae couple. They're very nice, gentle. Nicer and gentler than many humans. I wanted you to see more than just the Black Tower while you're here." He met her gaze. "You were very sweet with them."

She frowned. "What did you think I was going to do? Beat them?"

He said nothing for a moment, his gaze dropping to her mouth. Heat rushed through her body. "Of course not." He paused, meeting her eyes once more. "I was wrong to assume you were as bigoted as your father."

"Yes, you were." She looked away from him. "How do you know Eian and Lillian? I thought I read that brownies are more disposed to hang out with the Seelie, rather than the Unseelie." A dragonfly with vibrant blue, purple, and green wings rose up from the base of the lake and hovered near her nose for a moment. "Oh," she breathed and reached out to touch it. It darted away.

He looked down at the ground, saying nothing for several moments. "They are, but I have a special relationship with these particular Seelie-drawn fae."

She felt all delicious, loose, and relaxed. And here she was, unbelievably having the most enchanting—literally—time of her life. If it hadn't been for the beer and her surroundings, she never would have felt comfortable prying deeper. "What kind of relationship?"

He stood and walked around the lake. Finally, he stopped to look at her. "My twin brother tortured and killed their daughter."

That wasn't even close to something she'd thought he might say. Maybe that he played poker with Eian once a week, or that his aunt had been friends with Lillian or something. Not torture. Definitely not murder. She stared at him, at a loss for a reply.

Kieran walked toward her slowly. "You should understand this is not something many people know, especially people who think I'm their enemy."

"I've got good reason to think you're my enemy."

"I won't argue that. Regardless, you should know about this because of the situation we're in. Indirectly, you're a part of my past."

"What does that mean?"

"Are you going to let me finish?"

She nodded.

"A long time ago, the various fae races were at war with each other. You know all that, but what you might not know is that during the wars the Wild Hunt ceased to come for those who murdered." He paused. "And there were those who took advantage of it. My twin brother, Diarmad—"

"Took advantage?"

Kieran nodded. "He was a soldier, as was I. We fought in the war on the side of the Unseelie, but Diarmad targeted the troop, specifically the Seelie-drawn fae, like the brownies. Innocents." He went silent for a moment, studying the floating orbs around him. "There had always been something off about him, something dark. Ever since we'd been kids he'd been that way. I guess it was making his first kill in the war; it pushed him over the edge. He started killing for fun."

"He was like some kind of fae serial killer."

Kieran nodded. "A fae with the ability to tear flesh with his mind."

She put a hand to her mouth. "That . . . makes me want to throw up and then become a vegetarian."

He smiled, his eyes glittering. "Because of that psychic connection I told you about, I had the misfortune to experience every single kill he made. It was like I bathed in their blood when he did. He loved it. He lived for it. And every time it happened, a part of me died."

She swallowed hard. While she thought he was evil for what he'd done to her, she didn't think he was *that* kind of evil. "Didn't having that kind of a connection make you insane?"

"It did. It made me so insane that I was going to kill my own twin. Someone else beat me to it." He raised his eyebrows. "Emmaline. Remember her?"

She blinked, trying to reconcile the image of the smiling, extroverted Emmaline with the killer of a fae psychopath. *"Emmaline?"*

"Back then she was an assassin for the Summer Queen, which is a story for another day. The important part is she killed Diarmad just after he'd slaughtered Eian and Lillian's daughter. He was going to kill them, too, but she saved them."

She shook her head. "But I still don't understand how you became friends with Eian and Lillian after that. Don't they associate your face with the one they must see in their nightmares?"

"They are remarkable fae. They understand I'm not Diarmad and I never was. They understand that I need to make amends for the pain my brother caused, even though nothing I can ever do will make it better. I still carry a lot of guilt for not stopping Diarmad sooner. Eian and Lillian, along with the families of other fae Diarmad harmed, have been gracious and bighearted enough to allow me to help them in any way I can. And I have done so. For centuries."

She eyed him, suddenly suspicious. "Are you telling me all this so I'll like you?"

"I don't care if you like me or not. In fact, it's better if you don't like me. No, I'm telling you all this so you can see the humanity"—his lips quirked—"so to speak, in the fae." He reached out and touched a miniscule green and blue orb. "And the beauty."

"You're trying to get me to be less . . . bigoted." She winced on the word.

"Now that I've spent a little time with you, I don't think you're a bigot. However, I do think you've spent a lifetime listening to your father's revulsion of us. While you are intelligent enough to have drawn your own conclusions about the fae rather than inheriting his hatred, you still fear us. I'm trying to ease that fear and make you more amenable to having those memories accessed."

Her jaw locked. She almost told him about the nightmares, but that was far too personal a thing to share. Instead, she looked into the beautiful blue water. After a moment she thought she saw a woman's face on the surface. She shook her head and it disappeared. Sheesh. No more fae-brewed beer for her.

The face reappeared, this time much more solid. It was a young woman with a delicate visage, the long white-blond tendrils of her hair waving out around her head in a watery halo. She gazed up at Charlotte with dark blue eyes. Her skin was a pale pink, the color of the underside of a seashell. A slender body encased in a long white gown materialized as well.

Charlotte darted off the rock and straight to Kieran's side. "There's a woman in the water."

"She's the Lady of the Lake. She guards this place and she's benevolent, don't worry. Well, unless you try to harm her territory, then she gets a little tetchy."

"Tetchy." She put a hand to her head, which had begun to throb dully.

"If you should ever meet a horse in these woods, by the way, never ride it. No matter how tempted you may be."

"Should I ask why?"

"They're water horses. You may know them as kelpie. They'll ride you straight into the nearest body of water and drown you."

Just then the Lady of the Lake emerged from the water wearing a flowing white gown that rustled in the wind as though dry. She blinked her large, watery eyes. "My name is Áine. I ask of the female if I may be of service?"

Charlotte stared at the woman, mouth hanging open. "Kieran?"

"Yes."

"I'd like to go back to the Black Tower now."

GIDEON walked to his office, his shiny black shoes tapping on the polished floor of Phaendir Headquarters. All of his people were in their offices, heads down, working hard. Just the way he wanted it.

A tall, thin, narrow-nosed man came down the corridor opposite him. Brother Merion, the one he was grooming to be his second-in-command. Gideon met his shiny bright blue eyes, eyes that held respect for him and his cause, reverence, even awe.

Brother Merion inclined his white-blond head a little. "Greetings, Brother Gideon. May Labrai guide your every step."

Gideon inclined his head. "As He guides yours."

Brother Merion was one of his people. They were all *his* people. The moment he'd ousted Brother Maddoc, he'd taken stock of all the Phaendir, even the secretaries and janitors, who worked in this building. He'd removed the ones who didn't suit him, the ones who had followed Maddoc a little too closely for his liking. The ones who wanted mercy for the fae. There were way too many of them, that being Maddoc's doing, of course. After he'd weeded out the weak and the nonbelievers, he'd replaced them with his own people—the righteously motivated.

They had serious work to do and there was no place for the faith-challenged in it.

He had almost everything he wanted, almost everything he'd been working toward his entire life. If only the U.S. government would see his reasoning, then he'd have it all.

In the hallway outside his door—*his* door, not Maddoc's—he took a moment to admire the plaque with his name on it. He would have reached up and touched the smooth gold lettering, but he worried someone might see him. He needed to act cool and aloof—in control.

A folder sat on the top of the heavy oak desk. He settled into his comfy leather chair and flipped it open, examining some of the work he had to do that day.

His life was perfect, but for a few notable exceptions. There was the issue of Emily, to be sure. Her real name was Emmaline Siobhan Keara Gallagher. He'd fallen in love with her and she'd turned out to be a stinking fae. Once he'd found that out, all the adoration he'd felt had instantly transformed to white-hot hatred, so she hadn't broken his heart as much as she'd made him want to take several hot showers to get the taint off.

And kill her. That was still on his to-do list.

Then there was his agenda regarding the fae. He knew it would be difficult to push it to the U.S. government, but, really, the problems he was having were ridiculous. Didn't they understand what a threat the fae posed to them? Maddoc had let things spiral out of control. The fae now only lacked one piece of the *bosca fadbh*. They already had the Book of Bindings. If they were able to open the back of that book, they would find the power to break the hive mind of the Phaendir and destroy the walls of Piefferburg.

Humanity would once again be prey to the goblins, boggarts, killmoulis, red caps, and nagas. Was that not cause for alarm? Yet they sat on their hands, they stalled legislation, they argued, debated, held town meetings, and lobbied. Both sides twisted the issue to support their own causes and ended up doing nothing.

Honestly, dealing with the U.S. government was like having Maddoc back in charge. Ineffective, soft, and far too merciful.

Then there was the damn HFF. David Sullivan and his Labrai-damned followers. They marched on Washington every time the government sneezed in a positive direction toward one of the bills that could mean effective action against the fae. When they weren't marching on Washington, they were assaulting Protection City with their slanderous filth. It was that stupid amendment in the constitution that allowed it.

Gideon had been around when they'd written that thing. He'd had contempt for it then and nothing had changed.

Now that Maddoc was gone, he ruled the gates of Pieffer-burg City with an iron fist. The government would not allow him to completely prevent humans from entering if they wished. That stupid freedom thing again. But he wasn't ever going to make the same mistake again. Emily—*Emmaline* had fooled him with her glamour. He'd checked her background, of course, but she'd done a good job of covering her tracks. In the end she'd made a simple slipup that had outed her.

But the Phaendir learned from their mistakes. Now they went much, much deeper into all the backgrounds of the humans they admitted. The most recent one had been easy. The Bennett family was well known to the Phaendir. Charlotte Bennett's father was a major donor to their cause. All the same, they'd double- and triple-checked her. Made sure she was truly who she said she was before they'd let her in.

On top of it, they had spies in Piefferburg. Fae that would do anything for a little money, even turn in their own people. In some cases, enough money could even buy the destruction of someone. The fae wouldn't assassinate outright. The fae couldn't murder other fae without serious repercussions from the Wild Hunt. That was all right; there were plenty of other ways to neutralize the unwanted.

If only he had a way to neutralize David Sullivan. He was working on it, though. Oh, yes, he was. Damned man didn't realize who he was messing with. Humans against an immortal race of druids would lose every time.

He settled into his chair, sipped at the cup of tea an underling had left on his desk, and considered the work he had to do for the day. Most of it involved doing all he could to further his agenda in the U.S. Congress. It felt a lot like beating his head against a brick wall. He wouldn't stop doing it, though. Gideon was playing for keeps in the name of Labrai.

The fae would be exterminated, one way or another, before they had an opportunity to break those walls. Even if it meant the Phaendir defied the wishes of the government and took the matter into their own hands.

The phone rang and he picked it up. He'd gotten rid of his secretary after the fiasco with Emil—*Emmaline*. He didn't trust anyone anymore. "Gideon P. Amberdoyal."

Nothing.

"Hello? You've reached the archdirector of the Phaendir. Please don't waste my time."

"Amberdoyal." The voice was low, male, and made the hair on the back of his neck stand up.

"Yes?"

"We have a mutual goal, you and I, making sure the walls around Piefferburg don't fall." He had a slight Irish lilt to his voice.

Gideon rolled his eyes, tossed the pen he held onto the top of desk, and leaned back in his chair. "There are many people in the world who support our endeavor."

Silence.

Gideon leaned forward, making his chair squeak. "Listen, I've got a lot of work to do—"

"Many people, yes." Pause. "Few fae."

Gideon processed what that meant for a moment before replying. "You're telling me you're fae."

"Yes, Amberdoyal, we are."

We? "And that you're beyond the confines of Pieffer-burg?"

"Is it so hard to believe that some of us may have been missed during the Great Sweep? The Phaendir is hardly in-fallible." His voice carried no small amount of contempt.

He knew firsthand some of the fae had been missed. Em-maline had managed to stay hidden because of her skill with glamour. Still . . . "I don't believe you."

"I don't care what you believe, Amberdoyal." His voice was now a venomous hiss. "I don't like you. I would like to kill you. The only thing keeping you alive is that we share a common goal. We can help you achieve that goal."

"How can you help?"

"We know where the last piece of the *bosca fadbh* is located."

Gideon went very still and silent.

"Amberdoyal?"

"I'm here." He wasn't sure if he believed anything the man on the other end of this line had to say, but he couldn't discount it. Not now. "Where is it?"

The man laughed. "Do you really think I'd tell you the location?"

"No, of course you wouldn't. Not when you're lying."

"Why would I lie about something like this?"

"There are a million different possible reasons. This could be a trap. You could want something from me. It could be pure hatred for me and the Phaendir. You could be HFF. It could be—"

The man blew out a frustrated breath. "I want to tell you location of the last piece of the *bosca fadbh* so you can help us ensure that none of the fae from within Piefferburg are able to obtain it."

"None of the fae *can* obtain it. That's the nature of the wards, you see? None of them can leave Piefferburg."

"You're so naïve. And Emmaline Siobhan Keara Gallagher? How did she do it?"

"That was a mistake of my predecessor. I'm in charge now."

The man only laughed. "Of course. And *you* never make any mistakes."

Gideon's fingers curled around the receiver of the phone and his blood heated with fury. He could feel the veins in his temples pop out and the plastic of the phone crack. His voice came out a low hiss. "I don't make mistakes where Piefferburg is concerned, *fae*. I am Labrai's tool, His right hand. Everything I am is dedicated to the destruction of the fae, as my Lord wills. I will give my dying breath to see them all dead." He paused. "You included."

Silence reined between them for several moments. "Why do you hate us so much, Amberdoyal?"

"If you think I'm going to spill my deepest secrets in your ear, fae, you will be waiting until I whisper them over your time-whitened bones."

"Crazy fuck." He laughed. "Meet my associate in Protection City tomorrow. On the steps of the Cathedral of the Overseer. Noon."

Gideon sputtered. He rose from his seat. "You would dare to enter Protection City, fae? You would defile the steps of the Cathedral of the Overseer?"

"We do it all the time. *Be there*." The line went dead.

TEN

KIERAN watched Charlotte as she sat in the living room holding her head, a mug of tea on the coffee table in front of her. The beer buzz had apparently worn off, leaving her feeling headachy. Her long black hair hung mussed and tangled from their bike ride and the events of the day. As he studied her, she bowed her head further, closed her eyes, and rubbed the bridge of her nose.

Her boots lay discarded near her. She'd braced her bare feet on the floor to bring her knees up a little, pink painted toes nestled in the soft area rug. She had absolutely no comprehension of how lovely she was.

He shook his head. This was not a good line of thought.

"I'm never drinking alcohol again," she groaned.

He sat down in a nearby chair. "It's because it was fae-brewed. It packed a fae-sized wallop that most humans can't endure."

"Thanks for telling me that *before* I drank an entire mug of it."

He shrugged. "It would have been unforgivable to turn it down."

She looked up at him. "I have a feeling Eian gave me that beer on purpose."

"Like many of the fae, Eian does like to sow a little chaos now and then, like Lillian said, but he also has a keen insight into what people need. Maybe he saw that you needed to loosen up a little."

She waved her hand at him. "I don't need to loosen up."

Kieran grunted.

"What's that supposed to mean?"

He gave another shrug. "You just seem a little high-strung, that's all."

"Oh, and I have no reason to be high-strung? I've been *kidnapped*, Kieran."

"We're not going to hurt you."

"Correction. You have no *plans* to hurt me. That's not the same thing."

He caught her gaze and held it. "I will protect your life with all I am, Charlotte. I vow it."

She snorted. "Why would you promise that to a woman you think hates you?"

"I don't believe you hate us. I think you've been influenced by your father to fear us."

She sat up, dropping her hands into her lap. "So now I'm weak-minded and believe anything anyone tells me?"

"That's not what I meant." He sighed and rubbed his hand over his face. "Do you ever stop fighting? You're exhausting me."

"For your information, my father is an upstanding member of our community. Everyone looks up to him and *I love him*. He's the one who raised me. He's the one who—"

"Taught you everything from the cradle." He nodded. "Exactly."

"My father has good reason to hate the fae. They targeted his line specifically for extinction."

"Yes, so your father has claimed. Do you know why?"

She shrugged. "We don't know. All we know is the fae hunted his ancestors down."

"How do you know it's true?"

She crossed her arms over her chest. "Why would my father lie?"

"I'm not saying he's lying. It could be a fabrication someone in your family made a long time ago, something passed on like truth."

She narrowed her eyes. "Anything is possible, but that seems unlikely."

"I've been alive a long time and I've never known a human family to be targeted that way by the fae."

"And you know everything."

Kieran groaned. "Woman, you are impossible."

"Kieran . . ." She sighed. "I'm tired of fighting with you. My father hates the fae, really *hates* them, okay? As far back as I can remember he's warned me away from them, told me horrific stories about them. Despite all that, I don't think all the fae are evil and bad the way he does, but some of you scare me."

"Some of us?"

She slumped down against the couch. Closing her eyes for a moment, she began to speak. "When I was a child, right after my mother died, I had recurring nightmares about the fae every single night. I can remember snippets of those dreams even now. When I see one of the fae species that were featured in them, it's all I can do not to have a full-blown panic attack."

He studied her. Dreams were something he knew a lot about. Sometimes recurring nightmares were powerful enough to make fissures in a person's emotional body. "Which fae species were in your nightmares?"

"Goblins, red caps, and joint-eaters."

He wasn't surprised. Those were definitely the kind of fae most kids would have nightmares about. They were the most misunderstood of the fae races. "What do you think triggered them?"

She rolled her eyes. "My father's endless stories about the evil fae, I would imagine. He started really harping on their danger after my mother died." She shuddered. "That's when the nightmares started. I had them for months."

He leaned toward her. "I won't say they were 'just dreams,' okay, Charlotte? I know better than anyone how real and powerful dreams can be, especially if they were coupled with something as traumatic as your mother's death."

She met his eyes. "Thank you for not making me feel dumb." She licked her lips. "Every time I see a goblin or a red cap, I want to crawl out of my skin."

He held her gaze for a long moment. As a dream wraith, he had the power to smooth over and heal fissures like the ones Charlotte might have.

Maybe she would let him, maybe not. Judging by the tight set of her shoulders and the thin press of her lips, now was not the time to ask.

He stood. "I'm making dinner. Are you hungry?"

She looked away, shrugging. "As long as it's not poisoned."

He turned away with a grunt and a short laugh. "Sometimes I'm just a little tempted, woman."

CHARLOTTE had to admit the bed in the guest room was much more comfortable than the couch. Kieran had offered her a mystery novel by one of her favorite authors before she'd gone to bed and she was now snuggled under a thick blue eiderdown and reading by the light of a small lamp on the nightstand.

The fact Kieran had known what book to give her had been a little disconcerting, but on the scale of disconcerting things that had happened to her lately, it was on the low end. When he'd handed the novel over, he'd told her that he wanted her to be as at ease here as possible and to make herself at home.

She was pretty sure that offer didn't extend to leaving his apartment.

That said, as kidnappings went, this had to be one of the

milder ones, at least where her fear level was concerned. Despite everything Kieran had subjected her to so far, she had to admit she wasn't scared of him.

Of course, she had no idea if the "remembering" magick they planned to use on her would be as benign. They wanted her to recall things she had no business recalling—memories that weren't hers, locked away in her genetic material. It was just flat out weird. At the moment she was trying to roll with it—and not think too much about it. That way lay insanity.

Outside her door she could hear Kieran moving around his apartment even though it was very late. It was really too bad, all of this. Had he been human, and not the dark fae he was, she would have found him extremely intriguing. Of course, even if Kieran had been human, he wasn't exactly the kind of man she could bring home to meet her father. No long-haired, motorcycle-riding, beer-offering men for daddy's little girl.

Her father, bless him, was not of the opinion there were many men in the world worthy of his only daughter. She'd been groomed for greatness, and his expectations were high for everything she did in her life. The only man her father would find palatable was a high-ranking conservative politician, doctor, lawyer, or CEO.

He'd expected her to become a doctor or a lawyer, herself, or at least something well-respected and high-paid. He'd never expected her to go into accounting, but the fact she'd done so well for herself in the field seemed to mollify him. The job suited her because logic and numbers had always come easily to her. Plus, going into accounting had been her one little rebellion against her overbearing and iron-handed father. Pretty sad, really, since that had been her only rebellion. She'd never really defied her father, not ever. Not even as a teenager, the time when even the most dutiful daughters were expected to do so.

So bringing home a long-haired, motorcycle-riding man to her father would have shocked dear old dad right into a coma—never mind that Kieran was a dark-magick wielding fae.

She blew out a breath. Why was she even thinking about this? It had to be because of that stupid dream. It had been just the thing to make her undersexed brain go bananas with unrealistic possibilities. She wished she could shut off the part of her brain that liked to replay all the especially good parts—which was pretty much the entire dream.

Frowning, she set the book aside and flipped off the light. What were Kieran's magickal abilities anyway? He'd said the bond and the dream invasion were just a part of them. Was his magick anything like his brother's? She shuddered. He was Unseelie, after all.

She snuggled down into the soft mattress and pulled the covers over her. Turning on her side, she looked out the window that gave such a pretty view of Piefferburg Square. Big raindrops had begun to splat softly on the glass with the dark sky as a background. It looked beautiful and lonely, not unlike Kieran. There was something really sad in him.

She supposed that was not unexpected, considering his past and the evil that sat on his shoulders. The threat of damnation for falling in love. She couldn't imagine living her life under that kind of weight. She'd never known love of the romantic variety, but she hoped one day she would. At least she had hope. Kieran didn't . . . *couldn't* even have that.

Her eyelids drifted closed and soon she found herself floating in that place between sleep and wakefulness, her mind caught on Kieran.

One minute she was drifting to sleep and the next she was wide awake, her adrenaline pumping almost too fast for her veins and heart to handle.

Someone was in her room.

ELEVEN

A dark shape moved past the window, sized like a big male, but it wasn't Kieran.

Her fingers clutched the blankets and she resisted the silly urge to throw them over her head like a two-year-old. She couldn't hide from what was coming. The person in her room knew she was there. Hell, she was probably the reason he'd broken in.

The only thing within reach she could use as weapons were the lamp and the book on the nightstand. Of course, her biggest weapon was the tattooed Unseelie fae in the bedroom next door. She had a feeling he wouldn't want this man menacing his best shot at the next piece of the *bosca fadbh*. In this case, the enemy of her enemy was her friend. Time to call Kieran on that promise to protect her.

The man moved toward her bed and she knew she needed to do something fast. "Kieran!" she yelled, lunging for the lamp.

The man bolted toward her, wrested the lamp from her

fingers, and smashed it against her head. Pain exploded, making her cry out. The world went dark and she swam for a moment on a wave of threatening unconsciousness, fighting to stay topside. The man was so strong. She fought, but it was like trying to free herself from the grip of a grizzly.

He pulled her off the bed, sheets, comforter, and all. Full consciousness returning on a flood of self-preservation, she howled and pushed against him, kicking and screaming, at least until the cold metal of a very sharp knife made contact with her throat. It nicked her. Hot blood welled and ran down her throat.

She went very still.

Her breath came out of her in little pants. She tried to ask the man what he wanted, but no words came out. The knife pressed deeper and she closed her eyes. So this is how her life would end. Not in her sleep as an old woman with many grandchildren and a husband who loved her. No. It would end tonight because she'd been caught up in a war she wanted no part of.

Her knees went weak. God, she didn't want to die yet. She had too many regrets. Too many things she still wanted to do.

The door burst open and Kieran stood framed in the archway, backlit by the light behind him.

The man holding her backed away instantly, the knife leaving her throat. She staggered forward, suddenly free. Her attacker held up his hands, the blade glinting silver and deadly looking in the light. But the man seemed scared. "Wait. Don't—"

"Too late." Kieran's voice came out a low growl that chilled her blood even more than the knife had. It contained an edge of . . . *evil*. Pure and absolute. Kieran raised his hand.

The man screamed. This was no manly bellow. This was an inhuman high-pitched shriek of perfect terror that made her hair stand on end. The scream of a man who knew he was about to die. In the darkness, her attacker seemed to collapse. His screams became gurgly and wet-sounding, descending slowly as his body did. Oddly, it reminded her of the scene in the *Wizard of Oz* when the Wicked Witch meets her end.

The sound of liquid being spilled across the floor met her ears.

"Charlotte!" Kieran's voice was sharp. "Come here."

She got off her knees, not even realizing she'd fallen to them, and hurried over to him. She made the mistake of looking back at her attacker. This time it was she who screamed.

She saw now that the man had not collapsed. He'd . . . melted. The viscous substance that was her attacker was now leaking from underneath the clothes he'd worn and pooling on the floor. The knife lay in a little river of fleshy goo that snaked away from one of the man's shoes.

Sharp nausea rose. She pressed her hand to her mouth and closed her eyes for a moment, mastering it. Her gaze flew to Kieran and she pointed at the mess on the floor. "You did that. You melted him. A full grown man. And you just—" She sputtered, putting a hand to her throbbing head. It competed with the wound in her throat for highest pain honors. "How?"

Dark circles marked the flesh under his eyes. She wondered what kind of toll expending that kind of magick took on him. "I'm an Unseelie Tuatha Dé Danann, Charlotte. My magick doesn't bake cupcakes, it kills."

"It melts."

"My brother could tear flesh with his magick. My power is much the same."

Yes, as she'd wondered right before she'd fallen asleep. Now she was sorry she knew.

He held out his hand. "Come on. You're injured."

She eyed his hand with trepidation. "You act like you kill a man every night."

"I only kill to protect. Just because I have this ability doesn't make me evil, Charlotte. A human man would have shot a gun to kill. I use magick. The result is the same."

Casting a glance at the man on the floor, she decided this was worse. Still, she took his hand allowed him to lead her from the room.

Stunned, she sat on the couch. He'd flipped on the lamp nearest his bedroom, but now he turned on more, flooding the room with a bright light she was grateful for. In the kitchen she heard him on the phone with someone. Then he came back into the room with a first aid kit.

"How's your head?" He sat down next to her.

"It hurts, but I'm okay. How can you be so calm?" Her question blurted out high-pitched on a swell of posttraumatic panic.

"Tip your head to the side so I can see the wound. The man came during the night because he knew what I could do. He'd been hoping to catch you asleep, so you wouldn't raise an alarm and bring me running."

He dabbed disinfectant on the wound and she winced. "Why did he want to kill me?"

"I'm not sure he did. He had plenty of time to slit your throat and he didn't."

She touched her neck. "You think he wanted to kidnap me? Why?"

He stopped treating her cut, looked at her, and raised his eyebrows. "You're a smart woman. Can't you guess?"

She didn't answer. Yes, of course, she could. She licked her lips and swallowed hard. "Because I possess the location of the last piece of the *bosca fadbh*? Who, besides you, would want me because of that?"

"Lots of people." He smoothed a bandage over the cut, then used a warm cloth to wipe away the drying blood on her skin. "It could be someone sent by the Phaendir. They would strip you of that memory with their hive magick and then kill you. Individually they have little potency, collectively they're a powerhouse."

All her strength seemed to leave her in a rush. The Phaendir. They would kidnap and kill her, a human, to prevent the fae from getting the last piece? But she was on their side. Stupidly, she felt betrayed.

She shook her head. "They don't know why I'm really here."

"They might by now."

Panic shot through her at the possibility. "No, I don't think so. Anyway, how would the Phaendir find a fae here in Pief-ferburg to do their bidding?"

He shrugged. "Wouldn't be the first time there was a turn-coat fae in Piefferburg. We suspect Gideon Amberdoyal of having quite a few of us in his pocket, actually."

"Could it be anyone else?"

He didn't answer for a moment. "It could be the Summer Queen. She could have found out about your presence and sent someone to take you. If it was the Summer Queen, we have a problem. She has a much farther reach in here than the Phaendir. If it was her, we can expect more attacks."

"Great."

"Yes, especially since she knows how to defeat me."

She raised an eyebrow. "The Dark Lord of Melting Flesh can be defeated?"

"The Dark Lord's abilities are not limitless." His lips quirked. "Now look at me."

Her gaze found his and held. His eyes were warm, mes-merizing. He held up a finger and she had trouble tearing her gaze away from his eyes to track the digit as he moved it from one side to the other.

Kieran dropped his hand to his lap and held her gaze once more. He said nothing for a long moment and her heart started to beat faster. This man was incredibly intriguing despite his faeness. Hell, maybe because of it.

Finally he looked away. "I don't think you have a concus-sion, but you'll probably have a nice bruise on your head."

She touched the bandage on her throat. "Thanks for this."

"Don't thank me. I'm the one who dragged you into all this, remember?" His voice sounded gruff. He pushed up off the couch.

"What about"—she motioned vaguely at the bedroom, not wanting to think too much about the mess on the floor in there—"that in there. Will the Wild Hunt come for you now?"

He shook his head. "I was protecting you. No matter how brutal his death, it wasn't cold-blooded murder. I don't think the hunt will come for me tonight."

She sat staring out the window while Kieran moved around the apartment. The reality of what had just happened pressed through her shock and made her want to take a shower. She felt violated. Brushed by pure hatred. Unclean. She hugged herself.

Pure and utter evil had touched her tonight and it hadn't been Kieran. She didn't care what Kieran said about kidnapping; that man had wanted her dead either tonight or later. Whoever had sent him—they'd wanted her lifeless on the floor, her blood running. Idly, she rubbed at the bandage, an odd, heavy feeling of dread settling deep into her.

If she'd died tonight, she'd have done so without having accomplished any of things she wanted for herself. A satisfying career, a marriage filled with love, children. She'd never felt that she'd been wasting her life before, but now that unsettling thought lurked on the edges of her mind like a lion looking for easy prey.

Someone knocked on Kieran's door and he answered it. A tall, thin blond man with an androgynous appearance walked in, followed by a short, ornery-looking woman with dark red hair.

The woman jerked her chin at Charlotte. "That the human?"

The human in question rose from the couch to face them, wearing her bloodstained pajama top like a badge of honor. She'd just faced death and lived to tell the tale. She wasn't going to let some redheaded battle-ax of a woman intimidate her. Plus, she was cranky. She frowned at the new comer. "Yes, I'm the 'human.' Who are you?"

Kieran pushed a hand through his hair tiredly and then extended it toward the redhead. "Melia and Aelfdane, meet Charlotte Bennett. Charlotte, meet Melia and Aelfdane. They're here to clean up the mess in the bedroom."

Melia gave Charlotte a cool look, then gave her attention

to Kieran. "There are guards in the corridor, so I assume you told Queen Aislinn."

"Yes. The guards are going to stick around for a while."

Aelfdane studied Charlotte. "Of course you know what this means."

"Yes." Kieran glanced at Charlotte. "I do."

Charlotte straightened. "What? What does it mean?"

Kieran ignored her, jerking a thumb in the direction of the guest bedroom. "It's in there. I only regret I didn't keep him alive. It would have given us some idea about who'd sent him. My temper got the best of me."

"You didn't get a look at him?" Aelfdane asked Charlotte.

She shrugged. "It was dark. All I saw was a big guy. Then there was a knife, then panic . . . and melting."

"He didn't use any magick?"

She shook her head. "His magick came in the variety of a very large blade."

Aelfdane nodded. Then he and Melia made their way to the guest bedroom.

She narrowed her eyes at Kieran. "What does this mean? Answer me this time."

He walked toward her. "I'd convinced the queen and her counsel to give me time to show you the fae aren't as bad as you've been led to believe. I thought that by breaking through your misconceptions it would be easier for you to access those memories we need. Easier for us, easier on you." He paused, his eyes growing cold. "But this changes things. We need to get those memories from you *now*."

Yeah, like, before she was killed. That's all they were worried about. *Great.*

If Kieran was looking to ignite any warm and fuzzy feelings toward the fae, it wasn't working.

"YOU need to relax." Emmaline sat down next to her, a concerned expression on her pretty face that Charlotte didn't believe. "It will be worse if you don't."

"What do you care?"

Emmaline's brow knitted. "Of course I care. We're not heartless, Charlotte."

"Could have fooled me."

Kieran spoke as if with acid on his tongue. "This isn't going to kill you."

"How do you know? You've never done this before, have you?"

"We've done this lots of times, just never with a human."

She sputtered for a moment and gestured at him in frustration. "Yeah, and that would be me. *Human*."

Risa, a slender fae with pale skin and deep red hair that reached the middle of her back—and who apparently had off the chart psychic abilities—cleared her throat. She was the one who was supposed to go memory diving in her head. "Partial human."

Kieran rounded on her and yelled, "She's not ready for that yet!"

Risa blinked, unperturbed by his violent reaction. "She has a right to know."

Charlotte lunged to her feet. "What? What is she saying? What's going on?"

Everyone in the room went silent.

"I'm so sick of you all keeping secrets from me. I—"

Kieran faced her. "You've got fae blood. Not much, but a little. Your human ancestors' relations with the fae weren't all bad."

That meant her ancestors had been really friendly with the fae at some point. *Really friendly.* She actually felt the blood leave her face. "Does my father know?"

Kieran shrugged. "We have no idea. He's full human and therefore we don't know much about him save for his interactions with you. Some of us have magick enough to follow fae blood outside the walls of Piefferburg *if* we have a way to locate the fae-blooded in question. We found you through Unseelie Court records and bribed a *Faemous* TV crew member to get your address to us. Once I had your exact location, I used my bonding ability to draw you here. We have absolutely no access to the fully human-blooded at all, or the fae-blooded who conceal themselves."

"So that means the fae blood is on my mother's side."

Kieran nodded. "Even though your mother didn't possess much fae blood, it was powerful in her."

"I don't understand."

"It doesn't work like human genetics. A drop of fae blood in a human might show a lot or only a little. The only time I saw any evidence of faeness in you was in the dream. In the dream you were wild, free, passionate. *Fae.*"

She winced. "Don't talk about that."

"Come on, Charlotte, it must make sense."

She hugged herself. "No. It doesn't make any sense at all." She hadn't known her mother long. She'd died when Charlotte had been very young. She had no idea if her mother had been wild, free, and passionate. She had no idea *what* her mother had been and it was a source of never ending pain for her.

"I would bet money your mother knew about her fae blood, Charlotte. I bet she was wild and beautiful and I bet anything that's why your father was attracted to her. She probably always felt like she was different than others. She was probably lonelier than you could ever imagine." He paused, his gaze holding hers. "I don't know for sure, but I bet that's why she—"

"No! No, Kieran." She turned her face away. "Don't make excuses for her. Just don't. You don't know anything about her and neither do I. She ensured I never would." Charlotte couldn't mask the bitterness in her voice.

"All right." He plunged his hands into his pockets. "Anyway, that's how I know this won't kill you. We have done this before—"

"With the fae," she practically spat out. God, all of a sudden she felt as if she didn't know herself at all. She'd never felt like she'd known her mother, but before now she'd never been more divorced from her memory.

"With the fae." Kieran's eyes went hard. "You're one of us, Charlotte. If only a little."

"Only a little. Little enough that the assassin last night wasn't at all worried about being collected by the Wild Hunt if he killed me."

Kieran blinked slowly at her. "You're fae enough for this. I would never allow it if I thought it was dangerous."

Did he expect her to trust him? She folded her arms over her chest and made a scoffing sound. This, coming from the man who'd melted someone and barely blinked an eyelash.

Risa stood. "Are you ready?" She held out a narrow snow-white hand. "Maybe what we're about to do will give you some answers. I assume you've been searching for them for some time, regarding your mother."

"No. I stopped searching long ago." She'd simply accepted what had happened, but not without bitterness.

Risa's smile was touched with sadness. "Will you do it anyway?"

"Well, it's not like I can say no, can I? Somehow I don't think you would let me walk out of here." Not taking Risa's hand, she followed the woman across the room and lay down on a fainting couch. Just like being at the shrink's, but with magick.

Risa pulled up a chair next to the couch, turned so she was facing her. "This should be quite painless, Charlotte, as long as you don't fight me."

Emmaline brought a steaming cup over and gave it to Risa.

Risa held the cup out to Charlotte. "This will help you let go a little, okay?"

Charlotte eyed it. "Do I have to drink that?"

"No, but I highly recommend that you do. I suspect, at least for the first time, this won't be as pleasant if you don't."

She hesitated a moment, then reached out and took the cup. "Fine. Whatever." The beverage was warm and sugary, not bad tasting at all. She downed it and immediately felt a sweet lethargy steal over her limbs, a little like taking a tranquilizer.

Risa's soothing voice washed over her, telling her to relax and open her mind. Charlotte let her eyes drift closed as whatever magick Risa was mojoing threaded through her. She floated in a place of absolute peace and silence, a relaxing state of mind that she could remember experiencing only a few notable times in her life. Her body went numb, but her mind stayed awake. Yet even though she was aware of the room and everyone in it, her concerns and cares were something that existed far from her.

Magickally, Risa knocked on the door of her deepest consciousness and Charlotte let her in.

Images of her life flitted through her mind's eye, like a movie on rewind. The beautiful glen that Kieran had taken her to. Lillian's face. Falling into the ravine in the Boundary Lands. Opening the door and seeing Kieran's face for the first time. Gideon at Phaendir Headquarters. The plane ride and snatches of the bonding dream. Her father's craggy visage. It went back and back, through getting the job at Yancy and Tate, buying her first house, graduating college. Her high school prom. Her sixteenth birthday. Running through a sprinkler with a neighborhood friend.

Her mother's funeral.

The nightmares. Images of her waking night after night, pale-faced and screaming, crowded her mind. Emotion filled her, choking her throat with the memory of crying for her mother but her father coming instead. Disappointment. Fear. Deep grief.

The images slowed when they got to her mother when she'd still been alive, and for the first time Charlotte saw that Risa was controlling the speed of the memories.

Anguish bubbled up from the depths of her. Tears she was only vaguely aware of trickled out of her closed eyes and down her cheeks. She could barely ever think of her mother and not cry. Involuntarily, she tried to turn away and avoid the painfulness of seeing her mother's face, but she didn't have control of her mind now, Risa did. Charlotte chafed at that control, trying to push Risa from her head, trying to avoid the pain.

Risa buckled down on her, like a rider attempting to control a wild horse. It gave her the sensation of having a huge man pin her to the ground so she couldn't move—except it wasn't her body held hostage, it was her mind.

These memories were from when Charlotte was probably about five, a year before mother's death. Her mother had been so loving with her, brushing her long black hair out at night—the same hair she herself had possessed. Charlotte could see her mother's reflection next to her—same eyes, same nose, same hair. It made a knot form in her stomach.

Her mind riffled through memories that she hadn't even known she'd had—going swimming at a community pool and sharing an ice cream cone with her laughing mother, a birthday party with a big yellow cake, her mom reading to her before bed and then tucking her in. In all the memories warm love shone in her mother's eyes. Charlotte had edited that loving light out over the years to fit the image of her mother that her father had presented.

That was the most jarring thing. The impression her father had given her was nothing like the memories that Risa was digging up from the recesses of her mind. Which was the reality?

Suddenly the memories began to rewind again, going faster and faster until they were a blur. Charlotte caught snippets of her mother when she'd been much younger . . . then even younger. Charlotte cried out in her head for Risa to please slow down so she could see them, but the rewind continued unabated.

The memories grew more frenetic and fast. They began to bounce all over the timeline of Charlotte's life. It was almost as if Risa was looking for a doorway somewhere and couldn't find one. She skipped into the memories Charlotte had of being told her mother had died and the pain-filled days that followed.

Then Risa lost control and her personal line of memory drove smack into a brick wall. Pain ripped through her head and everything went black.

TWELVE

"CHARLOTTE?" Kieran's voice flowed over her.

She moved her head from side to side, pain throbbing dully in her temples. She could hear a woman moaning not far away. Risa?

"Charlotte?" Kieran asked again.

His arms were around her and she verified she was half in his lap. Her eyelids fluttered open and her gaze caught his. His dark eyes widened, the pupils dilating. His arms were strong and warm around her. She liked it.

Except . . . She winced. "My head hurts."

"Yeah, I'm sure it does."

She took stock of her surroundings by glancing around. "What happened? Why are you touching me?" She was much more concerned about that second thing than the first.

"Risa entered your memories and looked for a way into the record of your maternal line, but she couldn't find one. In fact, she hit a pretty big wall. Sent you both reeling."

His voice rumbled through her and the scent of him ignited nerves in her body that had nothing to do with pain. She touched her head. "Yeah, I remember that. All of it. You can let go of me now."

"Just don't do anything dumb like bolt to your feet, okay?"

"Like I could."

He eased away from her.

She pushed slowly to a sitting position and looked at Risa. "It was like having my mind pinned down and riffled through like a trunk of old things in an attic."

Holding her head and wincing, Risa glanced at her. "That's not a bad analogy."

"Some memories are buried for a reason." Charlotte choked on the words, emotion rising into her throat.

"I'm sorry I have to go there, Charlotte," said Risa. "I can feel how much you don't want to remember these things." She paused. "Although at the end, when I went faster, trying to find a way into your mother's ancestral memory . . . I had the sense you *did* want to remember some of that and you wanted me to go slower. Did you?"

Charlotte cleared through throat. "You went into memories of my mother when I was a very small child. I don't remember any of that consciously. I'm ambivalent about recalling that part of my life, but, yes, I do want to see it." She pressed her lips together, torn between needing to make them understand and wanting to keep her pain secret. "I want to know."

"Know what?"

Charlotte swallowed hard and looked away from both of them. "Whether or not she really loved me."

Risa dropped her hand into her lap, her face going softer. "I experienced all those memories, too, Charlotte, and I saw quite clearly that she loved you. It was all over her face whenever she looked at you. It was in the way she touched you and talked to you." She paused. "Your mother loved you very much."

Charlotte hugged herself. "I never knew that. My father told me . . ." She shook her head. "This hurts and it's confusing. All of it."

"Charlotte." Risa's brow knit. "You know that you'll soon be privy to all your mother's memories. Not only will you have access to your memories of her, you'll have access to your mother's memories of you, your mother's memories of your father, of her life." She paused. "There's no way to avoid it. You should prepare yourself because it's inevitable."

Charlotte swallowed hard. "I'm not sure how I feel about that."

"No matter how you feel, it will happen. We'll go through your mother, then your grandmother, and so on. But I will go quickly since we have to get through thousands of years of your genetic line to the ancestor whom we suspect had a part in hiding the third piece of the *bosca fadbh*."

"*Thousands* of years?"

Risa nodded. "The process is slow through the relatives you have conscious memory of—your mother, grandmother, maybe your great-grandmother. After that the memories will go so fast as to be a blur."

Charlotte frowned. "Why the wall? If we hadn't run into that, maybe we'd be done with this whole mess and I could be on my way home."

"Kieran was right to ask for time to get you acclimated to us. The wall is from your fear of the fae."

"No. I want to help you. Really. Because I know that the sooner I help you, the sooner I get my life back."

"It's a subconscious block, Charlotte. You might not think it's there, but believe me"—she put a hand to her head and grimaced—"we ran head-on into it."

"Is the queen any closer to discovering who attacked Charlotte last night?" asked Emmaline, perched on the armrest of Kieran's couch.

Kieran shook his head. "She set up a meeting with the Summer Queen for this afternoon, but, of course, Caoilainn isn't very forthcoming."

Emmaline nodded. "Well, you know I can defend myself and Charlotte, if needed."

Kieran raised his eyebrows. "Yeah, so what's your point?"

"Let us have a girl's day out." Emmaline smiled at Charlotte.

Kieran glanced between the two women. "I really don't think that's a good idea."

"It's a good idea and you know it." Emmaline gave him a hard look, narrowing her eyes.

He gave her a slow blink, clearly annoyed. "No. I really don't think it is."

Emmaline tilted her head to the side and grinned at him. "Aw, that's so sweet. You're growing so attached to her that already you can't let her out of your sight."

A muscle in Kieran's jaw worked. "Fine. When?"

Despite her irritation with Kieran and her raw emotions as a result of the memory rehash, Charlotte had to stifle a snicker at the easy way Emmaline had manipulated him with reverse psychology. She'd have to remember that trick for the future.

Emmaline gave him a winning smile. "How about tomorrow afternoon, right before the Ostara Ball? I would think your physical absence but the presence of your gold card should do nicely."

"Wait a minute." Charlotte held up her hand. "Ostara Ball? A real ball? Like music, dancing, big fancy dresses?"

Emmaline nodded. "I can't believe Kieran didn't tell you."

Kieran's voice came out a dangerous growl. "I didn't think it was relevant information considering the situation."

Emmaline waved a dismissive hand at him. "Men." She turned her attention back to Charlotte. "There are balls at the Rose Tower almost nightly, but the Unseelie only have them rarely. Usually just on the solstices and equinoxes."

Risa broke in. "Tomorrow is the celebration of the spring equinox. Yule, Samhain, and Beltaine are our biggest fetes, but Ostara is very important, too. I'm so happy you'll be able to attend."

"I never said she could," Kieran ground out.

"Oh, come on, Kieran." Emmaline slapped her hands on her jean-clad thighs. "It's a once in a lifetime chance for her."

"I don't know if it's safe." Kieran eyed her.

Charlotte remained silent on the matter. The fanciest event she'd ever been to was her high school prom. She couldn't even dance. Although the prospect of attending an actual, real, live faery ball was a little seductive.

"I don't know." Risa shrugged. "I think it's a good idea if she goes, Kieran. It might help tear down that block we just ran into."

"Anyway," Emmaline broke in, "she wasn't safe in your apartment. She might not be safe anywhere."

Charlotte scowled at her. "That's not a very comforting thought."

"Sorry, Charlotte." Emmaline gave her attention to Kieran. "But any enemy of yours would have to be crazy or desperate to pick an Unseelie ball as a location to attack. You'd have too many allies there. So, what do you say?"

Kieran studied Charlotte and rubbed his chin. "Okay."

"Great!" Emmaline clapped her hands together. She swept her gaze down Charlotte, taking in her scuffed boots, sweater, and jeans. "Got anything . . . else to wear?"

She lifted her brows. "To a ball? Emmaline, not even in my closet at home do I possess anything even remotely worthy of *a ball*."

She pressed her lips together. "This calls for massive amounts of shopping."

"With my credit card," Kieran growled.

Emmaline gave him an innocent look and echoed Charlotte's thoughts on the subject. "It's the least you can do for her."

GIDEON parked his car down the street from the Cathedral of the Overseer at a couple of minutes to noon. The city was filled mostly with Phaendir and their families—the small percentage of the brothers who chose to marry, anyway—and small groups of Worshipful Observers. He rarely came into Protection City, having made every inch of his life as close to Phaendir Headquarters and the gates as he could make it.

Even so, he knew the splendor of the Cathedral of the Overseer. It was the largest church in the United States and every block used in its construction was dedicated to the worship of Labrai. Most humans had not converted to the faith of the Phaendir. That was a pity, of course, and had to be rectified. First things first, however. All his attention had to be on the destruction of the fae. Once the world was free of their threat, Labrai's power would grow.

The church rose in the middle of the city on a hill that was terraced by hundreds of white stairs. Three domes rose at the top, the largest center dome being the church itself. At the very top of the middle dome rose a spire that reached all the way into the clouds as if to touch Labrai, Himself.

Gideon mounted the stairs, scanning the many people visiting the cathedral. Some sat on the stairs and talked, or were eating their lunches. Some were coming or going. Others were clearly tourists, cameras around their necks.

The thought of a fae on these stairs made him want to kill something.

He halted and let the rage wash through him. Before he'd come today, he'd done his morning worship with his cat-o'-nine-tails, scoring his back deeply and letting the blood run down his skin, purifying him, sacrificing for his God, showing Labrai the depth of his love and devotion. Now, in his anger, the wheals burned, broke open. Blood trickled freshly down his skin. He closed his eyes and lifted his face to the warm sun, letting the pain wash through him. It was glorious.

Feeling someone watching him, he opened his eyes and looked in the direction of the gaze. A tall, slim redhead with skin like a polished pearl stood about ten feet away. Her hands were on her hips in an oddly antagonistic posture. Hatred sat on her pretty face, diminishing her loveliness, like poison in a fine glass of wine.

Realization rushed through him. He could feel her faeness even from this distance. He frowned. He pointed at her, yelling. "You. *You* should not be here."

She glanced around her, then stalked toward him. "And

you need to shut up. My name is Máire." Like the man on the phone, she had an accent—heavily Irish.

"What's to stop me from dragging you to Piefferburg right now and throwing you past the gates, *Máire*?"

She smiled, but it was pure venom. "The information I have for you."

"Who are you people?" His brow twisted. He genuinely lacked understanding. "Why do fae want to keep other fae down?"

"Why do you care?"

"I'm curious. I need to understand my enemy."

She jerked her chin at him. "You can go on being curious. And I'm not your enemy, not in this." She grabbed his upper arm and started guiding him down the stairs. He shuddered at her hand on him. "We need to go somewhere to talk in private."

He jerked his arm away. "Don't touch me."

She leered at him. "Are you sure you don't want me to touch you? We know you have a weakness for redheads." She paused and smiled. "Fae ones."

"Listen, bitch—"

She rolled her eyes and hurried down the stairs in front of him. "Don't get your panties in a twist, Gideon," she threw over her shoulder. "Believe me, you're not my type."

He followed her down the stairs and into a nearby café. She ordered them both drinks, buying him the oolong tea he normally drank in order to prove an important—and unsettling—point. They knew a lot more about him than he knew about them.

Máire settled opposite him at a small outside table. She pushed the cup of tea toward him with a sickeningly sweet smile. "It's a beautiful day, isn't it?" She stretched and looked up into the brilliant blue spring sky.

He studied the container of oolong with mistrust. "Cut the chitchat and tell me why I'm here."

Her gaze found his and grew cold. She leaned toward him and spoke in a soft voice. "You fucked up last year, Gideon.

It was *my* people, not yours, who tried to stop Emmaline Siobhan Keara Gallagher from securing the second piece of the *bosca fadbh*."

He could smile poisonously, too. "And you failed."

She set her cup down. "My sister, Meghann, died trying to stop it from happening, Amberdoyal." Now there was no smile on her face, mocking, poisonous, or otherwise. There was murder in her expression, and for the first time since he'd met her, Gideon felt threatened. "And you did nothing. You let the assassin Emmaline roll right over you with her glamour. She danced in and out of Piefferburg and got them the second piece."

Gideon gritted his teeth. He didn't need to be reminded. Though it wasn't his failure, it had been Maddoc's. "Do you have a point?"

Máire sat back and sipped her tea. "You need help. Perhaps we would all be better off if we cooperated."

"The Phaendir don't work with fae."

"Oh?" She raised an eyebrow. "So you know the location of the third piece of the *bosca fadbh*, then? You don't need us?" She leaned toward him again. "That's the prideful way we thought last year, too. The free fae don't work with the Phaendir. Look where it got us."

He stared at his tea, now growing cold. He'd been poisoned via tea once—although it had been his own doing. No way was he drinking anything that had touched this woman's hands. "If you know where it is, why don't you take it, destroy it?"

"First of all, the *bosca fadbh* cannot be destroyed. Do you not read your history, Amberdoyal? Second, if we could take the piece, don't you think we would?"

"Why can't you take it?"

"It's spelled. Under a faery enchantment." She ran her finger on the top of the table. "Only a very, very special person can remove it." Máire raised her gaze to his. "It's like the sword in the stone, immovable but for the right hand."

"Whose hand?"

She smiled and then stood. "I think that's enough for today. Wait for Liam to call you again with further instructions."

Gideon rose from the table, enraged. The cup of tea jostled with the table, sloshing over the rim. "You can't order me around, bitch."

She leaned near his ear and whispered, "Looks like I just did, Gideon." And then she was gone.

"I'VE never taken any self-defense classes."

Kieran glanced at Charlotte. They were on their way back from having breakfast with Aislinn and Gabriel and had just turned down the corridor that would lead them to his apartment. He had no idea what had prompted that comment. "Okay."

She made a frustrated sound. "I meant that if I'm attacked again, I have no way to defend myself. You know how to fight. Emmaline knows how to fight. Me, I have no idea. I'm defenseless."

"You're human, Charlotte."

"Apparently not."

"You're mostly human. Human in all the ways that count. Even if you did know how to defend yourself physically, you'd still be about as threatening as cotton candy to most fae."

"You mean because I have no magick."

"Yeah. Especially here in the dark court where almost everyone has magick that can kill or at least harm."

"But it's the light court that's sending bad guys for me."

"We *think*. As you heard Aislinn at breakfast, we're no closer to knowing if it was the Summer Queen who sent that man or not. Anyway, even if it is the Summer Queen, she's not going to be sending fluffy fae who can only pull white rabbits out their hats. They'll be sending the bad asses, the rogue Unseelie for hire."

"I know I can't do much against forces like that." She blew out a breath, moving a tendril of long dark hair away from her face. "But Emmaline doesn't have magick that can kill or maim. Her power is with glamour. Yet she can still kick ass."

He stifled a smile. Her language was becoming more and more colorful the longer she stayed in Piefferburg. "She's a trained assassin. And even when she was a free fae outside Piefferburg, she worked with the HFF and was skilled in self-defense. As Seelie Tuatha Dé go, she's one of the more deadly."

"I'm just saying I would feel better if I knew how to defend myself. Maybe I wouldn't be able to take down some badass rogue Unseelie assassin bare-handed, but I could at least fight back. Right now all I can do is quote the tax code at them."

His lips quirked. "Okay. I can teach you a little."

She studied him. "Aren't you afraid I'll use it on you?"

"Do you think you could take me down bare-handed?" He raised an eyebrow at her.

Her gaze took him in from head to toe. "I might try."

He touched his face where he still wore her bruise. "You already have." They reached his apartment. He unlocked the door and they entered. "Anyway, if I teach you this, I expect you to try."

She entered the apartment and whirled around, hands in fists. "All right! Let's get going, then!"

He studied her boxing stance. Reaching out, he readjusted her fists. "Rule number one, princess. Always make sure your thumbs are outside when you punch, otherwise you'll break them." He frowned at her, remembering the nice uppercut she'd given him when they first met. "Thought you knew that already."

She grinned. "Just testing you."

He squinted at her, realizing something was missing. "You were wearing glasses before. Don't you need them?"

"I have astigmatism, but I can see without them. My glasses just make everything sharper, like going from regular to HDTV."

He jerked his head at the guest room. "Go change into

something you can move in. We have time before Emmaline is supposed to take you shopping."

She returned in a pair of black sweats, a plain white T-shirt, and bare feet. Her hair was twisted up and clipped at the back of her head. He hated that she looked really good.

He hated it even more that this endeavor was going to require his hands on her.

She stood in the middle of the area he'd cleared, her hands on her hips. He studied her. "Okay. Rule number two: in a confrontation, never back down. Display confidence, even if you're scared shitless."

She spread her feet, raised her hands, palms-up, and waggled her fingers toward herself. "Come on, I won't bite."

He was sure she was joking about wanting him to attack her, but he rushed her anyway, just to see how she would react. The surprised look on her face transformed to sheer terror within about half a breath, but she didn't scream and run, the way he'd expected.

She steadied her feet and tried to body check him as he made contact with her. He pulled his weight back at the last moment but couldn't quite stop himself completely. Knowing that he was the one body checking her, he wrapped his arms around her and swung her as they went down. He crashed to the area rug on his back and she landed on his stomach and chest, making him grunt.

He lay there, dragging air into his lungs and seeing stars while she sprawled on his chest, no worse for wear. That hadn't exactly been the way he'd meant for that to go.

"You didn't run." His voice came out a pained wheeze.

"Run? Why would I do that?" She lifted her head. Her face was only inches from his. Her eyes widened in surprise.

Lady, she was pretty. He loved the dusting of freckles across the bridge of her nose and the way her black hair set off her porcelain skin. "I admire that you stood your ground, but rule number three: if a man twice your size rushes you, you run. From a point of pure body mass, you have no chance against him."

"Emmaline can take men your size."

He flipped her and pinned her to the floor. Hovering above her, he growled into her face, "We talked about Emmaline's differences before."

She struggled against him. "Get off me."

"Since you think you can"—he raised his eyebrows—"*make me.*"

"Fine. *I will.*" She pushed against him, stronger than he would've guessed.

She almost dislodged him and they tussled. In the fray, his lower body ended up pressing very intimately against hers. She wiggled and he realized immediately this was a bad idea. His cock had gone hard as steel.

She went still, her pupils going dark and her breathing growing heavier.

He stared into her wide eyes. This reminded him of the dream and, judging by the look on her face, he wasn't the only one.

Her warm breasts rubbing against the bare skin of his chest, her whispers for more *in his ear . . . His hand caressing the round cheek of her rear, down the smooth skin of her thigh to the sweet back of her knee . . . Grasping her there and shifting her wider, spreading her thighs so he could slip between them . . . The press of the head of his cock into her hot, silken core . . . Thrusting deep . . . His mouth on hers, tongues twined as he pushed them both straight into ecstasy . . .*

His gaze dropped to her mouth, a heavy arousal settling into his body. He wanted to find out if she felt that good in real life. Did she taste as sweet as he remembered? His head dipped toward hers.

"Kieran?" Her voice came out a whisper, half entreaty, half protest.

He stilled. What was he doing?

"We shouldn't," she murmured.

No, we shouldn't. He backed off her like she was made of asbestos.

Rising, he shook his head, trying to rid himself of the images from the dream that were taunting him. "Sorry."

She pushed to her elbows, hair tousled, lips parted, and eyes heavy-lidded. "Forget about it."

That was going to be difficult.

Swallowing hard, she slowly rose to her feet and cleared her throat. "Okay, that was rule three. Now teach me rule four." Her voice sounded shaky.

Yes, better to pretend it had never happened. He liked that plan.

He spent the day teaching her the basics. How to target a man's eyes, throat, and nose. How to break a hold when someone took her from behind by jabbing her elbow into her attacker's solar plexus.

What Charlotte lacked magickally, she made up for in enthusiasm, and by the time they were done, he was black-and-blue and proud of his student.

But he still wanted her.

THIRTEEN

WHEN Emmaline came to collect Charlotte for their "girls' day out," she could barely move, let alone think about going to a ball. She smiled wanly at Emmaline from where she sat in Kieran's living room, freshly showered and totally exhausted. A night with a good movie and bowl of popcorn sounded much better than dinner and dancing.

Although, remembering the very close call she'd had with Kieran on the floor, maybe it was better she got away from him for a little while. If she hadn't stopped him—stopped *herself*—she had a feeling they would have done a whole lot more than just wrestle. In fact, she guessed self-defense training would have been forgotten entirely for a much more pleasurable pastime. A flush touched her cheeks.

"Come on," Emmaline said, gently slapping Charlotte's aching thigh, "Just think of me as your faery godmother."

Figuring this might be her only chance to ever go to a real faery ball, not to mention use someone else's credit card with impunity, she let Emmaline lead her out the door.

"Emmaline?" They stopped outside in the hallway at the sound of Kieran's voice. He jerked his head at Charlotte. "Be careful."

Emmaline pressed her hand to her chest and smiled. "I'll guard her with my life."

Kieran's gaze met Charlotte's for a lingering moment. Strange tendrils of emotion curled through her gut at the dark, tormented look in his eyes. "I'll see you tonight." Then he nodded and the door slowly closed.

She fell into step beside Emmaline. "He seems like a lonely man."

"Kieran? Oh, yes. It's not surprising, of course, considering his history. His life was pretty tragic before the curse, after the death of his brother . . ." She trailed off.

"I understand you're the one who killed him."

"Yes." Emmaline sighed. "I'm not saying that Kieran's twin was a good man who deserved to live, but I can say his death weighs on me. All the lives I took back in those days weigh on me."

"He also mentioned that you have a bright and shining new life."

Emmaline flashed a dazzling smile. "He means my marriage to Aeric. Yes, I'm very happy, though it took me a long, long time to get that way. Centuries."

She shook her head. "I can't imagine having the life span of a fae. You lived outside of Piefferburg for a long time, didn't you?"

"Yes. In fact, Aeric is not my first husband." Emmaline glanced at her. "I was actually married to a human man named David Sullivan for years. He works for the HFF. But it didn't work out." They reached the front doors of the Black Tower and exited onto the street. "My heart always belonged to Aeric, I guess."

Charlotte fell silent for a few moments, wondering what it would be like to share a love so strong it could endure centuries.

"David is a wonderful man, though." She grinned at her.

"Hey, maybe you should look him up when you get out of here. You two might hit it off."

Charlotte grimaced. "Thanks, but I think Kieran has put me off dating for a while."

Emmaline laughed.

As they walked, Emmaline told her more about David and her marriage to him. The small talk put her at ease. Finally Charlotte and Emmaline ended up in a section of stores near the Black Tower that seemed swanky, even by human standards.

"Here we are." Emmaline led her into a dress shop with a black-and-gold awning and matching paint in the front window that declared it Cecilia's.

Cecilia, tall and reed slender, was, in fact, on hand to actually wait on them. Charlotte was sure she could encompass the woman's waist with her two hands. Her hair and eyebrows were the color of sapphires. So bright it was like someone had crushed a whole pile of the gems and then wove it out into hair. If Charlotte had been anywhere other than in Piefferburg she would have immediately pegged the color as artificial. However, taken with the matching color of the woman's eyes, her tiny, tiny figure, and the gorgeous mahogany shade of her skin, she knew Cecilia was all strange, all real, all fae, all beautiful.

Emmaline greeted Cecilia with a kiss and a smile. "This is my friend Charlotte. She needs a dress for the ball tonight."

"Ah, yes," said Cecilia, walking around her with an index finger to her full red lips. Suddenly Charlotte felt like so much meat. "You have beautiful hair and skin."

"Thank you," Charlotte said with a smile.

"You have a nice body, too. Not overweight, yet not scrawny. You could use a little help in the height department, though."

"Not much we can do about that." Charlotte gave a nervous laugh, then imagined some of kind of magick that might stretch her out. Her smile faded. "Is there?"

"Shoes, my dear," said Cecilia, still circling her. "Magnificent shoes that will give you height. Hmmm . . . you need some help with your . . . um . . . chest area, too. A good bra will fix that." Cecilia continued the vaguely insulting tour of her person, tapping her free hand against her frowning mouth. "We'll have to do something about those bushy eyebrows."

"Hey!"

"That hair needs a good trim, too. Highlights wouldn't hurt. Hmm, let's see. . . . what else . . ."

Apparently she was not only getting a new gown, she was getting a whole makeover.

KIERAN slid his finger into the collar of his shirt and pulled, trying to loosen it. This was the first ball he'd attended in years. For a reason. He hated these things.

No one cared if he never came. This wasn't the frivolous Rose Tower. They had real work to do in the Black and socializing was not the purpose of being for the Unseelie. The only reason he'd come tonight was because Charlotte was attending and he needed to be near her.

He did agree that this ball might help relax Charlotte's opinion of the Unseelie. And the faster they got to the memories they needed, the faster Charlotte would be out of his life.

Not that she was all bad. In fact, he was coming to like her. She was intelligent and brave. All in all, she wasn't what he'd expected. In fact, she seemed to surprise him at every turn.

He definitely wanted her.

Remembering the feel of her body under his made him break out in a sweat. He'd wanted to push that so much further than it had gone. If she hadn't stopped him, he would have eased her pants off her and taken her right there on the floor. He'd seen the look on her face and had felt the way her breathing had quickened; she would have let him.

Maybe it would have been a good thing. Maybe fucking her would have ridden his body of the fever he felt for her.

He could've gotten it out of his system and his brain back on the job.

He gazed around, looking at the crush as a human might perceive it. Monsters everywhere. He shook his head, looking down at the polished tips of his black shoes. There wasn't much here to soften any human's opinion of the fae, especially one raised by a fae-hater like Jacob Arthur Bennett. For that they needed to head across to the other side of Piefferburg Square.

Yet here he was, standing in the crush of excited Unseelie who never had a chance to get dressed up. To top it off, he was wearing a freaking tux. The only good thing about tonight was the booze.

He ordered a vodka from the bar and turned to see Niall standing near him. He wore a standard black tux, same as him, his long onyx hair blending seamlessly with the material at the shoulders. Niall looked as bored as Kieran felt.

"Where's your date?" the mage asked before he swallowed down the rest of his drink.

"Please don't call her that."

Niall shrugged. "So where is she? I thought she was the whole reason you dragged your ass down here for the night."

"She's with Emmaline."

"Emmaline? What are they doing?"

Kieran took a long drink of his vodka. "Shopping, primping. Girl stuff."

"That's good." Niall nodded. "Emmaline will be able to protect her if anything happens before she's back in your care."

"That was the idea." He glanced at his watch and frowned. They should be here by now. Emmaline was highly trained and he trusted her as a capable bodyguard. Hell, he couldn't think of one other person, himself excluded, who he would trust more.

Still, worry niggled. Where were they?

"So, how's it going, babysitting the fae-hater?" Niall fingered his empty glass.

He took another drink of the vodka and stared down into the clear liquid. "She's not that bad."

"Really?" Niall's eyebrows rose. "She seemed pretty bad on the car ride in."

"She—" He looked up, searching the crowd. By the door his gaze caught on a woman walking toward him. Drop-dead gorgeous.

She wore a black velvet sheath dress that hugged every one of her curves, slit in the front to reveal her long, mouth-watering legs and a pair of matching black velvet stilettos. Pearls draped her slender throat, one of her wrists, and hung delicately from her earlobes. Her black hair was swept up from her slender neck and twisted in a chignon at the back of her head. Her skin shone a shade of pearly pink-white that made his fingers itch to stroke. Full ruby red lips pouted from a pretty heart-shaped face and her eyes . . . her eyes were . . .

"Charlotte?" he asked out loud. Then he recognized the woman who walked beside her—Emmaline.

"Fuck me," Niall breathed. "She cleans up a lot better than I could have imagined."

Now that Charlotte had drawn closer, he was amazed he could have mistaken her for anyone else. She had that same uncertain glint in her eyes and that same lopsided smile. She stumbled a little and Emmaline caught her. Clearly she wasn't used to being dressed up or wearing heels that high.

But, *sweet Lady*, if he'd thought she was pretty before, tonight she'd shot clear up to fuck-me gorgeous.

He rubbed a hand over his mouth. "I need another drink."

Niall pointed at his glass. "You still have an almost full one in your hand."

Kieran downed it in one swallow, letting the fiery liquid burn a pathway down his throat. He waggled the now-empty glass at Niall. "Like I said, I need another drink."

He walked back to the bar, filled up, and then returned to where Niall stood. Emmaline and Charlotte had joined him and were laughing at something Niall had said. Kieran figured it was at his expense.

Now that she was near him, Kieran could see they'd done something to her hair. Did they call that highlights? They'd lightened it a little from her natural blacker-than-midnight color. It was pretty like this, but he preferred it unaffected.

She looked at him and smiled.

He studied her face. Someone had put makeup on her, covered her cute freckles, altered her porcelain skin. He frowned. "You're different." He liked this new Charlotte less and less, no matter that he'd almost swallowed his tongue when he'd first seen her.

Charlotte's smile faded.

Emmaline hit him in the chest. "You have no idea how to act around women, do you? You might try offering her a compliment."

He blinked. "You're beautiful tonight, Charlotte. I picked you out of the crowd and didn't even know who you were at first. I wanted to rush over, pick you up, and take you back to my apartment immediately."

Charlotte turned bright red and Niall gave a bark of laughter.

Emmaline cleared her throat. "Wow, Kieran, you really ran with that compliment thing. That's a little more information than any of us wanted."

Kieran ignored everyone but Charlotte. He held her gaze. "But I like you better when your freckles are showing and your hair is pure black and loose around your face. You're beautiful tonight, but you're much more beautiful when you're natural." He couldn't say where that burst of honesty had come from or why any of it had felt right to reveal.

Everyone went silent. Charlotte's eyes had opened wide and her lips parted a bit as if stunned.

"Charlotte!" Risa came up on his side to join their circle. She wore a sleek green dress that set off her eyes and made her long, heavy red hair looked even more lustrous. "You look incredible!"

Charlotte inclined her head a little and smiled, clearly unused to receiving compliments on her appearance. "Thank you."

Risa held a champagne flute in one hand and swept the ballroom with the other. "Welcome to the Ostara Ball."

"It's dazzling." Her gaze met Kieran's for a moment. Her eyes were more brown than green tonight. Beautiful.

"Would you like to dance, Charlotte?" He jerked his head at the dance floor.

"Uh, sure." She gave him a tight smile.

He set his glass down on a nearby table and led her toward the dance floor.

"But you don't even know how to dance," yelled Niall from behind them.

"Is he talking to you or me?" Charlotte asked as he led her out onto the floor.

"Me. I don't come to these things very often."

"I don't know how to dance either. I guess we'll be bad dancers together."

He didn't care; he just wanted to touch her. It was a damned dangerous compunction to have, but he couldn't help it. He slid his hand around her waist and she caught her breath. He wasn't falling in love with her, but he had come to admire her. Tonight he lusted after her. Perhaps it was a dangerous combination, to be lusting after a woman he admired, but this was duty, not pleasure. He was keeping Charlotte entertained, as his queen had demanded of him. This was his job.

So he pulled her close and she came easily, molding her body to his and placing one hand on his shoulder and the other on his waist. She licked her lips and blinked a couple times in succession. He recognized the sign; she was nervous.

He swayed his body with the music, taking her along for the ride. After a moment, he understood that dancing was like sex and all he had to do was give himself over to it. Her hips moved with his and he decided he liked it.

"You said you haven't danced much?" he asked. "I thought human schools had all those social functions. What's that one event called, Sadie Hawkins?"

She laughed. "Yes, Sadie Hawkins. That's the dance where the girl asks the guy. We had one at our high school, but I didn't go. I was too shy to ask anyone."

"I would think the boys would have been in a line waiting for you to get up the nerve."

She ducked her head and shook it. "No, but thanks for thinking that. What about you? You can't tell me a man as old as you has never danced with a woman. You must have done it at least a few times."

"Sure, but love curse, remember? It doesn't usually lend itself to romantic interludes. Dancing with a woman has been pretty rare for me."

"Right. I forgot. Love curse." She paused, pressing her lips together. "It must be so hard to live with that."

"Sometimes. I see Aeric and Gabriel, friends of mine who have recently married. They have someone to share their life with and I have no one, will never have anyone. I'm old enough now that I want a woman to love and love me back. I have sown my wild oats and have been ready to settle down for centuries now."

"That makes it even sadder."

He shrugged. "It is what it is. I've had time to get used to the idea."

"It's wrong that you were punished for your brother's actions."

"Is it?" He shrugged. "Maybe not. Maybe I could have done more to stop Diarmad than I did." Before she could pursue that line of conversation any further, he asked, "What about you? You've never had any serious relationships?"

She smiled tightly and glanced away. "I've been in several relationships, but only one of them could even remotely be called serious. His name was Charles and he was in advertising. I met him on the job, actually."

"It didn't work out?"

"I wanted children and he didn't. He liked the city and I wanted to live in the country. Those are only a couple of the many differences between us."

"Differences can sometimes complement."

"And sometimes they can be insurmountable."

"Not that I know much about it, but I suspect a strong enough love can surmount anything."

She looked up into his face, holding his gaze. "Except a curse?"

"Probably not that."

They danced deeper into the crush of people. Eventually she laid her head on his shoulder and he tried not to like it. The music lofted around them and they moved with it, the bright gowns of the women swirling around them and the sounds of laughter, conversation, and the gentle clink of toasts rising in the air like an embrace.

Charlotte raised her head and looked as if she were about to say something. Her lips were parted and her eyes were deeply green in that moment, full of unexpressed emotion. His gaze met hers and held. He had the crazy impulse to dip his head and press his lips to hers. Not just because he wanted sex from her, not in this exact moment, but because he wanted to share an intimate moment with a woman he had grown to respect.

His blood froze.

Charlotte must have seen something in his eyes because her expression went from inquisitive to concerned in a heartbeat. "What is it?"

Just then a man came up on their side. He had a head of long, wavy, bright yellow hair and black tattoos weaving their way over half his face. The man smiled and expression lines crinkled at his bright blue eyes. "I wondered if I could cut in? I would like to take a turn around the dance floor with your exquisitely beautiful partner."

Kieran stepped back from her immediately. "Of course." At the moment he couldn't get far enough away from her.

Charlotte looked confused and he hated himself for causing it. Still, she let the blond lead her into another song and they melted into the crowd.

He whirled and went for the bar.

Aeric O'Malley came up on his side as he was downing another vodka. "I've never seen you pound drinks the way you are tonight. Something wrong?"

He resisted the urge to turn around and order another. "I remember coming upon you one night when you were five sheets to the wind."

"Yeah." Aeric rubbed a hand over his mouth. "And the reason was female-related. That's why I'm asking, something wrong?" He glanced at Charlotte out on the dance floor.

"No." Kieran scanned the crowd and saw Charlotte whirling around in the arms of the yellow-haired man. He held her close and she was laughing. An unfamiliar, very unpleasant, sensation curled through his stomach, and he didn't like it. He tore his gaze away from the sight. "Where's Emmaline?"

Aeric pointed her out in the crush. "Talking to the Quinn brothers." She stood not far away with Ronan and Niall.

"Can you ask her to babysit Charlotte a little? I need some space."

"Ah."

Kieran glared at him. "What's that supposed to mean?"

Aeric held up a hand. "It meant *ah*. That's all. Swear. Listen, man, if you say you need distance from a woman, I'm all over that. I'll tell Emmaline." He turned and walked toward his wife.

A woman's scream sliced through the air.

"Sweet Danu!" It was Risa's voice. *"Charlotte!"*

FOURTEEN

KIERAN dropped his empty glass and bolted across the room toward Charlotte. The blond guy had her wrist in his grasp. She yanked her arm, trying to pull away.

"Let me go, you psycho!" she yelled, landing a solid punch to the man's jaw. Kieran remember her punch—it was hard. The yellow-haired man's head whipped to the side, but he didn't loosen his grip.

Kieran's blood boiled white-hot with rage. He moved before he thought, fully intending to kill this man right here, right now. He raised his hand, feeling his unique brand of killing magick bubble up from the depths of him.

Nothing happened.

The yellow-haired man yanked Charlotte against him, weaving an arm around her waist. A knife glinted in his hand. It flashed upward, to her throat. The press of it against her skin made her gasp. "Your magick won't work on me, Kieran Aindréas Cairbre Aimhrea. I'm a null."

A circle had formed around the couple. Aeric, Risa, Emmaline, Niall, and Ronan had come to stand next to him.

"A fucking null?" Niall spat. "Why send a null? They're useless."

"They're perfect for this." Kieran kept his gaze on the man as he spoke. "Our magick won't work on him; he can get her out of here and do whatever his boss wants him to do with her."

"What is your name?" came an in-control female voice from behind them.

Everyone looked toward the sound. Queen Aislinn cut a path through the crowd, with her husband at one hand and her best friend, Bella, at her other. Heavy, expensive black and silver cloth made up her voluminous gown that harkened back to the Elizabethan era. A black and silver crown glittered in her upswept silver blond hair and silver jewelry dripped from her earlobes, wrists, and throat.

The yellow-haired man faced the queen. Charlotte appeared more pissed off than scared. "You can call me Doc, but that's not going to tell you anything."

Aislinn smiled. "I'll be the judge of that. Who do you work for and what do they want?"

Doc jerked his head at Charlotte. "This one." He paused and smiled. For the first time Kieran noticed that he had bad teeth. "Dead *after* we've had our way with her."

Aislinn's face grew stony. "I'm disinclined to grant your employer's wish."

"Doesn't matter what you want." He pressed the edge of the blade into Charlotte's neck and a drop of blood welled. "And you're not getting any information out of me either."

"You know there's no possible way you're leaving here alive. It really was stupid to plan an attack right in the middle of a well-attended Unseelie ball. You have nothing but enemies here."

"Oh, you'd be surprised how many friends I have lurking about. Anyway, I think we'll get out of here just fine. See, Queen Aislinn, you get to choose; either you let me go with the girl, or you watch her die right now. The boss wants her alive for a time, but I tend toward flexibility on that point."

"And the Wild Hunt?" Kieran asked loudly. "How do you plan to avoid them once the woman is dead? Do you *want* to join the slaugh?"

"She's got exactly two drops of fae blood." He snorted. "The Wild Hunt won't bother for her."

"Really? Are you so sure of that, Doc?" Kieran raised his brows and glanced at Gabriel, the leader of the Wild Hunt. "Let's ask someone who knows for certain."

Gabriel's lips peeled back in a feral manner to show gleaming white teeth. "The Wild Hunt will come for you if you so much as draw a drop of blood from that woman."

Niall whispered near his ear. "Stall this bozo. I'll go do something to distract him." Then he disappeared into the crush.

Doc made a hissing sound. "You and I both know that's not how it works. The hunt hounds lead you, not the other way around."

"Still," Kieran broke in, "seems like an awfully big gamble to me. I'm not sure how the Netherworld would rule on a part-blood's murder. I sure hope you're getting paid enough for the risk, Doc, because all the money in the world won't keep you out of the slaugh. And I'm betting your employer doesn't care where you end up."

"Enough chitchat." Doc jiggled the knife, making Charlotte yelp. "You going to let me out of here without any trouble or do you want to watch her die?"

Kieran stepped toward Doc, drawing his eye. He affected a calm, cool composure, even though all he wanted was to leap across the room and tackle this man. "So, let me get this straight. You'll either kill the girl now or kill the girl later. You simply want us to let you go so we don't have to *watch* you kill her? I don't understand your logic." He narrowed his eyes. "You *do* realize which court you're in, right?"

Charlotte's eyes widened.

Doc hissed at him. He pressed the knife in a little more and Charlotte stiffened, gasping. "Want me to do it now, then?"

Kieran took another couple steps closer to the man, getting ready for whatever Niall's distraction would be. His heart rate had increased. This was a risky move. If he couldn't get to them fast enough, Doc might take the opportunity to plunge the knife into her throat and be done with it.

"You really aren't very bright, are you, Doc? Don't you realize what a hard situation you've put yourself in? You're surrounded by Unseelie who want to rip you apart. Not to mention you selected a victim who is more than capable of taking care of herself." Kieran paused and caught Charlotte's gaze. "Aren't you, Charlotte?"

He was hoping to drive her out of her shock and remind her of the defense training he'd given her. Once things started to happen, she would need to get away from Doc as quickly as she could. She'd only had an afternoon's worth of instruction, but it would have to be enough.

The ballroom plunged into darkness. Not just ordinary darkness, but pure, unrelenting black like the inside of a cave.

Amid the shocked gasps of the ball-goers, he heard a male grunt and the clatter of silver on the marble floor. Kieran leapt forward, tackling the man he hoped was Doc. Doc bellowed out a swear word and Kieran recognized his voice: *Jackpot.*

Doc's fist connected with Kieran's jaw. Pain exploded. They scuffled in the darkness, rolling over and bumping into people's legs. Kieran punched blind in the black, connecting with what felt like Doc's jaw and then the side of his rib cage. Doc howled in pain and doubled over while Kieran fought to hold on to him.

Something slammed hard into Kieran's head—Doc's forehead? Blinding agony burst through his skull and Doc wiggled out from under him and was gone.

"Stop him!" Kieran yelled, scrambling on the floor in the direction he thought he'd gone.

The lights came back on.

"Stop him!" Kieran yelled again as he pushed to his feet and scanned the crowd. At his eye level all he saw were brightly colored skirts and black tuxedo pants. Doc was nowhere to be seen.

"We'll get him. Take care of Charlotte," Emmaline yelled as she rushed past with Ronan and Aeric. She'd kicked off her heels and had hiked her dress up to run better.

Charlotte.

He turned and saw her sitting on the floor not far away, blood dripping down her throat. Bella and Risa sat beside her. He ran to her, coming to a sliding halt next to her. "Are you all right?"

She nodded, her face pale and her eyes wide. "I guess."

Risa met his eyes. "I think she's just shaken up. More angry than anything else."

Dread gathering in the pit of his stomach despite Risa's words, he peeled Charlotte's hand away and examined the wound the knife had made. There was a lot of blood, but the cut wasn't anything that wouldn't heal relatively quickly.

Charlotte smiled. "I landed a good elbow to his solar plexus, just like you taught me."

"Good. That's good." Gods, she'd been lucky. The element of surprise had probably helped her get away, but Doc could have just as easily jerked that knife in the wrong direction.

He reached out and took her by the upper arms, fastening his gaze to hers. "This place is no longer safe for you. I know now it never was."

Bella nodded. "If whoever is behind this has stones enough to attack you at an Unseelie ball, that means they're going to keep coming after you. This was a desperate, high-risk move."

"I agree. It's time to get you out of here and I mean right now." He helped her to her feet. "We won't tell anyone where we're going except those we trust the most."

"What about the whole memory thing?"

He glanced at Risa. "You'll have to meet us."

She patted Charlotte's shoulder. "I'll go wherever you direct me. Just keep her safe."

"You'll tell the queen, I hope?" Bella raised her eyebrows.

"That goes without saying."

Just then Emmaline and the others returned, out of breath and without Doc. "He got away," Emmaline panted.

Kieran pushed a frustrated hand through his hair. "Okay. At least we know what this one looks like and that he's a null. Surely we can track down some kind of lead, either to him or to his boss."

Ronan nodded. "We're already on it." He jerked his head at Charlotte. "I presume you're taking her away."

"Yeah. Right now." He glanced at Charlotte, who looked prepared to meet the challenge ahead of them. She looked strong. That was good; she'd have to be.

He wished like hell it wasn't him who had to take her away. The last thing he needed was to be secluded somewhere with a woman he was coming to appreciate more with every passing day. This did not bode well, but the bond he'd forged to bring her here wouldn't allow anyone but him to guard her for what appeared might be a long stretch of time. He'd just have to keep his distance as much as he could.

Ah, Danu. It was going to be hard.

He stared at Charlotte for a moment, jaw locked. "Stay with them. I have to talk with the queen."

A scant fifteen minutes later Charlotte sat on the back of Kieran's bike while they hurtled through the night at a speed that made her want to vomit.

After Kieran had talked to the queen, he'd rushed her back to his apartment and given her terse orders to pack whatever she wanted to take that would fit into a backpack. She hoped they had a Laundromat wherever they were going. Kieran wouldn't say where that was because he didn't want to speak the location out loud. Charlotte didn't ask why, but she thought she knew—in case someone was listening. This was faerie, after all. She supposed they had much more interesting ways to eavesdrop than by sticking bugs under coffee tables.

She clung to him as he drove the bike through a maze of inner city streets, backtracking and twisting and taking sudden turns. Trying to determine if they were being followed?

Finally they made it out of the city and he upped the speed even higher. The trees of the Boundary Lands zipped past in a moonlit blur as they rocketed down what passed for a Piefferburg highway.

Directionally challenged as she was, she couldn't tell which way they were headed. All she knew was that she was forced to cling to Kieran for a very long time. Felt like forever. In reality, it was probably only a couple hours and change.

Traveling to . . . well, wherever they were traveling to . . . was a little like wandering through a dream. Most of Piefferburg was rural, wooded, filled with the tiny sprae, evergreens, and nature fae. Piefferburg City—she knew from her schooling—was the largest city in the detention area. She could name their greatest imports and exports, too. They passed through quite a few little hamlets, most of them dark and asleep, but a couple of the villages seemed to be jumping as though it was bright daylight—clutches of nocturnal fae?

At dawn they rolled into yet another village, but they stopped in this one. They pulled up to a curb and Kieran cut the engine on the bike. Charlotte immediately dismounted, groaning as she stretched her legs. After she pulled off her helmet and sucked in a couple deep breaths of non-quickly moving air, she glanced around her.

Again she was reminded of Europe. The houses were all small, narrow, and had those funny curved clay shingles. The streets were made of cobblestone and a large stone church rose in the center of it all. Just as she was glancing around, the bell began to chime six in the morning.

"It's literally like a faery tale vill . . . age." Her bemused smile faded. "What are those?" Of course, she knew what the creatures were that were currently crossing the street. Goblins. A pair of them. Her stomach clenched and she fought an urge to take a step backward. "There are goblins here?"

"Welcome to Hangman's Bastion." Kieran breezed past her. "All *actual* faery-tale villages have them."

"I guess you would know."

"This is one of the Unseelie strongholds away from Piefferburg City. Goblins are more than welcome here."

"And we couldn't find a Seelie stronghold?"

"There aren't any. You don't find many of the Rose Court out in the country. They don't like bugs or dirt. Anyway"—he gave her pointed look—"I don't think you'd like the Seelie as much as you think you would. In fact, most goblins are far more interesting and trustworthy."

"I suppose that's true. You can always trust a goblin to have you for dinner."

Ignoring her, he walked down the narrow, flower-lined pathway that led to a small white building. The swinging sign out front read *Hangman's Bastion Real Estate*. Hangman's Bastion? Who the hell would want to live in a place with a name like that?

He glanced back at her. "Hurry up, they're probably about to close."

She followed him inside where a totally normal-looking woman with long dark hair and skin the color of café au lait glanced up from her desk. A smile that said *fresh man meat* flashed across her pretty face. A sign on her desk read Elina. Elina did not acknowledge Charlotte's existence. Of course, in her place, faced with a man like Kieran, Charlotte probably wouldn't acknowledge her existence either. He did sort of draw all the hormones to him.

Kieran flashed a charming smile at Elina, megawatts more charming than any smile he'd ever used on her. Charlotte scowled. He began to speak in an odd language that she had come to recognize as Old Maejian. A lengthy, laughing exchange occurred in which Elina blushed three times. Charlotte's scowl deepened.

Eventually the conversation produced a piece of paper, which Kieran signed. Then he pulled a wad of cash from his back pocket, turned it over, and received a key in exchange.

Finally, he walked to her, waving the key. "Time to go."

For the first time since she'd arrived, Elina appeared to notice her and offered a smile and a wave . . . which Charlotte did not return.

They left the building and walked back toward the bike. "What's wrong with you?" he asked, handing her the helmet she'd left on the cycle.

"Me? I'm fine. So, did you get her phone number?"

He stilled. "You sound jealous. Why would you sound that way, Charlotte?"

"I'm not jealous." She snorted. "God, I can't wait to be rid of you. Go lock me in that place you just rented and come back here for her. I couldn't care less." She pulled her helmet on.

He stared at her for a moment longer, then pulled on his own helmet. "If you say so."

"I say so. Let's go."

He drove the cycle though the very quaint downtown area and the other side of town. A small distance away, they turned down a narrow, wooded path. Finally the trees opened up, revealing a small house. Golden in color, with green shutters and door, it was nestled in among pretty spring flowers and greenery. He cut the engine of the bike, allowed her to dismount, and pushed the cycle around the back of the house.

While Kieran was around back, the door opened and a goblin walked out. Immediately he did what passed for a goblin smile—a scary grimace—and began to speak in Old Maejian as he walked toward her.

Charlotte stepped backward, panic curling through her stomach. She forced herself to halt by fisting her hands so hard her fingernails dented the skin of her palms. Smiling tightly, she dragged a breath in through her nose to calm herself.

This was fine. She could do this.

When all Charlotte did was frown at him quizzically as he continued to speak, he switched to English. "You must be Mrs. Dorian. Elina just called to let me know you were renting this place." He walked to her, spindly gray hand outstretched. "I came by to open the cottage and greet you."

She really didn't want to touch him, but she hadn't been raised in a barn either. Reaching out, she took his hand and shook it. His hand felt like any other hand, and she drew hers away surprised. "Yes, I'm Mrs. Dorian. Nice to meet you."

He pointed at the house. "I've been cleaning it up for you. Should be ready to go. I left fresh towels and there are groceries stocked in the kitchen to get you started."

"Thank you. I didn't catch your name."

"Leson. I lived for a long time in Piefferburg City, Goblin Town. Then I fell in love with a female from Hangman's Bastion and moved out here."

Charlotte smiled. "That's . . . nice." Goblins fell in love. Who knew?

Just then Kieran came around the side of the house.

Leson approached him and shook his hand. They talked for a few moments in Old Maejian, then switched to a guttural, clicking language that had to be Alahambri, then Leson waved a hand at her and headed down a path leading away from the house. "Have a wonderful honeymoon, Mr. and Mrs. Dorian."

Once the goblin caretaker was gone, she gaped at Kieran. "You told Elina we were newlyweds?"

"It was the most plausible story I could come up with." He grinned. "You thought I was trying to pick her up."

She waved her hand impatiently. "Whatever, you got our hideaway. Good for you." She hitched her backpack up and headed for the front door. "I just hope there's a working bathroom. I need to brush my teeth and shower."

"It's been a long night."

Yes, her moment of glamour at the ball had quickly turned into picking bugs out of her teeth on the back of a motorcycle. "It's been a long week. I just want Risa to get here and retrieve those memories so I can leave this place. I'm tired of having knives poked into my flesh."

He followed behind her as she entered the place. It was

small, but very cute. Very "honeymoonish," even though she and Kieran's trip couldn't be anything further from that. The living room had a huge stone fireplace. The furniture in the small sitting area in front of the hearth was dove gray and was that soft microfiber stuff that she always thought she'd buy if she ever had kids—easy to wash. The hardwood floor was covered here and there with white-and-gray-patterned area rugs and throw blankets. Soft pillows abounded.

To her left was a small, open kitchen done all in white. Straight ahead rose a carved wooden staircase that led up to a loft area where she could see a large bed and the entrance to what was likely a bathroom.

She stopped short. "Kieran, please tell me there's more than one bed."

"There's only one bed. No worries, I'll take the couch."

She set her pack down on the area rug near the couch. "That's very gentlemanly of you."

His lips twitched. "I don't think I've ever been called that before."

"I heard *bastard* was a more commonly used descriptor."

"Yeah, well, you did ride in with Niall. He's colorful."

"That's one word you could use to describe him." She walked around the living room, admiring the furnishings. "This place is lovely. If we really were on a honeymoon, you'd have one happy bride."

"Telling the rental agent and the caretaker that story will give us privacy."

"Good. I don't want goblins popping in very often."

"Leson seems very friendly."

"They eat people, Kieran. Surely you can see my concern. Look at it from my perspective."

"You talk like human beings are the main part of their diet. They don't eat people for fun. They eat them in time of war or in order to protect themselves."

Her lips twisted. "Yes, that makes it so much better."

"Goblins mostly eat—"

She held up a hand. "I really do not want to know."

"It's not pretty, but it's not a whole lot different from the meat diets of most of humankind. Their way of consuming is just—"

She shushed him. "Please stop. And you wonder why humans want to keep you in here."

"Ah, here we go. I figured we'd have this conversation sooner or later."

She rounded on him from where she stood in front of the fireplace. "Let's don't. I know where you stand on the matter, and you know where I stand. Let's agree to disagree."

"No." He came toward her, his dark eyes darker than she'd ever seen them. She took a step backward, hunger flaring low in her stomach. God, she hated how much she wanted this man. His voice felt like velvet against her skin when he spoke. "I know I can make you see our side."

"Our side? There's no *our* side."

His eyebrows arched. "You're forgetting something distinctly important."

Her blood went cold for a moment as she remembered. Her voice came out sounding defensive. "I'm far more human than I am fae."

"You're one of us, Charlotte. You might not have enough blood for magick, but we're still in your veins."

She made a frustrated sound. "Can't you understand why the humans don't want you free? You can melt people *with your brain*, Kieran."

"Okay, sure, I *can* do that, but not with my brain, with my magick."

She put her hand on her hip. "Semantics."

"I can do it, but I don't. Not unless it's in the defense of myself or another. Any human can pick up a handgun and shoot someone dead. Most of them don't. I fail to see the difference."

"The difference is a human has to pick up the weapon and use it. You *are* the weapon."

He shook his head. "Charlotte, take a close look at your species. Humans are no strangers to brutality and violence.

The fae were here long before humans ever were and we lived among them peacefully for thousands of years, policing ourselves, staying hidden, minding our own business. I watch human television, your news programs, and I wonder how it is that they're able to think *we're* the scary ones."

She sputtered, unable to come with any good response to that. There was no possible way to refute the argument that humans were a brutal and violent species. "Because you're so different. You're *other*."

"Ah. Because we look different, have different cultures, see the world from a different vantage point." He gave her a sad smile. "Charlotte, you need better reasons than that. All of those are simply advantages, as I view them. They're not reasons for dread. Yet people like your father preach hatred and fear where there should be none."

"Should we light a candle and sing 'Kumbaya' now?" Her voice came out snappish, mostly because they both knew she'd lost the argument. "You're . . . *scary*, Kieran."

"Ah. Your nightmares. Risa told me she saw the memories. She thinks, and I agree, that they're the reason for the block."

She turned away from him. "They were only nightmares. I was just a kid."

His hand closed over her shoulder. She closed her eyes at the warmth of his palm bleeding through the material of her shirt. "They may have only been dreams, but they left an emotional mark. I can help you heal it."

"How?" She pivoted to face him and found him disconcertingly close to her. The heat of his body radiated out and warmed her. The scent of his skin teased her nose. She wanted immediately to step back from him, but instead she forced herself to stand her ground.

He raised a brow. "Dream wraith, remember?"

She shook her head. "I don't want you in my mind again."

"Charlotte, I'm sorry for what I did to you. If I had been able to make another choice, I would have."

She peered up at him. "Really?"

"I don't enjoy bending another's will to my own. If you allow me to help you with your problem, you won't even know I was in your head. You'll just wake up feeling better, less afraid."

Chewing her lip, she considered him. "If you think this will remove the block, why are you asking my permission?"

"Because what I just said was true—I don't like barging into people's dreamscapes unless I've been invited."

"But you don't need permission."

He gave a loose shrug. "No."

She looked down at the floor for a moment. The thought of having him in her head again while he was also under her skin was not a pleasant one. Yet, if he could remove the block she'd be out of here all the sooner. "All right." She looked up at him. "I give you my permission."

"Good."

She walked over, grabbed her backpack, and started for the stairs. "I'm going to take a shower." Her exhausted legs protesting every moment, she made her way up the stairs.

Minutes later, standing under the hot, driving water, she pondered what Kieran had said about allowing the fae to be free. She wanted so much to cling to her anger because of the way they'd brought her here, and because she'd been attacked twice now. Yet, in their place, if messing with the life of one human had been her only hope for freedom, wouldn't she have done the same?

Or maybe she was simply falling victim to Stockholm syndrome.

Of course, she wasn't ready to fall in line with everything the fae espoused. It wasn't that she disagreed with the things Kieran had said downstairs about the freedom of the fae, it was just that agreeing with him made her feel like she was disrespecting her father. Her father had been there for her when no one else had. He'd been the one to dry her tears when she'd been small, after her mother had died. He'd been the one to give her advice while she was growing up, had been there to love her, guide her. She worshiped her father.

. . . people like your father preach hatred and fear . . .

It was difficult to think of him from another perspective.

She finished up her shower, dressed in a soft pair of PJ pants and an old sweatshirt of Kieran's. Then she eased under the fluffy eiderdown on the bed and fell asleep in about half a heartbeat.

FIFTEEN

WHEN Kieran didn't hear any more sounds coming from the loft, he edged his way up the stairs. Charlotte lay on her side in the bed, blankets tucked around her, hand curled against her mouth on the pillow, fast asleep. He rubbed his eyes, wanting to join her, but she'd given him permission to enter her dreams and attempt to undo the damage caused by the nightmares. Now was the best time to do it.

He eased down the stairs, closed the blinds and lay down on the couch. It had been a long time since he'd used his ability to heal a psychic wound made by recurring nightmares. He needed to enter her dreamscape and, once in, he needed to find the emotional residue left of the nightmare and remove it. That complex process meant finding the nightmare in her subconscious, replaying it, and convincing Charlotte's dreaming self to interact with the symbols of her fear in a different way.

Letting himself drift to sleep was the easy part. Once he'd

entered the dreaming state, he forced his conscious mind to become aware.

He stood on a windy beach, sand stinging his eyes and whipping his hair around his face. Before him stretched a storm-tossed ocean and rolling, lightning-streaked gray-black clouds above it. Thunder crashed through the heavens. Tossed waves and the sound of the wind ripping at his clothing filled his ears. This was his own dreamscape, reflecting his inner turmoil. Concentrating, he calmed the winds and seas, changing his dream while he stood in the middle of it, but this was not his primary objective—he needed to find Charlotte.

Glancing around, he searched for the best place to exit his private dreamscape and find a gateway to a community area. From there he could locate a door to Charlotte's scape.

Striding into the cold, violent water, he forced the crashing waves to conform to his will. The surf calmed and he walked in mostly unbuffeted until he'd submerged his entire body and head. For a moment all he saw was dark, churning water, then everything shifted. Light flickered. Figures moved. Yes, here was a doorway into a community area. In dreams, water and mirrors often were.

Underneath his feet, the sand became stairs and the sea a placid silvery pool. He walked up out of the water into a dark, open space. His hair, skin, and clothing dried the moment they hit air.

As always, entering the community dreamscapes was like checking himself into a mental ward. People—mental projections of their dream selves—milled around talking to themselves and interacting with unseen objects, all of them lost in their own imaginings.

A blond in a pale blue dress had stopped to watch him emerge from the pool. In a moment she would likely take that image of him and spin it off into her own creation, falling deeper and deeper into her dreaming mind.

The pool he'd emerged from dried up, turning into black concrete as he stepped out of it, and he walked forward, avoiding the sleepers as he went, concentrating on Charlotte in order to find a way into her private dreamscape, just the way he'd done the night he'd formed the bond with her.

He passed into the darkening edges of the room and glimpsed a light ahead of him, a door cracked open to emit the glow of the sun. He reached it and pushed it the rest of the way open. Ah, here was Charlotte's realm.

She lay on a sun-drenched hillside amid a hundred daisies. Drawn like a cat to nip, he walked to her. Her eyes were closed, a smile on her lips, arms outspread. She looked peaceful. Odd, considering her current emotional state. He studied her for a long moment while he remained unnoticed. She appeared as she had in the bonding dream. Her long midnight hair was fanned out around her head, contrasting with the white daisies. Her lashes shadowed pink-tinged cheeks and accented her full red lips.

His gaze dropped to her slender throat and the gentle swell of her breasts cupped by the bodice of her dress. When he'd first seen her back during the bonding dream, the need to touch her had immediately swelled within him. His desire for her had eclipsed everything else—even the knowledge of who her father had been and how much she likely hated the fae.

Looking down on her now, knowing her better than he had back then, the reaction was even more severe. Hands fisted, he fought not to kneel beside her, kiss her softly, and draw her into his arms. He was certain that she would come to him with little more than a sigh. Then he could drag his mouth down the luscious column of her throat, take that dress off her and give careful, thorough attention to each of her lovely breasts, lick her nipples into hard little points, then part her thighs and move lower . . .

Teeth gritted, he took a step away from her.

But in order to trigger the nightmare, he was going to have to touch her. Steeling himself against his temptation, he inched his way closer to her and knelt. Before he could make himself known, Charlotte's eyes fluttered open and she caught sight of him. She pushed up onto her elbows, but at the same time, the dream shifted radically.

His blood went cold as Charlotte's body morphed into a child's and the scape faded to a ruined plain of black and gray. Ragged edges, broken stones, storm-darkened skies. Armageddon Land. It looked like a nuclear bomb had hit.

Child-Charlotte seemed to not see him in this scape. She cowered behind a stone, her face streaked with dirt and her arms and legs scraped as though she'd been running. Her tangled black hair framed wide, anxious eyes.

He stood, realization slamming into him; he'd been thrust right into her nightmare without even having to draw it out. Perhaps talking about her nightmare had triggered a reappearance. Or maybe it had been the mere sight of him—a fae.

He stepped toward her and spoke in a reassuring voice. "Charlotte."

She looked up at him with her big hazel eyes. "Who are you?"

"My name is Kieran. I'm a friend." Somewhere in the distance, thunder crashed through the sky followed by a streak of silver lightning.

She peered over the top of the rock. "They're coming."

"Who's coming?"

She glanced at him, her fingers white on the rock she gripped. Tears streaked her cheeks. Her voice shook with emotion. "The monsters. They're coming. They—they killed my mother and now they're after me."

That gave him pause. So in Charlotte's nightmare the goblins, red caps, and joint-eaters kill her mother. Gods, no wonder she had a subconscious block against the fae.

"There!" she yelled and pointed over the rock. "They're coming!"

In the distance a shambling array of the ugliest faery-tale creatures moved toward them, shaped by the mind of a child who'd been told tale after frightening tale of their awfulness. He could hear horror movie sounds—sounds no true goblin, joint-eater, or red cap would ever make—growing louder as they approached.

Charlotte stood and stumbled backward, ready to flee. Before she could run, he grabbed her birdlike shoulders and held her steady. "Charlotte, you don't have to run. Turn and fight them."

"No . . . no!" She fought him, eyes wild, "I can't."

Fear had her in its icy grip. He had to break it. He had to convince Charlotte that she had control here. Once she learned she could change this dream to suit her will, she could stand up to the boogeymen that plagued her.

By the time he was done here, she would save her mother. Save herself. Take control. That was the way to remove the block.

The fae creatures moved closer and Charlotte ripped away from his grip. He watched her run from her dream monsters, tripping over the wasted debris of the scape as she whimpered and screamed. The problem was going to be convincing Charlotte she could stand up to her fears.

He closed his eyes, stopped the dream, and commanded it to start from the beginning.

It was going to be a long session.

CHARLOTTE woke to the scent of hot soup and murmuring voices wafting up from the living room. Blinking, she saw that twilight had fallen. She'd slept the entire day away, but it didn't feel like she'd gotten any rest at all. Bits and pieces of the dreams she'd had filtered back to her and she realized why.

Flopping over onto her back, she recalled her nightmare—the one she'd had so many times in her life she knew every moment of it by heart. Yet this time it had been different. This time, instead of watching the monsters tear her mother apart and then come after her, she'd fought them and won. This time she'd leapt between the fae and her mom, fought them off before they could harm her, and then escaped with her into a sun-drenched landscape filled with thousands of daisies.

"Huh."

Apparently Kieran had worked his dream wraith mojo. Now, instead of feeling sadness and dread, as she did every time she experienced that nightmare, she felt light and happy—empowered. Euphoria filled her chest instead of grief.

She needed to thank Kieran. Her lips curved into a smile. The nightmare had been eradicated, easy as pie. Or maybe it hadn't been easy at all, considering how exhausted she felt.

Flipping back the blankets, she sought a pair of socks, then walked to the banister that overlooked the living room for the source of the murmuring voices. Risa had arrived. Her stomach did a curious little flip-flop. She was intrigued to explore her latent memories a little more, but frightened by what she might find.

Especially now that perhaps the block to her mother's time-line had been removed.

As she made her way downstairs, the hunger rumbling through her stomach blotted out all traces of anxiety regarding Risa's presence. It had been close to twenty-four hours since she'd last eaten.

She stopped at the foot of the stairs and locked gazes with Kieran for a moment over Risa's head. "Thank you."

Dark circles marked the skin under his eyes and his hair was mussed as if from sleep. He dragged a hand through it and nodded once.

Risa smiled at her. "Good to see you alive, Charlotte."

"Me, too."

While Kieran and Risa talked in the living room, she grabbed a bowl, filled it with hot soup simmering on the stove top, and took a slice of the yummy crusty bread that had been cut from a loaf on a board. Then she joined them, sitting down on the couch and balancing the soup bowl in her lap.

"Are you feeling better?" asked Risa. "The ball was the talk of the tower this morning."

"As well as can be expected. Physically, I'm fine. But I'm kind of taking it personally that so many people seem to want to do me harm."

"Well, I say we work as quickly as possible to extract the memories we need so those people won't have reason to try anymore. What do you think?"

"Sounds good. I'm ready to go home."

"Are you sure you don't want to take a break today?" asked Kieran. "The dream work we did was taxing on us both."

She shook her head. "I feel great."

After she finished her meal, Kieran took her bowl, and Risa patted the cushion next to her with a hand that bore long, ice blue nails. She arranged herself the way Risa asked, hoping there wouldn't be anything nasty in today's session or that they didn't hit another wall.

Risa gave her a kind smile. "Do you want some of the relaxing tea you drank before?"

She shook her head. "I'm fine. After Kieran's aid with my nightmare, I'm feeling better about this process. I only ask one thing."

"What is it?"

She chewed her lower lip, framing her request in her mind before she spoke it out loud. "If you jump into my mother's memories and come across the one in which she dies, please fast-forward through it."

Risa nodded. "I'll do my best. Sometimes the emotion rolled up in the memory won't allow me to fast-forward, but if I can, I will."

"Thank you."

"Okay, relax your body and let me work my magick." Risa pressed her fingertips to Charlotte's temple. Power crackled into her head. Memories flashed through her mind's eye, flickering at first and then getting steadier, like an old filmstrip taking hold.

Soon the memories whirled like a roulette wheel, nauseating Charlotte. They slowed, and then stopped where they'd ended before, with Risa trying to jump the line of recollection from her to her mother. The muscles in Charlotte's body tightened, expecting to slam into another barrier, as Risa probed for a way to cross over. Having Risa in her head was a little like being chained to a train; she had no control at all if Risa suddenly decided she wanted to speed a hundred miles an hour into a wall.

Risa slowed to a crawl at a most interesting memory—Charlotte's birth. They hadn't jumped the line yet, so these were still her memories—albeit memories buried far, far in the recesses of her mind, ones she couldn't examine without magickal help. She watched in her mind's eye with fascination the moment of her entry into this world and the look of complete elation on her mother's face as she was placed in her arms. Tears swelled in Charlotte's eyes. So her mother had been happy to give her life. Charlotte had always wondered.

The look on her face was not the expression of a woman who would later commit suicide when her daughter was only six. This was the expression of a loving, doting mother who wouldn't leave her child at any cost.

In her effort to jump the line Risa replayed the memory over and over, like a video on rewind, until Charlotte wanted to break down and sob. Finally Risa must have found a crack or a bridge or something because suddenly they were in her mother's memories and Charlotte was a bump in her mother's stomach.

The memories were not linear here, jumping to various times during her mother's life. They skipped from Charlotte's third birthday, to the day her mother had met her father, to the day her mother had graduated from college. The way the memories played, it was almost as if Risa was trying to gain control of the timeline and go straight backward, but something wouldn't let her. Charlotte could feel her irritation though the psychic link they shared.

Sometimes the memories had sound and sometimes they

didn't. Really, it was like watching a defective DVD. One of the memories that did have sound was quite interesting—when her mother told her father she was fae.

Her mother and father had been lingering over lunch in a fancy, mostly deserted restaurant. Charlotte surmised her age at the time to be something like five or six, close to the time when her mother had died. Her mother had revealed the information about her fae blood to her father haltingly, as if she feared his reaction. From her mother's vantage point, Charlotte watched her father's expression go from utter shock to a flash of cold hatred to calm acceptance.

Acceptance?

Charlotte studied her father through her mother's eyes. No, that wasn't acceptance on his face—that was rage wearing a mask.

Before she could process any of that, they were off again with a lurch, tripping all over the memory timeline once again.

The memory trail caught on one specific event, Risa tried to move on, but it only caught again. Over and over.

Her mother and father entered the house she'd grown up in. Evening painted the sky dark beyond the windows. They were both dressed up, apparently home after having gone out. Through her mother's eyes, Charlotte caught flashes of the blue sequined dress her mother wore as she moved around the room. Toys scattered the swank living room.

Again Risa tried to move on, and again the memory caught. Charlotte felt Risa give up and just go with it. Now the memory moved in real time.

Her mother and father paid Lisa, the babysitter, Charlotte remembered. Her mother collapsed on the couch and toed off her sparkly blue heels while her father poured a drink. They spoke cordially of the evening in low tones, but a tension hung in the air. Charlotte was only privy to what her mother saw and heard, not her emotions, but tightness lay in their communication and body language. All was not well between them.

Her father handed a short crystal glass filled with amber liquid to her mother, who set it on the coffee table, saying she'd return after checking on cricket.

Cricket?

Her mom rose and walked into a darkened room that Charlotte immediately recognized as hers during childhood. Standing over the bed, Charlotte got a good look at her child-self in the bed fast asleep. Her mother stood, taking in the scene, before she knelt, brushed Charlotte's hair away from her forehead, and laid a tender kiss to her temple.

"I love you, cricket," her mother whispered. Then she rose and returned to the living room.

Her mother sank down onto the couch with a sigh and sipped the drink her husband had prepared. Once she'd drained it she immediately became confused, slurring her words and becoming shaky in her movements. Charlotte would have said her mother was drunk, but she'd been perfectly fine before her father had mixed the drink he'd given her. Completely sober. It was odd. It had only been *one* drink, after all. Not enough to make someone this inebriated.

A cold little knot tied itself in Charlotte's stomach. Had the drink been drugged?

The memory went on. Her mother became frightened and clung to her husband for comfort. Her father gave her a pill, telling her it would help. She swallowed it. Became more confused.

Then she swallowed more pills, all kinds of them . . . all at her father's gentle coaxing.

Her mother collapsed onto the couch and lay very, very still. The world from her eyes looked hazy, indistinct, all of it growing darker by the second.

Her mother reached out, grabbed the lapel of his jacket, and whispered, "Why?"

Through the memory, Charlotte's father's face swam before her mother's drugged gaze. His eyes looked colder than Charlotte had ever seen them. "It's either this or Piefferburg. I'm doing you a favor."

Her mother's hand tightened on the material of his jacket. *"Charlotte."* Her voice came out as a slurred wheeze.

His expression softened. "I would never hurt her, but she'll never know the truth. She's young enough that she'll hardly remember you. That's a blessing."

Her mother's eyes filled with tears, obscuring her vision, and her hand dropped away.

The line of memory went black.

"No!" Charlotte sat up, screaming. "No! It's not possible. That's not right. It can't be!" Risa was there holding her failing arms down. Such an odd mixture of emotion warred inside her. Disbelief that her father was capable of that. Anger that he would do it.

And relief that her mother hadn't left her willingly. She hadn't taken her own life.

She'd had it taken from her.

"Take a deep breath, Charlotte," said Risa, releasing her arms and sitting down beside her on the couch. "Couple deep breaths."

She breathed in and out several times until she regained enough of a hold on her emotions to calm down and speak clearly. "Is it possible that the memories could be wrong?"

Risa exhaled long and slow. "No."

Kieran paced in front of her. "What the hell happened?"

She took another deep breath. It was the only thing keeping her from jumping straight out of her skin. "My father told me my mother committed suicide, that she'd swallowed a bunch of pills one night, but that's not what I just saw." Swallowing hard, she looked away from him.

"What did you see, Charlotte?" he prompted in a gentle voice that seemed so oddly out of character for him. It made her want to break down sobbing.

"I saw my mother's memory of her death. It was pills, just as he told me, but it was my father who manipulated her into taking them." She paused, forcibly gaining a handle of her emotions. "She trusted him. She died trusting him, thinking he was helping her when, really, he was murdering her." She drew a ragged breath. "He took my mother away from me when I was only six."

The room went silent. She didn't blame them for not knowing how to respond. It wasn't every day someone found out their father was a cold-blooded killer.

"Why would he do it?" she asked, finally. "How could he?"

"She was fae." Risa reached out and stroked her hair. "I know you saw the memory of your mother telling your father of her genetic heritage. He killed her not long after and then spent his life raising you to hate them."

Yes, she knew all that. She'd witnessed the same memories that Risa had; she simply didn't want to acknowledge the truth in them.

Risa stood. "We're done for now. I'll give her some time to process this."

Charlotte was more than ready to be alone so she could work through all these revelations. Risa watched her with a sad face as she left the house.

Once Risa was gone, she rose and went to the window to look out at the forest surrounding the house. Hugging herself, she concentrated on the rich colors of the leaves and flowers, trying to put her attention on something other than the emotional tangle in her gut and the confusion in her head.

Kieran came to stand beside her. "I'm not really good at this, but—"

"It's okay, you don't have say anything. In fact, I wish you wouldn't. I don't really want to talk about it. It's kind of a shock, but the world's a bitch and then you die, right?"

"I know you don't really think that."

She shook her head. "Honestly, I feel sort of liberated. That memory proves that my father is a Class A bastard. He never deserved the pedestal I put him on and now he's smashed to smithereens at the base. I can now abandon all sense of duty and responsibility to him. It's sort of a relief. I feel a lot less . . . heavy."

Now she had a question to the mystery that had plagued her since she'd been six; why had her mother abandoned her?

Answer: she'd never had a choice.

Grief bubbled up from the depths of her. God, her mother had been so young, so alive. At the time of her death she'd been Charlotte's age right now—her life stretching out before her.

Kieran's warm hand closed over her shoulder. "That's a bunch of bullshit. You must feel betrayed beyond belief."

"I do." She hung her head for a moment, breathing in and out through her nose so she wouldn't pass out. "In actuality, my father was always my sun and stars. This is unbelievable to me. If I hadn't seen it in my own head, I never would have thought it possible."

KIERAN stared at Charlotte's profile, lit by the descending sun. He wished he was better at this. Wished he could even relate. The closest thing he'd had to a parent were the nuns at the abbey where he and his brother had grown up and that had been a long, long time ago.

"I'm sorry this trip has changed your life so much." He stared out the window, seeing nothing, trying to think of something intelligent to say.

She pivoted to face him. "I'm not. Right now I'm happy all this happened. I'm happy you found me, bonded me, forced me to come here." Her eyes were glittering, hard. The grief was gone, replaced by anger. That was good. In his opinion, rage was an emotion you could use. Sadness was anger turned inward—it did nothing but destroy the person experiencing it. "If I'd never come to Piefferburg I would never have discovered the truth. I would have gone on thinking my father was everything and my mother didn't love me enough to stick around. Thank you, Kieran."

His gaze caught hers and held. "I never thought I'd hear you say that."

He studied her lips, parted and full. The image of her on the hillside filled his mind. He dipped his head a little, imagining what it would be like to kiss her. What would she taste like in real life?

At the same time, she leaned toward him.

Their lips met. Soft. Warm. Searching.

SIXTEEN

IT was unexpected, but not unwelcome. A shock went through him at the contact, ripples of pleasure radiating through his body.

He should have pushed her aside. He should have walked away from her, spoken terse words and left the room. He definitely should not have pulled her closer and kissed her back with interest. Wrapping his arms around her, he dragged her up against his chest and slanted his mouth over hers hungrily while his hand found the nape of her neck.

He wanted to make her pain go away and there was one surefire way to do it.

That desire to soothe her via any means bothered him, but it was quickly pushed to the side when her kiss became more aggressive, her mouth pressing urgently against his. His hand slipped under the hem of her shirt and found smooth, warm skin—skin he wanted to run his fingers and tongue over at length.

She parted her lips and he slid between them, brushing up against her tongue to taste her heat. She found the bottom of his sweater and pushed up. He allowed her to pull it over his head and drop it to the floor. Her hands explored him, running down his back, his arms.

It had been so long since a woman had touched him. It was a little like a drug and soon he couldn't get enough. Reason evaporated and good sense dissolved. He moved her toward the couch. That would do. Anywhere would do.

They'd strip each other's clothes slowly, melt onto the couch, and act out everything they'd done together in that dream, but, this time, for real. He wanted to spread her thighs and slip his hand between them. He wanted to press his fingers inside her, hear her moan as he thrust them in and out. He wanted to cover her clit with his mouth, make her come with his lips and tongue. That was just for starters.

Her fingers found the button and zipper of his jeans and undid them. His hands tangled in her hair as he dragged her mouth up to meet his again, using his lips, tongue, and teeth to consume as much of her as possible.

She gently bit his lower lip and it heated his blood. There was a peek of the hellcat he'd seen during the bonding dream, the one he knew was waiting to be released from her soul. The fae glimpse of her.

"I want you," she murmured against his mouth, stepping up against his body and weaving a hand through his hair at the nape of his neck.

"I want you, too." His voice came out low and gravelly, pure need. Saying the words made him realize how badly he truly did want her. More than anything.

And his blood went cold.

Reason took form. Good sense returned.

It was like jumping into an ice bath. He eased away from her, his fists clenched. "We can't do this."

Her lips were swollen from his kisses, and her hair and clothes mussed from his hands. Her desire-heavy eyes widened. She swayed on her feet. "You're right. Oh, god, I'm sorry. I wasn't thinking. I just—"

He pulled her to him and kissed her again. "I want it as much as you," he whispered meaningfully against her lips. "But because I want it so much, we shouldn't do it."

She lingered there for a moment, her lips hovering against his. He could feel her warm breath against his mouth. His hands tightened on her and he fought with himself for one very dangerous and indecisive moment. Sleeping with her didn't mean they'd fall in love. In fact, it was ridiculous to think they would. Sex was just sex. It didn't automatically lead to anything more. They could do this and still be safe. . . .

Her breath hissed out of her as though gathering her strength. She backed away from him. "No, you're right. I totally agree." She looked as stricken by the cruel interruption of reality as he was. "Too dangerous. Slippery slope. All that stuff."

"Are you all right?"

She gave a bark of laughter. "I'm fine. Really." Taking a deep breath she ran her fingers through her hair.

"Are you? I'm not."

She looked everywhere but at him. "Is it safe for me to take a walk? I need some air and a little time alone."

"Besides us, only two people in the world know where we are and I trust them both. Go take a walk. Just don't go too far into the woods." He paused and smiled at the memory. "You remember the spriggan."

"There's no forgetting the spriggan." She offered him a weak smile and then went for the door.

"Charlotte?"

She halted. "Yes?"

"You need shoes."

She looked down at her stocking feet. "Shoes. Right."

He watched her slip her feet into the boots near the door and counted to ten slowly, trying to get his libido under control. There was still time to change the course of this, to pull her back against him, kiss her, drag her to the couch. They weren't going to fall in love; they were safe.

Then she was gone.

Kieran closed his eyes, tipping his head back, and let out a slow breath of relief.

CHARLOTTE walked through the fae green grass toward the little path that led into the woods. She wouldn't go very far, just far enough so no one could see her. She desperately needed to be alone.

Kieran had almost offered her a blessed oblivion from her thoughts and she would have taken it, even though it would have been temporary. He'd been correct to put a stop to it, though, curse or no curse. It hadn't been right and it wasn't her way—she didn't just sleep with men like that.

All the same, her body hummed with the state the encounter had left her in. It had been a very long time since she'd been with a man and Kieran, despite everything, was highly attractive to her. But she'd been confused, vulnerable. Kieran was a true gentleman for not taking advantage of that. Especially considering how very badly she'd wanted to trace that black tribal tattoo along his side with her tongue—then drop to her knees and worship other areas of his body with her lips and mouth.

As she walked, she touched the limbs of trees and the leaves of bushes. The sprae lighted on her hands and arms here and there, as though greeting an old friend. Stopping for a moment, she looked into the canopy of trees overhead. It was so beautiful here. She'd never expected the majesty and dignity of this place. It was a shame, really, that the humans couldn't experience it.

She jerked. For a moment there, she'd thought of herself as a fae. That was ridiculous. She had some fae blood, but it was a drop in the bucket of her genetic makeup. Just enough to draw the sprae. Not enough to give her any magick. No magick meant she was no real fae. Basically, she was caught between worlds, as her mother had been.

If her mother had been alive perhaps she would be able to help Charlotte deal with that reality, but her father had taken that possibility away.

Her fingernails dug so hard into her palms she nearly drew blood.

In a small clearing where the tops of the huge trees provided a canopy, she found a large rock and sat down on it. She felt numb. This was something that might happen to someone else, not her. Folding her arms over her chest because it had grown chilly, she bowed her head and closed her eyes.

Now what to do with this knowledge?

She wouldn't be in Piefferburg forever. Eventually she'd return to her old life. Her immediate desire was to tell the police what her father had done, but she had no evidence to back up her claim. It wasn't like they were going to believe that she'd discovered the crime through faery magick. Even if they did believe her, that sort of evidence wasn't admissible in court.

And wasn't there a statute of limitations? If so, did the statute of limitations apply to a crime as serious as murder?

Another option was to let it go, knowing that nothing could bring her mother back. She mulled that possibility like something she'd bitten into, exploring its flavors. It was bitter, hard, unpalatable.

No, she couldn't let this go.

Either way, her father was out of her life forever. She would see him one more time—to tell him she knew. After that, he was dead to her.

A wave of grief rose up from the depths of her, swamping her emotions with utter darkness. She put her hands to her mouth to stop from sobbing. She wasn't going to cry for him. Not one tear. She would cry for her mother instead and find a way to punish her father.

"Are you all right?"

She jerked her head up and looked in the direction the voice had come from. The goblin caretaker stood there. With the too-long sleeves of her sweatshirt, she wiped at her eyes. "I'm okay."

"You don't look okay, and on your honeymoon, too." He *tsked* as he walked toward her. "Everything all right with your man?"

Her man? Oh, he meant Kieran.

"Yes, he's great, actually." No sense giving anyone a reason to look in on them too often.

Leson nodded and sat down beside her. Her first inclination was to move away. She realized with a jolt how horrible that was and stayed put. This man had done nothing but be polite and concerned for her. Anyway, at this point she was happy to have something to distract her from her thoughts. Maybe alone time wasn't the thing she needed, even if her company was goblin.

"Seems like a nice guy, but you never know."

"Nice." She rolled the word around in her mouth trying to fit it with Kieran. "I wouldn't call him nice, really. He's Unseelie." She glanced at him. "I mean, not that the Unseelie can't be nice. He's not nice, exactly, but he's . . . honorable. At least most of the time."

"Honorable some of the time." The goblin nodded. "That's better than honorable none of the time."

She smiled. "He's protective and doesn't take any guff from anyone. He's intelligent and very interesting. He'd probably the most fascinating man I've ever met. Complex. Mysterious. Maybe even a little dangerous, but I feel safe with him." She laughed. "He's not always very good with women, but I find that sort of charming."

The goblin covered her hand with his for a moment. His words stole her surprise at the contact. "I can tell you love him very much."

She blinked and looked up at him. *Love him?* She barely kept from blurting out *I don't love him*, but caught herself just in time.

"I can feel it." He touched his chest with one long gray finger. "Most goblins can sense emotion."

"You can . . . *feel* that I love Kieran?"

He nodded. "Just as I can feel you're mostly not fae and that you're afraid of me. Just a little."

She let out a breath. "Wow. You're really perceptive." But

that love thing was a mistake. She didn't love Kieran; she'd only come to appreciate him.

"You *are* mostly human, aren't you?"

She nodded. "I have a bit of fae through my maternal line, but it doesn't show up very much in me. It was very prevalent and noticeable in my mother, apparently." She looked down at the grass. "I never knew her, so I don't know for sure."

The goblin stood and seemed ready to leave. Before he walked back down the path, he said, "It's in you, too. It's right there under the surface. All you have to do is let it free. If you do, I think you'll truly find yourself." He cocked his head to the side. "I'm sorry you're afraid of me."

"I'm not," she called after him, but he didn't turn. Charlotte watched him walk into the trees. "At least not as much as before," she whispered.

I think you'll truly find yourself.

This trip had been all about that very thing. Finding herself. It was ironic that it took being plunged into her worst nightmare for her to do it.

GIDEON entered his apartment, flipped the light switch on, and tossed his jacket onto a chair. He stilled, feeling the presence of someone in the room. A fae. Slowly, he pivoted.

Máire sat in an easy chair, her booted feet comfortably on the coffee table.

"What are you doing here?" he rasped.

She tipped her head to the side. Black leather encased her slim body, fading into matching boots. Her long red hair hung straight and sleek around her shoulders, perfect as a model in a shampoo commercial. He wondered if it was glamour. If she had escaped the Great Sweep, it was likely she possessed that talent. "What? You're not happy to see me?"

He undid his tie with angry jerks. "How did you get in here?"

She swung her legs down, leather creaking. "I have many skills, Gideon."

"I thought I was supposed to wait for *Liam* to call."

"Oh, but I missed you." She stood. "I like you."

"Really?" Gideon grunted. "I want to rip *you* apart with my bare hands."

She sauntered over to him and gently touched his cheek with her fingertips. "That's why I like you." Her eyelashes fluttered a little.

He jerked his head from her touch and she turned away, walking slowly around his living room as though she'd been invited and was merely waiting for him to bring her a drink or something to munch on. "Your place is very austere. Like a monk's."

"I've given my life to Labrai. Worldly possessions have little value to me. I am a monk."

"Ah." She glanced at him. "Yes, you are more than a little obsessed."

"Of course I'm obsessed with doing my Lord's will."

She tilted her head at him. "The destruction of my people is your Lord's will."

He narrowed his eyes and jerked his chin at her. "You don't seem all that eager to save them."

"I don't want them destroyed, necessarily." She shrugged and continued on as though the topic of the annihilation of the fae wasn't all that interesting to her. "I just don't want the walls to fall. We want them to stay where they are and for you to keep doing what you're doing."

"Why?"

She stopped in front of the many cat-o'-nine tails that decorated the walls. Reaching out to touch the leather of one, she gave him a look over her shoulder. "You like pain, don't you, Gideon?"

He shifted and made a sound of impatience. "*Why* don't you want the walls to fall?"

She turned. "I, like the rest of my merry little band, have

been very, very bad fae children. Once the walls fall, all sorts of nasty things will happen to us."

Realization dawned. "The Wild Hunt will come for you. You'll be reaped."

"With extreme prejudice." She touched the cat-o'-nine tails again and gave him a saucy sideways look. "Want to punish me, Gideon? Oh, no, that's right, you would want *me* to punish *you*." She gave him a coy look. "That works, too."

His gorge rose at the thought of engaging that way with a fae and he turned away. She laughed. It was a cruel and bitter sound. "Why are you here? Can you please get to the point so you can go away? Your very presence fouls my home."

"I'm here to tell you the location of the last piece of the *bosca fabh*."

"Why couldn't you tell me before?"

"We had to make sure you could be trusted. We've been watching you very closely since our last conversation and have deemed you . . . well, not worthy of the knowledge, but you know what I mean."

He rounded on her. "What did you think I was going to do?"

She shrugged. "Track me. Would have been impossible, by the way, thanks to my special skills. That's why Liam sent me. We thought perhaps you'd try to find me and my friends. Fruitlessly attempt to drag us into Piefferburg. You didn't do any of that."

No, but he'd sure as hell thought about it.

"Okay, so I passed your test. Where's the piece?"

She took a piece of paper from her pocket and unfolded it. A map. "Here. The location is marked with a longitude and latitude. Don't think about taking the piece and hiding it somewhere else. Like I said, it's a sword in the stone. You can send people to guard it, however. We want all the help we can get in doing that. We don't want another event like what happened in Israel."

He took the paper from her. Her hand brushed his as they

made the exchange. "How do I know if I can trust you?"

"You don't, but I know you want the rest of the fae to stay locked up as much we do, Gideon, so you'll accept this information at face value."

His face twisted with rage at her presumption. "You don't know anything about me."

She held his gaze and adopted a small, slightly mocking smile. "Oh, Gideon, yes I do. I know a lot about you. About you and your mother."

Shock rolled through him. "How could you—"

She pressed her fingers to his lips. "It's all right. Your secret is safe with me." Then she leaned in and pressed her mouth to his. Stunned at more than just the dry kiss, he allowed it, up until she nibbled a little at his lower lip.

He pushed her away and she laughed. Seeming unconcerned, she sauntered toward the door. Wiping his mouth with the sleeve of his shirt, he asked, "What about the spell on the piece? I need to know the details."

She halted in the doorway of his apartment. "But if I tell you that now, I'll have no excuse to visit you again." She tipped her head to the side and smiled.

"The piece—"

"Is safe. My friends are always watching it. Believe me, this spell is specific, yet also very general. It might be a hundred years before the right person comes along or it could be today. The spell is of little consequence. The piece must be guarded at all times. That's why I gave you the map. Send your people to help us."

He took a step forward. "I need to know more."

She smiled. "And you will when I decide the time is right. See you later, Gideon." The door closed behind her and he stood staring at it, the map limp in his hand.

SEVENTEEN

───❦───

KIERAN dragged Charlotte underneath him on the bed, covering her body with his. Her smooth skin rubbed his bare abdomen and chest, making his cock rock hard. His hand stroked along her hip and up her side to cover one round, delectable breast, his fingers teasing her nipple into a hard little peak. She moaned at his touch and he dropped his mouth to her lips, consuming the sound.

He slipped his knee between her thighs and they parted for him, allowing him to slide between her legs. The head of his shaft touched the hot heart of her, nudging her entrance. She shifted, practically begging for him to push inside her. . . .

Kieran came awake with a gasp. He sat up on the couch, the blankets a tangle around his legs. His cock was hard enough to hurt and perspiration marked his skin. His breath came in short little pants.

The dream had been very, very real. Just like the dream he'd used to bind her, just like the nightmare he'd entered to alter for her, though he hadn't initiated this one and had lacked control within it. Somehow his dreaming self had found its way to her private dreamscape and acted out everything he'd stopped himself from doing today.

From the loft, he heard Charlotte gasp awake just like he had. She swore softly, just barely loud enough for him to hear. She almost never swore and when she did it was mild. Clearly, she was disturbed.

He closed his eyes. They were sharing erotic dreams. *Great.*

He swung around and sat up, pressing the heel of his palm into his eye socket. He could forget sleep for the rest of the night. After a few moments, he heard Charlotte coming down the stairs. She went directly into the kitchen and filled a glass with water, then stood at the counter and drank it.

Standing up, he walked to her. "Charlotte?"

She yelped and dropped the glass. His hand whipped out reflexively and caught it before it hit the floor. "God, Kieran, you scared me."

He handed her the glass. "Did you have a nightmare?" Maybe he'd be lucky and her dream wouldn't be the same as his.

She glanced sideways at him, then took a long drink. Finally, she said slowly, "It wasn't exactly a nightmare."

He leaned against the counter. "Shit."

"What?"

He bowed his head and shook it, then put his finger and thumb to his temple. "Forget it."

"Forget nothing. You can tell me. We're sharing dreams, right? This one felt like the . . . other one. The bonding one."

Fuck him. "Yeah." And these dreams were going to kill him.

"But you didn't cause this one, right?"

"It was involuntary."

"Did you know this might happen?"

He lowered his hand and looked at her. The moonlight shining through the window over the sink caught in her hair and made her skin seem paler than it was. "It's probably because I've entered your dreamscape twice now. My subconscious knows where to find you and my id wants—" He snapped his mouth shut.

"Me?"

"Yeah." He let out a slow breath. "Bad."

She held his gaze for a long moment, full lips parted, then blinked rapidly a couple times and looked away. "Okay, well, no big deal. They're just dreams."

"Dreams of what we both want. Otherwise we wouldn't be having them."

She bowed her head and he was certain her face had flushed. "I'm flattered."

"You shouldn't be. I would think every man who sees you would want you."

She laughed. It was a loud, abrupt sound in the stillness of the house. She pressed a hand to her mouth and laughed harder. "Ah, no, Kieran. That hasn't been my experience."

"Then all human men are blind."

She sobered. "Thank you. That's really sweet."

Sweet? At the moment he felt far, far from sweet. He wanted to take that glass of water from her hand, lead her into the living room, force her down onto the couch, and do everything in that dream and more.

And why not?

He'd stopped himself earlier in the day because . . . why? He could barely remember the reason now. Because he'd been afraid sex might lead to love? Since when had it done that? Never. The fact he now drew breath was proof of that. He'd been alive for five hundred and three years and for most of them he'd been living under this damnable curse. He hadn't exactly been a saint during all that time. He'd been with plenty of women and never once felt in danger of the curse kicking in.

Was this woman any different?

He took a long, hard look at Charlotte. She'd turned back to the sink, facing the moonlight, and sipped her water as she gazed out the window at some unknowable thing in the distance. She wore a lightweight nightgown that Risa had brought for her. As usual, Charlotte had absolutely no comprehension of her attractiveness. Her long dark hair trailed loose and tangled over her shoulders. The nightgown she wore was long and billowy, but it clung to her breasts, showing the curve of the top of them and how her nipples had pebbled in the cool air.

Sighing, she set her empty glass in the sink. "I'm going to back to bed."

He yanked her to him and crushed his mouth to hers. Her body stiffened for a moment with surprise, but then she molded herself to him, her breasts pressing against his chest and making him insane. He broke the kiss and murmured against her lips, "Not without me."

"I thought you didn't want this."

"Not want it? This is all I want." At the moment what he really wanted was to hike her nightgown up to her hips, yank his sweatpants down, and take her right up against the counter. "I'm not sure we'll make it to the bed, though. I want you too much."

She shuddered against him. "I want you, too."

He moved her toward the couch. That seemed the closest soft place they could get to at this point. She deserved more than for him to simply take her up against the sink.

CHARLOTTE'S mind whirled and her body hummed. She'd managed to get the fire he'd started earlier under control, but all it had taken was a spark for it to flame back into glorious life. He kept moving her toward the couch and she kept letting him. They both knew this was wrong on so many different levels, but she couldn't make herself push him away.

His lips brushed hers when he spoke. "It's been a long time."

"Been a long time? *Oh*." For sex, he meant. With his body pressed against hers and his mouth so close, it took a while for all her synapses to fire properly. "It's been a long time for me, too." And she wasn't even close to being as experienced.

They reached the couch and his hand bunched in her nightgown, dragging it upward slowly. His knuckles brushed over the skin of her outer thigh and hip. Her ability to reason disappeared. Soon her brains would devolve into Jell-O.

"Do you remember the bonding dream?" He kissed her lower lip, dragging it slowly between his teeth, and rubbed his thumb along the skin of her hip.

Her knees felt a bit wobbly. "Yes," she breathed against his lips.

"I want to make it real."

And that was the worst thing they should do. He rested his hand on her hip, her nightgown caught in his fingers. His knuckles brushed over her bare skin, back and forth, back and forth. Mesmerizing. "Okay," she answered.

This was a mistake, but she couldn't help making it.

His mouth slanted over hers and his hand went to the small of her back, pushing a little and forcing her body to arch into his. She'd been kissed before, but never by a man like Kieran Aindréas Cairbre Aimhrea.

She melted against him, molding her body to his as his lips skated slowly back and forth over her mouth, sending shivers of need through her. His tongue tasted her lips, asking without words for her to part them. When she allowed him in, his tongue stroked up against hers, bringing to mind a bed, tangled limbs, and the brush of skin on skin.

Her body flared to exquisite life, like she'd only been sleeping up until now. In some vague, recessed part of her brain, she thought it was interesting that she'd bring a faery tale to mind. "Sleeping Beauty." Although she would not consider herself any beauty and Kieran was certainly no prince.

Mouth still on hers, he dragged her back and pushed her gently onto the couch. Kneeling between her legs, he lifted her nightgown over her head and threw it to the floor, leaving her completely bare. His gaze ate her up her in a most appreciative way.

For the first time in a very long while, she felt pretty. No, *gorgeous*.

Her breasts felt full and beautiful under his gaze. Her nipples were hard as diamonds and her breath came fast and heavy as she watched him watch her. He wanted her so much. Never had any man looked at her with this kind of hunger on his face. Her hormones were flaring so hard now that if they stopped, if Kieran got up and walked away, she'd probably curl up and cry. She couldn't remember the last time a man had ever affected her this way. On some level, that realization frightened her but she was too far gone to examine it closely.

She ran her palms over his warm, naked torso, trailing her fingers over the swirls and arcs of his tattoo. He had a curious soft/hardness to him that came from the solid muscle under his skin. He was stunning, all perfect, sculpted flesh, strong arms, and a washboard stomach. Just looking at Kieran made her feel safe.

He lifted his gaze to her face. "You're so beautiful, Charlotte."

She swallowed hard. He really sounded like he meant it.

She ran her palms over his muscled chest, down his arms, remembering the feel of him from the bonding magick, all this glorious hard, warm flesh. He was something—literally—from her dreams.

"So are you." Her voice had a breathy quality that completely revealed how much she wanted him. There was no masking it anymore.

She was naked in more ways than one.

Her fingers found the drawstring of the jersey sweatpants he'd worn to bed and caught in them. Biting her lower lip, she raised her gaze to his eyes. Instead he pulled her hand away and eased her down off the couch to the thick rug in front of it. He came down over her body and his mouth found hers.

Balancing himself with one hand on the floor near her ear, he sipped and nipped at her mouth and tongue while his hand covered her breast. Her nipple went hard against his palm and she arched her back, moaning, as he teased it, rolling it between his thumb and forefinger. At the same time, he captured her lower lip and bit just hard enough to make pleasure rush through her veins.

Smoothing his hand over her skin, he parted her thighs and touched her softly there, weaving a kind of magick that had nothing whatsoever to do with violence. As he slipped his fingers over her folds and around her entrance, she let out a small sound of helplessness. He found her clit and petted, drawing it from its hood and teasing it until pleasure rippled through her body with every little movement he made.

She'd been with men before, of course, but none of them had touched her like this. Kieran had lived many years, had been with many women, and knew where best to stroke her, how hard, and for just how long. He turned her into a panting mess on the floor in no time.

His mouth left hers and traveled down her chin, over her throat. He took one nipple into his mouth, laved it until it was bright pink and diamond-hard, and then moved to the other. She watched as he dragged the tip of his tongue over her abdomen and then moved between her thighs. The sight of him there nearly undid her, and he hadn't even touched her yet.

He bit her inner thigh and she moaned low, her body humming with need. His fingers brushed over her, then slipped deep inside her, first one and then a second, stretching her inner muscles. He stroked in and out as his mouth came down on her. His tongue found her clit and nestled down against it, sending waves of pleasure coursing through her.

Her head dropped back onto the carpet, her spine arching a little as she swallowed hard. He'd managed to balance her directly on the edge of ecstasy. She could barely think straight, her thoughts coming slow and sluggish, mired in heavy lust.

He pushed her harder and faster, his fingers thrusting inside her and his mouth working over her swollen clit. Clearly, he was done playing. Now he meant for her to come. Her body spasmed as her climax hit and rolled through her, pulling her under crashing waves of intense gratification. It completely stole her ability to think. All she could do was *feel*, to hold on and go for the ride.

The orgasm came to a stuttering halt. She pushed up, reaching for him, wanting to feel him inside her. He was already there, pushing his sweatpants down and away. Her fingers found his long, wide shaft and stroked him up and down.

He shuddered with pleasure, his hands making fists, and his head falling back on a deep groan. It was one of the most erotic sights of her life. She took in the image he made, knowing he was just barely holding on to control and secure in the delicious knowledge that she'd put him right there on the edge.

With a growl of hunger, he pushed her onto the area rug and flipped her so she sprawled on her stomach. His body came down over her back, warming her skin. He dragged her hips up to meet his pelvis and she arched her body to help him, seeking what he intended to give her. The crown of his cock nudged her entrance, making her shudder with anticipation. Little by little, he pushed inside and she moaned as the muscles of her sex stretched to accommodate him.

One hand braced on the carpet to hold himself up; his other hand slid from her hip over her abdomen and down between her thighs. There he found her slick, swollen clit and stroked it as he hilted inside her as deep as he could go.

Charlotte gasped at the sensation of him filling her so completely, her fingers curling into the rug. She bowed her head and closed her eyes, a moan tearing from her throat.

Then he began to move in and out of her and she saw stars. She shuddered, her hands fisting against the pleasure. He slid in and out of her faster and harder, every inward thrust as deep as he could go, sending ecstasy skittering through her. She'd never had sex in this position. It was animalistic, raw, wild, wonderful.

He took her in long, driving strokes, his fingers sliding over her clit from the front. Every inward thrust moved her forward a little on the carpet, filled, and possessed her body. She found the ability to brace her knees and rocked back against him. Together they found a rhythm that drove them both straight into rapture.

Her body shattered a second time in climax, the muscles of her sex pulsing around his thrusting length. He groaned low and shot inside her, whispering her name over and over. They both collapsed to the carpet, sated, and breathing heavy.

"Oh . . . wow." She closed her eyes and smiled. Her body still thrummed with pleasure.

It had never been like this for her before. Never so passionate. Never so raw and inhibited. Kieran made her feel so pretty that she didn't worry about her body, never once had been self-conscious while they'd made love.

Made love.

Her eyes opened. Well, they hadn't. That had been sex, pure and simple. Really good sex born of a mutual physical attraction and nothing else. For a moment her mind caught on the fact it had been unprotected, then she remembered he was fae. No need.

Kieran pulled her back against him and nuzzled her hair, his arm finding her waist and closing around it. "Are you okay? I didn't mean for it to happen on the carpet like that."

She stifled a laugh. Was she okay? Her body still tingled pleasantly from head to toe. "Oh, yes, I'm more than okay, Kieran." She snuggled down and closed her eyes. She might have a little rug burn, but it was a small price to pay. "I haven't been this relaxed in a long, long time. I needed that."

"Yeah, me, too."

And that's all it had been. A little stress-relief. No worries.

She fell asleep with his hand moving possessively over her body, stroking her skin as though it could provide sustenance of some kind. Her last thoughts before she drifted off were about how long she'd waited to find a man who would touch her this way.

And what a pity it was Kieran.

EIGHTEEN

KIERAN answered the door the next day and found Aeric O'Malley on the other side. "What the fuck."

"I'm happy to see you, too, Kieran."

Kieran blinked. "What the hell are you doing here?"

He pointed to the interior of the house. "Gonna let me in?"

Kieran hesitated for a moment, unsettled by Aeric's sudden appearance and the lack of warning. But it was Aeric. He'd known him for centuries. He pushed the door open farther, letting Aeric catch it. Then he retreated back into the living room.

Aeric followed him in. "The queen let me know where you were because she thought you could use some backup. I rented a place in town and I'll be hanging out a little. She didn't want to send Ronan or Niall because of their notoriety."

Ronan and Niall Quinn were the only two fae known in the world that had druid blood—Phaendir blood—and their faces were known pretty well all across Piefferburg.

Kieran snorted and pushed a hand through his hair. "You're

the Blacksmith, not exactly a ghost on the fae radar." He flopped down into a chair.

Aeric shrugged and sat down on the couch. "Maybe, but I'm not as known as the mages. Not by a mile." He glanced around the room. "Where's the woman?"

"Out with Risa. We had an eventful session yesterday. Risa wants to wait a little before going back in."

"What happened?"

"Charlotte found out her father killed her mother."

Aeric's dusky blond eyebrows rose into his hairline. "Shit."

"It wasn't a fun afternoon."

"Yeah. And yet . . ."

"What?"

Aeric eyed him up and down. "You've got the look of a man who has been fucked and I mean in a good way."

Kieran gave him a slow blink. "So?"

"Charlotte, right? Not Risa."

"Charlotte."

Aeric raised an eyebrow. "Aren't you worried?"

He snorted. "Just because I slept with her doesn't mean I'm going to fall in love with her."

"It's a slippery slope."

Kieran laughed. "There are no slippery slopes here, Aeric. Do you think I've stayed celibate since the curse was laid on me? No way. I've slept with lots of women, some of them multiple times. There's no risk here. Believe me."

"Hmmm. Kieran, how do you think I knew it was Charlotte you slept with and not Risa?"

Kieran met his gaze. "How?"

"Because you and Charlotte have a spark." Aeric snapped his fingers.

He snorted. "Of hatred."

"At first, but then it changed into spark of another kind. Not love, *not yet*. But, like I said, it's a slippery slope."

"There's nothing to worry about, Aeric."

Aeric studied him with hard glittering blue eyes. "If you say so. Just remember, it can happen fast and with the woman you'd least expect. You can be standing there saying you'll never fall for her and all the while you're falling for her." He studied him for a long moment. "I know what I'm talking about, right?"

Yes, he did. Aeric O'Malley had captured the woman he'd thought of as his worst enemy. He'd waited centuries for the chance to take his revenge on her. The second Emmaline had entered Piefferburg, Aeric had been on her with the darkest of intention. Yet, in the end they'd fallen in love.

"*Goibhniu*, Kieran." Aeric snorted. "And you don't even know what love is. Can't even watch for the warning signs."

"I guess if there were warning signs, it would be too late anyway. There's no going back, is there? Once it's started."

Aeric shook his head. "I don't know. There wasn't for me and Emmaline."

"So what do I need to watch out for?"

"Fear."

"Fear?"

"Fear lies at the heart of love. Fear you're going to lose it, lose her. Fear something will happen to her, that somehow you won't be able to protect her. How do you know if you're in love? It scares you shitless." Aeric grinned. "It's great, too, though. You look at the person you love and you know you care about them more than you do yourself, more than your very life. You would do anything for them, risk anything. Your chest feels warm and fills up with this wonderful sense of goodness and light. In that person you find a damn good reason for living."

"Sounds like a mixed blessing."

"Yeah, it is. More blessing than curse." Aeric smiled. Then his smile faded as he realized who he was talking to. "At least for most people."

CURLED up on the couch with a blanket wrapped around her against the unusually cold spring evening and a fire started in the fireplace, Charlotte should have felt warm and cozy instead of chilly and a little scared. Book forgotten in her lap, her gaze followed Kieran as he moved around the house. Apparently hot-blooded by nature, he wore only a pair of sweatpants. Just like the ones he'd been wearing in the middle of the night last night.

Just like the ones he'd taken off.

Her body still remembered every detail of that encounter.

Shivering, she looked into the fire, watching the logs snap and pop. That's what she was playing with, of course—fire. She didn't know the details of the curse Kieran was afflicted with, but what if she fell in love with him? Would the fact he didn't return her feelings protect her from the curse? She assumed *he* was the one the curse hinged upon.

And surely he wouldn't fall in love with her. Not a man like Kieran. Never.

So, if, as she presumed, the curse hinged upon his feelings, they were safe. At least, physically. Her heart was definitely *not* safe and she hated that. She wasn't the type of woman who could sleep with a man she didn't have feelings for. She hated the fact she was falling for him, a fae, one who had used dark magick to bind her and may have destroyed her career.

Of course, her career was something her father had wanted more than she ever had. It stung that she'd put so much work into something that might now be ashes, but it didn't hurt nearly as much as she'd assumed it would at the beginning of this mess.

Clearly she had some soul-searching to do. A lot of it.

Also, it really sucked that she might be falling for a man who would never be in love with her. It sucked even more that if, by some miracle, he did fall in love with her they would be doomed for eternity.

When she got out of Piefferburg, she was going directly to a therapist.

"Charlotte?"

She jerked, startled. Kieran stared down at her with a furrowed brow and his luscious, lickable chest aglow with reflected firelight. "Are you okay? I said your name three times."

She rubbed her face. "I'm fine. Just a little tired."

"I wouldn't blame you for having a lot on your mind." He meant the revelation about her father, of course, not her love life. "When Aeric and Risa left tonight, Risa asked me if you'll be ready to continue tomorrow."

She considered the question. The faster they got that damned memory, the faster she'd be out of here, and the faster she'd be away from Kieran. That would be a good thing. For both of them.

Meeting his eyes, she answered, "Chances are the worst is over, right? I don't think there are many other secrets that could rock my world more than the one we've already uncovered."

"I don't think it could get much worse. You're ready to jump the line into your grandmother's memories anyway. Do you think she has any skeletons in the closet?"

"At the rate I'm going? Probably. But, what the hell, let's do it."

"I'll let Risa come, but keep in mind this session will be long. She means to get the memory we need this time."

"Long? Risa said once we reach the ancestors, whom I have no conscious memory of, that the process will go faster. Like nanoseconds fast."

He took a seat in the chair opposite her and leaned forward, forearms on his knees. She tried not to stare at the way his biceps flexed and tried even harder not to imagine how those arms had felt around her the night before. "Once she skips into your great-grandmother's line it will go quicker, but we've got thousands of years to power through."

"I'm just happy I'll stop being able to see the memories."

"Most of them will be too fast for you to focus on."

She chewed her lower lip, considering him. She remembered the family name he'd mentioned back at Eian's house, *MacBrehon*. It meant nothing to her, yet had made the entire room go silent. "I'm still confused about how my maternal line is mixed up with the fae. I've never even heard the name *MacBrehon* before."

"We don't know either."

"But back at Eian's house, that name made everyone go speechless."

"Reverent."

"Reverent? What?"

"It made us go reverent, not speechless. Look, Charlotte." He caught her gaze and held it. "That name has been intertwined with ours for a very, very long time, but there aren't many of us left who remember why. All we know is that your human ancestors were intimately linked with ours in a very warm and good way."

"But my father said—" He gave her a look and she shut her mouth. "Right."

He looked out the window and went silent, as if hearing something from a great distance. "Do you want to attend something that's even more impressive than an Unseelie ball?"

"As long as it doesn't end with some random fae pressing a knife to my throat."

He looked back at her, eyes flashing dangerously. "Next fae who threatens you dies brutally."

She smiled. That was the most romantic thing any man had ever said to her. Then she frowned and gave her head a sharp shake. Yes, she seriously needed a therapist.

He stood, grabbed a black sweater, and found some boots. "Dress warm. We'll be outside."

She was already in jeans and a sweater, so she dragged on a pair of boots and found a coat. Together, they headed out the door.

He led her into the woods behind the house. She pushed branches out of her way, admiring the way the sprae seemed to make the forest luminescent in the places where they congregated heavily. "Is it safe to walk through an enchanted forest at night?"

"When you're with an Unseelie it is. It's not far away. Leson gave me an invitation earlier today."

"Invitation to what?" Just then she began to hear the music. It was foreign and vaguely discordant to her ears, but with traces of chaotic loveliness that held her spellbound. As they grew closer to the source of the music, she began to hear the guttural language of Alahambri.

The trees opened into a clearing. A huge bonfire roared in the middle of the open area and goblins danced around it. She stopped short and stared, unabashedly openmouthed. There were few sights she'd ever beheld that were as impressive as a full-on goblin party.

Kieran spotted her and backtracked to stand near her. "It's a celebration of their main goddess, Orna. They light a bonfire, have a feast, eat, and drink. It's a very happy event. Let's go say hello."

He started to walk toward them, but she caught his arm. "I don't want to interrupt them."

He looked back at her. "You're not afraid to go join the party, are you?"

She shook her head. "It's not that. I don't want to intrude. It's not my culture and—"

His eyebrow rose. "You want to respect them?"

"Yes."

"You've come a long way in a short time, Charlotte."

She gazed past him at the spectacle. Male and female goblins danced with joyous abandon, some of the male goblins with children perched on their shoulders and a few of the women with young girl goblins balanced on their broad feet. Other males and females danced slower, clearly seeing little more than each other. Charlotte took a moment to spot Leson with a female who had to be his wife, her stomach distended with child.

They were all tall, thin, gray—*alien*—yet they behaved just as many humans might, engaging in and celebrating with a love of life and a carefree abandon that she admired. The firelight reflected off their skin and seemed to make them sparkle.

"It's beautiful," she murmured.

"I thought you might find it interesting." He twined his hand in hers and she jerked, almost pulling away from him in surprise. He grinned. "Come on. We have an invitation, so we're not intruding on them or disrespecting them."

She allowed Kieran to pull her into the merry circle of firelight.

Leson immediately spotted them and walked over, his pregnant wife behind him. *"Yakueish!"*

"Yakueish," Kieran answered, embracing him briefly and slapping him on the back. Then Kieran turned to his wife, keeping his eyes averted, and bowed. *"Yakueisha."*

The female bowed in return. *"Yakueisha."*

Kieran straightened, touched Charlotte on the shoulder, and spoke very quickly in Alahambri. She assumed he was introducing her.

The female goblin bowed to her. "Welcome."

Charlotte bowed and said, *"Yakueisha."*

Everyone laughed.

She elbowed Kieran in the ribs. "What did I do?"

"Females don't greet females that way, only males. You just vowed to disembowel anyone who threatens her."

She grimaced. "Oh."

Kieran's strong arm came around her shoulder and he tucked her against his side. "You get points for trying, though."

"No one will eat me?"

He grinned at her. "No one will eat you. Oh, but stay away from the buffet. There are things—"

"Yeah, yeah." She waved a hand at him. "I get it. Don't elaborate."

They spent a good part of the evening at the celebration. Most of the goblins were very gracious and immediately switched to English when they realized she couldn't speak Alahambri, though she did manage to learn a few basic words of the language throughout the course of the evening.

While Kieran danced with Leson's wife, she sank to the

grass with a cup of krastan, a drink that tasted a little like tangerine, and sipped at it while she watched them. Leson sat down beside her.

"Kieran is very good with our wives and children. He never offers offense."

She watched him keeping a careful distance from the pregnant female, eyes always carefully averted. "He's a very considerate man. I'm afraid all this is very new to me. I've probably offered lots of offense."

"You're human, from outside the walls of Piefferburg. You don't know our ways."

She refrained from remarking that such latitude had not been given to the previously digested *Faemous* crew.

"More importantly," Leson continued, "you are trying to respect our ways and you're even attempting to learn our language. That is very considerate of *you*, Charlotte."

"Oh, well . . . it just seems right."

"You'd be surprised to know how many people don't think so." He looked up into the sky at the moon, which hung large and luminous over their heads. "When Orna gave birth to the world, she created the goblins as a test to the rest of the races. She made us ugly to the eyes of others and she made our diet and basic nature nightmarish to their sensibilities. We exist in order to show the world how to find commonalities when none seem to exist. Once those commonalities are found, it is easier to make the logical, and correct, jump to the notion that all the races are, in fact, one race."

Charlotte stared up at the moon. "I think that's lovely, Leson."

"Orna is a good goddess and we are all her people."

Kieran blocked her view of the moon and held out his hand. "Dance with me."

"Oh. I don't know—"

Leson slipped the cup of krastan from her fingers. "There is no question you should dance on this of all nights! Orna is looking down on you two tonight and will bless your new union."

Charlotte's gaze locked with Kieran's. Dark amusement shone in his eyes. She clasped his hand and allowed him to pull her to her feet, while saying, "Well, we certainly can't pass that up, can we?"

Leson's wife carefully sat down next to her husband on the grass as Kieran led Charlotte out to dance near the fire. The goblins had been feeding it all night and it was powerful and hot. It warmed her side as Kieran took her by the hands and began to dance to the discordant and chaotic melody of the celebration music.

Her feet moved slowly, her arms swinging only because she was holding Kieran's hands.

"Let go, Charlotte," he yelled over the mingled sounds of the fire and the music. The fire lit half his beautiful face and left the other half in shadow. "Dance like you'll die tomorrow. Just let the energy flow through you."

She bit her lower lip and then shrugged. Why not? At this point she had nothing to lose. She closed her eyes and felt the rhythm of the music through the soles of her feet. She tapped into the roar and the heat of the fire. Her feet moved, her body swayed. Faster and bigger.

She let go of Kieran's hands and danced. Opening her eyes, she threw her arms wide and looked up at the moon as she moved, letting her body flow with the music and the people around her.

Some thread of otherness seemed to pull through her. Wild. Ancient. Awakening. Her fae blood? She wasn't sure what affected her now. Hell, maybe it was the krastan. All she knew was that it felt good, intoxicating.

Right.

Whirling, leaping, moving with abandon, Charlotte smiled up into Kieran's face.

MESMERIZED, Kieran watched Charlotte dancing, her black hair swirling around her face, grass stains on her clothing, a gleam in her eye and a wide smile on her face.

She looked . . . fae.

Reaching out, he grasped her hands and pulled her against his body. She molded herself to him, lifting her face to his. He smoothed her wild, thick hair away from her cheeks, admiring the way the glow of the fire touched her skin. Looking at her made a spot of peace in the center of his chest—a sensation he didn't often feel.

It was a warning flag, but he ignored it. Just for tonight he wanted that peace, wanted her. Holding her close, he swayed as if to much slower music, his hips moving in a primal rhythm that both of them recognized.

Her smile flickered and then faded, but the heat grew in her eyes, turning them from hazel green to a rich, deep brown.

Winding one hand to the small of her back and the other to her nape, he angled her head toward his as he lowered his mouth to hers. Their lips touched and her breath shuddered out of her, warming his mouth. She softly slipped her tongue in to brush against his tongue. The action made every nerve in his body flare to life, made his brain turn to mush.

In that moment he wanted her. Nothing else mattered.

Breaking the kiss, she gave him a small smile and a beckoning tilt of her head. She backed away from him and melted into the surrounding woods.

It only took him a moment to follow. Pushing branches to the side, the sound of the goblin celebration fading behind them, he followed her deeper into the trees.

In a small clearing, he caught her and pulled her toward him, his mouth immediately coming down on hers. Wordlessly, lips meshing, they pulled at each other's clothing until wide swathes of bare flesh touched.

Walking her backward, he pressed her against a nearby tree. Finding the sweet, smooth back of her knee, he hiked her thigh over his hip and guided the head of his cock inside the silky clasp of her sex and thrust within.

Her arms tightened around him and her breath came out in an agonized rasp of pleasure as he pushed deeper inside her. Her slick, soft inner muscles clenched around his length, dragging a guttural groan from his throat.

He lifted her and she pressed back against the tree, winding her legs around his waist, his cock buried root-deep inside her. Their gazes met and held for a moment before he began to thrust. Clinging to each other, bodies straining and mouths sealed, they found a rhythm under the moonlight. Moving as one, they gave and took from each other, sharing pleasure.

He shouldn't be doing this, but nothing in the world could make him stop. Right then he knew he was losing it, that edge he'd cultivated for so many centuries. This odd, beautiful woman was ripping it to shreds.

He was in trouble.

NINETEEN

CHARLOTTE closed her eyes and let Risa guide her down.
It got easier every time they did it. If she didn't fight the
intrusive magick, she just spiraled down into the spinning
memories of strangers.

But, first, the person she knew. Her mother. They hadn't
yet jumped past her line.

Every time she saw them, her mother's memories made
emotion rise from a place so deep that nothing had ever been
able to touch it before. The memories rolled over her and
through her, displaying her mother's life, both the good and
the bad, and giving Charlotte an incredible gift.

She'd been a warmhearted, wild, wonderful person. Too
much for her father to handle. They'd been married young,
when her father had been a different person. More carefree.
Charlotte's father had been besotted with her, madly in
love . . . at least until he'd learned about her ancestry. Her
mother had known how he'd felt about the fae, but she'd
presumed he loved her enough to accept her anyway.

How wrong she'd been.

When the memory timeline jumped to her grandmother, tears came to Charlotte's eyes. She didn't want to leave the closest interaction she could remember ever having with her mother. Before now her mother had seemed like a cold, selfish person because she'd been seeing her through her father's words and her own pain.

Now, through Risa's magick, her mother felt like a friend she'd lost.

Once they made the jump, Charlotte saw how Risa had slowed down the memories of her mother for her benefit. Her grandmother's line went fast. In a blink, it was gone and replaced with her great-grandmother's timeline, then the lives of her other maternal ancestors. The snatches she saw were interesting from an historical viewpoint, but she had little emotional connection.

Back and back Risa went, pushing and pushing. It was like watching a movie on fast rewind. Risa stopped only occasionally to sift more carefully here and there for things that Charlotte couldn't comprehend.

Detached and fatigued, Charlotte settled back and let it all happen. She was merely the vessel containing what they needed—a filing cabinet or a computer. Sometimes she dozed, but it didn't seem to affect Risa's work at all.

And then they were there. Ireland. The fae. A very, very long time ago.

Risa didn't slow as Charlotte had expected. Instead she buzzed and jumped her way through countless lines of her maternal memory before slowing to a speed she could follow. Was this the period of history when Risa believed her ancestral line had begun to have interaction with the fae?

Charlotte had no idea what this period of history was. Surely it was before the Roman conquest of Britain. She suspected from the circular houses made of organic materials and the rudimentary clothing that she was looking at her Celtic ancestors.

An image flashed of a dark-haired woman who looked eerily like herself. Her great-great-great- well, super great-grandmother, perhaps. Charlotte had long ago lost count of the number of her maternal line that Risa had gone through. This one's name was Aithne. Risa focused in on her, perhaps because of the resemblance to Charlotte.

Aithne was a human woman, but she'd discovered the fae when she'd been a child, playing near the edge of a forest. As soon as Risa came across *that* particular memory, everything slowed as Risa sifted carefully. Charlotte was wide-awake now, curious.

A willowy blond Twyleth Teg male took a liking to Aithne, befriended her, taught her about the fae as Aithne grew up, and then eventually deflowered her under an oak tree deep in the forest. From that union, Aithne conceived a child, a thing unheard of in the fae world. Fae children—especially half-breed fae children—were very rare.

Life back at this point in history was not as cruel to unmarried young women with children and Aithne was still accepted in her village. However, because the child was half fae, the Twyleth Teg male took Aithne in, made her one of them. Married her for all intents and purposes. Eventually the child was born, a girl that Aithne named Caoimhe.

Charlotte's fae lineage began here.

Caoimhe grew up among the fae and fell in love with a pureblooded Seelie Tuatha Dé man. She, too, bore a female child and named her Keelin. It became clear to the fae, and in Charlotte's memories, that these women had the rare ability to bear fae offspring, so they were valued.

And so it went. Instead of skipping backward in Charlotte's memories, now she and Risa inched forward. Her female ancestors essentially were magickless fae, living among them, marrying them, and bearing their children—all female—until one day everything changed.

Ah, here! They were closing in on the memory they needed; Charlotte could feel it.

Risa withdrew.

Charlotte gasped and opened her eyes. "But we were just getting to the good part!"

Risa looked ready to fall over. "I can't." She touched her head and gave her a weary smile. "I can't go even one moment more tonight."

Charlotte glanced out the window. It was full dark. She didn't know what time it was, but they'd started early in the morning and had taken no breaks. She met Risa's eyes. "How will you find that memory again?"

"Don't worry, I marked it."

She gaped for a moment. "You put a bookmark in my brain?"

Risa offered another exhausted smile. "Something like that. We'll get the rest of what we need tomorrow."

Charlotte sat up and groaned. Her stomach growled loudly. Rubbing the back of her neck, she watched Risa stand, stretch, retrieve her jacket, and walk to the door. "Will you be okay getting back to your hotel? We could call Aeric to come and get you."

"No." Risa paused. "I'll be fine."

"Risa?"

She stopped in the doorway. "Yes?"

"How did you know it was me who would carry the memory of where the piece was located?"

Risa sagged against the doorframe and regarded her with tired eyes. "I've been looking for memories of the piece among the fae for a long time now. A fae I happened upon had memories of one of your ancestors. She's distantly related to you, a Twyleth Teg. I looked up some of the records from that time period and came across mentions of your ancestral line. Eventually the name MacBrehon came up. I knew how intertwined that human name was with the fae, so we used the Unseelie ancestry records to track the line to you. It wasn't easy."

"So I have relatives here among the fae."

"Very distant ones, yes." She smiled. "You truly *are* fae, Charlotte."

She watched Risa leave the building and go to her car. The fire was dead in the hearth and a chill had set into the small house. Kieran wasn't inside, but she was sure he was close by. He hadn't left her unguarded, either by himself or another, since she'd been attacked that first night.

Walking around the living room, she turned on a few lamps. Finally the door opened and Kieran came in. "Enjoying the evening?" she asked.

"The stars are really bright tonight." He stopped. "How did it go?"

"We're really close. We should have the location by tomorrow."

Kieran let out a pent-up breath and closed his eyes, tipping his head back. A tension she hadn't known was in him seemed to leave his body. "Thank the Lady."

She studied him, chewing her lower lip. "You really care about your people, don't you?"

"The fae need to be free, Charlotte. Don't you see that?"

"I do . . . now."

"You mean, now that you know you're one of us, if just a little."

She shook her head and crossed her arms over her chest. "It's not just that. The fae are at the mercy of the Phaendir in here. If Gideon Amberdoyal gets his way and the government lets him, you're like lambs at slaughter between these walls."

Kieran's eyes glittered in the half-light. "We're not that helpless."

"Maybe not. Probably not." She looked out at the window at the sky. He was right about the stars.

"You never cared before."

She turned toward him. "I was afraid of you before."

"And now you're not?"

"I think I understand you better now." She paused. "Anyway, no race of people deserves what's been done to you. I've seen terrible things in here, but I've also seen beauty." She went back to gazing out the window. "How is that any different from humanity?"

"It's not."

She shook her head. "No, it's not." The ideas her father

had tried to instill in her had clearly not been buried very deep. They easily lifted away to reveal the truth the moment she lost her respect for him . . . the moment she'd ceased wanting his approval.

She glanced at the kitchen. She was really hungry, but eating something meant spending more time with Kieran and it was better if she didn't. She was coming to like him way too much. Better to keep her distance. By tomorrow maybe all this would be over and she'd be on her way home. "I'm going to bed."

"Charlotte, finding that memory came just in time. The bond magick between us has run its course. We're free to separate now."

"Oh." She swallowed, glancing away from him. Being able to leave whenever she wanted should make her happy, but, strangely, all she felt was sorrow. "That's great."

Kieran took her by the arm as she brushed past. He pulled her against him.

Her heart skipped a beat as his gaze caught and held hers. So much for keeping her distance. He reached up and very gently pushed her loose hair behind her ear, then he lowered his head and kissed her.

Turning toward him, she closed her eyes and gave herself to it completely. After all, there wouldn't be many more kisses like this to enjoy. Soon she'd be back in her old life . . . just the thought of Yancy and Tate felt so foreign to her, another world. A boring world.

His lips moved slowly over hers, back and forth, making her legs feel weak. Then he slanted his mouth across her mouth and slid his tongue within to meet hers. Their tongues tangled hot and she imagined what might happen next. The slow removal of clothing, the brush of bare skin against bare skin. His chest pressed against her breasts. Limbs entangled. Hands caught in each other's hair and mouths fused.

He crushed her to him and deepened the kiss. For a moment Charlotte thought her imaginings would become real. After all, she didn't have the ability to resist him if he nudged her in that direction. Her defenses where this man was concerned had been knocked down a while ago.

Instead he ended the kiss, pressed his lips to her forehead, and murmured, "Sleep well."

Relief and disappointment warring inside her, she pulled herself away from his embrace and hurried up the stairs before she could do something really stupid.

For a third time.

THE next morning, with Risa's help, Charlotte slid easily into the depths of her ancestors' memories. Today both Kieran and Aeric were in the living room and would stay there until this was finished. Everyone seemed on edge, waiting for the fruit of their labor. Their additional presence receded into the background as Charlotte pushed deeper into her maternal memory.

The timeline picked up almost immediately where they'd left off the previous evening. Aithne and her fae descendants, all female, had lived in peace among the fae for over a century. Until one day everything changed.

The Phaendir attacked.

Up until then the relations between the Phaendir and the fae had been frigid, their races locked in a type of cold war that Charlotte didn't understand. Now relations were far from cold—they were boiling.

The rise of the Phaendir god, Labrai, had caused murderous fervor in the Phaendir. Through His prophet, Bedwyr, Labrai had told His people that the fae needed to be cleansed from the earth. War erupted when the Phaendir attacked the main fae stronghold in Ireland.

But the Phaendir got the worst end of the deal.

Even though they'd taken the fae by surprise, the Phaendir lost badly. The images in her mind's eye showed them dead and bloody all through the forested area and the system of caves where so many of the fae lived. Of course, she knew that the Phaendir had eventually accomplished their major goal in the fifteen hundreds, during the fae wars and the on-set of Watt Syndrome. But in this part of history, they really got their asses handed to them.

Charlotte and Risa saw all of this through the eyes of Saraid, one of Charlotte's ancestors who had the same inky black hair and hazel eyes.

After the Phaendir were beaten back and the bodies col-lected, the object of power, the *bosca fadbh*, a magickal thing that had been created jointly by the fae and the Phaendir back in the days when the races had been allies, was removed from its hiding place. It was decided by the Seelie Queen and the Unseelie King that the puzzle box should be taken apart and hidden all over the world so the Phaendir could not use it against them.

Meetings were held between only seven fae: the Summer Queen and her chosen, the Unseelie King and his chosen, and one representative each from the troop, wilding, and sea fae. Saraid, a valued member of the Seelie Court because of her ability to procreate, sat in on all these meetings as the Summer Queen's choice.

One piece of the *bosca fadbh* was buried deep in the side of a mountain. Charlotte assumed this was the piece that Ronan Quinn had eventually stolen from a government facil-ity at the request of the Phaendir, and then smuggled into Piefferburg.

One piece was put into a charmed box that could only be opened by a fae using a charmed key. The box was sunk to the bottom of the Mediterranean Ocean near the ruins of Alit Yam off the coast of the country that was now Israel. This was the piece Emmaline had retrieved.

The final piece was hidden by Saraid, her very own ances-tor, and only Saraid had known its location. This piece was also charmed. Charlotte's breathing quickened as she learned of the spell put on the final piece. It was stuck in a massive hunk of stone in . . .

"Charlotte!"

Charlotte's eyes came open to see the silver flash of a

knife coming down toward her chest. Instinctively, she flinched away, squishing herself as far from the blade as she could, up against the cushions of the couch. The knife sliced through her upper arm. She felt nothing at first, only shock at both the blade and Risa's face twisted with hatred. Then blinding pain exploded and blood gushed from the wound.

Kieran grabbed Risa, wrenching her to the side and snatching the knife away. Four strange men burst into the small house and Aeric turned toward them, ready to fight.

Charlotte gripped her upper arm, a river of blood streaming between her fingers. God, there was so much of it. Her arm was laid open . . . glistening red. She knew she had to get up and fight. There were too many bad guys in here, not enough good guys. She tried to stand, sat back down. Her vision wavered, the world went white, whiter.

Gone.

TWENTY

CHARLOTTE woke in a dark, unfamiliar room with low, male voices emanating from beyond the closed door. The memory of what had been happening right before she'd passed out slammed into her. Panic made her heart rate ratchet into the stratosphere.

There had been five bad guys and only two good guys, since her butt had been passed out on the couch from blood loss. Who had been victorious? Had the bad guys won? Had she been kidnapped . . . again?

Was Kieran dead?

She moved her injured arm and winced. Someone had bandaged it. Well, that was an argument against having been kidnapped. Somehow Charlotte doubted bad guys would have taken the time to dress the wound they'd inflicted.

She shook her head, still unable to believe that Risa had tried to kill her.

Pushing away the deep grief she felt at having someone she'd trusted attack her, she glanced around the room for weapons to use. She didn't know what the hell was going on, but she wasn't going to take any chances.

Glimpsing a long iron poker near the fireplace, she rolled quietly off the bed, ignoring the twinge of pain in her arm, picked it up, and snuck over to the door. She'd seen enough movies to know how this was done. Stand and wait until someone opened the door, then clobber him over the head and escape. The flaw in her plan was that her right arm hurt like hell and did not want to wield an iron poker.

Someone finally opened the door. She brought her poker down, but Kieran caught it before it could make contact. His eyebrows rose in appreciation. "Nice, Charlotte."

She lowered her weapon and let out a sigh of relief. "Thank God."

He eased the poker from her fingers. "You're bleeding. I hope you didn't pull your stitches out." He led her to sit down on the bed.

She glanced at her arm, seeing the slow red seep of blood through the bandage. "I figured I was with friends since someone had bandaged my wound, but I didn't want to take the chance." She swallowed hard, feeling horrible for a moment as the grief rushed back. She felt betrayed. Violated. "What happened? Where's Risa?"

"Risa is tied up and unconscious. We'll bring her back to the Black Tower with us." Kieran's voice sounded rough and his eyes had gone violently dark. "Little did we fucking know we were bringing the enemy down here with us."

"What about those other guys who rushed in right before I passed out? What happened to them?"

He undid the last of her bandage with hands much, much gentler than the look on his face. He didn't answer her and he didn't need to. They were dead.

She swallowed hard. "Left the cottage in kind of a mess."

A muscle worked in his jaw as he examined her wound. "I don't think we'll get our deposit back."

"What are you planning to do with Risa?"

He gave her a grim look. "Get what we haven't been able

to get from anyone else who has attacked you. Answers."

"Has she revealed anything yet?"

He shook his head. "That's why we're taking her back to the Black. There are people there who are very good at that. You didn't pull your stitches, but be careful how you move, okay?"

She nodded, wincing as he cleaned up her arm with some supplies on the table near the bed and bandaged her back up again.

Then he knelt in front of her, his warm, strong hands on her thighs. "You need to tell me where the piece is. You and Risa are the only two people with this information."

She frowned and rubbed her temple with the hand of her uninjured arm, trying her best to recount the mess of maternal memory in her head. "The last piece of the *bosca fadbh* is embedded in a large phallic-looking hunk of stone that was special in some way. It supposedly is able to select fae rulers by . . . *singing*?" She shook her head. "It's somewhere in Ireland. I'm sorry, I don't know where and I can't tell you anything more specific. I could draw you a picture of the rock, if you wanted. I can still see it in my head—"

"It's the Lia Fáil, the fae coronation stone. It's been moved from its original location, but now it stands for tourists in Tara, Ireland. Teamhair." He shook his head. "I've seen Lia Fáil and there's nothing resembling a chunk of iron stuck in it."

"I don't know, but that's what I saw in the memory."

"Okay. It must be there somehow." He rubbed his hand over his mouth. "Too bad it couldn't conveniently be hidden somewhere in Piefferburg. Instead, it's wedged in stone, in one of Ireland's busy tourist locales. Fantastic."

"There's more." She drew a breath to tell him the worst part.

"What?"

"The piece is spelled."

"I'm not surprised considering the last two pieces were also charmed. The first could never be touched by Phaendir, which is partly the reason the Phaendir enlisted Ronan Quinn to help them get it. The second was locked in a charmed box. Do you know how this piece is spelled?"

She held his gaze for a long moment, not wanting to reveal this information. It hit far too close to home. "The piece is embedded in stone and can only be drawn out by a human." She drew a breath. "A lost human who has found her way, dying for the love of a fae."

Kieran held her gaze, his eyes growing bleak and distant. "Really."

"Yes."

He stood and turned away from her. *"Fuck."*

Charlotte said nothing. She only stared at the edge of the area rug that lay partially under the bed. What could she say? That maybe *she* was the human meant to pull the piece? She still didn't believe Kieran would ever fall in love with her.

And if he ever did . . . well, that was bad.

The spell probably had nothing to do with her at all. It was just a coincidence that she was a human involved with a man who had a love curse on him.

She swallowed hard. "Tough break, right? Where will the fae ever find a human to fit that bill?"

He didn't answer her.

"So, am I out of this yet? You got the information. Can I go home?"

Kieran stayed where he was, his shoulders tight and his head bowed. "I wish I could let you leave right now, Charlotte, but, no. You can't go yet."

"Why not? I've—"

He rounded on her. "You can't go. Not yet. Your fate is for the queen to decide, not me." The words came out on a snarl and he stalked out of the room.

GIDEON woke in the middle of the night to a face hovering close to his own, a beautiful, pale oval in the moonlight framed by a fall of bloodred hair. Yelping, he scrambled backward on his narrow bed, tangled himself in the blankets, and fell off the other side.

A clear, attractive tinkling laugh filled his bedroom. The laugh of a fae.

He pushed to his feet. "Máire."

She tipped her head to the side and smiled, her teeth bright and sharp in the half-light of the room. "Hello, Gideon."

"How did you get in here?"

"What a question." She shrugged. "I'm fae."

"What the hell do you want?" he snarled. He was not ever in the mood to play games, especially with a fae, but right now it was particularly unwelcome.

She only grinned, and then crawled across the bed toward him, her hips rolling. Her tongue stole out to wet her lips. "I thought you might be able to tell by now."

His stomach roiled. "I don't touch the fae. I certainly won't fuck one. Go whore yourself somewhere else." He turned to leave the room. She still had information he needed, but he wasn't going to dance this dance with her.

She appeared directly in front of him, blocking the door. He jerked back, startled. "Sorry. I never told you my particular brand of magick, did I?"

Rage surged through him. He could feel the veins in his head stand out. "Get out of my way." Normally when others saw him in this condition, so very angry, they immediately backed off. Máire seemed nonplussed.

She reached out and touched the top of his button-down pajama top. "I'm not asking for love, or for you to marry me. I'm asking for one night, Gideon. Just one." Her gaze strayed to the cat-o'-nine-tails curled so seductively on his nightstand. It was the one he used at home for his worship. "I would make it so much fun."

He grabbed her hand and yanked her forward a little, taking her off balance. "I wouldn't let you touch me with that— or anything else—for anything in the world."

"Ah." She smiled. "I doubt that very much. You know I have things you need." She took his hand and pressed it to her breast. "It could be nice."

He fought the urge to squeeze the warm, full orb pressing against his palm. "You're a fae—"

"—who hates fae."

His jaw worked. "That doesn't change your genetic heritage."

"My cunt is the same as any other woman's."

He twisted away in revulsion, but she caught his upper arm and turned him toward her. Her strength was much greater than it should have been for a person of her slight stature. A thrill went through him.

She put her mouth to his ear and whispered. "I love it when you play hard to get." Her teeth rasped over his earlobe, making him shudder. He loathed himself for it, but this excited him. "Ah, see? I knew you'd give in to me eventually."

"I'm not giving in to you." He turned his face and spat.

"Sure you're not." She smiled and nipped his lip, then bit down. Sweet pain exploded. Salty blood dotted his tongue and his knees went a little weak.

She pushed him back toward the night table with the pressure of her mouth on his. His own blood filled his mouth, blending with her saliva as she forced her tongue between his lips. Separating her mouth from his, she wound her fingers hard through his hair and pulled as if trying to detach it from his skull.

His breath caught in his throat and he stifled a moan.

She smiled. "Let's get business out of the way so we can focus on the pleasure, shall we? The only person who can pull the piece is 'a lost human who has found her way, dying for the love of a fae'."

A human? But that could mean *any female*, inside or outside of Piefferburg. "What does that mean?"

"Don't ask me. I don't know and I don't care. Our defense is guarding the piece at all times. If we ever find out, don't worry, we'll tell you." Her lips curled seductively. "Now that we have business out of the way . . ." She reached for the cato'-nine-tails, caught the handle, and flicked the leather straps so they cracked in the air.

KIERAN, Aeric, and Charlotte drove Risa back to the city the next day. Charlotte rode in Aeric's SUV because of her arm and Kieran took his bike, riding like a dark sentinel next to the SUV the whole way.

She *hated* that she hated he was away from her.

Risa was kept sedated and sprawled, handcuffed, on the backseat of the vehicle. It seemed like the drive took twice as long as it should've, but eventually they ended up back in Piefferburg City in front of the Black Tower.

It was interesting how here in Piefferburg no one seemed to look twice when a bound, unconscious woman was extracted from a SUV and brought into a building. It was like it happened every day.

As soon as they entered the tower, the unconscious Risa was placed into goblin hands and then disappeared into the depths of the structure. Charlotte harbored no love for the woman who had attempted to kill her, but she didn't envy the event Risa would soon be caught up in, either. They meant to get information from her and the way they'd do it wouldn't be pleasant. These were the Unseelie, though from what she understood, the Seelie Queen could be even more ruthless—and often was.

Kieran caught her arm as she gazed after Risa. "Come on."

She turned and followed him.

He led her up to see the queen. Charlotte's gut churned in anticipation of the queen's verdict regarding her fate. Nothing would make her happy. If the queen said she could go home, she'd be leaving Kieran. If she ordered her to stay, she'd be staying near him. It was a lose/lose situation.

Aislinn was dressed in full court regalia today. As usual her gown was of a style caught between Victorian fashion and gothic punk contemporary. Her bloodred and black skirts swept out behind her in a flounce that made her waist seem tinier than it was. The front of the dress cut up to her knee, revealing her shiny black thigh-high boots. The bodice had about a million shiny ebony buttons and pressed her breasts up to overflowing at the top. It was a beautiful garment but looked restrictive as hell. Ruby jewelry hung at her ears and throat, and glittered from her wrists.

The Unseelie Queen's face appeared drawn and serious when she and Kieran entered the room. It was just the three of them. Even the handsome king, usually always by her side, was absent today.

The queen motioned them to sit on a pristine white couch in her large receiving room, then seated herself in a nearby chair and crossed her boot-clad legs. "So, I understand you didn't escape all the excitement when you left for Hangman's Bastion. Instead you took it with you."

Kieran nodded. He'd been a man of few words since the revelation of Risa's betrayal.

The queen's gaze moved to Charlotte. "I don't think we will ever be able to repay you for what you have done for us."

It's not like she'd had a choice. A smile flickered over her lips and she touched her bandaged arm, remembering the blade coming toward her. "I don't think you will either."

"I apologize for the trouble we've caused you and the disruption to your life."

"Thank you." She glanced at Kieran. "Despite how I was brought here, however, I don't regret coming."

The queen's eyebrows rose. "Really?"

Charlotte inclined her head. "Risa did try to kill me, but her magick before that point revealed truths to me I needed to know. If I'd never come to Piefferburg, I would have lived my life in ignorance until my death."

"Ah." The queen considered her for a moment, apparently not knowing how to respond to that. "Thank you for all you've done. Your work is complete now."

Kieran's head snapped up. "You're letting her go?"

"I see no reason why she should stay. The charm is for a human who has found her way and is dying for the love of a fae. Charlotte, you sound a little like you've found your way, but are you dying for the love of any of us?"

"No. I mean, I feel perfectly fine." She glanced at Kieran. "But the curse. Me. Him. It seems—"

"Very fitting, doesn't it?" Aislinn smiled. "And yet you two are not in love, correct?"

"*No*," Kieran said forcibly. "We're not."

Something in Charlotte's chest pained her for a moment, then was gone. She didn't expect anything from him. Hell, love with Kieran meant death anyway. The fact he'd just stated that she meant nothing to him should make her happy. But, damn it, it didn't. Steeling her expression, she raised her gaze to the queen's.

"So, despite that she's the only human around who could conceivably be dying for the love of a fae, she is not. That means she's not the human who will pull the piece." Aislinn smiled. "Or do you two want to spend a little more time together and see if you can tempt fate?"

"*No*." Kieran's voice came out low and dangerous sounding.

The queen's gaze met Charlotte's. "Anyway, you're not entirely human, are you, Charlotte? Maybe not human enough for the spell."

"Everyone seems to think I'm human enough to kill without consequence. I don't see why I wouldn't be human enough for the spell."

The queen's eyes narrowed. "Are you saying you want to try?"

"Let her go home." Kieran's voice came out a harsh bark. He stood. "We've been waiting centuries to obtain the last piece of the *bosca fadbh*. Looks like we'll be waiting a little longer."

"But how will the fae get the final piece before the Phaendir are able to get their way with the government and hurt you all?" She couldn't bring herself to say *exterminate*. Charlotte found that she cared very much about the answer to this question. What a change from the first day she'd walked through the gates of Piefferburg.

The queen smiled. "With a charm like this one, there's no telling. The fae obtaining the book and first two pieces of the *bosca fadbh* feels a little like destiny. The stars aligned and those objects fell into our laps, though not without a significant amount of hardship."

"You and Gabriel almost died. So did Emmaline."

"And many fae *did* die when I took the Unseelie Throne and secured the Book of Bindings." The queen glanced out the window of the room and Charlotte had the sense she was remembering that war. "Many died, but we got the book and the two first pieces. I think that means we're meant to have all three pieces of the *bosca fadbh*, but I don't know how it will happen yet or when."

Kieran paced the room. "Even if we manage to get all three pieces that doesn't mean we'll have instant freedom. We will still need to determine how the book and pieces work and we'll have the Summer Queen to deal with. She might put up a fight."

"And the Phaendir," Queen Aislinn added, her expression going grim. "If we somehow end up with the book and the entire *bosca fadbh*, they'll want blood."

Charlotte shivered, remembering the fervor she'd seen in Gideon's eyes. She agreed with the queen's assessment. "Obtaining the last piece of the *bosca fabdh* is just the beginning of the battle."

"Yes." Aislinn's smile faded and her expression grew cold. "And there is an unknown element at work, as well. Fae, free and living among us, who apparently want to see us fail. That's why we need to get every bit of information out of Risa that we can. But you, Charlotte, it's time for *you* to go now. Your part in this is over." Aislinn stood and crossed the room to a polished onyx box, opened it, and took something out. Then she crossed the room and put the object into Charlotte's hand.

She looked down at the heavy piece of jewelry. It was an emerald and gold pendant in the shape of a gryphon.

"It's a fae piece, non-magickal, but worth a fortune because of its origins. You can keep it as a memento or sell it if you need the money. You should get at least one million for it at a human auction. It should go mostly unnoted by Gideon Amberdoyal when you leave. He's a long-lived Phaendir and will recognize it as an antique, but the pendant's origins are obscure enough that he shouldn't suspect anything."

One million? She rubbed her thumb over the smooth emerald body of the gryphon. It was beautiful, but yet so unassuming.

She held the jewelry out toward the queen. "I can't accept this."

"We brought you to Piefferburg against your will and you've risked your life three times while here. Please, this is the only way we can repay you for the valuable information you've provided."

Charlotte shook her head. "It's gorgeous, but no."

"Take it." Kieran's voice was a low, gruff lash. "You've earned more than that. Take the pendant and go home, Charlotte. Live your life. Be safe." He wouldn't look at her.

Okay, now she was really starting to feel hurt.

"He's right. You should go now. Pack your things and tell them downstairs you need a car to the gates. I've already left instructions for someone to drive you. Salvage what you can of your former life. I hope we didn't do too much damage."

She stared down at the pendant lying in her hand. "This experience ripped it apart, but, strangely, it's all right. I didn't know it, but it needed to be ripped apart."

The queen spoke in a warm voice, "I hope you have a good life, Charlotte."

She raised her gaze to Aislinn's. "I hope you get that piece."

"Thank you." She smiled. "Maybe we'll meet again one day, next time in your world instead of ours."

"I would love to see that. In fact, I'll be praying for it."

Silence descended. All that was left was the leaving. Odd how she'd thought she'd be jumping up and down in excitement when this moment came, but instead melancholy had taken her over. Melancholy and worry.

She walked toward the door, almost detouring to Kieran, but he wasn't looking at her. Her pride pricked, she made that slight hesitation in his direction look natural and just continued out the door saying airily, "Good luck to you both."

Fine, so she'd had her first one-night stand. Great. She was a big girl; she could do this. She could leave Kieran without saying good-bye or hoping he wanted to say good-bye to her. She had this.

Really.

Alone, she went straight to Kieran's apartment and found the door unlocked. Maybe they didn't care about guarding her anymore since she was of no further use to them. She opened the door slowly, not wanting any more surprises and definitely not wanting any more knives careening in her direction.

Someone pushed the door open forcibly from behind her, making her yelp in surprise. Kieran entered the room before she stepped in, obviously ready to handle anything that might be in there. His shoulders relaxed. "It's okay."

"Thank you."

His expression went stormy. "What were you thinking coming back here all by yourself, anyway?"

Entering the room, she shrugged. "You didn't look like you were going to follow me."

He turned away from her. "I had to talk to Queen Aislinn for a moment. Go on, get your stuff. I'll drive you to the gates myself."

"That's not nec—"

"*Get your stuff.*"

She glared at him, anger boiling through her veins. She

did not deserve to be treated this way, considering all she'd gone through for them. Especially not by Kieran, in view of the intimate nights they'd shared.

Pushing past him, she stormed into the bedroom where she'd slept, grabbed her bag and started cramming in the few things she planned to take with her. Fuming she turned and came nose-to-chest with Kieran, who'd been standing in the doorway, apparently watching her. She looked up at him. "What the hell is your problem, anyway, Kieran? Why do you all of a sudden hate me so much? What the hell did I do?"

He looked as angry as she felt. His jaw locked, eyes narrowed, he took a step toward her, saying nothing.

She made a frustrated sound. "Whatever. I just want to get out of here."

He caught her wrist almost painfully to stop her as she brushed past him.

She gritted her teeth. "Let me go, Kieran."

"That's the problem. I don't want you to go."

TWENTY-ONE

ELATION and panic raced through her veins like a rush of icy water. Stunned, she just stood there with his hand around her wrist, not knowing what to say or do. Her feelings for this man were so intense, more intense than anything she'd ever felt before . . . and they were poison. They could be the death of her.

"That's exactly why you need to go." He pulled her to the side, to face him, took her bag, and threw it to the floor. "You should leave right now. You should run as far as you can away from me, understand? If you were smart, you would do that."

She swallowed. How was it possible that ever since Kieran had stepped into her life, she'd felt more alive than she ever had, yet loving him meant she'd die? "I guess I'm not very smart, then."

He eased her hair away from her face, hooking it behind her ear. His mouth came down on hers and she returned the kiss with interest, her fingers finding and fisting in the material of his shirt, as if holding on to him this way meant he'd never leave her.

She allowed him to move her back toward the bed, her fingers undoing the buttons of his jeans as they went. Her arm still pained her a little, but that small hurt seemed to be drowned out in the flood of need she had for him. She wasn't naïve. This was the last time she'd ever be able to touch him. They'd do this, then she'd leave. Forever.

She was going to make it count.

He helped her push his sweater up and over his head. She skated her lips over the curves of his chest, inhaling the scent of his skin and trying to soak in the feel of his warm body against hers. She wanted to memorize it for when she left this place, so she had something to keep her warm at night when she was back in Portland.

Then his hands were on her, undressing her and following the slow reveal of her bare skin with his lips. By the time they were both undressed and had hit the mattress, Charlotte had forgotten all about the third piece of the *bosca fadbh*, the spell, the car to take her to the gates, the gryphon jewelry that made her a millionaire. Her mind was filled only with Kieran, the feel of his body on hers and his mouth crushed against her lips.

She spread her thighs and he slipped his hand between them to stroke her aching clit. He knew exactly how to touch her, how to apply just the perfect amount of pressure to make her moan. Her body tightened with need and she clenched a fist in the blankets against the rising tide of pleasure.

"Your body was made to be loved," he murmured roughly. "It drives me crazy to watch you get worked up, to hear you moan, to feel how wet you get when I touch you."

She shuddered at the coarseness of his words, excitement skittering up her spine.

He slid a finger deep inside her, then added a second and thrust in and out very slowly. At the same time, his head came down, hot mouth closing on one nipple, then the other. He worked his sweet magick over her until she was mindless with desire for him, begging him softly to take her. Her breath came fast and shallow, her body primed for him.

He parted her thighs wider with his knee and settled himself against her pelvis. Then, holding her gaze, he hilted his cock inside her to the base. His girth stretched her muscles and she gasped, her eyes widening, at the sensation of being so filled.

This time he was above her, missionary position. So intimate—mouth to mouth, chest to chest, sex to sex. He never moved his eyes from hers as he began to thrust. He took her that way, bodies fused and minds and hearts somehow joined by their gazes. Pleasure rippled through her with every inward thrust and warmth blossomed in her chest at the look on his face and in his eyes.

Ah, so this is what it meant to make love. She finally understood.

His body on hers, he touched her everywhere it felt the best. His hand between their bodies, his thumb found her clit, gently stroking it and sending waves of pleasure rippling through her. Lost in a sexual haze, her hands roamed his shoulders, arms, and back—committing him to memory.

He knew how to move, how best to make her come, and her pleasure built and built until it finally burst sweet as a berry on her tongue, making her back arch, her toes curl, and her head bow back into the pillow on a cry of total ecstasy as it crashed over and through her, stealing her ability to think.

As the waves of pleasure ebbed away, he kissed her long and slow as he leisurely thrust in and out of her. Tears fell down to the pillow from the corners of her eyes. She held him to her, ignoring the pain of her arm, tangling her fingers through his hair and curling her thighs around his waist as if to keep him inside her forever.

But eventually he whispered her name, groaned, and she felt his cock jump deep within her. Spent, he stayed inside her anyway, clinging to her as he eventually went flaccid still buried inside her.

They stayed that way until twilight began to steal the light from the sky. Then he rolled away, sat up on the edge of the bed, and said in a hoarse whisper, "Go, Charlotte. Please. Go now before I don't have the strength to tell you do it anymore."

Silent tears running down her face, she got up, dressed, picked up her bag.

And left.

KIERAN stood in the corridor, looking out the window that showed the area of the front doors of the tower. Charlotte was there, waiting for her car. She looked at ease standing there, such a change from two weeks ago when she'd jumped at the slightest movement seen from the corner of her eye.

She'd started to see the humanity in them and he'd begun to see the fae in her.

That and so much more.

Emmaline came to stand beside him, looking out the window with her arms crossed over her chest. "You love her, don't you?"

"I don't know for sure." He paused, watching the car pull up in front of the Black Tower. "But I think so. I just hope she doesn't feel the same."

If he fell in love with her and she didn't return his feelings, he was doomed, but she'd be safe.

"I'm scared for her. Got no reason to feel like she's in danger, yet I'm worried." He paused, rubbing a hand over his mouth. He couldn't remember the last time he'd feared so much for the welfare of another. "I didn't want to let her go."

Emmaline took a moment to reply. "Maybe her being gone will make you two grow apart. Maybe you'll forget her."

Kieran watched Charlotte get into the car and disappear down the road. "Haven't you ever heard the saying, 'absence makes the heart grow fonder'?"

CHARLOTTE climbed into the car and Niall flashed his handsome, dimpled smile at her. "Are you leaving us?"

"It's you! Oh, of course it's you." She sighed, staring up at the shining Black Tower through the back window. One last look before she left. "Yes, I'm headed up out of the rabbit hole."

He pulled away from the curb. "What are you going to do once you get out of here, Alice?"

Glancing down, she fingered the zipper of her bag and considered the question. Go home. Confront her father. Quit her job. Maybe not in that order. "I've got lots to do on the other side, Niall."

"You'll have to get through Gideon first."

Ah, so that's why he was driving her. He'd been sent to prep her for her "exit interview."

"I won't tell the Phaendir anything. I might've, before. But not now. I hope you all find that piece. I hope you break the walls, beat the Phaendir, and are free. I won't do anything to endanger that possibility. In fact, I'm praying you succeed."

In the rearview mirror, he smiled. "Good, I'm glad to hear you've come over to the dark side."

"The dark side isn't all that dark, Niall."

"Ah, come on." He grinned at her. "Don't break the illusion. That's no fun."

She settled back and watched the Boundary Lands go past. Closing her eyes, she said good-bye to them. Good-bye to the beautiful trees, the sprae, the lady in the lake, even the spriggan. She said good-bye to the Black Tower, to Emmaline and Aeric, to the king and the queen.

But she couldn't bring herself to say good-bye to Kieran.

"And your bit of jewelry? You know they'll search your person and your luggage when you leave."

Niall's voice startled her. She opened her eyes and found his gaze in the rearview mirror. "The gryphon? I have nowhere to hide it. I'll just have to tell them I bought it."

Niall mulled that over. "It might work. Your daddy is made of money, so it's in the realm of believability."

Made of money. Heartache, too, as it turned out.

The car pulled up in front of the gates and a couple of the red cap guards approached the vehicle as she got out. This time she didn't even glance at them. She leaned into Niall's open window and kissed him on his cheek, feeling the rasp of the stubble on his skin.

"See you later, kid," said Niall, putting the car into drive.

"See you." She watched him drive away.

After going through all the protocol to verify her identity, they finally opened the gates and let her out. Gideon waited on the other side. Her bandaged arm was out of sight under her shirt, so she wouldn't have to explain it, and, really, she had nothing to hide but a change of heart. Still, her pulse sped when she saw the archdirector of the Phaendir walking toward her. She would lie herself blue to protect the fae, but that didn't mean she'd enjoy it.

She frowned as she drew closer to him on the gravel road leading away from the gates. It was now evening, and by the dim glow of the streetlamps, she could see that Gideon looked . . . *thrashed*. His forehead sported a big blue bruise, and someone had split his lower lip. Barely healed cuts marked his throat and all his exposed flesh, the thin, angry marks disappearing under his shirt. He looked like he'd been involved in a fight and had come out on the losing end.

"Are you all right?" she blurted when she came up to him.

Gideon's face remained stony for a moment, then he cracked an insincere smile that she guess must've hurt. "I'm fine. More importantly, how are you?"

She hesitated for a moment, wanting very much to inquire further about what had happened to him. He really didn't seem like the bar fight type and the curiosity was killing her. "The job went well, but I'm glad I'm out of Piefferburg."

"I called the Piefferburg Business Council as soon as you contacted the gates to say you were leaving. They told me they've given your employer high praise for the work you did." They began to walk toward the Phaendir Headquarters.

"Your sacrifice will have some benefit in the end. I'm sure your superiors will be pleased and you will be rewarded."

He'd checked up on her. *Holy cow.* But apparently the Black Tower had been ready for it and she was covered. *Whew.* "Yes. They seemed pleased with my work. I'm just glad I'm all done and can head home to take my life back up again."

"Certainly. I've already called a cab to take you to the airport. You have made flight arrangements, I presume?"

She nodded. "I'll be on the first available flight to Portland. I'm sleeping in my own bed tonight."

"Excellent." They came to a stop in front of the building. The cab, just as he'd said, was parked not far away. He held out a hand. "But, first, I need to search your bag and pat you down."

"Of course." She handed her bag over. "Glad to have it done by you, the archdirector himself."

He flicked his gaze at her. "I don't trust anyone else to do an adequate job."

"Of course."

He rifled through her bag, immediately finding the pendant and holding it up. "What's this?"

"I bought it." She smiled. "It was so pretty. I couldn't resist."

He stared at it for a moment longer, then replaced it. "I didn't know you enjoyed fae jewelry." His voice seemed tight, displeased.

He didn't know anything about her; he only thought he did. "I don't, normally. That piece was just too interesting to pass up."

He grunted and zipped her bag up, then hand-searched her luggage, purchased in Piefferburg after her first suitcase fell into the ravine, and found nothing. Then somehow she suffered through his hands on her without shuddering.

She drew a breath of relief when they finally said their good-byes and she was able to head to her cab. Glancing back, she saw that Gideon's gaze stayed on her as she walked to the vehicle, got in, and drove off.

Now headed to Protection City and a plane bound for home, she settled back and tried to relax. Her nightmare was over. The bonding magick had lost its grip. She was free. She should be happy.

So why did she hurt so much?

TWENTY-TWO

~~~~~~~~

CHARLOTTE caught the last plane of the evening out of Protection City and made it back to her house in Portland just before one in the morning. She walked into the dining room and dropped all her things near her beloved polished Amish dining table and looked around the room.

Nothing was different than the day she'd left, yet everything had changed. The entire house felt like a stranger's.

Abandoning her things where she'd left them, but taking the gryphon pendant, she went upstairs and showered.

Rubbing the steam off the mirror when she was through, she stared at her reflection. Dark circles marked the skin under her eyes and she looked like she was coming down with something. Felt like it, too—weak and tired. No wonder, after the couple weeks she'd had, topped off with the late-night flight into Portland.

She squinted, taking a deeper look at her face.

Her face looked leaner than it had before, her eyes darker and sharper. Oddly, she hadn't missed her glasses at all. Was it possible for astigmatism to correct itself on its own? Was it silly to believe she could simply see better now—in more than one way?

Also strange, her lips looked fuller to her. She brushed them with her fingertips and closed her eyes, imagining Kieran's mouth rubbing over them. Cold longing made her chest feel empty. She dropped her hand and opened her eyes.

She would probably never see Kieran again.

Picking up the gryphon necklace, she slipped it over her head and settled it in the hollow of her throat. Running a finger around its edge, she told herself she'd sleep with it tonight and hope he visited her in her dreams.

Flicking the light off in the bathroom, she climbed into her bed and tried to sleep.

KIERAN woke the instant his sleeping psyche connected with Charlotte's in her dreamscape. The joining had happened spontaneously, just as it had back in the cottage in Hangman's Bastion. This time he'd been ready for it. As much as he wanted to see Charlotte again, no more contact between them could be allowed. He was too far gone.

He pushed the covers away, swung his feet down to the floor, and coughed. Rubbing his palm into his chest, he frowned, sensing the oddness that had settled into his body. He felt weak, as though sickness was trying to gain a foothold within him. It was a sensation not often experienced by the fae, who were almost never ill.

Terror rocked through him.

He wasn't too far gone . . . he was just *gone*.

Bowing his head, he ran his hand over his face. *Charlotte.* Sweet Lady, he hoped this was a one-way street. If she didn't return his feelings, she'd be safe.

Hopefully she'd left Piefferburg, and him, just in time.

THE first thing Charlotte did in the morning was confront her father.

She dressed, drank a little coffee, and left to go to his house with the gryphon pendant around her neck.

Her stomach roiled as she shouldered her purse and walked up the stairs to his door. Her father was a multimillionaire, a former CEO of a conglomerate who had given his life to his ambitions . . . and, ironically, to her. She still wasn't sure what she was going to do with the information she possessed. Take it to the police and try to explain how she knew what she knew? That's what felt right, even though it would be the hardest thing she'd ever done in her life.

But in order to get the police to believe her, she would need her father's help.

He would need to confess to the murder.

She walked up the fancy gray stone steps and rang the doorbell of her father's immense home. She remembered playing jacks on these stairs, remembered playing with her ball. She had lots of memories of this place, though in all of them she was alone.

Her father didn't answer the door. She frowned and rang again, looking over at the driveway where her father's Mercedes was parked. He had to be home.

She rang again. Still no answer. Maybe her father was in the shower or listening to opera really loud, as was his habit. It was a Saturday, so it was entirely possible.

She took out her keys and found the one she needed. Once she had the door unlocked, she pushed it open and went inside. "Dad?"

"I'm in here, sweetie," she heard him call from the family room.

Her whole body tight with the prospect of confronting him, she held her bag close and walked through the foyer into the family room.

He was standing near his bar, pouring himself a scotch. She frowned. That was out of character. He kept the liquor there for guests and rarely drank it himself, especially not on a Saturday morning.

"Dad, we need to talk."

He walked toward her. "Yes, we do." His voice sounded stern. "It's not like you to just run off that way without telling me. I had to call your boss to find out where you'd gone."

So he knew where she'd been.

She closed her eyes for a moment, knowing this was going to be hard all the way around. Of course he'd worried when she hadn't called. She usually spoke to him at least once a week. *Of course* he'd called her boss and asked them if she'd been in. "Then you already know I was in Piefferburg."

Rage enveloped his face. "Piefferburg, Charlotte! You took a job in that *mecca of evil?*"

She held up a hand. "It's a long story and it's not important."

"Not important?" he roared, the amber liquid in his short, chunky liquor glass sloshing over the rim with his movements. "How can it not be—"

She interrupted him, raising her voice, anger surging through her veins. "The important thing, the thing I came here to talk about, is that I had some very interesting revelations while I was there." She dropped her purse onto a plush, dark green couch and glanced around the room at the furnishings, anywhere but at her father.

This was the room where he'd murdered her. Sorrow rose up into her throat.

She summoned her rage to war with her grief. Rage she could use. Grief would only handicap her. "Revelations about you."

"About me? What are you saying?"

She frowned. What was that dark brown spot on the white carpet near the edge of the couch? Was that . . . blood? Actually, there was more than one spot. And, wait, over there . . . was that . . . a shoe? It was an expensive shoe, by the looks of it, and there was a foot still in it.

Oh, no.

TWENTY-THREE

HER stomach dropped to her feet and her mind fell into a black hole. She paused, taking a moment to process the situation. That was her father's fancy designer loafer. And if her father was lying there, on the floor, bloody, then who was standing here pretending to be him?

The blood in her veins turned to icy slush.

She looked up from the shoe with wide eyes, completely incapable of hiding her shock. The person—the fae—wearing her father's image dissolved it. A good-looking woman with dark red hair and pale, perfect skin stood before her. The woman's green eyes were cold and hard and she wore a mocking smile on her lips.

"Hello, Charlotte. My name is Máire. I think you must know my sister, Maeve? Wait, you know her as Risa. I wasn't expecting you so early, but all's well. Your arrival has saved me from having to hunt you down."

Another shiver of shock ran through her. She took a step backward.

"I know, but it's not as confusing as you must be thinking. I'm sure you've heard of us, the Three Sisters? We're practically famous in the world of the fae for the miracle of our births. Not unlike your friend, Kieran, and his twin brother, right? My sisters and I . . ." She paused. "Well, my *sister* and I have the same ability Kieran and Diarmad had— that ability to experience through each other. It only works in times of intense emotional spikes. Times of intense fear, pleasure, or rage. In fact, when that bitch of a fae, Emmaline, killed our oldest sister last year in Israel, both Maeve and I experienced it."

Charlotte fought through her shock and forced her mind to follow the logic. When Risa/Maeve had tried to kill her, this woman, Máire, had seen it through her eyes.

Charlotte drew a breath, marshaling her panic. "Then you must know your *bitch* of a sister, Maeve, is clapped in charmed iron right now."

Pain flashed through her eyes. "They've done a whole lot more than just clap in her charmed iron, girly. One of my sisters is dead and the other is being tortured. The latter is a fact for which I'm inclined to make you pay."

Oh, shit. She glanced around the room, looking for a weapon. Then she remembered the old antique charmed iron sword her father kept in his library. Could she get to it? It seemed like her only shot.

"So," said Máire, sauntering toward her, "I saw my sister try to kill you. I saw her battle with Kieran Aindréas Cairbre Aimhrea and the Blacksmith afterward. Since then I've experienced bits and pieces of my sister's conversation with both of them and with her torturers. I know who you are, Charlotte." She cocked her head to the side. "How are you feeling these days? Sick at all? Are you dying yet, for the love of a fae?"

She shook her head. "I feel fine. Kieran and I aren't in love. The curse hasn't been triggered. I'm not the human who can pull the piece."

Máire laughed. "Bullshit." She motioned to Charlotte's father. "I came here and searched his memories, looking for anything about you I could use. I saw your pathetic childhood and boring adulthood. Any woman with a history like yours would be immediately enamored of a dangerous, captivating fae man like Kieran Aimhrea, so cut the crap and talk to me like a woman to a woman."

"It takes two to trigger the curse. He doesn't love me so . . ." Kieran's words rang through her mind. *In a confrontation, never back down. Display confidence, even if you're scared shitless.* She shrugged carelessly, smiled, then her voice went low and dangerous. "So back off, bitch. You've got the wrong woman."

"Oooo, the kitten grew claws in Piefferburg. That's good. You're going to need them with me." Her gaze focused Charlotte's throat. "The gryphon? Where did you get that?"

Charlotte touched the pendant. "You can't have it."

"I'll take anything I want, little one." Máire lunged toward her.

Charlotte turned and ran. She had to get to the library, had to get that sword.

Behind her, Máire laughed. "That's right, you better run, girly."

Footsteps sounded right behind her even though she was running faster than she'd ever run before. She rounded the corner into the foyer and nearly slipped on the marble floor. Máire probably thought she was going for the front door, but she swerved at the last minute and lunged into her father's library, slamming and locking the door behind her. Going out the front door would have meant she'd be murdered on the front lawn. Charlotte had no illusions about her chances against a fae, no illusions that Máire cared whether the neighbors saw her committing murder.

Máire hit the library door from the other side and swore. That door was heavier than most, but Máire seemed to be extra strong. Charlotte was sure she'd find a way through.

Charlotte found the sword above the mantle over the fireplace and pulled it out of its sheath. She tested the blade. It wasn't very sharp, but it would have to do. She didn't know much about sword fighting, but she was pretty sure she could stick the pointy end in Máire if her life was in danger.

Máire continued to throw herself against the door. The wood around the frame cracked ominously. It wouldn't be long now.

Weapon in hand, Charlotte went to a window and pulled up the shade. Her car was parked next to her dad's Mercedes, but her keys were in her purse . . . which she'd left back in the family room. *Damn it!* She fumbled at the window's lock. Maybe she could get outside and hide in the woods that surrounded her father's house.

Just as she'd pried the window open a little, the door behind her crashed in a shower of splinters. So much for that idea. Time to fight. *Oh, god.*

Charlotte whirled, sword in hand, feet apart, trying her best to look fierce. The effect was probably ruined by the fact that she was quivering like a leaf in a very strong wind.

Máire stood in the ruined doorframe looking dangerous. "So you have a sword. My, my. What do you plan to do with it, girly?"

"Kill you."

"Really?" She raised a bloodred eyebrow. "How many people have you killed before, dearest? By the look on your face I would say . . . none." She smiled, showing very white teeth. "Guess how many I've killed?"

"Guess who's got the sword?" Charlotte lunged toward Máire.

Máire spun to the side, laughing, and picked up an iron poker from the fireplace. She took up a convincing posture in the middle of the room and they circled each other. Damn it, Máire looked like she actually knew how to fence.

Charlotte circled warily, both hands on the grip of the sword.

Máire moved with total confidence, one hand on the poker and the other on her hip.

Suddenly Máire feinted, knocking the poker into the blade.

Charlotte gasped, holding on to the sword with everything she had as the hit reverberated down her arms and into her hands. Sensing Charlotte's weakness, Máire pressed her advantage, moving forward and hitting the sword's blade over and over until Charlotte backed herself up against the wall. It was all she could do just to hold on to the hilt, never mind swing it.

Time seemed to slow as Máire lifted the poker higher and Charlotte knew what was coming—the next slash wouldn't be aimed at her sword . . . but at her face. With Máire's strength, it would tear her head right from her shoulders. Up until now Máire had just been having fun.

This was it. Charlotte knew she needed to make some kind of move, or she'd die.

Panic coursing through her veins, she gave a shout of mingled rage and terror, stepped forward and pushed her arms straight out as hard as she could. The tip of the sword found Máire's soft stomach and slid in.

Charlotte used all her strength to push it in even farther and then let go, backing away, totally shocked she'd found her mark . . . and that Máire wasn't made of steel but flesh and blood just like everyone else.

Máire's eyes and mouth opened wide and her skin went white.

Then she collapsed. Blood pooled around her folded body. She stretched out a red-coated hand still clenched around the handle of the poker, as if trying to hit Charlotte with it. The poker dropped to the floor with a *thunk*. Máire took a long, shuddering breath before she stopped breathing altogether.

Charlotte stood over Máire for a moment, her hand to her mouth, staring at the protruding sword. How many people had she killed?

One.

She backed away, hit the wall, and jumped, startled. Her mind was a tangled mess, reviewing what had just happened with disbelief. But she didn't have time for this luxury. She needed to move, get out of here. Maybe Máire hadn't been alone.

That thought spurred her to action. She ran into the hallway, back to the family room. Kneeling beside her father, she felt for a pulse and got nothing. She shook her head, her eyes brimming with tears. Of course she didn't get a pulse; his eyes were open, unseeing. He was dead.

She bowed her head over his body for several minutes, dragging in huge gulps of air, and tried to calm herself. Tried to reconcile grief, shock, confusion . . . and a worrisome niggle of relief she wished was not present.

Raising her gaze, she looked at her father's face. This was a man who had loved her in his own twisted, harsh way. This was also the man who'd killed a young, vibrant woman and let his daughter grow up thinking her mother had never cared about her. This man was a murderer.

And now he was dead. She would get no confession, no explanation, no revenge, no closure. *Dead.*

She wasn't sure what to do with all the emotions crowding her brain at the moment, so she focused on the physical things she needed to do. Getting out of here was primary on her list in case Máire had summoned others.

Leaning forward, she closed his eyes. Then she rose, retrieved her purse, and left the house.

KIERAN watched Risa squirm in her chair, eyes closed, as though enduring a bad nightmare. Blood tracked down her temple and arm from where the people getting information from her had tried to . . . *persuade* her. Nothing so far had worked and the queen was struggling to give the order to go further. Aislinn would need to give it soon or risk looking weak. That was a dangerous thing for an Unseelie queen.

What Risa was doing now—thrashing in the chair where they'd tied her, her head whipping back and forth and her spine arching—had nothing to do with the persuasion. This was new. Risa was being tortured by something that had nothing to do with the knives and syringes surrounding her. It looked as though she was dreaming, or experiencing something happening purely within her mind.

Kieran frowned, memories teasing him. It looked damn familiar to him, this waking torture she was going through. He leaned in, studying her. It had been a long time, but his memories never died.

"What the hell is happening to her?" asked Niall, entering the room and going straight toward her.

Kieran held up a hand to stop him. "No, let her be. I think I know what this is."

Risa's head snapped back and she let out a shriek of anguish and then broke down sobbing and muttering "No, no," over and over. Finally she slumped in her chair and went still and silent except for her crying.

"So what is it?"

Kieran considered the sobbing woman a moment longer, then approached her. "Risa?"

She looked ready to pass out.

He shook her shoulders. "Risa!"

Her head lolled back and forth for a moment, then her tear-wet eyes found his. "Don't call me that. My name isn't Risa."

"What is it?"

Her eyes squeezed shut and a wracking sob shook her slim body. "My sister is dead."

Kieran took a step backward. So it was what he'd thought. "You just experienced her death."

Her gaze caught his and rage flared in her eyes. "My sister Máire is dead."

Máire. He put that information together with the suspicion that he recognized what she'd just undergone. "Your name is really Maeve, isn't it? You're the youngest of the Three Sisters."

"You know what it's like, to experience your sibling die." Her eyes went unfocused. "I've had to do it twice now."

Twice now? So the two sisters who had been missed by

the Great Sweep were dead now and the one who'd been captured by the Phaendir was sitting here in front of him. Mystery solved.

Maeve gobbed spit at him, which he only barely missed being spattered with. "And it was your girlfriend who killed her."

Shock rippled through him. "What? What did you say?"

Maeve just smiled, her eyes glittering with mingled tears and malice.

He leaned forward, hands tight on her forearms, and got into her face. She winced and gasped at the pressure he applied to her arms, her face going pale. *"Tell me."*

"My sisters are dead. I'll tell you everything. There's no one left for me to protect."

"Good. Start with Charlotte."

Maeve slowly licked some blood from her lip and looked like she enjoyed it. "Untie me first."

"You're not in a position to bargain, Maeve. No way."

Her face crumpled in a new wave of grief. She squeezed her eyes shut and a tear slid down her cheek. "It doesn't matter."

"Good. Go on."

A muscle worked in Kieran's jaw as he waited for her to speak. "Máire must have seen me try to kill Charlotte through our link. Only the most emotionally charged experiences make their way through, but you know that, right, Kieran? Through our connection, Máire must have figured Charlotte might be the human to pull the piece, so she sought out her father and gleaned all the memories of his daughter she could, but Charlotte showed up unexpectedly. I didn't see anything through Máire's eyes until Máire attacked Charlotte." Her face twisted in rage and her voice came out a snarl. "Charlotte killed her! And now Máire is a ghost walking the human world, just like Meghann. It's worse than the slaugh."

He rubbed his hand over his face, absorbing this information. How had Charlotte managed to kill Máire?

Kieran leaned toward her, fists clenched. "You and your people tried twice to kidnap Charlotte instead of killing her outright. You waited until you had the location of the third piece of the *bosca fabdh* before you tried to stab her. *Why?*"

"My people here in Piefferburg all have loved ones on the outside whom we want to protect from the Wild Hunt. We wanted the location of the third piece as much as you did—to keep you from ever finding it." Her lips curled in a feral smile. Even the tears tracking her cheeks couldn't make her look harmless. "I didn't know until I experienced Máire's death throes that the fae on the outside already know the location. They know it and they're protecting it. If your precious Charlotte tries to pull that piece, she's going to die."

Kieran backed away from her, his veins gelling with frost.

"What the hell do you know that I don't?" Niall's face looked brutal in the small amount of light.

Kieran grabbed his arm and led him out of the room and into the corridor beyond, closing the door behind them. In the small chamber where they were keeping Maeve, her anguished, crazed scream reached them.

Kieran rubbed a hand over his mouth, trying to gather his thoughts enough to brief him. "Risa is actually Maeve, one of the Three Sisters. You and I both know how rare fae siblings are and the kind of bond they might share."

"You know better than me."

"I do. And that's how I recognized that Maeve was in the throes of a shared experience with her sister, Máire, who lives—lived—beyond the walls of Piefferburg."

"And apparently Charlotte killed Máire."

Kieran nodded, feeling his chest tighten in pain suddenly. He fisted his hands and swore. "That means that the free fae out there, that Danu-damned group of free fae who don't want the walls to fall, could know about Charlotte. They could be hunting her. She's all alone out there, Niall. You heard Maeve just now, if Charlotte tries to pull the piece, she's dead."

"But she's not going after the piece. We let her go because

we didn't think she had anything to do with this other than holding the memory of the location."

Kieran bowed his head in utter and total defeat. "Look at me, Niall. Take a good, long look."

"You look like shi . . . *Kieran*."

Kieran raised his head. "I only hope it's not affecting Charlotte."

"Can it work that way?"

He pushed a hand through his hair. "I think so. If I fall in love with her and she doesn't fall in love with me, I'm the only one who takes the hit."

"But if that's the case, she wouldn't be dying for the love of a fae and she wouldn't be able to pull the piece."

"I hope so."

"I'm sorry, Kieran, but that scenario would leave us nowhere." Niall shrugged at the look on Kieran's face. "These are serious, brutal times. Sorry, man, but I hope to hell she *is* in love with you."

"I hope Charlotte doesn't go after that piece."

"Damn. You really do love her."

"Yeah." Kieran rubbed a tired hand over his face.

Niall clapped a hand on his shoulder. "We're going to the Piefferburg witch to see if we can break this curse."

"I've been already, too many times over the centuries to count."

"Yeah, well, we're going again."

THE police kept Charlotte most of the day, asking her questions and re-asking her questions. She'd called the attorney her father had always used, gone to the police, and told them everything with the attorney advising her. A neighbor verified her story about her arrival time, and the fae woman in the library was hard to overlook. That's the thing that really set the police on edge, the fae woman. It was so rare to find a fae who had escaped the Great Sweep.

It was because of that, Charlotte presumed, their prejudice

about the fae, that they let her go with no charges. They'd called her act one of self-defense. They'd said it was clear what had happened. The fae had broken into her father's house for whatever reason—maybe because he was the head of the HCIF—killed him, and then Charlotte had surprised her and been forced to defend herself.

Because who wouldn't defend themselves against a wild animal like a fae woman? It was a good thing that fae was dead, dangerous thing that she was.

In this case, they'd been right.

It was evening by the time she left the police station. They told her not to go too far, that they might have more questions for her. Charlotte assumed that translated to something like, *don't leave town, we might charge you with something later*. It didn't make her feel warm and fuzzy. Of course, nothing about today had made her feel very warm and fuzzy.

Plus, the little tickle she'd had in her throat was developing into a hell of a racking cough. Her chest hurt from it. Since the only sleep she'd had in the last twenty-four hours had been a few fitful, Kieran-free hours she'd snatched last night and she'd had very little food or water, she assumed it had to be a bug.

God, she really hoped it was just a bug.

She sat in her car, wondering what the hell she should do. The moon was full tonight, hanging big and golden in the sky right down near the horizon. It looked like an alien thing. Her life felt alien, too. The only thought that gave her any comfort at all right now was Kieran. Talking to him in the dead of night when the stars shone overhead, dancing with him around a bonfire at a goblin celebration, the feel of his body against hers on a soft bed. God, she missed him.

How ironic.

She wished he was here with her now and could advise her. She was ill-prepared to deal with this kind of intrigue on her own. Spreadsheets and numbers she could wrestle into submission. But this? Her old job was starting to look appealing, but she knew she couldn't go back there. She couldn't go home, either. There had to be more fae loose in the human world than just Máire. Did they know anything of what had transpired in her father's house today? Did they want to kill her because they thought she was the human who could pull the last piece of the *bosca fadbh*?

Was she being hunted?

And what role did the Phaendir play in all of this? She couldn't imagine a fae/Phaendir alliance, but what if there was one? Did she need to be wary of the Phaendir as well?

She pressed the heel of her hand to the socket of her eye for a moment while her heart ached for Kieran. She had nothing here now. Her family was all gone. She had few friends. Her career meant so much less today than it had a few weeks ago. It was like her trip into Piefferburg had completely destroyed her.

The only question was how would she rebuild herself?

The tickle in her throat turned violent and she doubled over in her seat, coughing until she was nearly blind with agony. Her lungs felt cut to ribbons on the inside. When the pain eased and she could breathe again, she pulled her hand away and saw blood on her palm. She stared at it for a long moment, feeling strangely calm.

Of course she wasn't just coming down with a bug. She loved Kieran, and apparently he loved her back. As unbelievable as that was . . . *he loved her back*.

Elation rushed through her, followed by a cold wave of terror.

The curse was upon them. They were both going to die and be claimed by the slaugh.

Well, wasn't *that* just the cherry on the cake of her day?

She needed to get back to Kieran. This changed everything. It didn't matter if she was charged with a crime from today. Nothing mattered now.

Correction, the only thing that mattered was that she could pull that damn piece. Maybe she could do something good before she kicked the bucket. Feeling a determination she'd never experienced so strongly before, she put the car in drive.

She wasn't going to do this alone, however, not while she was *dying for the love of a fae*. Luckily, thanks to Emmaline, she knew just who to call for help.

TWENTY-FOUR

GIDEON stretched, enjoying the delicious pain that came from any movement. It was a guilty pleasure. The whole night had been. He vacillated between wanting to torture Máire slowly until she bled out on the floor of his apartment and wanting to call her again for another lusty round.

He hated her for making him want it.

Luckily, he'd probably never see her again. He shoved more clothes into his suitcase and checked his watch. It was almost time to go to the airport. He had a flight to Dublin today. It was time he checked out this piece of the *bosca fadbh* for himself. He wanted to touch the cursed thing, even if he couldn't pull it. He wasn't sending any of his men to guard that piece until he saw the lay of the land, made sure it was true.

The piece was lodged in a hunk of rock called the Lia Fáil, also known as the Stone of Destiny, near Tara in Ireland, supposedly guarded by a number of these free fae who were so afraid of Piefferburg's walls coming down. That would mean

talking to more fae. Goody. As long as none of them were
Máire he might be able to choke down a conversation or two.

He'd get to Dublin, rent a car, and drive out to the for-
saken Irish countryside, the last place in the Labrai-damned
universe he wanted to go. A headache stabbed into his eyes
and he sat down on his bed.

He hadn't been back to Ireland since Piefferburg had been
built. These were memories he didn't want to revisit.

The doorbell rang. That would be his driver.

After a moment of staring off into space, hating what he
was about to do, he stood, grabbed his suitcase, and left for
the airport.

Labrai give him strength.

TWENTY-ONE hours later, Charlotte took her first steps
onto Irish soil. Before she'd left Portland, she cleared out most
of the money in her accounts—an action that would surely
make her look guilty of a crime to the police—and driven
straight to the airport for the first ticket to Dublin she could
buy. She'd figured looking guilty to the police was the least
of her troubles at this point.

During her layover in New York, between coughing fits,
she'd bought new clothes, trashed her old ones, and eaten
two cheeseburgers, about a pound of french fries, and drank
a gallon of cola. The sickness of the curse certainly hadn't
affected her appetite. She'd been starving.

She stood at the baggage carousel in Dublin, even though
she had no checked luggage, and coughed into a Kleenex.

"Charlotte Bennett?"

She got herself under control and turned to look at the
man who'd come up beside her. He was a good-looking guy
with reddish blond hair, brown eyes, bit of stubble on his
chin, and a strong build. "David Sullivan?"

"I am."

She narrowed her eyes. "How can I be sure you're really
him?"

"You can't. How can I be sure you're really who you say you are?"

Charlotte gritted her teeth, on edge. "I guess we'll both have to be careful of each other."

"I guess so. I can also guess from your mistrust that you've had a run-in with a fae lately, one who can use glamour."

She fell into a coughing fit again. "You would be guessing right," she rasped when she could speak again.

He smiled, laugh lines crinkling at the corners of his brown eyes. "How are you doing?"

"Me? I've been better." She gave a humorless laugh. "Emmaline told me about you when I was in Piefferburg, so you were the first person I could think of who might be able to help me."

"And I wouldn't be here right now if you hadn't known details about my relationship with her." He gave her a critical look. "You have dark circles under your eyes and you look feverish. Long flight, or are you ill?"

"David, we've got a lot to talk about."

They found a Starbucks and Charlotte ordered a coffee that she needed big-time. Then they settled in and she told David everything. She had no choice; she had to trust him. There was no way she could handle this next part on her own.

David sat back in his chair with a sigh when she was done, and pushed a hand through his spiky hair. He looked like someone had just shown him a flying pig. "It must have been her older sister . . . Meghann? . . . who toyed with me in Israel. She pretended to be this woman I cared about, then she attacked me, drugged me up, and went off to try and murder Emmaline. Emmaline killed her underwater when they fought for the piece."

"Red hair? Nasty demeanor? Enhanced strength and the ability to use glamour?"

"Oh, yeah."

"That was her. I had the pleasure of making the youngest sister's acquaintance in Piefferburg." She paused, remembering, and then shuddered. "She's the only one still alive."

David sat forward, rubbing his chin and frowning. "Maeve must have been trying to protect her remaining sister, Máire. She must have known Máire would be reaped by the Wild Hunt if the walls ever broke. So Maeve got the location of the piece from you, but tried to kill you before anyone else learned it."

Charlotte nodded. "And since the sisters have that psychic link, Máire saw it when Maeve tried to kill me and tracked my father down in Portland. The only thing that doesn't make sense is that Máire told me the free fae know where the piece is already, so why go to all the trouble chasing down the buried memory in my head?"

"Perhaps *Maeve* wasn't aware that the free fae know the location."

"Maybe." She rubbed her hand over her face and slouched in her chair. She was so tired.

David took a sip of his coffee and stared off into the distance with his eyes unfocused. "That group of fae knew where the piece in Israel was, too, they just weren't able to raise it themselves. They can't take this one because *you're* the only one who can." He shook his head. "I have no idea how they come by this knowledge."

"I care less about that than I do my immediate problem." She leaned forward and caught his gaze meaningfully. "How I am going to pull the piece from the stone when it's clear all the bad guys know the location? It's not like I can just walk in and take it."

David opened his mouth to reply just as his cell phone rang. He held up a finger and fumbled for it. "We're at the Starbucks near baggage claim," he said into the receiver, then snapped it closed.

She watched him slip the phone back into his pocket and folded her arms over her chest, hating how alone and vulnerable she felt. "Who was that?"

He glanced up at her. "A friend. Don't worry."

"Kinda hard not to worry." She coughed into her hand. Her head pounded and her chest felt tight.

"How is Emmaline, by the way?"

She looked up at the note of pain in his voice. "She's good."

"In love with this man, Aeric O'Malley? The Blacksmith?"

"Uh." *Damn it.* She didn't want to hurt this guy. "They're actually married now. Yes, they're very much in love."

He nodded. "Good. I want Emmaline to be happy."

A hulking man with a scruffy beard came up on David's side. "Are you still mooning over that woman?" he asked in a booming voice that had half of the customers in Starbucks looking over at them. "You got to let her go, man."

David hung his head for a moment and smiled. Then he looked up at Charlotte. "Charlotte, please meet Calum. Calum, Charlotte."

Calum reached out and shook her hand in a grip that made her wince. "Hey! Happy to know you!" he boomed.

Charlotte liked him immediately.

"Charlotte, do you want to fill Calum in?" David asked.

She nodded, drew a labored breath through a chest that ached nonstop, and dove in, telling him everything. "The piece is supposed to be stuck somewhere in the Stone of Destiny."

Calum stroked his beard. "Thing is, I've seen the Stone of Destiny. I've touched every inch of that rock and I've never seen anything lodged in it that wasn't a part of the stone, itself."

"That's what Kieran said." She sat back in her chair, deflated. Here she was, dying, and perhaps on a useless errand. She could be spending this time with the man she loved . . . a man who apparently loved her back.

David shook his head. "Don't discount it. I've seen lots of fae magick in my time. It can be powerful."

"Well, there's no checking it out till nightfall." Calum looked at David. "That's for certain."

Charlotte sat up a little. "Why not?"

David's gaze met hers. "We both almost died trying to get the second piece of the *bosca fadbh* because of this group of rogue fae."

"And that fae bitch sister," Calum added. "She cut me up so bad I almost couldn't put myself back together again."

"We go under cover of darkness." David nodded. "We intend to take every precaution going after this one. We'll make sure every advantage is ours."

"If the piece is even really there."

"I think it is. I think that the final piece of the *bosca fadbh* is within our reach." David leaned forward and covered her hand with his. "The HFF crew is going to help you pull that piece and get it back into Piefferburg. I'm aware you don't have much time—"

"Before I die."

He gave her a rigid smile. "I was going to say you don't have much time to get back into Piefferburg and find some kind of way to break this curse."

"There isn't a way."

Calum caught her gaze. "If I was you, I'd die trying."

"THERE is no cure." Priss, the Piefferburg witch, in her guise as a comely young woman—the Maiden—gestured and spoke as though Kieran and Niall were simpleminded. "You've asked before and I've always told you the same thing; I know of *no way* to break the curse set upon you."

"What about the family that laid it? Can't they take it off?" Niall asked.

"They're dead," Kieran and the witch answered in unison.

"We've already been down that road," Kieran finished, turning away and rubbing a hand over his weary face. "Even if they were alive, it's doubtful they could reverse a curse this strong."

He walked to the grimy window of the witch's shop and stared out at the serpentine alleyway that wove its way around the base of the Black Tower. This was the same alley he'd chased Charlotte down the day she'd arrived. Now he wished she'd managed to escape. It seemed forever ago, not just a few weeks. His chest twinged with pain and he pressed his palm to it. The curse eating at him was growing worse by the hour. How was Charlotte doing?

"Kieran Aindréas Cairbre Aimhrea has come to me before," the witch was saying to Niall. "I have looked through every book I own, consulted with every one of my colleagues, including your brother, Ronan. I cannot find a cure."

Kieran turned from the window. "What about the woman? Can you find a way to break her free of this? Some way to break the curse just for her? She wasn't the one it was laid on; she's blameless."

The Piefferburg witch smiled. "You were always blameless, too, and I can't find a way to break it for you."

"Find a way to break it for her." He roared it, suddenly terrified and enraged all at once. "Do whatever you can. You know I'm wealthy. I'll pay you whatever you demand. *Just do it.*"

GIDEON gained a better grip on his bag and walked toward the sliding exit doors of the airport. A distance away a large, bearded man boomed, *"Well, all right, let's get going!"* to his companions. Dear Labrai, that man was huge. Gideon squinted, looking at the man's companions. The woman had long dark hair. The man had short reddish gold hair and a muscular build. The big man's booming laugh accompanied them as they walked through the exit doors about twenty feet ahead of him.

Deep in thought about his upcoming adventure in the country of his birth, Gideon watched the three disappear outside before heading to the car hire businesses. He wanted out of this place and he wasn't going to waste any time.

He got his car and, even though he was exhausted, drove directly out to County Meathe, about a forty-minute trek to the north. His hands tight on the steering wheel the whole way, he was finally forced to pull off onto a little used road in the countryside, get out of the car, and rest on a nearby hill in order to collect himself. He sat in the grass and held his hands out in front of him. They were shaking.

Coming here was worse than any of his nightmares.

Ireland looked different than the last time he'd been here, of course. But time couldn't completely change the way the land rolled or how it smelled. As soon as his feet had hit Irish soil, the past had risen up to smack him in the face. No amount of change could mask the fundamental soul of Ireland.

He could still remember the way her skirts had felt in his hands. Her laughter had sounded like bells. He still recalled how she'd run her fingers through his hair and say sweet things to him. She'd always smelled of flowers, even in the middle of winter. Loss opened up like an enormous mouth in the center of his chest, sharp teeth nipping away tiny, bloody chunks of his heart.

Gideon closed his eyes, trying to banish it all. Once he touched that grief deep inside, nothing but huge amounts of time could heal him. Time was something he didn't have.

Squeezing his eyes shut, he recited a segment from the Book of Labrai. "In the time before things were recorded, when monkey-men and pretend gods walked the Earth, demons ruled humanity. They entered the hearts of the weak and exploited their frailty, turning men on each other, causing chaos and allowing wickedness to rule. Humanity put their trust in the fae, the dark gods of selfishness and sorrow. One day unto a human woman a child was born and his name was Labrai, the light-bringer. He was Phaendir in a womb where no druid seed had been sown and spoke great truths before he walked. He—"

"Hello, ye not looking horrid well up there. Can I call someone?"

Gideon stopped muttering to himself and forced himself to focus on his immediate surroundings. A young man had turned down the small road he'd stopped on and had pulled up alongside his rental car.

"Did ye hear me, then?" The man leaned out his open car

window. "Having car trouble?" He narrowed his eyes as he
caught sight of Gideon's bruises. "Do ye need me to call for
help?"

"No. I'm fine. Thanks."

"Ah! An American!" He smiled as though that explained
all.

"American now, yes." Gideon forced himself to smile. He
hadn't always been. "Thanks for stopping, but I'm fine."

"Have a good day, then!" His tiny car motored off down
the road.

Gideon sat on the hill, staring off into the brightening day
and let the feel and scent of his homeland sink into him. A
door he'd shut tight and locked a long time ago opened a
little and he couldn't stop it. Not all the religious recitations
in the world could prevent that door from swinging wide and
letting all the memories flood back in.

*He could still remember the way her skirts had felt in his
hands. . . .*

He'd been ten when his mother had met Odran. Gideon's
father had been dead for several years and he guessed, now
that he looked back on it, his mother had been lonely. His
father had been Phaendir, of course, and his mother human.

The new man was fae.

The Phaendir and the fae were mortal enemies, Labrai having put His hand on the Phaendir as His chosen people. Apparently his mother, even though she'd been with a Phaendir
and had a Phaendir as a son, hadn't received the memo. The
fae man's name had been Odran Roarke ó Séaghdha and he'd
belonged to the Seelie Court. His magick had been the ability
to make crops grow stronger and faster. A mundane skill in
these times of chemicals and high-tech farming equipment,
but it had been highly valued back in those days.

Gideon remembered peering from around the bushes near
his mother's house at the two of them laughing and kissing,
the rage boiling up from the depths of his stomach. He had
hated Odran so much that his head would throb in pain as he
thought about all the ways to rid him from his mother's life.

When Gideon had asked his mother how she could stand to let a fae touch her, she'd always said he was Seelie and good, of the light court.

But not all had been good and light in their relationship. They had seemed to hate each other as much as they loved each other and their relationship had been full of drama and occasional violence. Gideon would return home some days to find his mother trying to hide a bruise on her face or her arm, sometimes a split lip or a cut she would explain away by saying she'd tripped or done something clumsy. Gideon knew what was happening, yet she always took Odran back after they fought.

Gideon had been only eight, but he'd plotted Odran's murder endlessly. One night when Odran had been sleeping beside his mother, he'd crept into the room and held a rusty blade to Odran's neck, but he hadn't been able to bring himself to cut down into the flesh. He'd been too young back then, too weak. He'd worried too much about his mother's heart and how she would look at him if he murdered her lover. His hand had shook and he'd run crying from the room.

That night haunted him. He should have done it, and if he'd been able to see what had been coming, he would've. Even now he fantasized that the night had gone differently, that he'd stabbed the fae in the throat and watched his blood gush.

But he hadn't, and one day Gideon had come home to find his mother broken on the floor of the middle of their house, a shard of pottery sticking out of her head above her open, unseeing eyes.

Gideon had gone to live with the Phaendir.

Odran Roarke ó Séaghdha had not lived to see the construction of Piefferburg. When he'd been caught he'd had a bad case of Watt Syndrome, but that's not what he'd died from. Instead he'd suffered an . . . accident. It had been Gideon's first such arrangement, definitely not his last.

Gideon lifted his head from where he'd dropped his forehead onto his knees and realized his cheeks were wet with tears. Looking up into the sky he saw that he'd been sitting there until well after noon. He had no time for this. He pushed to his feet, brushed the grass from his pants, and walked down the hill to his car.

His flight wasn't until tomorrow morning. He'd go check out the piece in the Lia Fáil, meet with whomever there was to meet with, then go sleep in his hotel room until it was time to leave this Labrai-forsaken place.

TEAMHAIR na Rí, the Hill of Tara, was empty of tourists on this weekday afternoon. Gideon stood looking at the so-called Stone of Destiny and curled his lip. This was the fae coronation stone, said to "sing" when the rightful heir to the fae throne touched it. It was one of quite a few fae artifacts that humans loved to ooh and ahh over when on their vacations, all the while paying the Phaendir huge sums of money to keep the fae well away from them in real life.

Stonehenge was, of course, the greatest of all sacred fae sites. Once upon a time it had been a portal to other places and times. Now it was a bunch of big, broken rocks, but that didn't stop the humans from dropping their jaws over it. Little did the tourists know that the Phaendir had had as large a part in the construction and magicking of those standing stones as the fae. Because the construction had occurred when the fae and Phaendir had been allied, it was a shameful thing for the Phaendir and not talked about—those dark times before Labrai had shone His brilliant light upon His people.

He circled the Lia Fáil, looking for some hint of the *bosca fadbh*, but he could find nothing. The Stone of Destiny just looked like a big rock. That's all. Frowning, he knelt and examined the base of the stone. Still, nothing.

Blowing out an exasperated breath, Gideon flipped open his cell phone to call Máire. Had the bitch been toying with him? Had he made this trip, forced himself to explore painful memories, for nothing? Was this some sick, twisted game of a sick, twisted free fae? He wouldn't doubt it.

He'd hunt her down and tear her to shreds for wasting his time and making him revisit his homeland.

"Well, and if it isn't the great archdirector of the Phaendir here to look at our pretty stone."

Gideon stilled, mid-number punch. He recognized that voice as the one who'd called him before Máire had met him at the Cathedral of the Overseer. The heavy Irish accent. How the hell had the man come up behind him so fast? The fae had made no sound and there weren't exactly a wealth of hiding places around here. No matter.

Gideon snapped the phone shut and pivoted. The man was huge—tall and broad—seeming twice the size of Gideon's own medium frame. He had thick, wavy red hair, pale skin, and blue eyes. "Liam."

His red eyebrows rose into his hairline. "I am Liam. Liam Connall Deaglan Mag Aoidh."

"Another damn fae who escaped the Great Sweep."

"Be proud to meet me. There are not many of us." His tone and the smile that accompanied them were mocking.

"Why did you give me your full name, Liam Connall Deaglan Mag Aoidh?" He made sure to pronounce every syllable perfectly.

Liam made a scoffing sound. "Once knowing the full name of a fae meant something, especially to our enemy, the Phaendir. Those days are over." He inclined his head. "I honor you with my full name, Gideon P. Amberdoyal, as a sign of trust. What does the *P* stand for?"

Gideon's eyes narrowed. He wasn't going to honor this fae with his full name in return, not for all the money in the world. He gestured angrily at the hunk of rock behind him. "Máire told me the piece of the *bosca fadbh* is stuck in the Lia Fáil, but she lied. Typical." He spat the last word.

"You don't have the eyes to see, Amberdoyal. You're too blinded by hatred."

"Are you some of kind of guru? Do I have to listen to

some vague spiritual bullshit now? Will you tell me the secret to inner peace?"

"You're well past such things now. There's no hope for you."

"And I'm supposed to respect what you say? Máire told me why you don't want the walls to fall. You'll be reaped by the Wild Hunt immediately for murdering your own people." He snorted. "You have no right to take any sort of spiritual stance."

Liam shook his head. "You don't have the slightest clue what you're talking about, man. And Máire, by the way, is missing."

"Missing?"

"She's missed her check-in. Have you heard from her?"

Gideon didn't care. He shifted impatiently. "Where's the damn piece. I'm not sending any help from the Phaendir until I see it with my own eyes."

"Then you'll have to come after dark. You're in luck. There should be moonlight tonight."

Gideon rubbed his face with both hands and counted to ten. "Goody. I can't wait to spend more time with you people."

"I know all you want is to toss the lot of us into Piefferburg, but that would be unwise. We're on the same page on this, Amberdoyal. We can help you. We *have* been helping you."

"How do you know I don't have fifty Phaendir stationed around this hill right now, ready to make you show us where the rest of you are?"

Liam smiled wolfishly. "First, because we've had you followed from the airport, Amberdoyal. Sitting on that embankment for so long was really boring for my people, by the way." He tipped his head to the side. "Although I have to admit I'm curious to know what you were crying about."

Gideon glowered, his hands flexing.

"Second, we own this hill and the surrounding area. It is ours. Every inch. No one gets near the Stone of Destiny that we don't know about it." He raised his eyebrows. "Meet you here at midnight?"

Gideon nodded. "Fine. Midnight."

"IT'S almost midnight. We should leave soon." Charlotte went into a coughing fit at the window overlooking the street in Kilmessan where they'd rented rooms for the night. David came up behind her and braced her upper arms as if to stop the racking coughs that were tearing her lungs to shreds.

When her hands came away, they were bloody.

She stared at her red palms, despair growing in the pit of her stomach. She was going to die in her midtwenties. She'd finally fallen in love and what was her reward? Fucking death.

God, it made her so angry.

Calum brought her a damp washcloth and she used it to wipe her skin off. "I can't believe this." Her voice shook.

"I can understand your fear."

She rounded on David. "Oh, this isn't fear. *This is rage.* This is so unbelievably unfair! I haven't done anything but fall in love. Kieran never did anything but have the misfortune to be born a twin to a psychopath!"

David held up a hand. "I know." He glanced out the window at the silent streets of Kilmessan. "So let's get this done and get you back into Piefferburg to Kieran so you can find a way to break the curse."

Charlotte stood for a moment, fists clenched. Then she collapsed back to sit on the edge of the bed. She stared at the floor for several moments while Calum and David studied her. "There's no way to break the curse."

Calum spread his hands. "In faerie, there's always a way to break a curse."

She took in a deep, steadying breath. Maybe he was right. Maybe there would be a way out of this mess. Maybe there would be a happily-ever-after for her and Kieran.

Maybe.

Hope sprang eternal.

"It's almost midnight, like you said," said Calum. "We should go."

She stood. "Then let's go get it."

SOMEONE knocked on Kieran's door. When he got up to answer it a coughing fit assailed him. He leaned against the couch and coughed until blood marked his palm.

He stared at it. "Damn it," he whispered.

Was this happening to Charlotte? He'd had centuries to get used to the idea that this might be the way he'd exit, centuries to adjust—if one could adjust—to the idea of joining the slaugh.

Wherever she was, Charlotte had to be terrified.

"Come back to me." The whisper sounded pained to his own ears.

The knocking sounded again. He straightened and answered it. The Piefferburg witch stood on the other side, grinning at him. Kieran glowered back. If she hadn't come with a solution to this mess, she needed to leave. Now.

"What?" he barked at her.

"I found a way to break to the curse for your lady, but you're not going to like it. If you do this, Charlotte will be set free. You, however, will not."

Relief surged through him. He would do anything to get Charlotte out of this. "What is it?"

"You must kill yourself before the curse kills you. If you do that, Charlotte will go free."

TWENTY-FIVE

THE hill was dark when they reached the base, though bright moonlight bathed the area, bleaching everything pale silver. Charlotte, David, and Calum had come prepared with charmed iron weapons. Weapons, David said, they'd dug up from the stores of fae artifacts kept by the HFF after his experience in Israel. Apparently he never left home without them now.

She didn't blame him.

Creeped out, she held tight onto her own charmed iron dagger, something that had likely been made either by Aeric O'Malley or his father many centuries ago. The edge had been sharpened to the point of hellishness and that made her feel good. An extra one was snuggled in a leather sheath on her belt. That made her feel even better.

By the time they reached the top of the hill her chest throbbed and her breath came shallow. If they were jumped by any hostile fae she was probably dead meat.

Not that it would be much of a change from her current state.

They made their way to the Stone of Destiny, a tall chunk of stone rising in the moonlight.

David's eyes seemed unnaturally bright. For a human, he seemed to care so much about the fae and obtaining their freedom. It was clear how excited he was by the prospect they might be closing in on the final piece of the *bosca fadbh*. Three weeks ago someone like David would have confounded her. Now she shared his joy.

He licked his lower lip. "Okay, let's get looking."

They circled the stone, looking for some hint of the final piece. Calum ran his hands over it, muttering to himself in the ancient language she'd come to recognize as Old Maejian.

"Nothing." Charlotte rocked back on her heels. "I don't see any—*Wait*." Her gaze had been caught by the tiny glint in the moonlight, a sliver, really, at the base of the stone. "What's that?"

David and Calum hurried over to her.

"Where? Oh, there," Calum whispered in near reverence. "Sweet Lady. There it is. I can't believe it."

It was almost completely embedded in the stone. To get it out someone would have to take a sledgehammer to the rock itself, though she doubted even that would work, considering the enchantment it was under.

"Touch it," David urged.

Hesitant, not knowing what to expect, she reached out and put her index finger on the moonlit sliver. Immediately the chunk of metal strained toward her, pushing through the rock as though it were butter. Startled, she snatched her hand away. "Oh, my god."

"*Indeed*. Fancy meeting you here, Charlotte."

Charlotte froze at the sound of Gideon Amberdoyal's voice behind her. Fast as lightning, she jerked the partially extracted piece into her hand. It left a hole in the stone and rock crumbles on the ground. She pushed it into her bra. "Run!"

She, David, and Calum bolted.

Only to be stopped short by four huge fae men. She came nose-to-massive-chest with a hulking, red-haired monstrosity. Her hand tightened on the handle of her blade, but this would be the second person she'd stabbed in the last twenty-four hours. The image of Máire's dead face still haunted her. It made her hesitate.

The red-haired man grabbed her wrists in a grip so hard it made her vision go dark for a moment. To either side of her, Calum and David fought. The clang of charmed iron against whatever weapons the rogue fae carried rang through the air punctuated by gasps, groans, and curses.

Looked like Calum and David were losing.

Gideon walked toward her. "Charlotte, meet Liam. Liam, Charlotte."

How the hell had Gideon known the piece was here? Apparently the rogue fae and the Phaendir were working together now? Did that mean she'd never get back into Piefferburg? Her mind spun out a hundred different questions in about a second and a half.

"You have something of ours." Gideon held out his hand. "Hand it over and maybe we'll let you live." He smiled. "Oh, that's right, you're not going to live, are you, Charlotte? *You're dying for the love of a fae.*" He leaned in and snarled into her face. "Serves you right."

No, it doesn't serve me right. None of this is right. Rage boiled up from deep within her. The bad guys were not going to win this one. She was through hesitating. Through with mercy. Hell, she was going to be joining the slaugh soon, anyway. She might as well give this everything she had.

She brought her knee up hard and fast, nailing Liam's balls with every ounce of strength she had. The bigger the man, the bigger the balls. Releasing her, he doubled over, bellowing with surprise and pain, then went breathless. Wheezing, he dropped to his knees. She brought the blade down into his massive body. Her aim wasn't the best, but it served.

The dagger sank into the back of his shoulder so deep she couldn't pull it out again.

She whirled to face Gideon who had gone from innocuous to criminally insane in under two seconds. The veins in his receding hairline pulsed, his eyes were narrowed to slits, and a muscle in his tightly clenched jaw jumped. Charlotte had no doubt he was thinking very gruesome thoughts about all the ways he wanted to torture her to death. She was certain that, if given the chance, he'd act every single one of them out.

"Give me the piece, Charlotte." His voice was low and he enunciated every syllable clearly. He lowered his weak chin and looked at her from the top edges of his eyes. *Oh, crap.* And she'd thought he couldn't get any creepier looking; now he looked like something from a horror movie.

She took another step back.

Behind her one of the fae men lunged for her, only to be blocked by Calum, who gave a roar similar to something she would imagine a Celt warrior in battle might emit, sending the blade of his charmed iron short sword though the man like a hot knife through ice cream.

She didn't have a sword, but she did have an extra dagger hidden in a sheath under her coat. She yanked it and held it up to Gideon. "Don't come any closer. I've stabbed two people in the last twenty-four hours. Don't think I won't do it again."

Gideon took another step closer to her. Apparently he thought she was bluffing. "I'm not fae. Charmed iron doesn't work on me."

"But I bet the blade wouldn't do you much good."

"Let's see how you do with it sticking out of your heart." He ran toward her.

Her breath seized in her throat and she twisted away from him. He couldn't get hold of her weapon. She had no doubt that would not go well for her. He grabbed her by her collar and, oh, man, he was stronger than he looked. She shrieked as he whipped her around and tried to punch her.

She blocked his punch with her forearm and staggered

back. She needed to call on the training that Kieran had given her, the small amount of it there was. Except . . . she couldn't remember a thing.

He lunged at her again, his eyes all crazy and his deceptively strong arms coming around her, long, thin hands reaching for her dagger. She tried to twist away from him, but it was like freeing herself from concrete. She flailed and kicked as hard as she could.

His hand closed around her hand, fingers inching to the handle of the weapon. Panic lodged her heart behind her tonsils. She managed to find some wiggle room and brought her elbow back hard into his solar plexus. Gideon *oofed*, probably more in surprise than anything else. Either way, it gave her the ability to twist free of him.

She rounded, her heart pounding and her chest tight and painful from the exertion. While she had a slight advantage, she raised the knife. In the same moment David came from the side and tackled him. They rolled on the ground at the base of the Stone of Destiny, punching and kicking until Charlotte couldn't tell who was on top and who was on the bottom. Then, suddenly, they both lay still.

Everything went still.

Dark mounds scattered about her, like a battlefield after a war. She looked around, trying to locate Calum. Then the mound with Gideon and David shifted. Someone moaned, started to stand . . .

Her grip tightened on the handle of the knife.

The man groaned again, put a hand to his head and straightened. "Charlotte?" David's voice.

Relief poured through her. She coughed a few times and staggered toward him. Gideon lay motionless in the moonlight, blood soaking his white shirt. "Is he dead?"

"I don't know. Calum—" David knelt by a nearby fallen man.

Charlotte rushed to his side to watch him turn his friend over onto his back. Calum had a charmed iron dagger stuck into his chest.

"I don't think . . . I can . . . heal this one. Too deep. Hit something . . . I need." His words came out on agonized puffs of air.

"No, Calum." David's voice broke. "Come on. You've been through worse than this."

Calum smiled. "Been . . . a good . . . run, man." Blood dribbled from the corner of his mouth.

"No, Calum!"

"Break those . . . walls for . . . me." The light faded from his eyes and they went glassy and cold.

"*Calum.*" David collapsed over Calum's body, his head bowed. "Damn it."

Charlotte pressed a hand to her mouth and rose, feeling responsible for this. "I'm so sorry, David."

David said nothing for several long moments. Finally he lifted his head and closed Calum's eyelids—reminding her acutely of finding her father.

Had that only been a day ago? It felt like forever.

He stood. "Calum knew the risks when he made the decision to come along." He raised his gaze to hers. "You have the piece?"

She touched her breast. It was uncomfortable and bulky tucked in her bra. "Yes."

He began to stride away from the Stone of Destiny. "Then let's not let Calum's death be wasted. Come on."

"What about his body?" Charlotte hurried after him, her breath coming in shallow, painful gasps.

"It's just a husk. Calum's not in it anymore. He wouldn't care what we did with it, but I'll call the local HFF. They'll come and take it away. Give him a proper burial. Now it's more important than ever we break those walls, Charlotte. We need to get you back into Piefferburg."

"How? The Phaendir know I'm their enemy now. They'll never let me back in."

He shook his head. "We don't know that. Gideon seemed pretty surprised to find you here. I know I wounded him really badly. I may have even killed him." He glanced down at his blood-covered shirt and pants. "All this is his. You might still have a shot, but we need to hurry."

"Why is it more important than ever that we break the walls, David?"

He stopped and looked at her. "You don't know? Any fae that dies outside the walls of Piefferburg walks between the worlds because the Wild Hunt can't reap them. Calum won't be able to get to the Netherworld until the walls break."

Horrified, she looked back at the body. Calum would be like a ghost, but it was better than becoming one of the slaugh. Maybe.

"Don't you want to check to see if Amberdoyal is alive?"

"Why? If he's still alive, do you want to finish him off?" He gave a bitter laugh at the look on her face. "Yeah, I thought not. Listen, I know what a snake he is, but not even I'm that cold. No way could I slit a dying man's throat, not even Gideon P. Amberdoyal's."

She stared at Gideon's body.

When she looked back at David, he was already striding away from her, toward the rental car. She followed him, coughing into her hand so hard her breath came out an agonized wheeze.

"YOU want to . . . what?" Aislinn appeared serene as she sat in her high-backed chair with her hands folded in her lap and her black and silver skirts arranged artfully around her. Her eyes reflected her emotional reaction to Kieran's words, however. Turmoil.

He understood. That's what he felt, too.

"It's the only way to free Charlotte."

Aislinn shifted in her seat, her heavy gown rustling. "This is your only option?"

"I wouldn't be mentioning it if I had any other. This isn't exactly the outcome I wanted."

"I wanted you to find love and be able to live to the end of your natural life span. The whole package. Happily ever after."

"Unrealistic, as it turns out."

Aislinn's breath caught and she looked away. Kieran thought he'd glimpsed tears in her eyes. Clearing her throat, she looked back at him. "When do you want to do it?"

"Soon."

"Don't you think Charlotte might come back to Piefferburg?"

"Maybe." He pressed his lips together. Seeing her again and then having to leave her. *Lady.* It would be hell. "That's why I want to do it soon."

"You have no idea if she's suffering the effects of the curse?"

He shook his head. "It's possible I'm the only one in love. In that case, she'd be unaffected."

"If you don't know whether or not she's affected, why—"

"Rush it? Why not? My death is going to happen sooner or later, and I can't take the chance."

Aislinn bit her lower lip for a moment. "Right."

"I don't know what's going on with Charlotte and it's killing me. All I know is she had a run-in with that rogue fae, Máire, whom she somehow killed, and that her father is dead. She hasn't come back to Piefferburg, and not knowing if she's all right is driving me insane."

"Maybe she *is* suffering under the curse and she's gone to pull the final piece of the *bosca fadbh*."

The thought had crossed his mind and it chilled his blood. If Máire had known where the piece was through her connection with her sister, it was possible other rogue fae knew the location, too. Charlotte wouldn't stand a chance against odds like that, especially if the curse was making her sick.

"Maybe," he answered. "There's no way to know."

"How do you want to . . . do this?"

"I don't know. All I know is I can't do it on my own."

"What do you mean?"

"I can't do this by myself." He couldn't even bring himself to say the word *suicide*. He loved life too much. "I can't take my own life by my own hand, not even under these circumstances."

"You want to put that on someone else, Kieran? That's a horrible weight to have to bear—"

"There are plenty of fae in the Black Tower who would be happy to do it and you know it, lots of Unseelie whose magick yearns to spill life."

She looked down into her lap and nodded. "You're right. I'll find someone."

"Thank you."

"You say soon. So, when?"

He drew a breath. "Tomorrow."

TWENTY-SIX

DAVID and Charlotte took the first available plane out of Dublin in the morning and arrived in Protection City late in the afternoon. It had been a twelve-hour flight all in all, with a stop in New York, and Charlotte was exhausted. She'd slept fitfully on both flights and hadn't been able to eat much. The effects of the curse were increasing.

She was glad David was taking charge because she felt—literally—dead on her feet. He rented a car and took her to a motel, where he rented a room, told her to sleep, and that he'd be back soon.

Her head hit the pillow and she was out.

It seemed like two seconds later he woke her, pushed her into the bathroom after shoving several shopping bags into her hands. "I bought you fresh clothes. I think I got the size right, but it's been a while since I bought clothes for a woman."

She took them with a tired smile. "I'm sure they're fine." Then she disappeared into the bathroom.

He'd done great. The jeans and sweater fit perfectly. He'd

even nailed the undergarments. He'd gone with a sports bra—wise. The boots were a little big, but she'd survive. After she'd dried her hair and put some moisturizing lotion on her face, she almost felt human again.

"Better?" she asked, stepping out of the bathroom.

"I bet you feel better." He was sitting at the little table, looking tense. She didn't blame him. "You're presentable enough for the Phaendir. Where do you intend to put the piece?"

She blinked. She'd forgotten the policy to search everyone's bodies and belongings. "Right. Good question." She wasn't exactly on top of her mental game at the moment.

He frowned at her. "You have very pretty, thick hair."

She touched the end of a dark, curling tendril. That was an odd change of subject. "Thanks."

"Ever wear it up?"

"Yes. I always did . . . before." Her voice went soft. She'd only started wearing it down after Kieran had complimented her on how beautiful it was and told her she shouldn't hide it.

"The piece isn't very big. If I helped you, you could probably conceal it in your hair."

Oh. She nodded. "It's worth a try."

After another trip to the store for bobby pins and a few fumbling attempts, they managed to do it. The piece was now secreted on top of her head, in an artful mass of tangled curls that looked a little formal for jeans and a sweater, but would work.

She glanced longingly at the bed.

David guided her toward the door. "You can sleep when you get to the Black Tower."

She could sleep when she was dead. Oh, no, wait, she couldn't. She'd be part of the slaugh. Probably not a lot of sleeping involved with that.

She half turned toward him once they got outside. "I wish you could come in with me."

A wistful expression overcame his face for a moment. "I wish I could, too. However, I'm on the Phaendir's most wanted list."

She grinned. "I bet."

"In fact, I can't go any farther than Protection City. Even coming here was a huge risk. I called you a cab. It will take you to Phaendir Headquarters. Time is of the essence. We don't know if Gideon is alive or dead. If he survived, he may have already alerted headquarters not to allow you in. If he's dead, they may have been notified and will be on guard. That wouldn't be good either."

Truth was, this was a huge risk for her, too. She had no idea what to expect when she arrived at Phaendir Headquarters. Of course, the risk was worth it—this was the fae's last chance at freedom. If someone had told her a month ago she'd be in this position, would care so much about the outcome of the situation, she'd have told them they were smoking something.

David gave her a sheaf of papers in a manila envelope, her excuse for needing to go back into Piefferburg. Apparently he'd worked on it while she'd been sleeping. She'd taken a peek and they looked pretty damn convincing . . . as long as no one really examined them.

The cab pulled up, they said good-bye, and she got in. David stood in front of the door of the room, his hands in the pockets of his jeans, fading into the distance.

Next stop, Phaendir Headquarters.

GIDEON opened his eyes to white. Panicked, he started to sit up, only to be pushed back down.

"You just settle in there, sir. You've been stabbed almost clean through. Amazing you're even drawing breath."

His gaze fixed on the human nurse scowling down at him. "Where am I? What happened?"

She set her hands on her very wide hips. "Well, now, you're the one going to have to be telling *us* what's going on. You were dumped in front of our hospital sometime during the night."

"Dumped?" he echoed, slumping against the pillows. Pain stabbed through his side and he cried out.

The nurse adjusted something on the IV drip, muttering to herself about how she never thought she'd be giving comfort to the head of the bloody Phaendir.

"You know who I am."

She jerked her chin at him. "Had your wallet on you, luckily. Archdirector of the Phaendir, right?"

He nodded.

"You're not real popular over here, right? We're wantin' you to give us back our fae." She turned away from him, moving angrily. "Sucked the magick out of this land, you did. Expect your doctor shortly. The garda, too, I have no doubt." With one last hostile glance at him, she left the room.

Gideon searched his memory for clues to what had happened. This wasn't the first time he'd woken in a hospital room, except the last time he'd been the one to put himself there. He'd poisoned himself in order to set up Brother Maddoc for attempted murder. The last thing he remembered from the previous night was rolling around on the ground near the Stone of Destiny with that damned HFF man, David Sullivan. Then the sharp pain. Hot blood. Realizing it was his own spilling out of him.

So, he'd been stabbed and brought to the hospital by some unknown party. Not David, surely. Not . . . Charlotte Bennett.

Charlotte.

Charlotte Bennett had been there last night. She'd pulled the piece.

He glanced out the window. It was full dark. He had no idea what time it was, or even what day it was. Ireland was five hours ahead of Protection City. It might still be afternoon there.

Charlotte could be back already. With the piece.

Spying his clothing on a nearby chair, he lunged out of bed, only to be stopped short by the IV hooked up to him. He leaned over, his wound screaming with pain. He had to get to his cell phone in the pocket of his slacks. He had to call headquarters and warn them not to let Charlotte Bennett into Piefferburg. He stretched as far as his IV would let him, but his pants were just out of reach. The tips of his fingers barely grazed the fabric.

Making a frustrated, grunting noise, he gripped the end of the IV, intending to rip it out, when the doctor walked in.

"Whoa, wait a minute," she said, rushing toward him with her arms out. "You don't want to do that."

"Yes, I do," Gideon gritted out.

"Get back into bed right now." She was small, but she had presence. She loomed over him, her dark eyes snapping. *"Right now."*

He slumped against the side of the bed, his dressing gown flapping open. "I need my cell phone. In the pocket of my pants."

"Are you insane? Is the call you have to make worth your life?"

"Yes." He nodded. "It is."

She sighed and pointed at the bed. "Lay down and I'll fetch it for you."

"But—"

"Do it, or I'll throw your phone in the toilet."

Rage enveloped him for a moment, but he knew better than to argue. He climbed back into the bed and pulled the covers over himself. His wound shot fresh bolts of pain through him. Light-headedness made him sag backward. The room spun.

The doctor fished out his cell phone and slapped it into his palm. "I don't want to see you out of that bed again."

Ignoring her, he flipped it open and speed-dialed headquarters, hoping it wasn't already too late.

"I just need to deliver these papers to the Business Council." Charlotte handed over the manila envelope to Brother Merion, apparently Gideon's second-in-command.

Merion took her envelope and peered down his narrow

nose at her. Thick black glasses half hid his husky blue eyes. "You're not on our list."

"I wasn't expecting to have to come back. Believe me"—she turned her head and coughed, hoped like hell she wouldn't have an attack right now—"I don't want to be here. I'm feeling under the weather and would much rather be at home on my couch. However, as you know, there's no mail service between Piefferburg and the rest of the world. I have to take this in by hand. It's the tail end of the project I did for them."

"Yes." He drew out the word so it sounded like *yeeeesssss*, but she was pretty sure he hadn't heard a thing she'd just said. He'd pulled the papers from the envelope and was now looking over them.

Charlotte fought the urge to fidget as she sat stiffly in front of his desk. She was just glad no one had taken her into custody yet.

After what seemed like an eternity, he put the papers aside, folded his thin, knobby hands on the desk, and looked up at her. "We can expect you to exit tomorrow morning?"

No. Never, actually. "Perhaps sooner than that, this evening, if I can. I'm sick and want to spend the night in a nice, cozy hotel room in Protection City. Traveling has done me in. As long as the Business Council doesn't need me for anything else, I'll drop these papers and be right back out."

He laughed knowingly, a fake sound that raised all the hair on the back of her neck. "I can understand that. No one wants to spend more time in there than they must."

"You said it."

"I'll accompany you to the gates."

Great. She rose. "Thank you."

They left headquarters and started toward the gates, walking down the gravel road that led past the creepy Phaendir graveyard and church that always had black vultures circling in the sky above it. They made small talk along the way, the kind you make with people you don't know in order to avoid uncomfortable silence. How she loved to talk about the weather when she was days away from dying and had a piece of the *bosca fadbh* stuck in her hair.

They finally reached the gates. This time, instead of being the last place on Earth she wanted to enter, they were the gateway to love . . . if only for a little while.

"Only one more thing," said Brother Merion turning toward her.

"The search of my belongings."

"Yes. My apologies. We can't be too careful."

"I totally understand."

His thin, ghoulish hands on her during the pat down made her vomit a little in her mouth, but he never checked her hair. He didn't even say a word about the griffin pendant around her neck. After he'd rummaged through her purse and found nothing, he signaled the Phaendir guards and the gates slowly began to swing open.

"Well, thanks for everything." Charlotte clutched her fake sheaf of papers and shouldered her purse. "See you soon."

"Be careful in there."

"Oh, always." She tossed a careless smile over her shoulder and walked toward the gates. Only fifteen feet and she was in the clear.

Behind her, she heard his cell phone ring. Brother Merion answered it and his voice immediately rose in alarm.

Oh, no. That didn't sound good. The gates were ten feet away. She quickened her pace. Maybe Merion's distressed tone of voice didn't have anything to do with her.

"Wait!" called Merion. "Close the gates! Stop her!"

Or maybe it did.

The gates in front of her creaked to a halt and reversed direction. *No way.* She bolted. Every step she took seemed to close the tiny space even more. Panic ripped through her, making her heart pound. Two guards stepped in front of her, but she hadn't come this far to be stopped now. She barreled right into them, thrusting the heel of her hand into one of the men's noses, and barely slipped through the narrow space of the closing gates to the sound of agonized bellows of pain and Merion shouting obscenities at the Phaendir guards.

She hadn't been fast enough.

The other guard grabbed her arm and yanked her toward him before she could get all the way to the Piefferburg side. She gave the Phaendir a vicious kick to free herself and he grabbed her ankle instead. With a shriek of surprise, Charlotte went down on her stomach, pain screaming through her body, and the guard pulled her toward him. Her fingers dug into the gravel as she was dragged backward, out of Piefferburg. The red caps grabbed her hands and pulled her in the opposite direction, trying to keep her in. For a moment she felt like taffy. The gates were almost closed by now. She kicked her shoe off and the Phaendir guard's grip went with it. His hand, with her shoe, disappeared into the rapidly closing space.

She flipped over just in time to see Merion peering into the sliver of area still between the gates, his face and eyes livid. The red caps put themselves between her and him, looking one hundred percent their bad reputation. Charlotte could see Merion's angry glare through the crack right before the red caps slammed it the rest of the way shut with a smile.

She collapsed, the world going darker as the red caps peered curiously into her face. Then everything went black.

TWENTY-SEVEN

GIDEON'S hand clenched on his cell phone. Plastic cracked. He gritted his teeth, the blood rushing to his face, roaring through his ears. Rage poured through him, making his veins bulge and a hard rushing sound surge through his head.

The phone cracked again in his hand and the screen went dark. He threw it across the room where it hit the opposite wall and shattered. If Merion had been anywhere close to him in this moment, he'd be dead.

Vaguely he noticed that his wound throbbed with pain. No matter. He almost ripped the IV from his arm, but good sense reigned at the last moment and he pulled it out carefully instead, but it was an effort. He had no patience right now.

No patience and no mercy.

He needed to get back to Protection City *now*.

ONE of the hulking red cap guards laid Charlotte onto Kieran's bed. Kieran leaned over her, touching her forehead and throat with his fingers. She felt warm to his touch, her breathing shallow.

He rounded on the guards. "What the hell happened?"

"We're not sure. All we know is she was hell-bent on getting into Piefferburg and the Phaendir were hell-bent on trying to prevent it. She barely made it in. Once she was in, she just passed out."

He glanced at her and pushed a hand through his hair. "Okay. Thanks for your help."

They nodded and left the room.

He turned back to Charlotte, sinking down on the bed beside her. Cupping her cheek, he moved her face toward him. "Charlotte? Charlotte, baby, wake up."

She roused a little, her eyelids fluttering open. "Kieran?"

He wrapped his arms around her and held on like he never had to let her go, like in an hour he hadn't planned to doom himself to an eternity without her. He buried his nose against her skin and inhaled as though he could hold on to her scent forever. Her being here was going to make things much, much harder.

Cradling her face in his hands, he slid his lips over hers slowly, savoring her. She shivered against him and pressed her mouth more firmly to his, asking for more. He was willing to give it.

When he'd kissed her enough to content himself—for the moment—he rested his forehead against hers. "Charlotte, what are you doing back here?"

Gently she pulled away from him and put her hand on top of her hair, pulling bobby pins out and dropping them onto the bed. Little by little her thick, pretty hair fell in curling tendrils around her shoulders.

Then the final piece of the *bosca fadbh* lay in her palm.

He stared at it, the blood leaving his face and the breath vacating his lungs. *"Ní chreidim é."* Finally, he looked up at her. "I don't believe it."

"I pulled it out of the Stone of Destiny."

"How did you do it?" He pressed his hands to hers. *Lady,*

this meant she was suffering from the curse, too. Fuck. That's probably why she'd passed out and why those dark circles were under her eyes.

"It's a long story."

"I know about Máire and your father."

"How?"

"Long story."

After they'd caught each other up on what had happened while she'd been gone. He pulled her against him. "I'm not sorry I met you, Charlotte, but I'm fucking sorry you ever met me."

She looked up him. "I'm not sorry."

"You're dying."

She touched his cheek. "I'm still not sorry. You're the first man I've ever loved. Lots of people go to their graves never knowing what it is to be truly in love. At least I can say I've experienced it. That's a precious thing, maybe something worth dying for."

"I do love you, Charlotte."

"I love you, too, Kieran." She paused, drawing a breath. "There's a bright side." She looked up at him, smiling, though it didn't reach her eyes.

"What's that?"

"At least we'll join the slaugh together."

His lips twisted. "I don't think that's much of a bright side."

"No. You're right, not really."

He dropped his head to hers, rubbing his lips slowly over hers, savoring the taste of her, before he parted her lips and slipped his tongue in to rub up against hers. She shifted on the bed, making a sound of hunger in the back of her throat. Her hands came up around his shoulders, her fingers curling into the hair at his nape. He clasped her waist and slanted his mouth over hers, kissing her deeper.

Gods, this was cruel.

He broke the kiss and sagged against her, the strength going out of him. It had been hard enough knowing he'd never see her again. Now that she was back, it was going to be hell having to say good-bye. He wanted to stay with her, find out everything there was about her. He wanted to learn all the ways to make her laugh, to make her moan his name in passion. He wanted years with Charlotte, centuries.

They only had hours.

"Are you okay?"

He looked down into her concerned face. "Not really."

"Yeah, me neither." She pressed her lips together. "We need to deliver the piece to the queen."

He kissed her forehead, tightening his arms around her. "Soon. I want a little time with you first, as much as we can get."

She smiled and snuggled against him. "I never would have thought you and I would end up this way, not after I punched you the first time we met."

He chuckled, running his hand up and down her arm. "The *first* time we met you definitely didn't punch me."

She looked up at him, blushing. "You mean the dream? That doesn't count."

"Princess, I can't get it out of my head. It counts in my book."

She rested her head against his chest. "Sadly, that dream sex was the best sex I'd ever had." She paused. "Well, until I had the real thing with you."

"Me, too, Charlotte."

"What?" She glanced up at him. "Come on, you must have been with hundreds of women over your lifetime." She scowled. "In fact, I don't even want to think about how many."

He tipped her chin up, forcing her to look at him. "But I've only ever loved one." He grinned. "Do you need more proof?"

"No. I only need you."

He kissed her again and held her for a long time in silence, pretending they weren't both afflicted by a curse and they didn't have the final piece of the *bosca fadbh* to deliver.

That they could just be a man and a woman in love, enjoying the warmth of each other for a few tender, blissful minutes.

AISLINN looked down at the piece Kieran had laid in her lap and began to sob.

Kieran stepped back, dumbfounded. He'd only known Aislinn since she'd taken the Shadow Throne. Since that day she'd been completely poised and, while compassionate, mostly cool and detached. This reaction was nothing at all like detached. This was complete and total relief and joy.

Gabriel knelt at her side and pulled her against him, as though hating to see her cry—even though Kieran was certain these were tears of happiness.

Kieran went to stand near Charlotte, curling her hand protectively in his. The four of them were the only people in the room, something he was sure Aislinn was probably thankful for. This display of emotion completely destroyed the image of composed, controlled leadership she'd attempted to project to the Black Tower.

The Shadow Queen wiped her eyes with a tissue her husband had given her and looked up at Charlotte. "I have no idea how we can repay you for this. You risked your life to get this piece for us, and you did it when you don't even consider yourself fae."

Gabriel stood. "We consider you fae, Charlotte. You're one of us."

She tightened her grip on Kieran's hand. "Thank you. That means so much to me. I never thought it would, but it does."

The queen looked down at the copper piece in her lap. "We have to move quickly now that we have the book and all three pieces of the *bosca fadbh*. The Phaendir will be fast to act to prevent us from opening the back of the Book of Bindings. I need to meet with the Summer Queen immediately." Steel resolution entered her eyes. That was more like the

Aislinn he was accustomed to. "I hope she doesn't give us trouble."

She knew, as did they all, that this was the moment of truth. Would the Summer Queen cooperate with them? Or would she, for reasons only she knew, block the union of the *bosca fadbh* and try to prevent the opening of the Book of Bindings? This was the question they'd been waiting to have answered. Kieran would bet money there would be a fight. He'd been alive a long time and had rarely seen the Summer Queen be cooperative. He'd seen the Black and Rose towers allied even less frequently.

"Kieran, after I've talked with the Summer Queen, you and I will need to meet. Alone." She gave him a meaningful look. "I'm assuming recent events have altered things?"

Charlotte looked at him curiously.

Kieran inclined his head. "Yes, my queen."

Aislinn turned her gaze to Charlotte and her face softened. "Charlotte, I just don't know what to say to you. 'Thank you' seems so weak and empty. Is there anything we can give you?"

"The only thing I want is this damned cursed lifted from me and Kieran."

The queen bit her lower lip. "I wish with everything I am that I had the power to grant that."

Charlotte glanced at Kieran. Her fingers found and played with the gryphon pendant she wore around her throat. "If I can't have a future with him then I want time. I would like for us to spend whatever period of life we have left together."

Kieran pulled her against his chest, one hand going to her nape and the other around her waist in a gesture of protection. Emotion welled up inside him—grief, dark and viscous. He kissed her forehead hard, closing his eyes as her arms came around his waist. "Of course we'll have that," he whispered against her skin, but the words were like heavy stones in the center of his heart.

When the queen spoke next, her voice sounded heavy with tears. "You can have anything within the realm of my ability to give. A quiet place, orders to not disturb you, anything."

Kieran pulled Charlotte out of the room with him, his heart feeling bruised about what had to come—and come soon. They were both battered by the effects of the curse, exhausted, dark circles under their eyes, labored breathing, and pains in their chests. He knew Charlotte had been coughing up blood, just as he had. The symptoms would be getting worse very soon, then even worse. Until neither of them could move, eventually until neither could breathe.

Charlotte's arrival had only delayed the inevitable and made this so much harder. He would make the arrangements with the queen tonight. Charlotte didn't know it, but they only had one more night together.

Tomorrow morning, before Charlotte woke, he would be gone.

CHARLOTTE curled up next to Kieran after a late dinner of roast chicken and vegetables. It had been the first decent meal she'd had since she'd left Piefferburg. Kieran had started a gentle blaze in the fireplace of his bedroom—something she'd noticed many fae seemed to have. They loved their wood burning fireplaces.

With the room lit only by the light from the hearth and the crack and snap of the logs filling the room, they lay together on the bed, talking softly. The only subject they didn't speak of was the obvious one—the slow and inexorable failing of their bodies. It was nicer to pretend that part wasn't happening, though it was hard to ignore.

Charlotte lay on her back. He rested on his side, stroking her hair. He dipped his head and kissed her, his lips skating slowly over hers and igniting warmth throughout her body. He cupped her cheek as he did it, his thumb rubbing her skin.

He broke the kiss and stared into her eyes. Turmoil made them seem darker than they were, matching the emotion that twined so bittersweet with the tenderness she felt for him.

"I never knew love could feel like this," she whispered. "I would do anything for you, sacrifice anything." Without saying it, she meant the curse. She didn't want to die, but the alternative was worse—not sharing love with Kieran.

A haunted look entered his eyes. His gaze shifted, his pupils dilating, and for a moment it appeared as if he were looking past Charlotte, maybe to a future she couldn't see.

She opened her mouth to ask him what was wrong, but he dipped his head and kissed her. "I know exactly what you mean, Charlotte," he murmured against her lips. He caught and held her gaze, speaking fiercely. "I love you so much that I would do anything for you, too, sacrifice anything."

She swallowed hard, the weight of what was to come a little more than she could handle when he looked at her like that—with such love and protectiveness in his eyes and in his voice. "Let's promise one thing, Kieran. Let's do this together, you and I. When the time comes, we'll stay together and face whatever fate befalls us."

His pupils dilated and seemed to turn into black holes for a moment as anger swept over his face. It was gone in a flash, replaced by grief. He dropped his head to the curve of her throat. "Charlotte, I—"

"Promise me." She forced him to look at her. "Please."

He held her gaze for a moment before speaking. "Of course. We'll always be together."

"I just wish we had more time."

He closed his eyes for a moment. "I do, too."

They lapsed into silence. Then Kieran kissed her and soon they couldn't stop. Both of them were sick, yet all that physical pain seemed to wash away in their need for each other. Desire overcame the curse . . . at least for a little while.

Ravenous for the feel of him, Charlotte pushed him back against the mattress, straddling him and pulling her sweater over her head, wanting to feel her bare skin sliding against his. Cupping his face, she lowered her head and slowly rubbed her mouth across his.

With a groan of need, Kieran flipped her and slanted his

mouth hungrily over hers, delving his tongue between her lips. She pulled at his clothes, yanking his shirt up and sliding her hands beneath to find the smooth, warm, muscle-tight skin of his lower back. Then her fingers found the button and zipper of his jeans and undid them, slipping inside to take his length into the palm of her hand.

Slowly, lips exploring every inch of bare flesh revealed, they undressed each other. Once their clothing was just so much material piled on the floor, they touched each other like they could derive sustenance purely from their fingertips on each other's bodies. Kieran stroked her breasts and slipped his hand between her thighs; igniting her until the only sounds she could make were breathy entreaties for more.

Her hands slid down the bunching muscles of his back and upper arms, traced the curl of the tribal tattoos along his side, skated over the curve of his luscious rear, and around to stroke his length until he groaned her name.

Then he slipped between her thighs, cupping the back of her knee as the head of his cock found her entrance and slid deep within. She gasped at the way he stretched her muscles, closing her eyes and arching her spine. Kieran held her gaze steadily as he began to thrust in and out of her. He took her slow and then even slower, his strokes deep into her body and with their gazes locked.

Tears pricked Charlotte's eyes at the intimacy of the act. Not only were their bodies joined, but their hearts and minds, too. How bittersweet to know they could share in something as powerful as this, but that it would only last a short time.

They came together in a powerful climax, backs arching and mouths meshing.

Afterward they twined around each other and Charlotte fell asleep in his arms, ironically feeling happier than she could ever remember feeling.

KIERAN woke a few hours later and pulled himself gently from the tangle of Charlotte's limbs. The light from the dying fire bathed her face and he stared at her in wonder for several minutes. Dark circles marred the skin under her eyes. Fatigue and sickness sat in the lines of her face, but none of it diminished her beauty. Not to him. Her long, dark curling hair fanned out around her face, caught on one bare, dusky nipple. In sleep her lips were pouted, perfect for catching between his teeth.

All he wanted was to crawl back into bed and pull her up against him, make love to her again and again. For the rest of their lives.

But it was time to go. Time for him to take that fatigue and sickness from her body. Lift the curse that he'd put on her.

He cupped her cheek and brushed his lips whisper soft against her skin. His fingers caught in her hair and he took a moment to try and memorize the feel of it, the scent of it. Then he stood, dressed, took one last look at her, and left the room.

It was the hardest thing he'd ever done.

He expected what he was about to do next would be even harder. He was not the kind of man to take his own life. The only thing that would make it go easier for him was the reason he was doing it. This was for Charlotte. He hoped she'd understand that when she discovered what had happened. He hoped eventually she would move past this event, get over him, and find love again—this time with someone who could give her forever.

Sweet Danu, he was jealous of that faceless man.

His legs feeling like he had anchors attached to them, he walked through the corridors to the queen's chambers. They'd met briefly the night before to organize this. On his way to get dinner for himself and Charlotte, he'd stopped in to see Aislinn—to arrange the manner of his death.

One of the queen's hallway attendants spotted him approaching the Shadow Queen's apartment, recognized him, and opened the door. "She's expecting you," the attendant said.

"Thank you."

It was only just after sunrise and the queen still wore her dressing gown, but even that had the pomp and circumstance expected of the Shadow Queen. No T-shirt and pajama pants for her. Long, silky, and jet-black, her nightgown enveloped her slim body like a passionate embrace, cupping her breasts perfectly at the bodice. She wore a lacy black silk robe with a high collar and her silvery blond hair fell loose around her shoulders. Any other man would have thought her incredibly beautiful, but Kieran didn't think she was a fraction as pretty as Charlotte.

"Hello, Kieran." Aislinn's voice and face were somber. Resigned.

Gabriel walked into the room wearing a pair of jeans. As he entered, he pulled a gray T-shirt over his head. "Kieran, are you sure about this?"

He nodded. "It's the only way to free Charlotte." He glanced around the room. "Where is he? The Unseelie you asked to do this."

Aislinn said nothing, she only moved to a nearby table. "Take a seat, Kieran."

He took a seat on the couch and Gabriel walked into the room, his face pensive. Aislinn went to the bar on the far end of the room, opened the refrigerator, and clinked glasses.

"I can feel the curse working inside me." Kieran rubbed a hand over his face. "It's eating away at me and Charlotte, whittling us down to death. It won't be long now. I think this sickness we're suffering from is about to get much worse. I want—*need*—to save Charlotte from this, from this anguish and from the slaugh."

Aislinn turned with two glasses in her hand. She gave one each to Gabriel and Kieran, and then returned for her own drink.

Kieran looked at his glass. "Orange juice for a dying man?"

Aislinn gave him a wan smile. "Yours has vodka in it. I figured you could use it before . . . everything."

Gabriel lifted his drink. "To selfless acts of love." His voice broke on the words.

"To Kieran." Aislinn lifted her orange juice to him, voice shaking and tears streaming unchecked down her cheeks.

Kieran looked at his glass. "To Charlotte," he murmured, "and to the love she helped me know for the first time in my miserable life." He tipped the beverage to his lips and drank the vodka and orange juice to the dregs, barely even stopping to savor it. Maybe Aislinn was right; maybe a stiff drink would help him get through what was to come.

Immediately he knew something was wrong. Aislinn had put something more than just vodka in there. *Poison.* Panic washed through him because, even though he'd sought this, he didn't want it. It was the primal reaction of a man who wanted to live. Ah, Danu, he'd lived the equivalent of ten human lifetimes, but he still wanted more time.

His gaze flew to Aislinn. She sat on the couch, sobbing, her hand pressed to her grief-stricken face. They'd agreed that a death-bringer Unseelie fae would come here and do the deed. He'd never expected this. But maybe that was the point. Maybe Aislinn had thought it would be easier on him if it were a surprise.

Whatever the case, he was done for. The poison rushed through his veins as though he'd been injected with hot metal, headed straight for his heart.

The glass dropped from his fingers and hit the carpet with a *thunk*. He fell onto his knees beside it, his vision going black at the edges and his head feeling oddly light. No pain burned through his body. He never gagged. This was more like a heavy curtain coming down on him. He lost feeling in his fingers, hands, then his arms and through his chest. His feet and legs went cold and then numb. One by one parts of his body shut down as the poison sent him hurtling toward death.

Charlotte. Every inch of him filled with the thought of her. The knowledge of his loss was the most painful thing about this. "I love you," he whispered. "Be well."

His eyes went unseeing; the entire room plunged into blackness. His body listed to the side, hit the carpet, his head impacting hard because he lacked the ability to protect it. His eyes closed.

He knew no more.

TWENTY-EIGHT

"OH, my sweet Danu." Aislinn went down on her knees beside Kieran's body. Her whole body shook and tears dropped onto the rug where he lay. She tried to touch him, roll him over, but she drew her hands away. She'd been strong enough to pour the foxglove, highly poisonous to the fae, into Kieran's drink, but she wasn't strong enough for this. "Why does it have to be this way? It's so unfair." Her voice broke on the words and tears streamed down her cheeks.

Gabriel came down on Kieran's other side and gently rolled him over. "This is what he wanted. I would have done the same if I were protecting you." He felt for a pulse and looked up at her. "He's gone."

She rocked back on her heels, pressing her hand to her mouth. She knew that already. The moment Gabriel had begun checking for a pulse, she'd felt the presence of Kieran's soul in the room.

She was a necromancer, able to sense and communicate with souls before they passed over into the Netherworld. Or, in this case, were claimed by the slaugh. Gabriel was Lord of the Wild Hunt and would reap Kieran when they rode tonight. She could see and talk with Kieran right now. Gabriel wouldn't be able to sense him until he reaped him.

Sometimes, when it involved people they cared about, their gifts really sucked.

Gabriel looked up at her, understanding. "You can feel him?"

She nodded, not wanting to turn around and see. Once that happened, this nightmare would be real. She closed her eyes.

Aislinn? Kieran's voice.

She hesitated, then stood and turned. He looked like all other souls did, wispy and insubstantial. A pale silver cord attached him to the Netherworld. She closed her eyes for a moment and swallowed hard. "Kieran, I'm sorry I tricked you."

It was easier that way. I never saw it coming.

"Are you . . . all right?" What a dumb question.

I'm resigned to what comes next.

Aislinn swallowed the lump in her throat. She knew what came next.

Tell Charlotte I love her more than I have ever loved anyone.

A bright light began to glow behind him. Pressure filled the room, making Aislinn's ears pop. That was odd. She'd been conversing with spirits for many years and had never seen anything like this.

Gabriel stepped forward. "What is that?"

"You can see that?"

"No, but I sense something."

Kieran glanced at the light growing behind him. *Tell her I want her to go on and have a good life.*

"I will." Aislinn watched the light grow bigger and brighter. Warmth had begun to fill the room. "What is that light, Kieran?"

The slaugh. They're coming for me.

Panic sliced through her. "No. *No!*" Aislinn fisted her hands at her sides, lifted her head to the heavens, and yelled, "Danu,

hear me! This is wrong! Kieran Aindréas Cairbre Aimhrea
has done nothing to deserve this fate! Spare this man from
the slaugh, Danu, I beg you!

The light exploded in a bright flash that made both Gabriel
and Aislinn close their eyes and turn their heads away.

When they looked back, Kieran was gone.

CHARLOTTE woke slowly, warm and comfortable in
Kieran's bed. Her body, heart, and mind felt sated as a well-
fed cat. Smiling, she stretched. Her body had none of the aches
and pains of the previous night. It no longer hurt to breathe
and the weakness and fatigue were gone. It took her a moment to realize that she felt . . . *good*. That hadn't happened
since the curse had kicked in.

How odd. She had to tell Kieran. Reaching out, she fanned
her arm through the rumpled blankets, looking for warm skin,
and came up with nothing. Frowning, she sat up and found
the bed empty. Disappointment sat like a little ball of lead in
her stomach. Dawn was just pinkening the horizon through
the large windows of Kieran's bedroom. Why hadn't he stayed
with her?

"Kieran?" she called and got no answer. Maybe he was in
the kitchen and couldn't hear her. Coffee would taste really
good about now.

She got out of bed and yanked on her clothes against the
chill in the apartment, marveling at how good she felt. Yesterday it had hurt to pull a shirt over her head, her muscles
protesting the movement. Today she moved freely, without the
constant background ache. The pain through her chest was
gone, too. It was a welcome change, but a strange one. Uneasiness settled around her like a winter coat. There was something wrong; she could feel it.

The doorbell rang. Charlotte walked into the living room
expecting to see Kieran answer it, but the room was empty.
"Kieran?" The kitchen, too, seemed quiet and cold.

No response. The doorbell rang again.

She answered it and took a step back, recognizing the old woman she'd seen when she'd fled down the alley to Goblin Town the first day she'd arrived—the old woman who wasn't really an old woman, at least not all the time.

"I'm looking for Kieran Aimhrea." The strange lady squinted at her and then smiled somewhat maliciously.

"He's not here."

She nodded. "Not here because he's out or not here because he did it?"

A fist clenched in the pit of her stomach. "Did what?"

"You don't know?" Her voice had a mean and playful lilt to it, as if the old woman thought Charlotte's ignorance was amusing and she was just dying to divulge the secret.

"No." Charlotte spoke carefully, that mantle of uneasiness growing a little heavier. "I don't know."

"You are Charlotte Lillian Bennett, the mate of the cursed, are you not?"

She blinked at the odd phrasing. "I am."

The old woman's mouth split into a grin and her black eyes glittered. "He'd planned on killing himself to free you."

"He . . . *what*?" Cold shock washed through her. True realization took a second to dawn. It made sense. She'd woken alone. She felt so much better—back to normal.

Curse-free.

Charlotte staggered back, a hand to her throat. For a moment she thought she might pass out. Then she lunged forward, pushing past the old woman, and ran down the corridor to the queen's chambers, the most logical place to find Kieran.

Behind her, the strange lady cackled.

When she reached the ornate double doors of the queen's chambers Niall was standing outside, talking to the guards. Charlotte pushed past them, trying to get into the room, but Niall grabbed her and pulled her away.

"No." She shoved at him. "I need to get in there. I need to find Kieran. Let go of me."

Niall held her tight. "Charlotte, you don't want to go in there right now." His voice sounded rough with emotion. Grief.

She paused for a moment, the implication settling into her bones. Finally, she moved. "No!" She fought him, shoving him back. *"Where's Kieran?"*

Niall's arms dropped helplessly to his sides. "He's in there, Charlotte." His voice was disarmingly gentle, too gentle for a man like Niall Quinn.

And, then, she truly knew.

"It's too late. I got here too late." The words fell out of her mouth like stones. Her body had gone numb, cold. She staggered to the side and he caught her before she collapsed and righted her on her unsteady legs.

He shook his head. "You never would have been able to stop him anyway. He was hell-bent on saving you from the curse."

She stared at him, feeling the blood drain from her face. Then she pushed past him and bolted for the door. The guards moved to stop her, but Niall barked at them to let her through. She burst into the room and saw the one thing she'd never wanted to see in her life, Kieran's lifeless body on the floor.

"Charlotte," came the queen's shocked voice.

Charlotte barely heard her, barely saw the king standing near her. She ran to Kieran's side and took him by the shoulders, shaking him like she could wake him up. She knew he wasn't alive anymore. She felt it in the pit of her stomach and in the vigor of her curse-free body. It was in the heaviness of him and the cool that seemed to be fast settling into his limbs.

"What did you do, Kieran?" she yelled at him. "How could you?" Tears streamed down her face. "You promised me!"

A strong hand touched her shoulder, trying to pull her away, but she shrugged Gabriel off. She slumped down over Kieran's chest and came apart completely, feeling grief bubble up out of her like thick, black sludge.

"I didn't want it to be this way, Kieran," she whispered. "We were supposed to do this together." Tears dripped onto Kieran's shirt, making it damp. "You lied to me."

The queen knelt beside her, placing a hand on her back. "I'm so sorry, Charlotte. I can't express how much we'll all miss him. He told me to tell you he loved you and that everything he did this morning, he did for you. He asked you to forgive him."

Charlotte straightened, wiping her eyes. "No," she snarled. "I won't forgive him. I will never forgive any of you for this." Rage poured through her at the unfairness. It didn't make any sense. They'd been in love. Innocently. Purely. Deeply.

And Kieran had died because of it.

After a moment, the queen rose. "She needs a little time. Let's leave her alone," she whispered to her husband. They left the room.

Charlotte slumped down at Kieran's side and sobbed quietly. Grief, thick and dark drudged up from the depths of her, coated her, made everything hazy and gray. What was she supposed to do now? How could she go on without him? She didn't *want* to go on without him, even though she knew that was exactly what Kieran had intended. He'd ended his own life prematurely so that she could keep hers.

"Oh, Kieran," she breathed, closing her eyes. She lay down beside him and put her head near his. "Why couldn't you just have told me? I could have been here with you. I could've said good-bye."

But, of course, he didn't answer.

She knew why he hadn't told her. He'd known she would have fought him, tried to stop him. That assumption would have been right. If she had known he was going to do this, she would have tried everything to prevent it.

Now he was gone.

PRISS, the Piefferburg witch, shuffled into her shop and residence nestled at the base of the Black Tower. Stopping in the doorway and staring up at the massive polished black quartz of the tower, her lips split in a smile.

Everyone thought she was a chaos-sower, a lover of strife

and conflict. It was not an untrue assessment of her character, yet every once in a while she did someone a good turn. Sometimes even without their knowledge. She liked to stay unpredictable.

Her sleek black cat twined around her ankles. The feline lifted her silky head. *"Murreep?"* •

"I think it will work, Sekhmet." She shuffled farther into her shop, the scent of dry herbs rising like an old friend's embrace. "He could not be told beforehand. He could not have known because his decision needed to be completely unselfish, but I think it will work."

"Murrup," Sekhmet agreed.

Priss took a jar of dried mandrake from a shelf and shrugged. "And if it doesn't work, well, at least I freed the woman."

Sekhmet, apparently now bored with the silly activities of fae and humans, trotted off into the roomy darkness at the back of the building.

Her home was much larger than the outside would lead one to presume, existing in a double pocket of reality—both in the *ceantar dubh* and in the Boundary Lands. If she looked out the window and shifted her vision just a little, she would be able to see trees and the vibrant, shining sprae.

But today she had no wish for greenery, preferring the cold, black vista of the tower as she imagined what would soon might be occurring in its highest reaches. . . .

TWENTY-NINE

CHARLOTTE stirred, realizing she'd cried herself into a fitful, grief-laden sleep. Her head pounded and her throat ached from her misery. She wasn't sure how long she'd lain draped over Kieran's body.

The last thing she remembered was praying to God and to the fae's main deity, Danu. Since she had mixed blood, she figured she needed to cover all her bases. Then she guessed her mind had simply shut down and dragged her under. Sleep was a blessing, really, a respite from the sudden nightmare her waking reality had become.

A small noise drew her attention. For a second her heart stuttered, thinking it came from Kieran. In the moment she realized it couldn't have possibly come from him, her heart shattered into a million pieces all over again. She doubted she would ever be able to put it back together.

Then Kieran moved.

Charlotte shot up and looked at him. His eyelids fluttered, and her heart pounded. Was she still asleep? Dreaming? That had to be it. But, no, if this was a dream it was the realest one in the history of the world.

Kieran groaned.

"Kieran?" she whispered.

Nothing.

Oh, God, she'd gone insane. That's what it was. She'd wanted Kieran's death to be some mistake. She'd prayed until her voice had gone hoarse that he be given back to her, or, at the very least, he be spared the slaugh. He didn't deserve that fate. He was a good man. Now she was imagining that her first wish had been granted.

She shook her head, slowly backing away from him. This was not healthy. Kieran's body was not Kieran. Kieran's soul had left the building. Still, it was very, very hard to remember it was just a shell. She had to leave it. Somehow, someway, she was going to have to find the strength to leave his side. . . .

His hand reached out and caught her wrist.

She screamed.

Gabriel and Aislinn burst into the room just as Kieran's eyes came open. He groaned.

"*Danu,*" Aislinn breathed, her hand going to her mouth.

If Aislinn could see this, too, that meant Charlotte wasn't imagining it. Her mind hadn't cracked. That meant—

"*Kieran?*" Her breath came out a whisper, half unbelieving that he might be alive, half filled with hope.

"Charlotte?" His voice sounded faint. His gaze found hers, unfocused at first, then it sharpened. "Charlotte." Now his voice was a little stronger.

She collapsed over him, kissing him. His skin felt warm, flush with life, under her fingers and lips. She stroked his skin, absorbing the wonderfulness of it. Her mind stuttered and restarted fifty times in the span of a few seconds trying to figure out how this could be. Finally she stopped trying and just enjoyed the feeling of Kieran alive.

Slowly, he sat up and enveloped her in an embrace that

seemed warmer and more secure than any she'd ever experienced before. Nestling her head in the curve of his neck, she inhaled the scent of him and smiled happily. They clung to each other like they would never let each other go again.

"How?" she whispered against his skin. "What happened?"

He held her tight while he spoke, his voice gravelly. "I died and was taken to the Netherworld." He paused. "I don't remember much. I remember waiting to be included into the slaugh. I remember white light. I remember . . . a woman's voice." His voice broke. "The sweetest voice I have ever heard. It was like a champagne glass filled with sunshine and gold. The voice told me that because I had sacrificed my life for love, the curse was broken, and that it wasn't time for me to go to the Netherworld yet." He paused again. "There was more but I don't remember it clearly. The next thing I knew I was falling into blackness and my body hurt."

She pulled away from him. "Do you still hurt?"

"Not like I did before. This is different." He cupped her face in his hands. "The curse?" His pupils narrowed. "How do you feel?"

"I feel fine. Wonderful." She laughed. "Perfect."

"Your body is processing the poison, Kieran," said Gabriel in an awed voice. "That's the pain you feel. Somehow you're surviving it. Something has given you the ability."

"Not something, someone. The goddess Danu," came Aislinn's wonder-filled voice. "She sent you back."

Charlotte agreed. Danu was real and she had lifted the curse on him because he had sacrificed his life to save the one he loved.

She took him by the shoulders, starting to cry again. "Don't you ever do something like that again, Kieran Aindréas Cairbre Aimhrea. Do you hear me? Never. Whatever life throws at us, we go through it together. All right?"

He gave her a lopsided smile. "From now on." He took her hand pressed it to his heart. "Forever."

"I don't want to live without you," she whispered.

He pulled her against him and they clung to each other for a long time. When they finally looked at something other than each other, they saw that Gabriel and Aislinn had discreetly left the room.

GIDEON climbed out of the taxi in front of Phaendir Headquarters, grimacing and grunting. The painkillers they'd given him at the hospital had long since worn off during the trip back to the States. Since he'd left without telling the doctor, all he had now were over-the-counter drugs, and they weren't cutting it. It was a good thing he'd trained himself to endure pain over the years to the point of finding it pleasurable. He only wished he could enjoy it.

At the end of the gravel road, he could see that the gates leading into Piefferburg were swarming with news crews. Damn it, someone had leaked the info about the third piece. The media was worse than the vultures circling the sky around the nearby church.

One of the reporters spotted him and headed toward him at a fast clip, followed by the rest of them. Good thing that road was a long one. Gideon threw his money at the driver and dragged himself toward the front doors of headquarters as fast as his injuries would allow. As he approached the entrance at a limping pace, the reporters a galloping herd behind him, he motioned impatiently to the guards to let him in.

"Keep them out," he grunted as he passed, sweat breaking out across his forehead. The clamor of the reporters reached his ears as the doors shut in their faces. Gideon didn't look back. He headed straight to his office.

Brother Merion had received word the archdirector had arrived and was already sitting in Gideon's office, head bowed, hands folded in his lap. He expected punishment, as well he should.

Gideon entered slowly, staring at the back of Merion's head. Rage burned in his veins as he thought about sedation, hot knives, and smooth skin. Unfortunately punishment of that sort wasn't politically correct, not these days. Too bad.

Instead he stalked into his office and stood behind his desk. Every minute of silence probably made Merion more nervous, though he didn't show it. Gideon stared down at him for a long moment and then sank into his chair with a grimace of pain.

He organized a few papers on his desk before speaking. "You are hereby relocated to the Phaendir station in Ulan Bator, Mongolia." Merion's head snapped up. Gideon continued without looking at him. "Enjoy your new home."

"But—"

Gideon held up his hand. "You leave on the first flight that can get you there. Go pack. You don't have much time." He picked up the phone. "I'm making travel arrangements now."

Brother Merion paused for a moment, sputtering. Then he slowly rose and shuffled, beaten, out of the room.

Gideon punched the number of the person in charge of making travel arrangements while glaring at Merion's back as he left the room. The man was weak. Too weak to be a Phaendir. If he could cull him from the herd without risking prison, he would. Mongolia was the second best option. Merion was lucky to be getting out of here with his life. Well, such that it would be. He hoped Brother Merion liked yaks.

Once travel arrangements were made, he picked up the phone again. He had a total of seventy-five messages, probably reporters. Sighing, he dialed another number. Congressman Reynolds.

It was time for the U.S government to act to protect themselves. If they didn't, if the government showed its tendency to bog down in bickering, posturing, and back-and-forth endless reams of paper . . . Gideon looked out the window at the main gates and the human reporters roving like ants around it. Well, then, the Phaendir *would* act. And act quickly.

Congressman Reynolds needed to say the right words. He needed to give Gideon access to the president and the president needed to act to give him the ability to be ruthless. Gideon hoped to procure that license, but it didn't matter one way or other.

Either way, this was war.

KIERAN spent the day recovering. The poison that should have left him dead merely made him sick for a few hours. The whole day passed in a euphoric haze of bliss despite the dregs of toxin still left in his body. All his dreams had come true. They had the piece. The curse was gone. He'd been touched by Danu, herself.

He had his love.

He wondered if Priss had suspected that sacrificing his life for Charlotte's would break the curse and give him a return ticket from the Otherside. Asking her was on his list of things to do.

But not for today.

Charlotte had fallen asleep next to him on the couch. The fire before them crackled and soft music played behind them. She'd spent the day trying to make him comfortable, but all he'd wanted was her near him. The scent of her skin. The feel of her hands on him. The sound of her voice in his ears.

He sat up, slipped a pillow under her head, and gazed down at her, studying the curve of her cheek and the shape of her lips. Every time he looked at her, his chest swelled with love. He didn't know how it was possible to care about someone this much, to want everything for that person no matter what it might mean for yourself.

He might be centuries older than Charlotte, but she'd taught him more about himself in their time together than anyone else had since the time of his birth.

He wasn't alone anymore.

Walking to the window, he gazed out over Piefferburg Square. Twilight painted the horizon in a tangled splash of reds, oranges, and pinks. It was the leading edge of night, but it felt like a whole new day.

His gaze strayed to the Piefferburg Securities Exchange where Queen Aislinn was now meeting with the Summer Queen about the *bosca fadbh*. One would have thought the Summer Queen would have jumped the moment the Shadow Queen had sent word that the final piece was in her possession, but that had not happened. The Summer Queen had delayed. That either meant Caoilainn Elspeth Muirgheal planned to give them trouble regarding her two pieces of the *bosca fadbh* or she was attempting to gain control by making the Shadow Queen wait for the glory of her presence. Knowing the Summer Queen, it could be either.

Kieran bet it was the former.

A warm hand touched his shoulder. He pulled Charlotte against him and she sighed, her body warm from her nap. He tipped her head to look up at him, her mussed dark hair curling around her face. "You let me fall asleep." There was a teasing note of accusation in her voice.

He twined his fingers through her hair and brought her mouth to his for a deep kiss. "You needed it after all you've been through in the last few days."

She let out a long sigh against his lips. "I still can't believe you're here with me."

He dragged her up against his chest and buried his nose in her hair, inhaling the scent of her. He wanted to savor every moment he had with her now, knowing how all their moments had almost been taken away.

Pulling her back, he guided her to the couch and found her mouth with his. His lips moved over hers, his tongue finding its way into her mouth to tangle with hers. She made a small sound in the back of her throat that made his cock go hard. He wanted to feel her under his body right now, wanted to feel the blood pumping through his veins. He wanted *her*. Every sigh of pleasure he could get from her, every moan. He wanted to slide his hands over every inch of her skin and memorize all of her curves.

And this time it wasn't because he was going to lose her, it was because he would have her for the rest of their lives.

She pressed her hand to his chest. "Kieran, we need to discuss something very important."

He nuzzled her throat and made her moan. He ran his fingers down the goose bumps he'd raised on the back of her arm. "What could be more important than this?"

"It's just that . . . you're going to live now." She sighed and slipped a hand beneath his shirt. "For a very, very long time, and I'm—" She broke off on a moan as he nibbled the skin beneath her earlobe.

"What was that?" he murmured against the curve where her neck met her shoulder.

"Never mind," she sighed.

His hands found the hem of her sweater and he pushed beneath it, finding smooth, warm skin. He wanted her naked, soft, and spread beneath him.

She smiled against his mouth. "I thought you were feeling sick."

He nipped at her lower lip. "I'm feeling much better now that you're here." He pulled her sweater over her head and discovered she was fully, deliciously, bare underneath it. Making a little growling sound in the back of his throat, he lowered his head and sucked one rosy nipple into his mouth while slowly running his fingers over the other to excite her. It went hard against his palm and she let out a low moan, her fingers curling in his hair.

He walked her backward until her calves hit the side of the couch and then moved his hands down, unbuttoning her jeans. She wiggled out of them and went to work on his clothes, kissing and nipping at his skin as she undressed him. They said nothing. The only sound was their breathing and the rustle of clothing hitting the floor.

Wanting to play out the fantasy he'd had in his head for so long, he turned her so that her back was to him, then bowed her over the armrest of the couch. Running a hand down the smooth skin of her back, he admired the curve of her spine and the delicious shape of her rear. Parting her thighs, he slipped his hand between them and found her wet. Locating her swollen clit and the entrance of her sex, he made her even wetter. He slid one finger inside her and thrust, then added another, stretching her muscles.

Charlotte grabbed hold of the cushions of the couch and moaned out his name. "Please, I need you."

As he needed her.

He stroked himself from tip to base; he was hard as a rock and couldn't wait to slide inside her. She spread her thighs, her lovely buttocks tipped up in invitation. He pushed the head of his cock inside her. The sensation of her tight, velvety walls clasping his length made him arch his back and groan. She felt like heaven. She *was* heaven.

In this position, he was able to leverage himself in just the right way to drive deep and fast into her. He pushed them both hard, loving the way Charlotte squirmed and moaned beneath him until she finally shattered in climax, the muscles of her sex pulsing and releasing around his shaft as he thrust into her.

When she was limp from the throes of her first climax, he pulled her up, sliding his hands over her breasts and nibbling at the back of her neck and ear with his cock still lodged deep inside her. Then he pulled free and guided her to lie on the thick carpet in front of the fire, enjoying the sight of the light playing on the aroused, rosy flush of her skin and licking at her beautiful, hard red nipples.

He came down over her, kissing her deeply, driving his tongue into her mouth as if starved for the feel of her tongue against his. She shifted beneath him, forcing his rigid cock inside her once again. He drove deep, making her gasp with pleasure and shiver as though he was completing the missing part of her.

As she completed the missing part of him.

As one, joined, they moved together. He caught her gaze and held it as he thrust slowly in and out of her. Her eyes were filled with as much emotion as he felt coiled tight within his chest. Contentment was finally his, after so many years. He wanted to tell her *thank you*, but was loathe to interrupt the soundless communication of their bodies.

Instead, he gave her pleasure. Slipping his hand down between them, he found her swollen clit and stroked it with his thumb. Her eyes fluttered shut and her back arched, her breath coming faster.

Monitoring the way she moaned, breathed, looked at him, he pushed them both to flirt with the leading edge of ecstasy and held them there, prolonging it, building it to a shattering crescendo when he finally decided to push them both over the precipice.

She shuddered, then cried out, her face flushing and her back arching. Pleasure rose up from his balls, exploding over him. They cried out each other's names as they came together. He poured into her and hoped, for a fleeting second, that Danu would grant them a child.

They collapsed together in a tangle in front of the fire, breathing heavily.

She curled around him and knotted her fingers through his hair.

"I love you," he murmured.

Tears glistening in her eyes, she kissed him. "I love you, too," she whispered against his lips.

He stroked his hands over her body, leaving no inch unexplored, and drove her to one last quiet orgasm there on the carpet. He never wanted to leave the rug, never wanted the fire to sputter and die. At the moment, all he wanted was Charlotte. The rest of the world could go to hell.

"I want to marry you." The words came out rough with emotion.

She pushed up on her elbows. "What?"

"I want to tie my soul to yours in the way of the fae. I want to bond with you right now."

She laughed. "I don't understand."

"I want to give you my soul by saying the Joining Vows. They're the magick-laced words of the traditional Tuatha Dé wedding ceremony."

"Magick-laced?"

"They'll give you the life span of a fae."

Her brow wrinkled. "How would that be possible?"

"You have fae DNA in you, Charlotte. Not that much, but you do have it. I don't know for sure if it will work, but it should. I will give my soul to you. When you die, so will I. You don't have to say them back to me, but if you do, your soul will be forever linked to mine."

"And when you die, so will I."

He nodded. "It's a hell of a commitment."

"That's what I wanted to talk about before, the difference in our life spans. When I left Piefferburg I didn't know you loved me. When I came back, we were both going to die, so it wasn't an issue. But now . . ." She licked her lips. "I don't even have to think about it. Yes. Yes, of course, I want this."

He gave her a head-to-toe sweep with his gaze. They were both still naked in front of the fire. "Do you want a real ceremony? A dress? Flowers—"

She put her fingers over his mouth. "Everything I want is right here, right now."

THIRTY

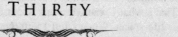

CHARLOTTE wept with joy as Kieran took her hands in his. He stared into her eyes and spoke in Old Maejian first, then in English so she could understand.

I give you my blood, bone, and breath.

I give you my soul and the spirit it rides in.

Should you be discarded by others, I will cherish you.

Should danger come, I will give my life to protect you.

Should your honor be lost, in mine I will cloak you.

Should you become sick, I will heal you.

Should you be lost, I will find you.

Ask me never to leave you. Stop me not from following after you.

Where you go, I will go. Not even death shall part us.

I am yours.

A warm, tingling magick enveloped her, making her eyes close, her chest swell with gentle heat, and tears stream down her cheeks. In that moment, she felt what Kieran felt for her.

All the love she saw glimpses of on his face and in his eyes, all of it became an actual, tangible mantle of peace and warmth that settled around her shoulders.

It was what she felt for him, mirrored back at her.

When she opened her eyes, she felt different. Stronger. Healthier. Happier.

Practically immortal like a fae?

It seemed likely. Now she didn't have to worry about growing older and dying before Kieran did.

They could be together now. Forever.

She squeezed his hands and began saying the Joining Vows back to him. They came to her in Old Maejian easily, even though she didn't speak the language. They simply poured out of her mouth with the intention of giving herself completely to him. The magick swelled and Kieran bowed his head, accepting her gift.

They were one.

CHARLOTTE came out of the bedroom, rubbing a towel through her wet hair, to the sound of someone pounding on the front door of Kieran's apartment. It brought back bad memories of the morning that she shook off. That nightmare was over. Kieran was fine.

And she was married, literally, to her soul mate.

Kieran wore only a pair of blue jeans, a look she found exceedingly distracting. The visitor pounded on the door again and he shot her an expression that said, *This probably isn't good*, and answered it.

Niall stood on the other side. "We've got trouble. Heaps and heaps of pure, black trouble." He leaned in and waved at Charlotte. "Trouble. Got it? Feeling better? Hope so. Can you come with me?"

And just like that another nightmare began.

Kieran grabbed his shirt and a pair of shoes by the door. "Charlotte, you coming?"

"I wouldn't miss it for the world," she said dryly, finding her own shoes. She could only imagine what kind of danger was headed their way now.

Niall led them to the queen's chambers. Entering, Charlotte looked at the place where she'd knelt by Kieran's lifeless body only hours ago and suppressed a shudder.

Gabriel and Aislinn stood by one of the huge windows that looked down over Piefferburg Square. The rest of the group Charlotte had come to recognize as Aislinn's advisors were assembled in the room. The entire Wild Hunt—Melia, Aelfdane, and Aeric O'Malley, plus Bella, Emmaline, Ronan, and Niall.

Aislinn looked at Kieran and Charlotte pointedly. "All right?"

"More than all right," Kieran answered. "We've shared Joining Vows."

The queen smiled. "We'll have to celebrate after we deal with this new crisis."

Kieran walked toward her. "Did the Summer Queen give you the two pieces of the *bosca fadbh*?"

"Of course not," Gabriel growled. His fists were clenched. "But that's not our primary concern at the moment."

"Are you ready for war?" That came from Niall, who still stood near the door. "The old-fashioned kind. The kind we used to have, way back when. Remember?"

Kieran's body tensed beside her. "I've done a good job forgetting."

"Well, you better remember," said Ronan from his place on one of the white couches. He had an arm wound protectively around Bella's shoulders.

"The red caps report activity at the gates." Aislinn pursed her lips, pausing for a moment. "The Phaendir are massing to enter Piefferburg. Not only can the guards see it, it's all over the human TV news. The Phaendir mean to act without consent from the U.S. government."

"What?" breathed Charlotte. "They wouldn't dare."

"The HFF is there, too," continued the queen. "There are

protestors and riots starting already in Protection City. The government is calling in the National Guard—"

"But we don't know what side the human military will end up on, right?" Kieran rubbed his chin, caught in thought.

Gabriel nodded. "We don't know if the National Guard is coming to control the Phaendir . . . or us."

"And the Summer Queen?"

"Is balking."

Kieran swore in Old Maejian. "The bitch. I knew it, but the majority of Tuatha Dé Danann in both courts won't stand for it." He turned, pushing a hand through his hair. He glanced at her, fear in his eyes. Fear, she knew, for her. He didn't want her caught in a fae versus Phaendir war, maybe with U.S. military thrown in. "We need to get those pieces from her. *Now*."

"We're working on it." Gabriel nodded at Niall. "We have the best thief around, after all."

Niall gave a bow with a mocking flourish. He didn't look the least bit worried, but why would he be? He had no one he loved to fear losing to warfare.

Charlotte cleared her throat. "How well can the fae handle a conflict like this? Trapped here in Piefferburg?" Piefferburg was large area. Still, it seemed like it would be shooting fish in a barrel.

Emmaline bared her teeth in a feral grin. "Oh, we're stronger than we seem, Charlotte. We're not sick this time with Watt Syndrome, we're not weakened by widespread internal strife. We have magick and, mostly, unity. The humans had better watch out. The Phaendir . . ." Her grin got a little more brutal. "Well, a lot of us have been waiting for a chance to fight them."

"I'm making an announcement to the Black Tower today," said Aislinn. "We're opening the arms cache. Weapons for all." She gave Aeric O'Malley a pointed look and raised an eyebrow. "I guess it's fortunate that our Blacksmith has kept his secret forge hot all these years. The charmed iron won't work on the Phaendir, of course, but the pointy parts will."

Aeric blinked and jerked a little, clearly surprised that the queen knew about his secret work. Creating charmed iron weapons had been outlawed, but the former Shadow King had created a forge for Aeric to make them in anyway.

"You think I didn't know, Aeric?" Aislinn gave him a cold smile. "Bring all the weapons you've made over the years. We'll need those and more. You can train others to help you, since the weaponry doesn't need to be charmed it just needs to be able to kill. We aren't going down without a fight." The queen raised her voice, the tattoo of the Shadow Amulet flaring black against her pale skin. "We're not going down at all."

Slowly, they filtered out of the room. Aeric tapped most of them to help with the weapons. Before Kieran and Charlotte made their way into the bowels of the tower to Aeric's apartment, Kieran pulled her aside.

They stood in silence in front of a large window overlooking Piefferburg Square. They couldn't see the gates from where they were, but Charlotte could imagine the chaos beyond them. She knew better than anyone in Piefferburg the mix of fascination and fear that humankind had for the fae. The threat of the walls coming down would be rippling through human society like the explosion of a nuclear bomb on American soil.

"You need to leave, Charlotte." Kieran's voice was hard, resigned.

She slipped his hand into his. "I'm not going anywhere."

He rounded on her, cupping her face between his hands. "You have no magick. You can't defend yourself and Gideon will be gunning for you. *You need to leave.*"

"What makes you think Gideon won't kill me the moment I set foot past those gates, Kieran?"

He shook his head. "He can't. You're human, a U.S. citizen. You've broken no laws. He can't lay a hand on you with the world watching. But if the Phaendir break into Piefferburg, if there's war within these walls and we can't break the warding, he'll come after you and kill you. You know he will."

She covered his hands with hers. "I'm not leaving you. I'm never leaving you again, Kieran. Do you hear me? Our souls are twined now. Where you go, I go. Where you stay, I stay. Weren't you listening to the vows we just said?"

He closed his eyes. "Danu, woman, what am I going to do with you?"

She smiled. "Love me? Kiss me? Make love to me tonight?"

He set his forehead to hers and sighed. "Aeric was right."

"About what?"

"Love isn't all puppies and sunshine. It makes you scared as hell."

She went up on her toes and pressed her lips to his. "Yes, isn't it wonderful?"

He kissed her deep, his tongue dipping in to twine with hers, as his hand went to the small of her back and pressed her body up against his. "Yeah, it is," he whispered against her lips. "Thank you for showing me all of its sides, even the jagged ones."

Then they linked hands and walked down the corridor to a future they'd face together.

Dear readers,
Curious where Piefferburg is located?

Visit my website for an interactive map:

www.anyabast.com

GLOSSARY

Abastor The mystic black stallion that leads the Wild Hunt.

Alahambri The language the goblins speak.

Black Tower A large building on one end of Piefferburg Square that is constructed of black quartz. This houses the Unseelie Court.

Book of Bindings Book created when the Phaendir and the fae were allied. The most complete book of spells known. Contains the spell that can break the warding around Piefferburg.

bosca fadbh Puzzle box consisting of three interlocking pieces. Once was an object owned by both the Phaendir and the fae, back when they weren't enemies. When all three pieces are united, they form a key to unlock part of the Book of Bindings.

Boundary Lands The area where the wilding fae live.

ceantar dubh Dark district. This is the neighborhood directly abutting the Black Tower.

ceantar láir Middle district. Fae "suburbia," it also borders a mostly commercial area of downtown Piefferburg where the troop live and work.

charmed iron Iron spelled to take away a fae's magick when it touches the skin. Used in prisons as handcuffs and by the Imperial and Shadow Guards, it's illegal for the general fae population to possess it. Charmed iron weapons were a major reason the fae lost in the war against the Milesians and Phaendir in ancient Ireland.

Danu The primary goddess of the Tuatha Dé Danann, both Seelie and Unseelie. Also followed by some other fae races. Danu is accompanied by a small pantheon of lesser gods.

Furious Host Those who follow the Lord of the Wild Hunt every night to collect the souls of the fae who have died and help to ferry them to the Netherworld.

Goblin Town The area of Piefferburg where the goblins live. The goblins are a fae race with customs that differ greatly from the other types of fae.

Great Sweep When the Phaendir, allied with the human race, hunted down, trapped, and imprisoned all known fae and contained them in Piefferburg.

Humans for the Freedom of the Fae (HFF) An organization of humans working for equal fae rights and the destruction of Piefferburg.

Humans for the Continued Incarceration of the Fae (HCIF) An organization of humans working with the Phaendir to ensure the fae are never given freedom.

iron sickness The illness, eventually fatal, that occurs when charmed iron is pressed against the flesh of a fae for an extended period of time.

Joining Vows Ancient, magick-laced vows that twine two souls together. Not often used in modern fae society because of the commitment involved.

Jules Piefferburg Original human architect of Piefferburg. The statue honoring him in Piefferburg Square is made of charmed iron and can't be taken down, so the fae constantly dishonor it in other ways, like dressing it up disrespectfully or throwing food at it.

Labrai The god the Phaendir follow.

Netherworld Where the fae go after they die.

Old Maejian The original tongue of the fae. It's a dead language to all except those who are serious about practicing magick.

Orna The primary goddess of the goblins. Accompanied by many lesser gods.

Phaendir ("Fane-dear") A race of druids whose origins remain murky. The common belief of the fae is that their own genetic line sprang from them. The Phaendir believe they've always been a separate—superior—race. Once allied with the fae, they're now mortal enemies.

Piefferburg ("Fife-er-berg") Square Large cobblestone square with a statue of Jules Piefferburg in the center and the Rose and Black towers on either end.

Rose Tower Made of rose quartz, this building sits at one end of Piefferburg Square and houses the Seelie Court.

Seelie ("Seal-ee") Highly selective fae ruling class, they only allow the Tuatha Dé Danann into their ranks. Members must have a direct bloodline to the original ruling Seelie of ancient Ireland and their magick must be light and pretty.

Shadow Amulet The one who wears the amulet holds the Shadow Throne, though the amulet might reject someone without the proper bloodline. It sinks into the wearer's body, imbuing him or her with power and immortality, leaving only a tattoo on the skin to mark its physical presence.

Shadow Royal Holder of the Unseelie Throne.

Sídhe ("Shee") Another name for the Tuatha Dé Danann (Irish) fae, both Seelie and Unseelie.

Summer Ring Like the Shadow Amulet of the Unseelie Royal, this piece of jewelry imbues the wearer with great power and immortality. It also sinks into the skin, leaving only a tattoo, and may reject the wearer at will. This ring determines who holds the Seelie Throne.

Summer Royal Holder of the Seelie Throne.

trooping fae Those fae who are not a part of either court and are not wilding or water fae.

Tuatha Dé Danann ("Thoo-a-haw Day Dah-nawn") The most ancient of all races on earth, the fae. They were evolved and sophisticated when humans still lived in caves. Came to Ireland in the ancient times and overthrew the native people. The Seelie Tuatha Dé ruled the other fae races. When the Milesians (a tribe of humans in ancient Ireland) allied with the Phaendir and defeated the fae, the fae had to agree to go underground. They disappeared from all human knowledge, becoming myth.

Twyleth Teg ("Till-eg Tay") Welsh faeries. They're rare and live across the social spectrum.

Unseelie ("Un-seal-ee") A fae ruling class, they'll take anyone who comes to them with dark magick, but the true definition of an Unseelie fae is one whose magick can draw blood or kill.

water fae Those fae who live in the large water areas of Piefferburg. They stay out of the city of Piefferburg and out of court politics and life.

Watt syndrome Illness that befell all the fae races during the height of the race wars. The sickness decimated the fae population, outed them to the humans, and ultimately caused their downfall, weakening them to the point that the Phaendir could gather and trap them in Piefferburg. Some think the syndrome was biological warfare perpetrated by the Phaendir.

Wild Hunt Comprising mystic horses and hounds and a small group of fae known as the Furious Host, led by the Lord of the Wild Hunt, the hunt gathers the souls of all the fae who have died every night and ferries them to the Netherworld.

wilding fae Nature fae. Like the water fae, they stay away from Piefferburg proper, choosing to live in the Boundary Lands.

Worshipful Observers Steadfast human supporters of the work the Phaendir does to keep the fae races separate from the rest of the world.

Turn the page for a preview of
the next paranormal romance from Anya Bast

MIDNIGHT ENCHANTMENT

Coming January 2012 from Berkley Sensation!

BLIND, pissed off, and holding a rope embedded with cold iron. *Yeah.* This night couldn't get any worse. Niall's ear twitched and the hair on his nape rose as something scraped along the boulder to his left. He went still, his eyes searching the endless black for some sign of his quarry.

Find her. Trap her. Do whatever he had to in order to locate the two stolen pieces of the *bosca fadbh* and get the fuck home. Those were his objectives.

Too bad Elizabeth Cely Saintjohn's objectives directly opposed his.

Footsteps sounded on the path behind him. He turned, cursing the lack of moonlight and Elizabeth's habit for traveling only at night. To his right, movement caught his attention and he stilled, growling in frustration. Light, ringing laughter echoed around him.

Rage clenched his gut. She was playing with him. *Again.*

"Must be nice to be able to see in the dark and move like the wind, huh?" he snarled into the empty air. Not to mention dissolve into water and move anywhere she wanted within the bounds of Piefferburg. Neat trick.

His hand tightened on the rope, especially designed to trap a fae like her. He wore thick black leather gloves to prevent the charmed iron from touching his skin and leaching his magick. It was meant to bind Elizabeth, an asrai, before she escaped him. Unfortunately, roping this woman was harder than catching a weasel in vat of olive oil. He'd never so much as caught a glimpse of her yet since it was always dark.

Usually, it went this way—she toyed with him for a while, making him think he might have her . . . then she escaped. *He* was usually the one doing the toying where women were concerned. Having the tables turned sucked.

"Come on, Elizabeth. Don't play hard to get. Just give me the pieces and I'll stop hunting you."

"I kind of like it when you hunt me," came her lilting voice from somewhere farther up the path he walked. She had a sexy voice, whiskey-rough and sweet.

He ground his teeth together and readied a spell in his head that would give him a little light. It wouldn't last long, so he needed to draw her closer to him before he released it. He was a mage, capable of versatile magick not unlike that of the Phaendir. Except his magick wasn't born of the creepy hive mind that the Phaendir used—his was all inside him. Independent. Powerful.

And that's why he'd been sent after the asrai. He was the most qualified for it. Best at thieving—or thieving *back*, in this case. Best at mind-fuck magick. Best at tracking, capture, and torture. Best for this job. Or, at least, that's what everyone thought. That had been days ago. The Shadow Queen had sent him out the moment the Black Tower had learned the Summer Queen had passed off her pieces to Elizabeth. He was no closer to trapping her now than he had been on the first day.

"Why are you doing this?" he called. "Why keep your people from freedom? The Phaendir are at our gates right now. We don't have time to lose." His voice grew a degree lower and a lot more hostile. "Why work for the Summer Queen, a nice nature fae like you?"

"Who said I was nice?" The words breezed past his ear and were gone.

He lunged toward the direction of her fading voice with his rope and got nothing but air, a cool breeze and the light floral fragrance of the soap she used. Staggering and swearing a blue streak, he barely caught himself before falling on his face. Straightening, he laughed mirthlessly. "Come on now, don't go away so fast, baby. At least give me a kiss before you fuck me."

And then she was there, the warmth of her presence at his elbow, taunting him with her proximity. The brush of her silky hair against his skin. That soapy, light flowery scent of hers teasing his nose.

Ah, good. He'd been gambling her arrogance might be her end.

"*Arendriac,*" he murmured. The charm burst from him with a little pop, lighting their immediate area with a golden glow. He reached out to pull her close in the same moment, rope in one hand ready to trap.

His fingers brushed her waist as she backed away. For a moment she stood motionless. Her lush lips were parted, ruby red hair lofting around a pale, beautiful, heart-shaped face, and green eyes flecked with gold and wide with surprise.

He stared back at her, sharing an equal measure of astonishment. She was the most stunning woman he'd ever seen. He hadn't been expecting that.

Niall took a step forward, rope in hand. She dissolved as soon as he moved. A vision of beauty one moment, gone the next. He looked down at his feet and saw the puddle of water she'd become. Then even the water disappeared, soaking into the earth, traveling through it to find a river, a stream, whatever flow would take her away.

Swearing under his breath, he knelt and touched the barely damp soil where she'd been standing only a moment ago.

Gone yet again.

"Damn it," he cursed under his breath. The pretty lady with the pieces was out of his reach for another night. He wasn't sure which he mourned more—the loss of the pieces or the woman. The witch enticed him and had even before he'd caught a glimpse of her. Why couldn't she be some un-alluring hag without the clever wit she displayed in the woods every time he chased her, without that constantly teasing scent? It was fucking distracting.

Especially since he sort of liked the woman.

Too bad he was probably going to have to kill her.

Turn the page for a sneak peak of

DRAGON BOUND

a breathtaking new paranormal romance
by Thea Harrison

Coming May 2011 from Berkley Sensation!

PIA was blackmailed into committing a crime more suicidal than she could have possibly imagined, and she had no one to blame but herself.

Knowing that didn't make it easier. She couldn't believe she had been so lacking in good judgment, taste, and sensibility.

Honestly, what had she done? She had taken one look at a pretty face and forgotten everything her mom had taught her about survival. It sucked so bad she might as well put a gun to her head and pull the trigger. Except she didn't own a gun because she didn't like them. Besides, pulling the trigger on a gun was pretty final. She had issues with commitment and she was so freaking dead anyway, why bother?

A taxi horn blared. In New York, the sound was so common everyone ignored it, but this time it made her jump. She threw a glance over one hunched shoulder.

Her life was in ruins. She would be on the run for the rest of her life, all fifteen minutes or so of it, thanks to her own foolish behavior and her *shithead* ex who had screwed her, then screwed her over so royally she couldn't get over the knifelike sensation in the pit of her stomach.

She stumbled into a narrow, trash-strewn street by a Korean restaurant. She uncapped a liter-sized water bottle and chugged half of it down, one hand splayed on the cement wall while she watched the sidewalk traffic. Steam from the restaurant kitchen enveloped her in the rich red-pepper-and-soy scents of *gochujang* and *ganjang* sauces, overlaying the garbage rot of a nearby Dumpster and the acrid exhaust from the traffic.

The people in the street looked much as they always did, driven by internal forces as they charged along the sidewalk and shouted into cell phones. A few mumbled to themselves as they dug through trash cans and looked at the world with lost, wary eyes. Everything looked normal. So far so good?

After a long, nightmarish week, she had just committed the crime. She had stolen from one of the most dangerous creatures on Earth, a creature so frightening that just imagining him was more scariness than she ever wanted to meet in real life. Now she was almost done. A couple more stops to make, one more meeting with the shithead, and then she could scream for, oh, say, a couple of days or so while she figured out where she would run to hide.

Holding on to that thought, she strode down the street until she came to the Magic District. Located east of the Garment District and north of Koreatown, the New York Magic District was sometimes called the Cauldron. It was comprised of several city blocks that seethed with light and dark energies.

The Cauldron flaunted caveat emptor like a prizefighter's satin cloak. The area was stacked several stories high with kiosks and shops offering Tarot readings, psychic consultations, fetishes and spells, retail and wholesale sellers, imports, those who dealt with fake merchandise, and those who sold magic items that were deadly real. Even from the distance of a city block, the area assaulted her senses.

She came to a shop located at the border of the district. The storefront was painted sage green on the outside, with the molding at the plate-glass windows and door painted pale yellow. She took a step backward to look up. The name DIVINUS was spelled in plain, brushed-metal lettering over the front window. Years ago, her mother had on occasion bought spells from the witch who owned this shop. Her boss, Quentin, had also mentioned the witch had one of the strongest magical talents he had ever met in a human.

She looked in the storefront. Her blurred reflection looked back at her, a tired young woman built rather long and coltish, with tense features and a pale tangled ponytail. She looked past herself into the shadowed interior.

In contrast to the noisy, none-too-clean surroundings of the city street, the inside of the shop appeared cool and serene. The building seemed to glow with warmth. She recognized protection spells in place. In a display case near the door, harmonic energies sparked from an alluring arrangement of crystals, amethyst, peridot, rose quartz, blue topaz, and celestite. The crystals took the slanting sunshine and threw brilliant rainbow shards of light onto the ceiling. Her gaze found the single occupant inside, a tall queenlike woman, perhaps Hispanic, with a gaze that connected to hers with a snap of Power.

That was when the shouting started.

"You don't have to go in there!" a man yelled.

Then a woman shrieked, "Stop before it's too late!"

Pia started and looked behind her. A group of twenty people stood across the street. They held various signs. One poster said, MAGIC = HIGHWAY TO HELL. Another said, GOD WILL SAVE US. A third declared, ELDER RACES—AN ELITIST HOAX.

Her sense of unreality deepened, brought on by stress, lack of sleep, and a constant sense of fear. They were yelling at her.

Some of humankind persisted in a belligerent disbelief of the Elder races, despite the fact that many generations ago, folktales had been proven as the scientific method was developed. The Elder races and humankind had lived together openly since the Elizabethan Age. These humans with their revisionist history made about as much sense as those who declared the Jews hadn't been persecuted in World War II.

Besides being out of touch with reality, they were picketing a human witch to protest the Elder races? She shook her head.

A cool tinkle brought her attention back to the shop. The woman with Power in her gaze held the door open. "City ordinances can work both ways," she told Pia, her voice filled with scorn. "Magic shops may have to stay within a certain district, but protesters have to stay fifty feet away from the shops. They can't come across the street, they can't enter the Magic District, and they can't do anything but yell at potential customers and try to scare them off from a distance. Would you like to come in?" One immaculate eyebrow raised in imperious challenge, as if suggesting that to step into the woman's shop took a real act of bravery.

Pia blinked at her, expression blank. After everything she had been through, the other woman's challenge was beyond insignificant; it was meaningless. She walked in without a twitch.

The door tinkled into place behind her. The woman paused for a heartbeat, as if Pia had surprised her. Then she stepped in front of Pia with a smooth smile.

"I'm Adela, the owner of Divinus. What can I do for you, my dear?" The shopkeeper's face turned puzzled and searching as she looked Pia over. She murmured, almost to herself, "What is it . . . There's something about you. . . ."

Crap, she hadn't thought of that. This witch might remember her mom.

"Yeah, I look like Greta Garbo," Pia interrupted, her expression stony. "Moving on now."

The other woman's gaze snapped up to hers. Pia's face and body language transmitted a CLOSED sign, and the witch's demeanor changed back into the professional saleswoman.

"My apologies," she said in her chocolate-milk voice. She gestured. "I have herbal cosmetics, beauty remedies, tinctures over in that corner, crystals charged with healing spells—"

Pia looked around without taking it all in, although she noticed a spicy smell. It smelled so wonderful she breathed it in deep without thinking. Despite herself the tense muscles in her neck and shoulders eased. The scent contained a low-level spell, clearly intended to relax nervous customers.

While the spell caused no actual harm and did nothing to dull her senses, its manipulative nature repelled her. How many people relaxed and spent more money because of it? Her hands clenched as she shoved the magic away. The spell clung to her skin a moment before it dissipated. The sensation reminded her of cobwebs trailing across her skin. She fought the urge to brush off her arms and legs.

Annoyed, she turned and met the shopkeeper's eyes. "You come recommended by reputable sources," she said in a clipped tone. "I need to buy a binding spell."

Adela's bland demeanor fell away. "I see," she said, matching Pia's crispness. Her eyebrows raised in another faint challenge. "If you've heard of me then you know I'm not cheap."

"You're not cheap because you're supposed to be one of the best witches in the city," said Pia as she strode to a nearby glass counter. She shrugged the backpack off her aching shoulder, pulling the tangle of her ponytail out from under one strap, and rested it on the counter. She stuffed her water bottle inside and zipped it back up.

"*Gracias*," said the witch, her voice bland.

She glanced down at the crystals in the case. They were so bright and lovely, filled with magic and light and color. What would it be like to hold one, to feel the cool, heavy weight of it sitting in her palm as it sang to her of starlight and deep mountain spaces? How would it feel to own one?

The connection snapped as she turned. She looked her own challenge at the other woman. "I can also feel the spells you have both on and in the shop, including the attraction spells on these crystals as well as the one that's supposed to make your customers relax. I can tell your work is competent enough. I need an oath binding spell, and I need to walk out of the shop with it today."

"That is not as easy as it might sound," said the witch. Long eyelids dropped, shuttering her expression. "This is not a fast food drive-through."

"The binding doesn't have to be fancy," said Pia. "Look, we both know you're going to charge more because I need it right away. I still have a lot to do, so can we please just skip this next part where we dance around each other and negotiate? Because, no offense, it's been a long, bad day. I'm tired and not in the mood."

The witch's mouth curled. "Certainly," she said. "Although with a binding, there's only so much I can do on the spot, and there're some things I won't do at all. If you need something tailored for a specific purpose, it will take some time. If you're looking for a dark binding, you're in the wrong place. I don't do dark magic."

She shook her head, relieved at the woman's businesslike attitude. "Nothing too dark, I think," she said in a rusty voice. "Something with serious consequences, though. It's got to mean business."

The witch's dark eyes shone with a sardonic sparkle. "You mean a kind of I-swear-I-will-do-such-and-such-or-my-ass-will-catch-fire-until-the-end-of-time type of thing?"

Pia nodded, her mouth twisting. "Yeah. That kind of thing."

"If someone swears an oath of his own free will, the binding falls into the realm of contractual obligation and justice. I can do that. And have, as a matter of fact," the other woman said. She moved toward the back of her shop. "Follow me."

Pia's abused conscience twitched. Unlike the polarized white and black magics, gray magic was supposed to be neutral but the witch's kind of ethical parsing never did sit well with her. Like the relaxation spell in the shop, it felt manipulative, devoid of any real moral substance. A great deal of harm could be done under the guise of neutrality.

Which was pretty damn self-righteous of her, wasn't it, coming fresh as she did from the scene of her crime and desperate to get her hands on that binding spell? The urge to run pumped adrenaline into her veins. Self-preservation kept her anchored in place. Disgusted with herself, she shook her head and followed the witch. Here goes nothing.

She really hoped that wasn't true.

They concluded business in under an hour. At the witch's invitation she slipped out the back to avoid more heckling from the protestors. Her backpack had been lightened by a considerable amount of cash, but Pia figured in a life-or-death situation it was money well spent.

"Just one thing," said the witch. She leaned her curvaceous body in a languid pose against the back doorpost of her shop.

Pia paused and looked back at the other woman.

The witch held her gaze. "If you're personally involved with the man that is intended for, I'm here to tell you, honey: he isn't worth it."

A harsh laugh escaped her. She hefted the backpack higher onto one shoulder. "If only my problems were that simple."

Something moved under the surface of the other woman's lovely dark eyes. The shift of thought looked calculating but that could have been a trick of the late afternoon light. In the next moment her beautiful face wore an indifferent mask, as if she had already moved on to other things.

"Luck, then, *chica*," the witch said. "You need to buy something else, come back anytime."

She swallowed and said past a dry throat, "Thanks."

The witch shut her door and Pia loped to the end of the block, then moved into the sidewalk traffic.

Pia hadn't shared her name. After the first rebuff, the witch knew not to ask and she hadn't offered. She wondered if she had TROUBLE tattooed on her forehead. Or maybe it was in her sweat. Desperation had a certain smell to it.

Her fingers brushed the front pocket of her jeans where she'd slipped the oath binding, wrapped in a plain white handkerchief. A strong glow emanated through the distressed denim and made her hand tingle. Maybe after she met with the shithead and concluded their transaction, she could take her first deep breath in days. She supposed she should be grateful the witch hadn't been more of a shark.

Then Pia heard the most terrible sound of her life. It started low like a vibration, but one so deep in power it shook her bones. She slowed to a stop along with the other pedestrians. People shaded their eyes and looked around as the vibration grew into a roar that swept through the streets and rattled the buildings.

The roar was a hundred freight trains, tornadoes, Mount Olympus exploding in a rain of fire and flood.

Pia fell to her knees and threw her arms over her head. Others screamed and did the same. Still others looked around wild-eyed, trying to spot the disaster. Some ran panicked down the street. The nearby intersections were dotted with car accidents as frightened drivers lost control and slammed into each other

Then the roar died away. Buildings settled. The cloudless sky was serene, but New York City most certainly was not.

Alrighty.

She pushed upright on unsteady legs and mopped her sweat-dampened face, oblivious to the chaos churning around her.

She knew what—*who*—had made that unholy sound and why. The knowledge made her guts go watery.

If she were in a race for her life, that roar was the starter pistol. If God were the referee, He had just shouted *Go*.

H E had been born along with the solar system. Give or take.

He remembered a transcendent light and an immense wind. Modern science called it a solar wind. He recalled a sensation of endless flight, an eternal basking in light and magic so piercing and young and pure it rang like the trumpeting of thousands of angels.

His massive bones and flesh must have been formed along

with the planets. He became bound to Earth. He knew hunger and learned to hunt and eat. Hunger taught him concepts such as before and after, danger, and pain and pleasure.

He began to have opinions. He liked the gush of blood as he gorged on flesh. He liked drowsing on a baked rock in the sun. He adored launching into the air, taking wing, and riding thermals high above the ground, so like that first endless-seeming ecstasy of flight.

After hunger he discovered curiosity. New species burgeoned. There were the wyrkind; Elves; both light and dark fae; tall, bright-eyed beings and squat mushroom-colored creatures; winged nightmares; and shy things that puttered in foliage and hid whenever he appeared. What came to be known as the Elder races tended to cluster in or around magic-filled dimensional pockets of Other land, where time and space had buckled when the earth was formed and the sun shone with a different light.

Magic had a flavor like blood only it was golden and warm like sunlight. It was good to gulp down with red flesh.

He learned language by listening in secret to the Elder races. He practiced on his own when he took flight, mulling over each word and its meaning. The Elder races had several words for him.

Wyrm they called him. Monster. Evil. The Great Beast.

Dragua.

Thus he was named.

He didn't notice at first when the first modern Homo sapiens began to proliferate in Africa. Of all species, he wouldn't have guessed they would flourish. They were weak, had short life spans, no natural armor, and were easy to kill.

He kept an eye on them and learned their languages. Just as other wyrkind did, he developed the skill of shapeshifting so he could walk among them. They dug up the things of the Earth he liked, gold and silver, sparkling crystals and precious gems, which they shaped into creations of beauty. Acquisitive by nature, he collected what caught his eye.

This new species spread across the world, so he created

secret lairs in underground caverns where he gathered his possessions.

His hoard included works of the Elves, the Fae, and the wyrkind, as well as human creations such as gold and silver and copper plates, goblets, religious artifacts, and coinage of all sorts. Money: now there was a concept that intrigued him, attached as it was to so many other interesting notions like trade, politics, war, and greed. There were also cascades of loose crystals and precious gems, and crafted jewelry of all sorts. His hoard grew to include writings from all Elder races and from humankind, as books were an invention he (only sometimes) thought was more precious than any other treasure.

Among his interest in history, mathematics, philosophy, astronomy, alchemy, and magic, he became intrigued with modern science. He traveled to England to have a conversation on the origin of species with a famous scientist in the nineteenth century. They had gotten drunk together—the Englishman with rather more desperation than he—and had talked through the witching hours until the night mist had been burned to vapor by the sun.

He remembered telling the clever, drunken scientist that he and humankind civilization had a lot in common. The difference was his experience was couched in a single entity, one set of memories. In a way, that meant he embodied all stages of evolution at once—beast and predator, magician and aristocrat, violent brute and intellectual. He was not so sure he had acquired humanlike emotions. He had certainly not acquired their morality. Perhaps humankind's greatest achievement was law.

Humans in different cultures also had many words for him. Ryu they called him. Wyvern. Naga. To the Aztecs he was the winged serpent Quetzalcoatl whom they called God.

Dragos.

When he discovered the theft, Dragos Cuelebre exploded into the sky with long thrusts from a wingspan approaching that of an eight-seater Cessna jet.

Modern life had gotten complicated. His usual habit was

to focus Power on averting aircraft when he flew or, simpler yet, just file a flight plan with air traffic control. With his outrageous wealth and position as one of the eldest and most powerful of the wyrkind, life scrambled to arrange itself to his liking.

He wasn't so polite this time. This was more a get-the-fuck-out-of-my-way kind of flight. He was blinded with rage, violent with incredulity. Lava flowed through ancient veins and his lungs worked like bellows. As he approached the zenith of his climb, his long head snapped back and forth and he roared again. The sound ripped the air as his razor claws mauled an imaginary foe.

All of his claws except for those on one front foot where he held a tiny scrap of something fragile and, to be frank, inconceivable. This tiny scrap was as ludicrous and as non-sensical to him as a hot fudge sundae topping an ostrich's head. The cherry on the hot fudge sundae was the elusive whiff of scent that clung to the scrap. It teased his senses into frenzy as it reminded him of something so long ago, he couldn't quite remember what it was—

His mind went white-hot and slipped from its mooring in time. Existing in his wrath he flew until he came to himself and began to think again.

Then Rune said in his head, *My lord? Are you well?*

Dragos cocked his head, aware for the first time that his First flew behind him at a discreet distance. It was a measure of his rage that he hadn't noticed. Any other time Dragos was aware of everything that happened in his vicinity.

Dragos noted that Rune's telepathic voice was as calm and neutral as the other male's physical voice would have been had he spoken the words aloud.

There were many reasons why Dragos had made Rune his First in his Court. Those reasons were why Rune had thrived in his service for so long. The other male was seasoned, mature, and dominant enough to hold authority in a sometimes unruly wyrkind society. He was intelligent with a capacity for cunning and violence that came close to Dragos' own.

Most of all, Rune had a gift for diplomacy that Dragos had never achieved. That talent made the younger male useful when treating with the other Elder Courts. It also helped him to navigate rocky weather when Dragos was in a rage.

Dragos's jaw clenched and he ground massive teeth shaped for maximum carnage. After a moment, he answered, *I am well.*

How may I be of service? his First asked.

His mind threatened to seize again in sheer incredulity of what he had found. He snarled, *There has been a theft.*

A pause. Rune asked, *My lord?*

For once his First's legendary coolness had been shaken. It gave him a grim sense of satisfaction. *A thief, Rune.* He bit at each word. *A thief has broken into my hoard and taken something of mine.*

Rune took several moments to absorb his words. Dragos let him have the time.

The crime was impossible. It had never happened, not in all the millennia of his existence. Yet it had happened now. First, someone had somehow found his hoard, which was an incredible feat in itself. An elaborate fake setup complete with state-of-the-art security was located below the basement levels of Cuelebre Tower, but no one knew the location of Dragos's actual hoard except himself.

His actual hoard was protected by powerful cloaking and aversion spells older than the pharaoh tombs of Egypt and as subtle as tasteless poison on the tongue. But after locating his secret lair, the thief had managed to slip past all of Dragos's physical and magical locks, like a knife slicing through butter. Even worse, the thief managed to slip out again the same way.

The only warning Dragos had received was a nagging unease that had plagued him all afternoon. His unease had increased to the point where he couldn't settle until he went to check on his property.

He had known his lair had been infiltrated as soon as he had set foot near the hidden entrance to the underground cavern. Still he couldn't believe it, even after he had torn inside to discover the indisputable evidence of the theft, along with something else that trumped all other inconceivability.

He looked down at his clenched right foot. He wheeled in an abrupt motion to set a return path to the city. Rune followed and settled smoothly into place behind him, Dragos's rear-right wingman.

You are to locate this thief. Do everything possible, Dragos said. *Everything; you understand? Use all magical and nonmagical means. Nothing else exists for you. No other tasks, no other diversions. Pass all of your current duties on to Aryal or Grym.*

I understand, my lord, Rune said, keeping his mental voice quiet.

Dragos sensed other conversations in the air, although no one dared direct contact with him. He suspected his First had begun giving orders to transfer duties to the others.

He said, *Be very clear about something, Rune: I do not want this thief harmed or killed by anyone but me. You are not to allow it. Be sure of the people you use on this hunt.*

I will.

It will be on your head if something goes wrong, Dragos told him. He couldn't have articulated even to himself why he pressed the matter with this creature who for centuries had been as steady and reliable as a metronome. His claws clenched on his implausible scrap of evidence. *Understood?*

Understood, my lord, Rune replied, calm as ever.

Good enough, he growled.

Dragos noticed they had returned to the city. The sky around them was clear of all air traffic. He soared in a wide circle to settle on the spacious landing pad atop Cuelebre Tower. As soon as he settled, he shifted into his human shape, a massive six-foot-eight, dark-haired male with dark bronze skin and gold raptor's eyes.

Dragos turned to watch Rune land. The gryphon's majestic wings shone in the fading afternoon sun until he also shifted into his human form, a tawny haired male almost as massive as Dragos himself.

Rune lowered his head to Dragos in a brief bow of respect before loping to the roof doors. After the other male had left, Dragos unclenched his right fist in which he held a crumpled scrap of paper.

Why had he not told Rune about it? Why was he not even now calling the gryphon back to tell him? He didn't know. He just obeyed the impulse to secrecy.

Dragos held the paper to his nose and inhaled. A scent still clung to the paper which had absorbed oil from the thief's hand. It was a feminine scent that smelled like wild sunshine, and it was familiar in a way that pulled at all of Dragos's deepest instincts.

He stood immobile, eyes closed as he concentrated on inhaling that wild feminine sunshine in deep breaths. There was something about it, something from a long time ago. If only he could remember. He had lived for so long, his memory was a vast and convoluted tangle. It could take him weeks to locate the memory.

He strained harder for that elusive time with a younger sun, a deep green forest, and a celestial scent that drove him crashing through the underbrush—

The fragile memory thread broke. A low growl of frustration rumbled through his chest. He opened his eyes and willed himself not to shred the paper he held with such tense care.

It occurred to Dragos that Rune had forgotten to ask what the thief had stolen.

His underground lair was enormous by necessity, with cavern upon cavern filled with a hoard the likes of which the world had never seen. The treasure of empires filled the caves.

Astonishing works of beauty graced rough cavern walls. Items of magic, miniature portraits, tinkling crystal earrings that threw rainbows in the lamplight. Art masterpieces packed to protect them from the environment. Rubies and emeralds and diamonds the size of goose eggs, and loops upon loops of pearls. Egyptian scarabs, cartouches, and pendants. Greek gold, Syrian statues, Persian gems, Chinese jade, Spanish treasure from sunken ships. He even kept a modern coin collection he had started several years ago and added to in a haphazard way whenever he remembered.

On the ostrich's head was a hot fudge sundae. . . .

His obsessive attention to detail, an immaculate memory of each and every piece in that gigantic treasure, a trail of scent like wild sunshine, and instinct had all led Dragos to the right place. He discovered the thief had taken a U.S.-minted 1962 copper penny from a jar of coins he had not yet bothered to put into a coin-collecting book.

. . . and on the hot fudge sundae atop that ostrich's head was perched a cherry. . . .

The thief had left something for him in place of what she had taken. She had perched it with care on top of the coin jar. It was a message written on a scrap of paper in a spidery, unsteady hand. The message was wrapped around an offering.

I'm sorry, the message said.

The theft was a violation of privacy. It was an unbelievable act of impudence and disrespect. Not only that, it was—baffling. He was murderous, *incandescent* with fury. He was older than sin and could not remember when he had last been in such a rage.

He looked at the paper again.

I'm sorry I had to take your penny. Here's another to replace it.

Yep, that's what it said.

One corner of his mouth twitched. He gave himself a deep shock when he burst into an explosive guffaw.

Don't miss a word from the "erotic and darkly
bewitching"* series featuring the D'Artigo sisters,
half-human, half-Fae supernatural agents.

By *New York Times* Bestselling Author

Yasmine Galenorn

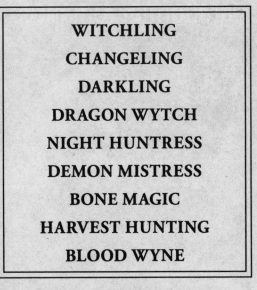

WITCHLING

CHANGELING

DARKLING

DRAGON WYTCH

NIGHT HUNTRESS

DEMON MISTRESS

BONE MAGIC

HARVEST HUNTING

BLOOD WYNE

Praise for the Otherworld series:

"Pure delight."
—MaryJanice Davidson, *New York Times*
bestselling author

"Vivid, sexy, and mesmerizing."
—*Romantic Times*

penguin.com

*Jeaniene Frost, *New York Times* bestselling author

M192AS0910